THE SECOND GATE

by

Brian Wyvill

THUNDERCHILD PUBLISHING
Huntsville, Alabama

THE SECOND GATE

ISBN-13: 978-1719243773
ISBN-10: 1719243778

Published by Thunderchild Publishing. Find us at
https://ourworlds.net/thunderchild_cms/

Maps: Rhea Lonsdale and Guy Pommares.

Cover photo by the author.

Acknowledgments

I have been working on *The Second Gate* for more than a decade or so (on and off) and finally trusted Dan Thompson of Thunderchild Publishing to publish this book. He gave me much helpful advice pointing out some historical and other errors that I was able to fix in time, as well as what to leave on the cutting room floor.

Several professional writers helped me along the way. A big thank you to Leina Pauls, a former English instructor at the University of Victoria who was my first editor and taught me that the comma was not something to sprinkle on the page at random via a comma shaker (similar to a salt shaker.) Thanks to the Banff Centre and Pauline Holdstock, who led me in one of their wonderful *Writing With Style* workshops. Thanks go to the Historical Novelists Society, and the Surrey International Writers' Conference, for allowing me to meet inspirational historical authors such as Jack Whyte, Diana Gabaldon, CC Humphreys and James Nelson. James, author of the excellent "Isaac Biddlecomb" books, and past skipper of a square rigger, put me right on some of the technical details and his books were inspirational. A huge thank you to my mentor Chris Humphrey's whose workshops are really worth it, and his novels get better and better. Speaking of whom, Chris, when are you going to write another Jack Absolute book?

Special thanks to my family, Shawna and my children Simon, Siomon, and Charlotte, who have had to put up with my enthusiasm for 18th century naval battles for a couple of decades, but continued to show their love and support. To Guy Pommares who taught me a lot about fighting with bladed weaponry and also added the figure showing the action between the galliot and the *Palerma*. To the staff at the Maritime museum at Greenwich, for giving me access to their charts and the logs of the *Vanguard*.

Thanks go to my climbing partner, and friend for many years, Geoff Powter, a professional author himself, for his comments and introducing me to Wilfred Thesiger's crossing of the Empty Quarter. To my in-laws and published authors, Joe Mahoney and Susan Rogers, for all the helpful advice to the guy who married their sister. Thanks to their parents Rosaleen & Tom Mahoney who chanced to send me a copy of "Master and Commander" and awakened my interest in the age of fighting sail. To all the many friends who read earlier drafts and made some comments: Joanne Wyvill, Paul Lalonde (Acadian French advisor), Kathleen Wiebe, Alyn Rockwood, Ahmad Nasri (who introduced me to riding camels), Don Chandler, Rory Macintosh (climbers and sailors). My students who put up with my ramblings about sailing ships; Pauline Jepp, Kaye Mason, Callum Galbraith, Kevin Foster, Martin Fuherer, Ryan Schmidt, Jeff Mahovsky, Erwin De Groot, Masamichi Sugihara, Zainab Meraj, Herbert Grasberger, Pourya Shirazian, Ji (Lucky) Li, Maurizio Kovacic, Mauricio Rovira Galvez, Ed Wisernig, Rodolphe Vaillant, and Baptiste Angels. With apologies to those whose names I missed.

Last but by no means least, many thanks to Rear-Admiral Kit Layman (RN ret.), author of the splendid book, *The Wager Disaster*, which explores the fate of one of Admiral Anson's ships wrecked in Patagonia. Kit not only read and made notes on an earlier draft of *The Second Gate*, but let me touch his collection of Nelson artifacts, and took me on a tour of HMS *Victory* in dry dock at Portsmouth. Who better to visit Nelson's old ship than with an admiral. Thank you Kit, for your inspiration.

Prologue

Wednesday 20th June, 1798. (2nd Messidor - Napoleonic Calendar) Malta 8 AM

Duncan burst through the door of an old ammunition shed into a sunny day in hell. He walked out into the courtyard of a castle, where black smoke billowed from windows at the ground level. Ahead, a few French soldiers ran towards the central keep of the old fort urged on by their sergeant whose bellowed orders added to the general chaos. Duncan stood there watching, momentarily stunned as they organized a bucket chain to fight the fire.

A second commotion by the castle gate drew Duncan back to further chaos in the castle grounds. A woman ran towards a man wearing a navy blue English lieutenant's uniform identical to his own. Together they headed for the castle gate. As he watched, one of the gate guards ran back to his sergeant.

"Sergeant Gaston, there's a prisoner escaping."

"Who the devil is that girl?" Demanded the sergeant?

"Monsieur, she works for the turnkey."

"Get that prisoner back to his cell. Leave the woman to me."

The sergeant ran towards the escapees, while Duncan looked at the fugitives more closely. His mouth and eyes gaped wide.

"Could it be?" He muttered. He shook his head knowing this was not the time to contemplate the other lieutenant. Instead, he called out; "Run, you fools!"

A sudden cold breeze brought with it clouds to block the sun. To Duncan it was a bad omen. He stood in an exposed position with nowhere to go, and he had just drawn the sergeant's attention.

"By the holy virgin, another Englishman. Is this an attack?" Gaston cried in astonishment with a glare at this second English lieutenant.

Behind the sergeant were four soldiers, armed with muskets. The odds did not look good to Duncan. Then, predictably things got worse as four more soldiers joined them from the barracks. Duncan drew his cutlass.

"You four follow me, and the rest of you keep your muskets trained. I prefer to take him alive, but shoot that man if he slips past us," ordered the sergeant.

Duncan sniffed rain in the air and felt the first droplets splash onto his outstretched hand. A roll of thunder bounced off the stone walls of the castle as if to announce the forthcoming battle. The guards spread out along the sergeant's left flank.

"To stop me reaching the gate," mused Duncan.

The first to gain his position was a gangly youth, who slipped and dropped his musket on the ground where it discharged with a loud bang. While his inexperienced adversary struggled to free his sword, Duncan charged.

The Englishman brought the hilt of his cutlass down on the boy's left ear, and the youngster fell to the ground with a groan.

Duncan felt the familiar glow from the adrenaline his system produced in abundance in battle. He felt invincible, but knew he must let his brain rule his body. It was his body that called out; "One down, three standing."

The other soldiers seemed stunned by the conflict and stood frozen until their sergeant brought them to life.

"You there," said the sergeant addressing the second soldier. "He's an enemy officer, bring him down."

With a war cry the second soldier charged, aiming the fine point of his sword at Duncan, who arched his back and side stepped. As momentum carried the Frenchman onwards, the Englishman slashed the sharp edge of his cutlass across a retreating hamstring. The soldier's cry changed to one of pain. He slid to the ground leaving blood spatters in the dust.

Angered by their comrades failure the next pair of guards moved in to attack, keeping their distance and circling him like angry hornets. 'Fat and Thin,' smiled Duncan.

"Arrêtez-les."

A cry from the castle gate drew the soldiers' attention. Duncan risked a glance towards the would-be escapees, who had reached the castle gate.

Two gate guards closed in tightly around the prisoner but, in a sudden fury of flying fists, the fugitive laid them out cold. On the threshold of freedom the couple came face to face with a young French naval-officer who barred their exit. The escaping man roughly pushed the French officer onto his knees, and the woman kicked him between the legs. He went down with a screech.

The officer's cry was almost lost in a crash of thunder and hammer of rain. The voice of the sergeant broke the standoff.

"Hit his sword arm; grab it, then pull him here for questioning. Have I taught you nothing." His voice had an angry tinge.

The thinner of the two held his sword tightly, the whites of his knuckles showed the Englishman that the man was a new recruit. Duncan sent his heavy navy-cutlass crashing into his opponent's out-flung blade with a loud clang. The guard's sword leapt out of his hand, and he dived after it. Without even trying Duncan slapped the hilt of his sword into the side of the man's skull, putting him instantly out of the fight. The fat one was right behind, and with the loose grip of a seasoned fighter cut at Duncan's right, trying to hit his sword arm. Expecting the blow, Duncan used the weight of his heavier cutlass to turn the fat soldier's sword just enough. Then the Englishman retreated slightly and crouched down, recovering his breath while his enemy regrouped. He reached down through the dirt to find a dry layer. His opponent came back for another try.

"Watch his left hand," cried the sergeant.

The warning came too late. The Englishman jumped forward with a handful of dry sand, which he flung at the fat one's eyes and, blinded, the guard slipped on the wet ground, falling backwards.

With a sigh the sergeant stepped forward, taking a swordsman's stance. Instead of engaging him, Duncan ran back towards the ammunition shed. With his pursuer only a few paces

7

behind, Duncan plunged through the wooden door. He tried to close it but the smiling sergeant seemed confident that he had Duncan trapped. Duncan pushed, but his weight was no match for the heavy sergeant, who had wedged his substantial French army boot in the opening.

As Duncan pushed, the sergeant's sword came thrusting through the gap, catching Duncan on his sword arm, just below the shoulder. Crying in pain the Englishman fell against the door. Taking advantage of the Englishman's injury, the sergeant grabbed his arm, and dragged the Englishman out into the rain.

At that moment an over eager musketeer pulled his trigger. There was a bang, then Duncan's arm was free. He looked up to see the sergeant lying on the ground his hand to his neck, where the musket ball had torn its way through. The soldiers ran to help their sergeant, and for an instant all eyes were on Gaston's last pathetic gurgles. Spots of blood appeared on his uniform, then a flood as the carotid artery let go when he tried to speak. As the sergeant bled to death on the ground, Duncan seized the opportunity to dash into the darkness of the shed and bar the door. A short way in he heard the soldiers gain entrance, and he could hear their clumsy progress. Despite his pain, he soon found his secret door, smiling as he thought about the confusion his mysterious disappearance would cause.

Chapter 1

The Professor

Wednesday 10th June 2015 5 PM Victoria, British Columbia, Canada

Sarah walked up the lovely but lonely Mystic Vale towards the university, enjoying the tranquility of the deep, narrow valley. This oasis of old-growth trees was a tiny hide-away separating the campus from a suburban neighbourhood. The afternoon had brought cold air in from the sea, and with it a mist that hung in the trees like colourless Christmas decorations. Sarah slipped easily into a familiar daytime dream, envisioning herself as the lady of a great 18th century house. Dressed in her riding habit on her daily inspection of the grounds, she would dispense with the side-saddle to ride unconventionally astride her Arab mare.

She sniffed something unpleasant that shattered her daydream, reminding her of unwashed clothes and bad breath. Was somebody watching her? The previously friendly valley had become unnaturally quiet, almost claustrophobic. She started walking again and crossed a rickety bridge anxious to get away from the smell. A raspy voice from behind made her stop again.

"Bonjour ma petite."

She looked back, but saw nobody at first. Then the branches shook and a scarred man's face thrust out from across the stream. The left side looked like stone chips had blasted it. A grizzled, empty socket marked where his left eye had once looked out on the world.

9

Shivering, she goaded her frozen muscles into unbearably slow movement. Mystic Creek blocked her escape on one side and a steep embankment closed the trap on her right. She reached a second bridge, and with fearful steps, quickened her pace towards the staircase that led out of the vale.

"Attend, ma petite!"

The voice was louder. The man was closer. She reached the first of the thirty-nine uneven wooden steps leading onto campus, and heard laboured breathing, very near now. Without turning her head, she started to run, but as she hopped from step to step she tired. Mud splashed her socks and she stumbled, heart thumping with panic. Hurrying breathlessly upwards she focussed her energy on not falling. This man was straight out of her childhood nightmares and she could hear him thumping up the stairs. Her movements seemed so slow now, and she wanted nothing but to look back. She must not linger but push harder for the top. She reached the third switchback and clung to the rail for a brief moment of relief from the pain in her lungs. Exhausted and out of breath, she turned to face her fate, however ugly. To her relief, there was nobody, nothing to disturb the peace of Mystic Vale.

She stumbled across the ring road and into a patch of grass alive with feral rabbits. Back among the students everything was normal, and her irrational fears seemed foolish.

At the Clearihue building she ran upstairs to find her history professor, but instead she saw her sister sitting at his desk.

"Annette, what're you doing here?"

"The prof had some sort of emergency, so he gave me his key and asked me to sit here until six . . . ." Annette paused; "What's wrong?"

Sarah, flush-faced and still shaking from her earlier encounter sat down and took a breath.

"Nothing. I'm just being an idiot."

"About what?"

"Some old homeless guy upset me. He had this raspy voice and a scarred face," said Sarah, head in her hands.

"Did he hurt you?"

"No, I'm fine, really." Sarah stood up, took out her assignment from her backpack and placed it on top of the pile on the crowded desk.

"No, you're not. You're shaking. What happened?"

Sarah shook her head.

Annette came out from behind the professor's desk and put her arm around Sarah. "Okay, kid. You tell me if I can help."

Sarah nodded, a faint smile lit her face. She glanced around the room and her attention was caught by a painting on the wall. "Wow! That's huge. How did prof Duncan get it in here?"

"You've never been to his office before?"

Sarah shook her head.

"Go ahead and take a look around. He's got some cool stuff. The painting's a genuine Nicholas Pocock."

"Who?"

"If you knew your 18th century Royal Navy a little better you'd know he's the one who painted all the famous ships and battles."

"Pocock? Okay, I'll make a note. Will it be on the test?"

Annette laughed and muttered a quiet, "Undergrads!"

Sarah inspected the painting. The title read, *The great cabin HMS Lively 1798*. It was wonderfully detailed, showing the luxury enjoyed by the senior man on board. She noticed the dark figure of the captain bent over his books. He looked lonely. Did the captain pay for his comfort with solitude?

The painting restored Sarah's spirits, and her curiosity was taken with the rest of Professor Duncan's collection. Floor to ceiling shelves held historical artefacts. She knew Duncan was an expert on the Napoleonic wars, particularly the naval engagements. She was drawn to a beautifully detailed model of a thirty two gun frigate of the British Navy. Several swords hung immediately behind the desk, in handy reach in case of late assignments, she mused. She moved on to inspect a ship's clock in a wooden case, and bent down to read a small inscribed plaque fixed to the base, "HMS *Lively* 1794 - 1798 wrecked at Rota Point." The polished wood was marked with two deep scratches at the front, but the clock still ticked away after more than 200 years.

"1798 again," said Annette.

"Your favourite year!" chuckled Sarah.

"The Battle of the Nile was that year. It was very significant, and the subject of my thesis."

"I know, I know. Take a pill!" Sarah said this with such a genuinely sweet voice that Annette laughed.

"Sorry, sis. I take my work far too seriously."

"I love rock climbing and playing piano, and you love old sea battles!"

"We aren't very lady like are we?"

They laughed and Sarah gazed at the clock.

"Take another look at the painting," said Annette.

Sarah looked closely, and there it was in the captain's cabin.

"It's the same clock! I wonder if it was the last thing the captain grabbed before leaving his sinking ship. How did Duncan get hold of it?"

"No idea, but it's in amazingly good condition," replied Annette.

"Well almost good condition. There's a broken edge on the right side of the case. It looks like it's missing the right-hand spiral."

"Actually it was stopped until recently. Duncan had me collect it from some guy called Charlie, downtown, who deals in antique clocks. He fixed it!"

"Well Charlie must be pretty good. It's ticking." Sarah said, her ear close to the clock.

"They built them to last," laughed Annette.

Sarah was about to move on when she saw a few old envelopes propped against the clock. The front one was addressed to Duncan care of a lawyer's office. The postmark was just discernible: Montreal, April 2000. Certainly not an antique. She wondered why he had kept them.

"It's six o'clock, time to go." Annette got up from the desk and stood beside Sarah who was inspecting some naval uniforms.

"These look nearly new, and those hats — " Sarah pointed to some naval hats on a shelf. She continued to look idly through the uniforms as if she was clothes shopping when Annette interrupted.

"Be careful, there's a chance they're genuine."

"What? The uniforms? Just hung up like this? No protective covers, nothing?"

12

"Surprising, isn't it? But take a look at the weave and the stitching. This cloth was not made on a modern automatic loom."

Sarah was not convinced. "How can you tell?"

Annette smiled, "Simple! The weave is not as tight and precise as that from a modern loom. Secondly, the thread is . . ."

"Okay, I believe you." Sarah put the garment carefully back on the rack, but the weight was too much for the wire hanger and it fell to the floor.

"I'm sorry."

Annette pushed her out of the way. "Just as clumsy as when you were a kid." She picked up the coat, then shuffled the others along the rack to find a better hanger. "Hey look! A door. He has some kind of annex through here. Maybe there's more to his private collection." She handed the coat to Sarah and tried the door handle.

"Do you think you ought to do that, Annette? Perhaps he had the door hidden for a reason."

"Always the good girl, Sarah. If he asks me to take care of his office hours, the least he can do is let me look at his museum." Annette went through, but Sarah would not cross the threshold.

"Nothing much in here," Annette reported over her shoulder.

Sarah looked into a small, bare, room. As her eyes grew accustomed to the low lighting, she noticed a window, but it was already dark outside. A slight seaside smell bothered her senses.

Annette turned sharply and ushered her sister out.

"What's wrong?" asked Sarah.

"That's odd." Annette pondered for a second and grasped Sarah's hand, her tone deadly serious. "Just before my mother disappeared, before your family adopted me . . ."

A voice interrupted her; "Anybody here?"

Emerging from the coat rack, they walked straight into Ken DiPalo.

Annette dropped Sarah's hand. "You complete jerk," Annette shrieked, and stepped out into the office hot with annoyance. Sarah sighed and reflected that as Annette grew older, she had stopped talking about her past. Ken had interrupted just when her sister was actually volunteering some information.

Ken shrugged unknowingly and addressed Annette. "Hey, what'd I say, Annie?"

13

"Ken, you dummy, you startled me and don't call me Annie, it's Annette, understand?"

"My apologies, dear lady." Ken bowed, losing the bright blue fedora from his head as he did so. He picked it up. "Clumsy me! Let me buy you a coffee in recompense for all my sins?"

Annette ignored his cheesy attempt at gallantry. "It's after six. I suppose that's your late assignment?"

"Well, we mortals have to try hard while you gods find life so easy," he said placing his assignment on top of the one marked Sarah Malette. He looked up to give her his sheepish look.

"Don't expect sympathy from me, Ken. You don't try nearly hard enough." Annette paused, "I mean in class," she added sharply, pushing Ken out of the door and locking it behind her.

"See you later, Sarah," said Annette as she walked off down the corridor.

"Hey Ken, you can relax. You and I are in the same research group, and Annette told me she's our T.A." said Sarah, noting Ken's crestfallen look. At this news Ken brightened.

"Thank you Professor Duncan! I get to work with the Goddess!"

Sarah sighed and walked away.

Ken lost his smile. "Wait a minute!" He ran past her to catch up with Annette.

"Hey, Annette, can I tell you about my project?"

"I know, it's about the South Sea Bubble. Another time, Ken. I have studying to do."

"Let's go for coffee?"

"Non!" said Annette emphatically and hurried off.

"Au devoir," sighed Ken as Sarah caught up.

"You're a funny man, Ken . . . "

"I take that as a compliment," he said, fedora in hand. "It's so cute the way she switches to French when she gets angry."

Sarah paused to take in Ken's hat and flowing white shirt. "Being the class clown doesn't work with Annette, but I could take pity on you and let you buy me a coffee." Ken's sad look had stirred her slightly.

"Why do French Canadians sound so sexy," said Ken.

"Well thank you, or do you just mean Annette?"

14

"Sarah, you just haven't got her accent!"

Sarah looked skywards and turned to go. The shoes dangling from her pack narrowly missed Ken.

"What are those? Your dancing shoes?" asked Ken.

"Rock climbing," Sarah replied with enthusiasm.

"That sounds like fun. I've done a bit, indoors at Stelly's climbing gym. I wouldn't mind trying it outside sometime."

"We could go Saturday. I know a great pub in Nanaimo on the way home . . ."

"D'you think Annette would come with us?"

"No, that really isn't her thing. What about you?"

"Saturday? No sorry, I have to . . . iron the cat! Yes, the cat's all wrinkly . . . " said Ken.

"You know what? Forget the coffee." Sarah reddened and walked away leaving Ken with a "What did I say?" look on his face.

As Ken and Sarah disappeared from sight, the man with the scarred face who had frightened Sarah in Mystic Vale, walked down the corridor and paused outside the door of Professor Duncan's office. He glanced up and down and when the door would not give, he took a plastic card out of his wallet and inserted it into the lock. At that moment, a loud groan came from inside. Startled, the man walked away.

Duncan, clad in an 18th century British navy uniform, staggered through the inner door. Pushing aside the coats, he grabbed at his desk, sending papers flying. He sank into his chair, wet, exhausted and with blood seeping from a wound in his right arm. In his wake he left a set of blood stained assignments like detritus from a battlefield. As he lost consciousness, the bloody sword he carried rattled to the floor.

Thursday 7th June 1798 8 PM — Abdul

Thirty-six oars pulled in perfect harmony in time with a deep throated drum beat to propel the *Murad*, a sleek Barbary Coast galley, swiftly through the water off the coast of Malta. Slaves and freemen alike worked their oars for fear of the whip.

15

Dip, Sweep, pause.

The steersman turned the *Murad* into the wind to intercept the prey, a small merchant ship. The captain or *rais* as he was known to the crew, was Mohammed Abdul al-Bashir. He watched with pride as the seventy two oarsmen worked to catch their enemy. The crew cleared for action, and the vessel creaked and groaned through her turn. The sail handlers ran to bring down the single triangular sail. The oarsmen pulled with a rhythmic pulse; dip, sweep, pause.

"Hands to the gun!"

A crew of eight ran the length of the vessel to work the heavy iron piece sitting on the reinforced bow deck pointing towards the enemy.

"Out tompion!"

With a glint of greed, the captain said quietly,

"More speed!"

The order was relayed with gusto by the first officer and so down the chain of command. The drum beat faster and to his delight, Ali the galley master laid on with his whip to make his sweat soaked *ciurma* (oarsmen) work harder.

A cooling breeze from the shore wafted across the bare backs of the slaves. To the northwest lay their quarry and to the east a small cape. Between them the wind pushed the water of the Mediterranean into sets of white capped waves.

The sound of the oars groaning in the leather thules made Abdul grin through his beard as he stood on his quarterdeck watching each naked pair pulling together. He consulted his English time-piece knowing that twenty minutes of back breaking work was all they had in them. Enough time to overhaul the infidels before the stronger men fell over with exhaustion, and weaker hearts failed.

He crossed to the weather side and observed the enemy closely. She was square rigged on the main and foremast, with fore and aft sails on the mizzen, a barque rig. He watched her sailors running in all directions throwing barrels of water and other loose objects over the side in a frantic attempt to lose some weight and gain some speed. Splash! Splash! Splash! Three, four-pounder guns hit the water. With insufficient men to fight they were better off trying to escape, and lose the guns. The tactic worked, and the merchantman started to pull away.

The rhythm of the galliot made the captain's pulse quicken; he was not going to let this ship escape. The *Murad* pulled towards the shelter of high limestone cliffs.

"Catch her quickly! Once the sun sets she'll escape in the dark."

His command rose above the noise of the wind, and the groans of the oarsmen.

"Aye, aye, Rais." The first officer shouted something to the galley master, whose whip answered with a crack. The unlucky oarsmen shrieked with pain and pulled all the harder. The spray came over the larboard bow as the galley turned to intercept the barque at an impressive six knots, fast enough to produce a bow wave. Rais Abdul stood on the stern platform with his officers around him.

"Master gunner."

At his right hand a heavy-set man with a great black beard bowed.

"Rais?"

The captain held up an old silver dirham; "Take out a spar and bring this chase to an end, and this silver will be yours. If you miss . . ."

Aziz Pasha the gunner, saluted, then bounded down the quarterdeck gangway, sprinting the seventy feet of deck past the rowers to the bow. The gun was a long nine, which could send a nine-pound ball more than half a mile. The crew of six had primed the gun and just waited for the command.

Aziz took careful aim, "A goat's testicle more to larboard . . ." His men set to with the handspikes to move the ton and a half iron cannon. "Enough!"

He leaned forward arching his back to anticipate the recoil of the huge gun, so to avoid the foot-crushing wheels. He applied the slow match and with a bang that brought blood to the ears of the oarsmen of the first bench, smoke and flame exploded from the long barrel. They watched for a splash; when it didn't come, the master gunner judged the ball had flown high through the ship's rigging and her hull had hidden the fall. He could see no change in their quarry's progress, so the ball had done no damage. The gun crew groaned

17

their disappointment, interrupted by a stern order from the master gunner.

"Silence fore and aft! Sponge! Reload! Run out your gun! Prime! Fire as they bear!"

It took a full two minutes of furious activity for the men to get the gun ready for the second shot. The whole company watched carefully as it exploded into life, sending the iron ball towards the target. It seemed to disappear again, but this time the barque's fore topsail lost its luff. Nobody cheered, but they had caused sufficient damage for the galliot to start to close the gap on the chase.

The first officer smiled, showing broken front teeth to his captain; "Allah has sent us good fortune."

The rais was not convinced. "Wait until we've boarded before you count your silver."

As he said this, he looked astern where a steep limestone promontory blocked his view towards the East. To the first officer he said, "Will we catch this barque before we lose the light? Or will our oarsmen fall over first with exhaustion?"

"Rais, it was an easy day for the ciurma. In this light breeze they will catch our prize. The shallow water is not far away; we have the advantage. We shall board her in five more minutes."

The captain was satisfied. The galliot's draught was considerably less than the laden barque, so their prey could not escape inshore. The cliffs afforded their vessel protection from the weather, and he could already detect an increase of perhaps half a knot as the wind diminished.

"Sail to leeward!"

All eyes turned astern where the lookout pointed. Two heavily armed frigates flying French colours rounded the small cape. They were piling on sail in the light winds to come to the aid of the barque. The Frenchmen had the wind on their beam, and they were far from the shoal water, but close enough for their broadsides to be effective.

"More effort unless you wish to rot in a French prison or die on their guillotine! Hold your course to windward." He turned to his first officer and said, "In a few more minutes the frigates will not fire for fear of hitting the barque."

They were within a pistol shot of the merchant ship's stern, close enough to hear the shouts of her sailors. Then a ranging shot from the nearer frigate splashed into the water ahead.

"We must reach the shelter of the barque. Do not spare the ciurma."

Ali cried, "You sons of whores pull harder, or die in their broadside!"

The galliot was now directly astern of the merchantman, with the leading frigate only a few cable lengths behind. She turned to form a right angle with the *Murad* so she could fire a raking shot down the length of the vessel.

"Get down!" From this range the frigate could not miss. Abdul threw himself to the deck in time to feel the draft from more than a dozen 18-pound iron balls flying over them like an attack of giant wasps. The rowers were in the most vulnerable position. A head came up a second too soon and was split from its body by French round shot. The same ball continued into the slave on the bench in front killing him instantly. The crash of splintering wood could not drown out the terrified cries of the injured men. In the pandemonium, the captain turned to see a bloody mess on the deck where his first officer had once stood.

"Keep pulling," he grunted to the galley master. "The next broadside will be grape!"

A raking shot with grape, thousands of steel balls, would kill them all. The frigate captain had been merciful, probably in an effort to spare the slaves. The crew watched fearfully as the second frigate manoeuvred into position to fire the final shot.

Thursday 11th June 2015 9:45 AM — Victoria

"Imagine what it was like on a ship, a British man-of-war in the year 1798. You're an ordinary seaman on a frigate, cruising in the Mediterranean, searching out French shipping. You did not choose this profession, but you were caught by a press gang and forced into the navy. Perhaps you are sick, or drunk, knocked on the head and by the time you wake up, you are already at sea. Sneered at

19

by the other men because you are a landlubber, sick for the first
month or two . . ."

Professor Duncan paused; Sarah in the front row had her
hand up. "Yes, Sarah?"

"What about women? Were they press ganged too?"

Duncan sighed, took a bottle off the desk and popped a
vitamin C tablet in his mouth.

"No, they were not. Women on board ship were frowned
upon by the navy, although some captains were more lenient on this
question than others. Some women passed themselves off as men
and lived successfully for years on board. The other sailors would
turn a blind eye to such a thing."

Sarah sat forward in her seat, noting that Professor Duncan's
face was grey and bruised. His left arm was tied up in a sling and
heavily bandaged. His breathing seemed shallow, and he was having
some difficulty speaking. She could hear more quiet chatter than was
usual.

"How'd he get that?" "What's he done to himself?" "He
looks tired."

Sarah, like the other women in the class, was not immune to
Duncan's charisma. He presented history as if he had personal
experience of the 18th century and his concern with the plight of the
ordinary sailor touched her. She stopped thinking about him, and
forced her attention back to the lecture.

"Imagine you are on a seventy-four gun ship of the line,
heading into the Mediterranean in June, 1798 with Admiral Horatio
Nelson. You have been at sea for several months now and have got
used to the beatings, the continual lack of sleep, damp clothes, damp
everything, as you work the larboard watch. Maybe you have some
aptitude, and one of the kindly top men takes you under his wing and
nurtures you along, teaching you the various knots, the names of the
hundreds of different sheets, lines and sails. Soon you are racing
fearlessly up to the maintop avoiding the easy route through the
lubber's hole, and climbing straight over the overhang on to the
platform, then up further to the crosstrees. Now you are out on the
main topgallant yard yelling, 'Laying on!' You have to take in a sail,
high up, well over a hundred feet above the deck. As the ship rolls
the tip of the mast whips through the air, and you cling on for dear

20

life because a gale is blowing. If you don't get the sail furled, you could endanger the ship. You are wet and cold, feet slipping in the foot-ropes, barely able to hold on, but work you must."

A strong silence marked the pause. Every face in the crowded lecture hall was rapt with attention, held by Duncan's deep, musical voice. Then his tone changed.

"Admiral Lord Nelson, later to become Britain's greatest ever hero, arrived in Alexandria near the mouth of the Nile River and, finding no French fleet, he left. He was less than 24 hours ahead of Napoleon without knowing it. A missed opportunity to destroy the general at sea and perhaps radically change history. It took Nelson another month to find the French fleet. At last, the British ships catches up with Monsieur Admiral Brueys in Aboukir Bay on the afternoon of the first of August 1798."

"*Goliath*, a seventy-four gun ship of the line under Captain Thomas Foley, leads the fleet. He notices the first French ship has anchored quite far out, and it may just be possible for an English man-of-war to sail between the French fleet and the shallow waters of the bay. The ship is put on the highest state of alert. You help clear for action and go to your assigned station below decks. Perhaps you are a member of a gun crew, firing eighteen pound iron balls from enormously heavy guns. You hope French round shot does not come through the side of the ship to send huge, sharp splinters flying through the air, spearing whoever gets in their path. Below in the orlop, the lowest deck, the surgeon prepares his table. You will have to carry your fallen comrades down there. Perhaps you will be ordered to hold them down while the surgeon removes a shattered arm or a splinter skewered leg. On the gun deck blood pours through the scuppers and your comrade's screams make you thankful it isn't you bound for the surgeon's table."

Duncan surveyed his spellbound audience. As he was about to resume, Sarah stood up. "Professor Duncan, under these conditions, why would anybody want to put to sea?"

Sarah saw a gleam come into Duncan's eyes. His whole body shifted and took on a different demeanour.

"The men had little choice, God save them. Indeed we will cover the 1797 fleet mutinies in the forthcoming week. For the officers, life was different. They wanted to rise in ranks, to become

21

captain. At the Nile they came away covered in glory. Foley's tactic worked, and the French fleet was mainly destroyed."

He paused again, his face showing some of the pain he felt. Unexpectedly he said, "No greater pleasure exists compared with command of a man-of-war under sail! Class dismissed."

As Duncan left the front desk, he was confronted by Sarah and Ken, who were anxious about their group assignment. "Do you have questions?"

Ken and Sarah spoke together, "Professor Duncan . . ." they stopped and Annette spoke for the group.

"Professor Duncan . . ."

"Yes, I know who I am," said Duncan.

"I was wondering if we had any choice over the research group for the next assignment?" said Sarah, looking pointedly at Ken.

"I'm their TA." Annette explained.

"Oh, I see." He paused. "The groups were chosen deliberately. So were the teaching assistants. I expect the TA will work with each group allocated to them, and help them. I will mark this assignment." He nodded his head and left abruptly.

Catching up with Annette outside the lecture hall, Sarah was on the point of renewing their conversation from the previous day when Ken interrupted again.

"Well since it's now official we are working together, can I tell you what I discovered?" said Ken, with an enthusiastic grin. Annette and Sarah exchanged a glance and sat down on a bench in the corridor.

"Go on then," said Sarah.

Ken straightened, set his fedora crookedly on his head and, ever the clown, started to pace back and forth in front of the bench with a determined look on his face in a reasonably good imitation of their professor. To finish the job he put on his best British accent.

"A small sum invested in the South Sea Company would make a huge return if the investor were to sell his shares before the fateful day in September 1720 when the crash occurred. Those who did not . . ." a look of triumph came into his eyes ". . . lost their shirts!"

"Who did? You mean lost their investment?" asked Sarah with a wide eyed innocent look.

"Isaac Newton for one!"

Annette shook her head. "Not everybody can have lost. Somebody must have made money."

"One person managed to buy low and sell on July 1st 1720 at the peak high, making around 20,000 British pounds, several million in today's money. His name was Masthead Duncan," declared Ken with a flourish.

Sarah shrugged her shoulders, "D'you think he was an ancestor of our professor? Duncan's British."

"They only list initials in the department directory; Duncan's is 'M'. Anybody know what it stands for?" Ken asked.

They exchanged shrugs.

"That's strange. I know the first names of all my other profs, but none of us know Duncan's?" Sarah mused.

What kind of name is 'Masthead,' anyway? Was it a common first name in the 18th century?"

"I have never seen it before," said Annette.

"I bet Duncan has some relevant records. He has stacks of stuff in his office," volunteered Sarah.

"No problem," said Ken, taking a key from his pocket. "You can buy these master keys from the engineers for twenty bucks."

Sarah was horrified, while Annette merely filed the information away for later.

"Is that your big discovery?"

"Yup!"

"I have an appointment with the professor. See you later," said Annette taking Sarah by the arm and walking away.

Sarah cast a quick look back, to see Ken in his blue fedora, staring at the ground his hands in his pockets.

"Annette, come in," said Duncan.

"Professor, are you all right?" She was shocked to see him looking so worn out.

"Fine, just a slight accident, but my shoulder is healing, thank you. I was just having a bit of a rest."

"I won't keep you long, Professor Duncan. I would just like your opinion concerning a question I have about the Nile."

He nodded, and she continued brightly, "It's a matter of navigation charts. If the French admiral Brueys had a really accurate chart perhaps he would have realized the possibility of an English ship of the line slipping between his ships and the shore. I want to compare the modern chart with the 1797 French chart, to see if the lack of detail was a factor in the decision to anchor the French fleet at that particular position, rather than somewhat closer to the shallow water. Did Nelson have any chart whatsoever of Aboukir?"

Professor Duncan made himself more comfortable behind his large custom oak desk.

"Nelson did not go into Aboukir Bay with much knowledge of the enemy. His strategy was 'up and at 'em!' "

Annette considered this for a moment, "Is it likely the British would have lost if Admiral Brueys had moored his ships closer to the shore? If Nelson's ships could only sail on one side of the French line, they wouldn't have had an advantage. I just wanted your opinion on the feasibility of my thesis?"

Duncan smiled at her. "If you present me with hard data to back up your theories in a well argued paper then you will get top marks, but you already know that."

Annette blushed and got up to leave. "Thank you, Professor."

Chapter 2

Malta

Captain Hardy came on board with intelligence that he had spoke a vessel that had left Malta yesterday. The master reported that the French had taken Malta on Friday last, that their fleet had sailed from there on Saturday leaving a garrison of their troops, but could not give any information of the destination of their fleet.

Navy Records Society Vol 2, p22., Logs of the great sea fights, Ed. T. Sturgis Jackson, 1898.

Sunday 10th June 1798 noon: The Grand Harbour

Five hundred ships of Napoleon's huge fleet lay spread out in Valletta's Grand Harbour. Throughout the island of Malta rumours spread of invasion and bloody encounters with French troops.

Lieutenant Reynard, commander of the French armed cutter *Active*, stood on the wharf by St. Barbara Curtain wearing ordinary seaman's clothes. He watched the locals huddled in groups, speaking in low voices, nervous, jittery, as if at any moment they expected to see the French army marching round the corner. Out in the harbour a Grecian brig unloaded a cargo of wheat.

Early that morning the political officer, Langon, had instructed him. It was a simple divide and conquer strategy. "We must turn the populace against the absolute domination of the ruling knights. The movement against the dictator, Grand Master

Hompesch, grows daily. Those that support the knights will turn on the Maltese revolutionaries and we will bring order to the ensuing chaos. We French must be seen as liberators, not invaders. Any kind of trouble gives us a suitable excuse."

Since Reynard spoke the local language his assignment was simply to cause trouble. Help the "divide" part of the French strategy. How he did this was up to him. Reynard had one advantage, he had learned Maltese from his mother. For the first time in his life, his non-French heritage was working in his favour. Perhaps he had found a short cut to promotion.

A boatload of sailors from one of the Greek ships landed at the wharf and stood idly gossiping while they waited for the next shuttle boat. To the left Reynard saw a group of Maltese harbour workers advancing towards him, their shift just finished. The Maltese workers halted at a flight of rough hewn stone steps leading up, into Valletta. Some of them sat down, others lounged. Reynard watched a shabby little man with several days of facial stubble.

"Hey Marjo, you better pay me the money you owe before the French arrive to steal it all."

Marjo took his friend seriously. "They say the French will liberate us from the knights. Are they really going to rob us, Dumink?"

The other laughed. "Come and buy me a drink, French or no French."

Reynard moved away, continuing along the wharf towards the Greek sailors, wondering how he could obey his orders. He could become charming when required despite his crooked nose and pointed features. The sailors seemed to be milling around aimlessly, so Reynard smiled and caught the eye of one whose over developed chest and spindly-legged body reminded the lieutenant of a barrel. The man spoke in Greek, but when Reynard shook his head the man tried French:

"Parlez vous Francais, Monsieur?"

"Oui."

So the barrel man continued. "Our group is new to your island. We wish to know if the taverns are open in such troubled times?"

26

Reynard spoke slowly, as an idea occurred to him. He may not be able to win the Maltese workers to the French side, but he could cause trouble. "Oui, Monsieur, the Taverna Hompesch is open. Turn right at the top of those steps." He indicated the stairs now crowded with dock workers.

"Hompesch? Like the grand master?" Replied Barrelman.

"Oui, Monsieur, named in his honour, but there are other taverns."

"Merci, Monsieur."

Reynard idly walked back to the Maltese dock workers. Dumink was lounging on the third step up, with his friends scattered in groups, blocking the whole width of the staircase. Reynard deliberately walked around Dumink to go up, but the dock worker jumped to his feet, standing tall on the next step up. In any language he looked threatening. He put his hand on Reynard's shoulder and said:

"So you know those Greek sailors?"

Reynard had a good knack with accents, and he had spent some time listening to the workers, so he replied in Maltese adopting the same intonation as Marjo.

"They are waiting for an agent from Hompesch. I think they could be helping the knights."

The men around Dumink abruptly broke off from their conversations.

"What is it, Dumink? Are the Greeks siding with the French invaders?"

"They should be taken to prison. Shall we call the watch?"

Dumink put up his hand for silence. "Hompesch controls the watch, and he is a traitor. We shall take care of these sailors." He nodded to Reynard. "Friend, can you speak Greek?"

"No, but one of them has some French," replied Reynard.

Marjo gasped. "French you say?" A burst of angry exclamations came from the crowd.

By this time, the Greeks had reached the bottom step, and Reynard, still held by Dumink, called to them in Maltese. "Who are you working for?" He looked directly at Barrelman, who looked back uncomprehendingly.

Reynard asked, this time in French: "Which tavern are you going to?"

The man replied: "Hompesch, like you said."

Dumink turned round and gestured to the Maltese workers who crowded together to block the Greek advance. They roared in protest upon hearing the sailor openly claim to be working for Hompesch. Dumink pushed his way through and loomed over Barrelman on the step below, seizing him by the collar. Marjo backed him up, positioning his large bulk right behind his smaller friend.

"We heard what you said. You would help Hompesch and his knights betray us to the French?"

The Greek shrugged his shoulders and looked towards Reynard who descended to the bottom of the stairs and said in French: "They want to know where you are going to drink."

"They look like they want trouble. Tell them we just want to pass into the town."

"That is just their way. Tell them the name of the tavern; they might buy you a drink."

"Hompesch, Hompesch!" he said. He turned to his friends, "These Maltese have short memories. They keep asking me where we are going to drink."

The sailors laughed, angering the dockworkers even more.

"We're making a citizen's arrest. You will all come with me," commanded Dumink.

Reynard smiled. At least he was succeeding in fermenting discord. While the Greek was speaking, Reynard weaved his way in behind the group and gave one of them a push into Marjo, who responded in kind by shoving the man back into the crowd. Then a giant among the Greeks stepped forward and grabbed Dumink by the scruff of his neck:

"Best leave my friend alone! We mean no harm."

In reply Marjo leaped forward and placed his very large knife at the big man's throat: "Best you leave go of my friend, Monsieur."

At that moment another great shove came from behind. Marjo, who had only intended to frighten the man, inadvertently fell forward, so that his knife sliced into the Greek's throat. As the large man lay dying, his blood spurting on to the quayside, a great cry

28

went out from the Greeks, and they surged forward, with knives drawn.

Reynard moved to the back of the crowd, sensing his presence was no longer necessary. As he backed away, he could hear the cries as the men laid into each other. He saw the water stained red where a bleeding man had been pushed over the edge of the dock. The shouting turned into grunts, the sounds of blows and then of pain. The dock workers outnumbered the Greek sailors by two to one. It was a massacre.

The Grand Harbour. Wednesday the 13th of June, 3 AM.

In the early hours of the morning a few days later, Antonio Barbaro slipped over the side of the sixty-four gun man-of-war moored in Valletta's harbour, and into a small skiff left by his friends for the purpose. Although only 21, he had been in the Maltese navy for nearly seven years as a midshipman, and was overdue for promotion to lieutenant. His slim build belied his strength; he handled the waiting boat easily. The ship he had left behind was in the hands of the French navy, and he had no wish to fight for France. Nor did his loyalties lie with Hompesch's knights.

Antonio rowed quietly through the darkness and reached the shore unobserved. He tied up the boat and made his way through a maze of narrow cobbled streets to a nondescript door on the side of an old house. Inserting a small key into the lock, he entered unobserved. Once inside, he paused to light a candle at the top of a flight of stone steps leading downwards. Closing the door behind him, he proceeded to the cellar. The flickering flame revealed stone walls covered in black mould fed by the alcohol seeping out of the wine and spirit casks covering most of the floor. He inspected three of the labels before he chose a particular stack of casks against the far wall. He was able to move them surprisingly easily, pushing them aside to reveal a second doorway. He entered and pulled on a rope attached to the lower cask, which enabled him to pull them back into place behind him.

The passageway led to the cellar of a nearby house. A candle flickered, revealing an old, but well-dressed man bent over his books. Antonio hesitated, not wanting to interrupt. He was bursting to tell his news, however, so he finally coughed.

The old man slowly lifted his eyes from his books. "Mr. Barbaro, it is you. You have something urgent you need to tell me?"

"Monsieur Le Comte, the forts at Tinge and Ricasoli have surrendered. Grand Master Hompesch has capitulated. The French are already landing their troops."

The old man showed no surprise, only resignation. "It is a wonder they can be so concerned about securing our island. It can be of little value to them, unless . . ." he trailed off deep in thought.

The young officer had done his duty, now what remained was for the old man to solve the problem.

"I spoke to Father Vie Cesarini last night," whispered the Comte. "He is of the opinion these French revolutionaries have come to rob our churches. We shall not die to defend the knights, but our sacred relics and the Baroque silver collections are guarded only by the priests. What shall become of them?"

Antonio waited until the silence made him uncomfortable. "The people are no friends of the knights. We should do what we can to safeguard the sacred treasures. The silver . . ."

"Tell them to paint it black. That will hold the French thieves for a time," interrupted the old man with a smile.

"Black? Yes. I will pass the message."

"This Napoleon, he has commandeered our ships?"

"The sixty fours and both frigates are closely guarded by the French navy," replied Antonio.

"Yet our merchant ships are free to leave port?"

"They are subject to search, Sir."

"Pass the word to collect as much of the church silver as can be gathered in a single day. We have very little time. The brig, *Palerma*, is moored in a quiet bay to the north. You must speak to captain Bondini. You know him?"

"Yes, Sir. You are speaking of the Ragusan snow?"

"Just so. Not Maltese and perhaps not subject to the same degree of search. If the French start tightening their hold on the merchant shipping the *Palerma* may not get away. She must be moved to a safe harbour. Load the vessel and report to me. I can trust you to carry out this task?"

The young man bowed. "I will do my duty, Sir."

He left the chamber, and the old man returned to his studies.

Monday 15th June 11 AM 2015 — Sarah

Sarah arrived at the "Bean There" a few minutes late. Annette, looking elegant in a knee-length black skirt and suit-jacket, sat at a table holding a small espresso in one hand.

Sarah, red-faced and out of breath, sat across from her.

"Hi!" Sarah said, ignoring Annette's unvoiced reprimand of her tardiness. "What's up?"

"I didn't hear you get in last night," replied Annette, moving her slim briefcase out of the way of Sarah's chair.

Sarah turned slightly away, brushing her unruly hair out of her eyes. She knew her ragged jeans, a somewhat wrinkled blouse and a generally unkempt appearance did not meet Annette's standards.

"Sorry I'm late. I tore something in my finger climbing on the weekend."

"Can you type?"

"Yes, it'll be fine."

After an awkward pause, Sarah spoke quietly. "Yesterday, before Ken interrupted us, you started to talk about your mother's disappearance. You've never really told me about it. When we were kids you sometimes seemed angry and . . . "

Annette smiled and put her hand out. Sarah took it.

"We've had our differences, yes?"

"Like Quebec sovereignty you mean?"

"I support an independent Quebec with all my heart!" Annette's eyes glistened with tears for a moment.

"Your mother believed this too?" Asked Sarah.

"My mother was a single parent when being a single parent was . . ." Annette paused, looking for the right word.

"Unacceptable?" Suggested Sarah.

31

"Yes, exactly."

"And you never knew your father."

"Except to say that he was English, Mother didn't want to speak about him. She never saw him after I was born, and he didn't help, you know, financially. Because she was French, she never got a decent job, so we were poor. She always said that the FLQ had it right."

"Wasn't the FLQ a terrorist organization?" Asked Sarah with a shocked look.

"Don't worry, I am not suggesting that violence is a good way to achieve equality, but independence is the right path for us as women and as Québécoise."

Sarah looked into Annette's eyes, hoping she would agree. "I want the same, Annette. I think we can get those things by remaining in Canada."

There was a quiet moment and Annette continued to hold Sarah's hand. Sarah plucked up courage. "Look, you hardly ever speak about the time before you came to live with us. I would really like to understand you more."

Annette squeezed her sister's hand and let it go.

"There isn't much to tell. As I said we had some hard times. This old leather bag is the only thing my mother ever gave me. She always insisted that it was a genuine 18th century antique. In fact it was my mother who first turned me on to history, especially the Napoleonic era."

Annette paused and it seemed to Sarah that a shudder ran through her. "That man you described yesterday in Mystic Vale sounded exactly like the man who terrorized my mother and me."

"The man you used to call Uncle André?" said Sarah, in an excited tone.

"My mother called him 'uncle' to make him seem less scary. What worries me is that he might still find me."

Sarah glanced up as Ken walked into the café, ordered an Americano and brought it carefully to their table.

"Ladies, I'm here!" He announced and was greeted with a cool look from Annette and a distant "Hi" from Sarah. Once again he had broken in on a rare personal moment.

Ken stood there, a look of pain on his face. "Er . . . Am I interrupting something?" He asked pushing his fedora back out of his face.

"You look like you were out drinking last night instead of working on your project." Annette sounded like his mother.

"I was getting healthy exercise in a sailing class!"

"You call that exercise?" muttered Sarah.

Ken sat down and knocked Annette's old leather bag off the back of her seat, "Oops sorry." He picked it up and handed it to her. "Hey, your name's burned into the leather."

"Thank you, Ken." Annette's voice was cool.

"Okay, here's the truth. I put in a long evening partying with my engineering friends. Later I had a panic attack about the project, but I stayed up most of the night surfing the internet for information about the South Sea Company."

"The internet. Your original source? Not exactly an archivable reference." Annette was not impressed.

"I looked at a few books as well." Ken sipped at his coffee and smiled.

"Did you guys hear the rumour about Duncan?" Sarah cut in.

"What about him?" Annette asked.

"He turned up at emergency with a knife wound."

"How do you know that?"

Sarah hesitated; she didn't want to betray the confidence of her friend at the hospital. "Uh, well, everybody's talking about it. You saw for yourself . . . his entire arm was bandaged."

"Yes, but what makes everybody think that Professor Duncan was knifed?"

"Perhaps an angry student attacked him. You know, upset about his marks?" Ken interjected.

"As long he can grade the projects," laughed Annette.

"Speaking of which, I found something really exciting." Sarah's voice was louder than she intended.

Ken put on his familiar professorial expression. "I know, you discovered the cure for scurvy!"

"Please tell us what you found, and ignore the bozo." Annette's tone brooked no reply from Ken.

She glared at him, and he sat back down and mimed the closing of a zipper across his mouth. "I was searching through some firsthand reports on scurvy; trying to figure out how it was eliminated. Anyway I found this in the London Gazette." Sarah held up a printed sheet and read aloud.

"Strange incident in the fight against Scurvy: In December 1757 captain James Gilchrest of the British frigate, HMS *Southampton* (32 guns), came to the aid of an English Indiaman. The Merchant Ship was an easy target as she was all but disabled. She had been attacked several months earlier by a French privateer, shortly before nightfall. The Indiaman lost her mainmast, but escaped in the night. She lost her remaining masts in a severe tropical squall, and the crew had no choice but to continue with their long voyage back to England, limping home under jury rig. After several months, the men were dying of scurvy. They were found by HMS *Southampton*. Lieutenant Masthead Duncan was sent aboard the Indiaman with the frigate's surgeon to give assistance."

With a sharp intake of breath, Annette chimed in: "What? Masthead? You're joking right?"

Sarah put the paper down. "This is no joke. The report actually says it was Duncan, not the doctor who gave the scurvy victims some small pills, and they all recovered in a matter of days, some in hours."

The three students started speaking at the same time, until Annette exerted her seniority.

"Listen! This is not the same Duncan as Ken found in 1720! It's thirty seven years later. It can't be the same person . . ."

Ken cut her off. "A strange coincidence, the name Masthead? Have you ever heard that used as a Christian name before?"

"Look, I'm not suggesting it's the same person. I'm just saying this is a weird coincidence. You and I both turned up something about a Masthead Duncan."

Annette drew out a large sheaf of notes from her leather bag. She set them down and fiddled with the clasp. It never did shut properly. The two women looked at Ken who offered no paper notes, but set his smart phone down on the table.

"What has that thing to do with our projects?" Asked Sarah.

"Everything! I have all the details of the French invasion of Malta in 1798." He glared at the women, and caught Sarah shaking her head. "At least I didn't spend my entire weekend rock climbing!"

"You know, I visited Malta last year. I learned quite a bit about the French invasion, the subsequent Maltese revolt against the French, and the British relief expedition Nelson sent a year later." Sarah responded.

Ken was unimpressed. "Oh yes, and I suppose you climbed the famous sea cliffs of Malta?"

"As a matter of fact, I did," she replied. "Look Malta is a really interesting little island. It's steeped in history from the famous siege way back in the 16th century to the ghost ship, which appeared during the French invasion."

Ken brightened at this interesting titbit. "What ghost ship?"

"It's an intriguing story. In 1798, on June 23rd, a brig, the *Palerma*, was found deserted, no crew, nobody, just floating close to Valletta."

"Why? What happened? How come you remember that date?" Asked Ken.

"June 23rd is my birthday! Anyway, nobody really knows what happened. Apparently the lost crew was mostly Malta locals, although the brig was from Ragusa."

"Where the hell is that?"

Annette shook her head. "It is part of Croatia today, but look at the 1798 Mediterranean map, it was a state back then, Napoleon took it around 1806."

"Nobody knows what happened to the crew," continued Sarah. "They were last seen on the morning of the 22nd by Nelson's fleet. Captain Hardy spoke to the vessel's captain, asking for information on the French fleet."

"Well, go on. What else do you know?" Asked Ken.

"Well it isn't real history, except the part about Captain Hardy."

"Who's he?"

"Ken? Are you serious? Only Nelson's flag captain at Trafalgar! It's in his log. Anyway, the ship was found abandoned the next day, and no explanation was ever offered. It was about the time when Napoleon took Malta on his way to Egypt."

"To fight the battle of the Nile!" Ken exclaimed. Nobody spoke for a few seconds, then Ken leaned across the table. "Annette, why're you so interested in that battle?"

Annette put down her pen. "If you must know the Nile was a key battle, a turning point in the war. It brought the British back into the Mediterranean, and cut Napoleon off in Egypt. I believe the history of Europe may have been very different if Admiral Brueys had defeated Nelson."

"Would we be any different today?" asked Sarah with no hint of sarcasm.

Ken jumped in. "D'ya think old Bony would have invaded England? Cut supplies to Canada and sent his fleet over to retake Quebec and maybe the rest of British North America too?"

"It's not beyond the realms of possibility," answered Annette.

"So what difference would it make to us if Canada had been all French?" Ken's tone was ironic.

"Perhaps you would be able to speak French properly," replied Annette.

"Maybe we'd have a better health care system?" Chimed in Sarah.

"And we would all be great cooks!" This last from Ken made Sarah laugh.

Ken glanced at Annette's stone face and changed the subject. "I found some great web sites, ship's logs, financial transactions, all sorts of source material, and downloaded them to my phone. I even found all the modern charts for the Mediterranean, including Aboukir Bay for you, Annette."

"That's kind of you," she said tossing her hair back. "You can't rely entirely on web sites for your research."

"What's your problem, anyway, Annette?"

"My problem is you! You are lazy and always looking for shortcuts. I wouldn't mind if it was only your future at risk, but it's not. Sarah's grade and my success as a TA are also at stake. We have no intention of putting our careers at risk because of you!"

"I'm doing my best. Stop being such a bitch to me!"

Sarah and Annette stared at him, then Annette picked up her things and left.

"Sorry, I didn't mean that the way it sounded," Ken stammered at her retreating back.

"Come and see me when you're ready to work," Annette continued walking, with her head held high.

"You complete idiot!" Sarah looked at Ken in disgust. "She's right, you know." She picked up her backpack and left, unaware of the rock dust that spilled out across the table.

For a moment, all Ken could think of was how very attractive Annette was, especially when angry. Earlier in the term he thought he might have some success if he asked her for a date. Not much chance now that she had marked him as a slacker. Sighing, he settled his hat more firmly on his head, and headed for the history department. He had to prove to Annette that he could be as much of a keener as she was.

Annette sat at a desk reading, "What do *you* want?" She asked barely looking at him. Ken tried not to notice her long black hair, or those perfect, petite features. He took off his hat and bowed.

"I came to apologize."

"Well?"

Ken looked up. "I am truly sorry. I promise that my work will, indeed, be up to your standards."

"Not good enough," but Annette's eyes had softened, and he seized his opportunity.

"Not only do I humbly beg your pardon, but I wish to make it up to you by inviting you, at no cost to yourself, to a slap up feast at La Quiche tomorrow night at seven. I'll bring along my work just to prove to you that I can contribute to the project."

La Quiche was not the best restaurant in town but probably the best Ken could afford.

"I accept if you invite Sarah, so we can get some work done together. Also I would like to borrow your phone to take a look at those charts," said Annette breaking into a smile. She knew she was not immune to his charms.

He fiddled with the phone then handed it over. "I disabled the passcode — it will go straight to the charts app for you," he said.

37

"Thank you. I'm working late tonight so don't forget to tell Sarah."

Ken left for his next class. His feet were not quite touching the ground.

Tuesday 16th June 2015 Victoria 7 PM — Ken

Ken made a special effort to arrive at La Quiche before 7 PM on Tuesday evening. It was certainly better than the lowly cafés he usually visited. The waiter lit the candle at his table and greeted him with a friendly bonsoir. Ken was feeling a little apprehensive about the evening, since, for him, this was a date, which is why he had indulged in the small subterfuge of not inviting Sarah. Annette arrived wearing a brown suede, calf length skirt and a low cut patterned blouse with a dab of pink. Some delicate silver earrings and only a hint of makeup completed her look, which had a remarkable effect on Ken. He stood up to greet her and stayed standing with his mouth open.

"Is there something wrong with your mouth, Ken?" Annette asked with a pretended girlish innocence.

Ken laughed. "Hi, you look great!"

She smiled at his awkwardness and even Ken realized how lame he sounded.

"Some wine?" He asked pointing to his near empty glass.

"No. Thanks."

"Anything else?"

"You could take your hat off."

Ken plucked the inevitable blue fedora from his head. The waiter presented the menu and Ken ordered a second glass of red wine in French. Annette chuckled.

"I try my best," said Ken, a little hurt his efforts had not met with more success.

He buried himself in the menu to hide his exasperation, thinking hard of something to say that would show him to be fascinating and intellectual. He leaned over the table with a show of nonchalance.

"I have made some interesting discoveries about Lieutenant Duncan."

As he said this, the menu he was holding bent closer to the candle flame. "I think he was an English spy against Napoleon."

"Oh really?" Annette was a little unsure if this was another of Ken's jokes. "You mean Duncan from 1757 on HMS *Southampton?*"

The menu started to smoulder.

"Yes, that one," said Ken, who wanted to get maximum effect from his bombshell.

Oblivious to the smoke curling un-noticed between them, Ken repeated his observation:

"You're looking very lovely tonight."

Annette laughed. "That's a non-sequitur. Are you trying to attract me with your boyish charm?"

Ken leaned right over and dropped his voice. "Sorry, couldn't take my eyes off you." He had not meant to lean over quite so far and they simultaneously realized he had given himself a spectacular view of her cleavage.

Annette sat bolt upright. "So I see." She sniffed the air. "What's that smell?"

At that moment the waiter came over to their table shouting something.

"Monsieur! Votre menu est sur la chandelle!"

Ken looked blank, so the waiter said in a loud voice: "The menu is on fire, monsieur!"

Ken jumped up from his seat, his attempt at being romantic shattered. Annette laughed and her annoyance disappeared. Ken reddened and looked sheepishly at the waiter.

"Désolé je ne savais pas su qu'il brûlait."

This only caused Annette to laugh again, this time at Ken's Acadian accent. "Why don't you Anglophones take some trouble to learn French?"

"You're wrong. I'm not an Anglophone."

Annette looked at him as if he were an out-and-out liar, so Ken continued.

"All right, my mother was English, but my father was originally from Turkey, although his mother was from Egypt. In fact I was raised in Cairo for the first seven years of my life, then we moved to Italy until I was fourteen, when we came to Canada. I learned French in New Brunswick when I was a teenager. I can speak French, Italian, Turkish and Egyptian Arabic thanks to my grandmother."

"Look, I had no idea. I'm sorry, okay? Tell me something, aren't Turkish and Arabic the same language?" Ken noticed her apologetic tone and was encouraged.

"Not really, Turkish is quite different. What about you? What's your background?"

Annette hesitated, then started to speak: "I was brought up by my mother who was French, from Paris. She came to Montreal shortly before I was born." Annette paused, then shaking her head said: "She left when I was ten."

"I'm sorry," said Ken.

She looked down at the table. Ken understood these were not happy memories.

"My mother was badly treated by an Englishman before I was born, so she taught me never to trust them. Can you say anything to change my mind on that subject?"

"Errr .. not as such. Is it so bad being French in Canada?"

"Perhaps not now, but in the past it was terrible. Why do you think I'm so passionate about my counter-factual history? If I could go back in time, I would change Canada to make it French!"

Ken's smile hid his discomfort. Annette was finally talking about something other than work, but he could think of nothing that wouldn't sound totally lame. There was a long silence and finally Ken broke the mood.

"I found another reference to Duncan. I mean to Masthead Duncan."

"Tell me, what did you find?" asked Annette, genuinely curious.

"I found it by pure accident. I was looking at the history of Malta and of course the French invasion in June of 1798. As you know Napoleon took the island in just a few days"

"You've done your homework, Ken. The Knights of Malta under Grand Master Hompesch capitulated."

"Yes but the French also captured a number of English people surprised by the invasion. One of them was a naval officer called Masthead Duncan," said Ken with a flourish.

"You're joking?" Annette's tone was incredulous.

"No, really, this was a reliable source."

"You mean we have never heard of this Masthead Duncan one day, and the next we find three references to him, in 1720, 1757 and 1798? If Masthead was say 20 years old in 1720, then he'd be 57 in 1757 and 98 in 1798! It can't be the same person."

"I suppose not," Ken acknowledged.

"Strange with a name like that? The last two were in the navy, 40 years apart." Annette sat back thinking.

"Perhaps it was a father, son and grandson?" Ken conjectured.

"Yes that's possible. Once a silly name is in the family they might use it again." Annette paused. "Wait a minute. The British navy had all but abandoned the Mediterranean before the Maltese invasion, so what was he doing in Malta?"

"I suppose he was spying; he was arrested!"

"Did the article say what happened to him?"

"No, it was in just a list of prisoners from the French records," replied Ken.

She looked puzzled and thought for a moment. "Let's ask Sarah her opinion when she arrives," and she stopped to consult her elegant wrist watch. "She's a little late now. I wonder what can have happened to her?"

A momentary look of guilt passed over Ken's face, and he turned away a little too late.

"You didn't ask her, did you?"

"I thought you'd see her first," lied Ken.

"Monday nights I'm always late getting home. I told you."

"I . . . I wanted you all to myself. I owe you an apology."

Annette stood up. "I do not date Anglophone liars!" She walked out of the restaurant, leaving Ken red faced and ashamed.

"I'm not an Anglophone." He said to her retreating back.

* * *

41

By Friday Sarah started to worry that Duncan's absence might affect their project grade. The professor had missed two lectures that week and, as he was now twenty five minutes late, most of the students had gone. Sarah stood up and walked over to where Annette was sitting studying her notes.

"Any idea where the professor has disappeared to?"

Annette was about to answer when Ken appeared from the back of the class, pushing past a small crowd of students to reach them. "Hi ladies!" he said smiling.

Annette ignored him. "I haven't seen the professor for over a week, since last Thursday afternoon. He didn't turn up to the last class."

"All three of us are here, so shall we meet anyway?" As Sarah picked up her pack, the contents spilled on the ground, including her rock shoes and climber's chalk.

Annette helped pick up Sarah's things, smiling at the lack of feminine purse. "Ken told you of his findings?"

Sarah nodded. "Yes, interesting but just a coincidence."

"Here's an idea!" Ken volunteered.

"Another of your ideas," Sarah sighed.

"No really. Somebody could just go and find out from the department office what's going on with Duncan."

"For once Ken has a good idea. Off you go," said Annette.

Ken blurted out. "Now? You want me to go all the way over to the Clearihue building?"

"If you go, we'll read your project and make some comments."

"All right then, if you gir. . . women gang up on me." Ken handed a sheaf of papers to Annette and ambled off.

About twenty minutes later, they had moved to a bench outside in the sun and were busy editing Ken's essay when he came running towards them, a broad grin spread across his face. He arrived breathless and flung himself down on the bench.

"The history department couldn't tell me anything other than 'Professor Duncan is indisposed'. The secretary apologized that she hadn't notified the class, but she had something, which got me excited."

He paused and Annette glared at him. "Are you going to tell us or not?"

"Sorry. She had his file out on the desk. I think they were looking up his home address; it was right there on the front."

"What are you talking about?" Sarah asked. "What was on the front?"

"His name!"

"Of course his name was on the front of his file!" Annette exclaimed.

Ken spoke the next few words very slowly. "The name on the front of the file was Professor Masthead Duncan, just like the one from 1720 and the Duncans from 1757 and 1798. In case you hadn't noticed it's 2015. The man's amazing!"

"Idiot! They can't be the same man!" declared Sarah.

"All right, but he does have all those genuine antiques in his room, in remarkably good condition."

"Maybe his ancestors left them to him."

"The only verified antique item I know about is the clock," said Annette.

"The clock from the picture? Is it really a couple hundred years old?" asked Ken.

"I'm assured it's genuine by an expert in the field. Well, a guy called Charlie."

Sarah laughed. "Professor Duncan seems to set great store by Charlie."

"He certainly seems to know a lot about 18th century clocks."

"It does match the clock in the painting of HMS *Lively's* great cabin in Duncan's office." Sarah said, wrinkling her nose.

Annette ran her fingers through her long black hair, lost in thought for a few seconds. Then her face drained of colour and she stopped arranging her hair. "Sarah, there's something else that's curious."

"What?" said Sarah and Ken simultaneously,

"You remember last week behind the coats, in Duncan's office? I saw something not quite right with the window in the little room. Now I understand what it was."

The others looked at her waiting. "It was 5 PM in June and daytime, yet through that window it was dark outside."

Sarah looked at her sister, not understanding. "What're you saying? Duncan's inner office has a magic window?"

"Wait a minute, let me get this straight." Ken said this with such authority that both women stopped to listen.

"First, we have the strange name of Masthead Duncan. A name none of us had heard before, turning up three times in the past, decades apart. Second, we have the modern Duncan and his strange knife wound. Third, the professor has numerous items including the ship's clock, that should look like antiques but, instead, look new. Fourth, the strange inner office with the window out of sync with the world."

Nobody spoke for a while, then Annette gave a slight cough. "I have one more piece of information, but I don't want to share it right now."

"Annette we are all in this together," said Ken with no hint of a smile.

"In what?" asked Sarah mystified.

"Finding an explanation that fits all the facts. Well I've got a theory, and I think Annette is on the same line or she wouldn't be so cagey."

Annette held her head high and wore an expression that told Ken she was not going to reveal anything that she did not want to.

"For goodness sake, people. What's everybody on about?" asked Sarah in a voice as tight as the tension she felt.

"So are you going to tell us?" Ken demanded.

"All right, but this goes no further. Is that understood, Ken?"

"I swear!"

"Before my mother left, she promised she would be back with me very soon. Sarah's family took me in while she was gone."

"Sarah's family? You grew up together?" Ken said astonished.

"It's something we usually keep between us. You will respect that, Ken?" Annette was very firm.

"Of course! Please continue."

"Well she never came back! She said that if she did not return, I should apply to the University of Victoria, and in June of

2015, I would find some kind of gate that would help me find her. I never knew exactly what she meant, but perhaps this is it. I have to take this chance, if I could find her . . ." Annette paused, then added: "It's worth it to me, no matter what the potential cost or danger."

"So you agree with my theory?" stated Ken.

"What theory? Look you guys I don't understand what you're saying?" Sarah threw her hands up, frustrated.

"It's obvious!" Ken cried. "Duncan's a time traveller! He brought that stuff here from the past. He made his money from the South Sea Bubble, he knew to give Vitamin C to cure scurvy, back when they thought it was a disease, not a lack of something. Those recent injuries of his weren't made by a knife attack, but by a sword wound from somewhen in the past."

"Are you serious?"

"Sarah, please listen. I keep reading about experiments where elemental particles react to others before they come into existence, and according to Stephen Hawking, black holes and worm holes criss-cross the space-time continuum. Perhaps Duncan found a wormhole."

"Where do you think Duncan is now?" Sarah asked, her tone sceptical.

"Suppose he went back to 1798, to Malta. My research material tells me somebody of his name was imprisoned there. Right now he could be stuck in a French prison in 1798."

"That's nuts, how can he be 'now' stuck in a French prison, if it's all in the past?" Sarah looked at Annette wide eyed.

"Yes confusing isn't it? But do we have to finish the projects?" repeated Ken.

The women glared at him. "Annette, do *you* believe time travel is possible?" Sarah asked ignoring Ken.

Annette held out her hand. "Ken, give me your illegal key. I am going to look in his office."

"Not without me you're not!" said Ken.

"Wait!" Sarah said louder than she intended. "You can't believe . . ." she stopped and looked at Annette, surely she of all of them would be the sceptic. Annette glanced at Ken, who used his trump card. "Come on, Annette. You can't get into his office without my key."

"Don't be so ridiculous. There's probably a perfectly ordinary explanation. The clock and its case are clever forgeries. You were mistaken about what you saw through the window. Time travel is simply not possible." Sarah was determined to introduce sanity into the conversation.

Annette looked at Sarah and shook her head. "Sarah, this is it. This is what my mother told me to look for before she disappeared. I think she was trying to protect me from Uncle André. Perhaps he has something to do with this business. She didn't tell me everything in case he ever found me."

"You want to break into Duncan's office? Is this worth jeopardizing your academic career?" asked Sarah.

"Yes — it is!"

Sarah held out her hand, and Annette grasped it in stunned silence. Nobody moved for a full ten seconds, then Ken broke the spell.

"That's good enough for me, let's go."

"He's a professor!" Sarah's words were wasted since Ken was already halfway across the quad and Annette, who had dropped Sarah's hand, was close on his heels.

Not far from their bench, a poorly dressed man with a scarred face emerged from behind a tree, and followed them across campus.

Chapter 3

The Slave Galley

Thursday 7th June 1798 8:30 PM — Abdul

Fortunately for the galliot a large wave hit the French ship, causing the gun crew to miss their timing as their ship rolled up. The shot passed harmlessly over the heads of the exhausted slaves, who pulled towards safety behind the shelter of the barque. Both frigates turned to follow, now out of position to deliver another broadside but with an intent to board the galliot. The frigates held enough marines and sailors to send a small army of men aboard to ensure its capture.

The wind was strong enough so that the French sailing ships could outdistance the *Murad* easily, but the frigates had a much deeper draft. Abdul steered his vessel towards the shallow water, as close inshore as the jagged rocks would allow. He kept the barque between his position and the frigates, so his attackers would not use their bow chasers. The gap was closing, when, in answer to the captain's silent prayer to Allah, the fickle shore breeze died. The sailing ships drifted slowly while the *Murad* made good her escape, hugging the shoreline to seek the darkening night's protective cover.

Nearly two weeks later on the 19th June, Abdul stood on his quarterdeck wrapped in a mood of deep frustration. His anger smouldered like slow match burning the fuse of his limited patience. He watched the crew working to complete the repairs to his vessel. Their ability to procure materials was hampered by the French

47

soldiers, who swarmed over the island. He turned to the watch officer, a young man by the name of Omar.

"The cursed French frigate killed one quarter of my ciurma, and my first officer is a smear on the deck. We lost a goodly prize with a hold full of valuable cargo. We started with 18 oars on the larboard side and now there are only ten. Damnation to those French ships!"

"Captain, the frigates were only the vanguard of a French fleet, come to take this island from the knights. Perhaps it was simply God's will." Omar said, trying to placate his captain.

Abdul paced the quarterdeck and looked shoreward. The rais was an imposing figure, tall with a weather beaten face, a typical Egyptian nose, and a massive red beard, which he wore most proudly. In his left ear dangled a large gold earring, giving him a piratical appearance; however, he was not just another Barbary Coast pirate. He was Mersa Bey's fleet commander, assigned to the *Murad*, the last oared vessel in the fleet. Perhaps, Abdul reflected, it was the last Egyptian galliot afloat.

They were at anchor in a small bay surrounded on the landward side by unscalable cliffs, some 100 metres in height, where he hoped they were safe from the French. He sniffed the sea fresh air, noticing the smell from the ciurma was not as bad as in earlier times. Now volunteers and debtors outnumbered the slaves; less than half of them were chained to the benches. He turned to watch the deck hands raise an awning supported by oars to keep the sun from their bare backs. Soon they started to make bean soup. Abdul let a faint smile cross his face when Manu, his servant, hobbled to the sternpost carrying a tiny cup of very strong Turkish coffee. The captain accepted the coffee from Manu, so loyal and still useful despite his age. A young boy, Manu's son, followed with a tray of food. The coffee helped Abdul concentrate on solving the current problem. After a while he turned to the young officer beside him,

"Omar Hassan al-Munari."

"Aye, aye, my rais."

"The first officer is dead, so I am required to decide on promotions." Omar and all the deck officers became alert. Abdul continued. "Our Bey has directed us to find out what we can about French fleet dispositions in the Eastern Mediterranean. Many sails were seen to leeward of those two frigates. A fleet this large must be an invasion force much too large for Malta; the question is who will they invade next? I need an officer to take a boat into Valletta."

Omar stepped forward. "At your command, my rais."

Abdul needed a more experienced officer to go with Omar; his gaze fell upon his second, Abu bin Samir, the younger son of one of the wealthier of Mersa Matruh's ruling class. The man had joined the crew at the command of the Bey, despite Abdul's misgivings. Samir performed his duty well enough, working with the galley master, Ali, to ensure the slaves were ready at all times to power their craft, but their cruelty was often counterproductive.

"Samir, take young Omar and bring me information. No, I want more than information. I want you to bring back a French naval officer, perhaps two. They can tell me what I want to know and provide extra hands for the oars. You may take Ali in case the Frenchmen cause trouble."

Omar did not look pleased at being sent out with Samir as his senior. Omar was the son of the Bey, and to be sent off as lackey to this evil eyed second son felt like an insult, but it was their captain's wish. The sailors launched a small boat and, as the officers stepped aboard, the captain called out to them.

"Samir, I hold you responsible for Omar's safety. Make sure the Frenchmen are both acquainted with the fleet movements, and wealthy. You understand me? French, wealthy, and knowledgeable!"

Four sailors rowed towards Valletta. Their small vessel passed unheeded in the shadows of the huge French fleet silhouetted against the night sky. The ships were on the move, and Omar was trying to count them when Samir leaned across to the Bey's son.

"Omar, do you know where to look for Frenchmen?"

The younger officer looked at him and shook his head, so Samir continued. "I will tell you. These Frenchmen pass their time imbibing alcohol. We shall seek them out in one of their taverns. Our rais is desirous they should be rich, and how else can we tell if a man has wealth without first examining his purse? Perhaps some of that wealth could be directed towards a more worthy cause?"

Omar's reply had a hard edge to it. "I am not a common thief. They must be wealthy for the ransom we shall extract and, most importantly, they must have knowledge about the fleet." With that he stood up and addressed the rowers. "Let me pass!" He pushed past the hands to the bow where he sat as far from Samir as he could. Samir laughed, then there was silence.

Time passed, and Omar started to drift off to sleep. The rhythm of the oars blotted out the whispered conversation in the stern.

"Are you my man, Ali?" demanded Samir.

"Sir, I am your man. I hope to see you as Bey one day."

"To command such a fine vessel as the *Murad* would be a grand thing indeed. Already the men and slaves fear me. It would not be difficult. A knife in the dark, a splash, and the rais would be gone."

Ali bowed his head in assent, and soon afterwards the boat gently bumped against a stone wharf, The Arab sailors alighted, leaving two men to watch over it. There were no guards to challenge them, so they proceeded towards the centre of Valletta. The five men slipped into the city and soon found what they sought. A cobbled street led to a dimly lit stone building, where a battered sign declared they were at the Taverna St. Ursula. The place was noisy and crowded with French soldiers.

Samir smiled at Omar. "The invasion is good for business." Then, turning to Ali, he said, "Take the hands and find the back entrance. You know what to do with any French officers who come out, understand?"

The men went out by the back door, leaving Omar and Samir to inspect the clientele, consisting mostly of uniformed officers.

"We shall wait to see if any of them exit at the back. We follow them out and let our men do the rest," Samir whispered.

Omar pointed to a pair of youngish looking French naval officers. "Those two seem very nervous. Perhaps we can encourage them to take the rear exit?"

"I have been watching them. One of them paid for that whole crowd of drunken army officers," Samir replied.

As he spoke, a fight broke out. Two of the officers were at each other's throats over a provocatively dressed woman. A table turned over, and the two young navy men who had caught Samir's attention jumped out of the way, and headed directly towards the back door.

"Allah has sent us these two. Let's go."

They followed the men into the darkness. The French officers were caught off guard by the galliot's sailors waiting by the door. Samir grabbed the nearest captive by the neck and showed him his knife.

"Make a noise, and I will cut out your tongue!"

In any language his threat was understandable.

Friday 19th June 2015 9:40 AM — Ken

By the time they reached Duncan's office, Annette and Ken were, once again, arguing.

"Ken, I am going in alone. No sense in both of us jeopardizing our careers. Just give me the key, and I'll return it later."

"Not on your life! If Duncan has some sort of time machine in there I want to check it out!"

Annette's eyes hardened. It was hard to argue when Ken had the key. After checking that the corridor was clear, Ken opened the door, bowing low as Annette went through into the office shaking her head.

"Look there's the clock in the captain's cabin," Annette said looking at the big painting.

"Wow! The detail is magnificent. You can see the wooden spirals on the case. Well actually only one spiral, just like the clock sitting on the Professor's shelf."

Annette stepped over to the actual clock, inspected it then went back to stare at the painting. "Look Ken, those scratches near the base. The artist has reproduced them faithfully. That's definitely the same clock in the painting. The case is either an incredibly clever forgery or else the real thing."

"Come through time!" Exclaimed Ken. "Where's this inner office? Let's check it out."

51

Annette moved in front of the hanging coats. "Oh no. You stay where you are. I'm not having a clumsy idiot getting in my way on this trip."

Ken glared at her and was about to say something when they heard somebody walking down the corridor. Annette let out a stifled cry, pushed Ken out of the office and pulled the door closed.

"What the hell're you doing?" he hissed, stopping short when he saw a university security officer approaching.

The man glanced at Ken, then addressed Annette, "Anything wrong, miss?" Clearly he had not seen them emerge from the professor's office.

"No, I am fine, thank you. We were just having a discussion, and we're going now." With these words, Annette grabbed Ken by the arm and propelled him down the corridor.

"Listen Ken," Annette said, once they were outside in the sunshine.

"What?"

Crowds of students were hurrying in all directions, and she made sure Sarah was not one of them before she continued. "If you give me your key, I'll go and look at the inner office to check the anomaly I saw before. I'll come right down to tell you what I see." Ken just stood there looking at her, so Annette added, "And I'll go on a date with you."

The young man's eyes grew wide, but he made no move to give her the key, so she added, "And I'll be nice. Agreed?"

He was speechless. She sensed he wanted another chance to make up for the disastrous dinner at La Quiche, but still he hesitated.

"I don't know," he said.

Annette held his arm again, only this time she pulled his head down so she could whisper in his ear. "If you give me the key I'll sleep with you, okay?"

Ken's mouth opened, but no words would come out. He held out the key, which she took with a smile.

"You're too much of a gentlemen to hold me to that one, aren't you?" Annette asked blowing him a kiss.

As she disappeared into the building, Sarah came out of a different door.

"Where'd you go? I looked upstairs, and all I saw was some security guy making his rounds. I thought you'd been carted off!"

"We got out before he arrived."

"So what'd you do with Annette?"

Ken could not keep the smile off his face. "I gave her my master key."

"What!" exclaimed Sarah, "You let her go upstairs by herself? By now she's gone back to the 18th century, and we'll never see her again. Why would you do that?"

"She said she would be nice to me." Ken did not sound so sure of himself now.

"Men!! You let her go and discover whatever it is on her own in exchange for a promise? Have you any idea what trouble . . ."

"She's gone to look in the inner office; then she will report her findings to us," interrupted Ken.

"Ken, you're an idiot! She's fanatical about her project. She wouldn't pass up an opportunity to see the 18th century first-hand. Why would she talk to us first?"

"She, uh . . . you're right!"

Sarah and Ken ran back into the building and up to Duncan's office. The door was shut and locked.

"She's pretty keen to keep us out, isn't she?" Sarah griped, her voice betraying her annoyance.

Ken knocked on the door but, predictably, there was no answer. He looked at Sarah with a sheepish expression.

"Well? What is it?" she demanded.

"Oh, nothing." As he said this, Ken dug into his pocket and produced another master key. "Why buy one when you can get two?" he asked unlocking the door and stepping across the threshold. Sarah stood outside for a second looking amazed until Ken stuck his head out. "Come on before security comes back."

She entered and stood in the office wondering what to do next, while Ken quietly closed the door behind her. Sarah made up her mind and crossed through the uniforms into the inner office. "Hey, Ken! Here we go!"

"Hang on." Ken held up a small leather pouch containing gold coins he found in the desk drawer. "Bingo!"

"You can't take the professor's money!" Sarah protested from the doorway.

"We'll need it! Gold was the only viable international currency back then. If I'm right about the South Sea Bubble, Duncan won't miss this little purse."

"You don't even know if you can operate whatever it is," said Sarah.

"Let's go and find out." Ken said as he pushed past her through the coats.

"It's dark, just like Annette said." Ken pointed at the only window. To the left was a door. "Sarah, this is it! He's got some sort of gateway here. Wherever it leads is certainly not Victoria at 10 o'clock in the morning."

"Wait!" said Sarah. "I have to go through that door and help Annette, but you've no reason to endanger yourself."

Ken just laughed. "First, as you so rightly pointed out, I am smitten by Annette, and I certainly don't want any harm to come to her, besides she's got my smart phone."

"What?"

"They had some Mediterranean naval charts she wanted. I gave it to her!"

Sarah smiled; she didn't want to go alone. "Ok then, if you want to come with me, then we need to prepare ourselves."

"What d'you mean?"

"If you're right about this we can't turn up wearing 21st century clothes!"

They returned to the outer office, where Sarah started to go through the rack of clothes.

"Are you going to the ball as a man?" Ken asked, in a shocked tone when he saw the uniform Sarah was holding.

"Of course," said Sarah, "I don't think it was much fun being a woman 200 years ago. Turn around while I change, Ken."

Ken turned his back and she quickly put on what turned out to be the uniform of an aspirant, the French equivalent of midshipman. Her sports bra helped keep her breasts from being too noticeable and her hair was tied back in a pony tail imitating the masculine naval style of the time. Her little turned up nose was cutely feminine but she could do nothing about that. Of the two, Ken was less convincing with his short hair, but the naval hat hid the 21st century styling.

Ken sadly left the blue fedora on Duncan's desk and they returned to the inner office to face the door, but there was no handle.

Sarah tried pushing, but it wouldn't budge. "Annette must have gone through, or we would've seen her."

"True! If she figured this out, then so can we." Ken thought for a moment. "Maybe it's some kind of voice activated device. It can't only be tuned to the professor's voice, because Annette managed to open it. What would she think of?"

"It has to be something really obvious."

A loud knock sounded on the outer door. An authoritative voice called: "Professor Duncan, security here. Somebody called in some suspicious activity."

"Security!" said Sarah in absolute panic.

"Quiet, they may not come through here." But Ken sounded just as worried. They kept silent as they heard the outer door open.

"Anybody here?" They could hear the security officer moving around the office, and then the sound stopped and they heard uniforms being shuffled on the rack.

"Christ!" whispered Ken, "He'll find the inner office."

"If only this door would open."

Ken screwed up his face concentrating hard. "Perhaps it's some catch phrase from history, like open sesame!"

Sarah gave him an exasperated look. "Don't be stupid! This isn't the 1001 Arabian nights." As she said this, the door in front of her slid silently to one side revealing a dark interior.

"See, I told you so!" Ken couldn't hide the excitement in his voice. The pair hurried through the door, which slid shut as the security guard entered.

Tuesday 19th June 1798 7 PM — Antonio

The solitary candle flickered as Antonio entered the chamber. After a few moments the old man looked up from his books. "You have succeeded in the task I set you?"

55

"As you anticipated, monsieur Le Comte, the French have looted a large number of the churches. They loaded their own ships with our silver, but they did not get it all. The priests were happy to cooperate with us when they saw the true intentions of these invaders. Where we had time, the black paint was sufficient to make fools of the soldiers, and we also removed three dozen crates filled with silver."

The old man looked pleased, then a cloud seemed to pass over his face. "Has General Napoleon's fleet yet sailed?"

"It is likely they will be under way by tomorrow morning."

"Were you discreet?"

Antonio paused, knowing he was at fault. "Monsieur Le Comte, I beg to report I have been unable to conceal our activities. At St. George's in Citta Pinto some of our men were caught moving the silver out of the great church. The French army arrived to take what they considered their own, and several of our men were incarcerated. I myself . . ." Antonio stopped again, trying to choose the right words to express his fears, without seeming to be a coward.

"You were being followed, Antonio?" The old man was ahead of him.

"Yes, Sir. I fear a French agent suspects I am involved in saving the treasures of our churches."

The old man chuckled to himself. "Don't worry, my young friend, others protect you. Use one more day to collect silver and load the *Palerma*. The French soldiers are none too bright. The black paint will continue to make fools of them. The brig must put to sea in two days at most, you hear me? We cannot risk more time, or the French will seize her. I have here a letter to our friends in Sicily to be conveyed by the brig. You will take these documents to her captain and tell him my instructions, but you will not go with the ship. For you I have other plans."

The Comte saw the look of disappointment in Antonio's face. "We have rid ourselves of the knights and, in time, we will overcome the French. You will get your promotion to lieutenant in the new Maltese navy. One day you will have your ship." Antonio took the packet and had turned to go when the old man spoke again. "Remember, she must sail by the 21st."

Chapter 4

The Gate

When Annette emerged from the disused munitions shed, she was surprised to find she was in a courtyard of what she thought was an old castle. Nobody noticed her as she stepped into a crowd of mostly female Maltese workers. A discerning observer would have noted that her gown, hastily selected from Duncan's collection, was too grand for this situation. The French castle guards, however, were intent on the change of shift, and just wanted to get the workers out of the courtyard and the gate closed for the day.

Unobserved in the crowd, Annette recognized the Maltese dialect. She was hot in the formal gown, but her joy at finding herself in Malta outweighed her discomfort. She had done it! She had travelled through whatever strange gateway Duncan had in his office, and ended up in a different place and time. The evidence from the articles suggested that the last place Duncan visited was Malta in the year 1798, but she had to be sure. She needed a way out of the procession to get her bearings.

Impeded by her formal dress and unused to the uneven cobbles, Annette soon trailed behind the domestics. In an effort to catch up, she increased her pace, which caused her to stumble into the path of two French naval officers. The shorter of the two grasped her arm and steadied her.

"Be careful Mademoiselle, such a pretty dress," he said in French.

Annette replied, in the same language. "Monsieur, you are too kind."

He bowed, but kept hold of her hand. "You are French?"

"Monsieur, I am the daughter of a Frenchman, but I was brought up here." As the words escaped she realized this story was a mistake. Being Maltese might cover her accent in French, but would not explain why she did not speak the local dialect.

"My apologies Mademoiselle, but you are a daughter of one of the nobles? Perhaps you will permit me to escort you to your father's house?"

As the officer bent closer, Annette's face flushed with shock, and her whole body pulsed with her beating heart. Although this man was much younger, he bore a strong resemblance to Uncle André. She forced herself to concentrate, remembering that she was two hundred years in the past. The officer in front of her was unscarred and, unlike Uncle André, had both of his eyes and a full head of hair. He could not be the same man who had haunted her childhood nightmares.

"Something is wrong? Do you feel unwell? Mademoiselle. . .?"

Unlike the husky rasp that had sounded so threatening to the young Annette, the officer's voice was clear, deep, almost enticing. The young man was waiting for a reply, and Annette had to think fast. She had stepped through the gate without taking any time to prepare a story to explain her presence here. She was in Malta and, judging from the style of the uniforms, it was sometime after the French invasion of the 13th June 1798. She needed to guide the conversation, to find out whether the fleet had yet departed for North Africa.

"Monsieur you are too kind, but my father is long dead, and I have been living with distant relatives. Unfortunately, they fled when the motherland relieved our island of the tyranny of the Knights. I am . . . quite alone."

Annette hoped this speech might arouse some sympathy. Perhaps this officer could help her to change the outcome of the forthcoming battle.

"I am deeply distressed to hear of your pitiable state. Perhaps I may escort you into the city?"

Annette smiled. The same charms which had seized the hearts of men in the 21st century seemed to work equally well in the 18th.

"You have my gratitude, Monsieur. My name is Annette . . ." A sudden panic seized her, should she give her mother's name? It had an aristocratic sound to it and this revolutionary officer might be averse to helping if he thought she was an aristocrat. She settled for using the name she used at the University. "Annette Salvigny." It was the name she had used when she and her mother were fleeing from Uncle André.

"I am Lieutenant André Reynard, commander of the cutter *Active*."

Hearing the name André made her heart beat faster but, mercifully, Annette's apprehensive memories of the man who stalked her in the twentieth century were interrupted when the other officer made a polite cough.

"May I introduce my first officer, Lieutenant Granon," said Andreé, taking the hint.

"Enchanté Mademoiselle," said his taller companion in a strong voice.

He bowed his head, then looked straight into her eyes. The thrill she felt was a complete surprise, and she also bowed her head as much to acknowledge the introduction as to hide her excitement. When she looked back Granon was smiling. Had he felt the connection?

"Mademoiselle, may we escort you somewhere? These are dangerous times," warned Granon.

"Thank you, Monsieur, but . . . I am taking you away from your duties. Are you preparing to sail with the fleet?"

"We must go where the admiral orders us. As you no doubt saw this morning, the fleet has sailed without us."

Annette smiled, now she knew it was the 19th of June, 1798. Without thinking, she murmured, "The 1st of Messidor."

Reynard turned in surprise, "Mademoiselle, you are acquainted with the general's revolutionary Calendar?"

"I read a great many books, Monsieur."

The excitement she felt on discovering how close she was to Admiral Brueys and the Napoleonic fleet gave her confidence and a bold exhilaration. She decided all she had to do was bide her time and win the heart of this eager young commander of the French cutter. Perhaps she could persuade them to take her to the Admiral. Was it possible that she could actually change history? As they came into the town of Valletta, Reynard stopped and indicated a nearby inn.

Reynard turned to her. "The Taverna St. Ursula, Mademoiselle. My first officer and I will be taking dinner here. You would do us a great honour if you would share our table?"

"Thank you, Monsieur. I would be most pleased to dine with you."

The officers escorted her to a quiet private dining room away from the noisy public areas and took over the task of ordering their meal.

"So Monsieur Lieutenant, you command a cutter. How grand! You have fought the English with this cutter?"

"Indeed, I helped capture the *Active* from the English almost ten years ago, but she is built to a French design, very slim, very fast and armed with 12 powerful guns. Each gun is capable of sending a four pound ball through the side of an English ship."

"You helped to capture the vessel? How very brave you must be!"

Annette settled back to allow her companions to control the discussion. Reynard was pleased with her flattery. She smiled and took in everything they said, hoping for any nugget of information that might further her quest. As they finished their meal, Annette overheard one of the waiters speaking French. Excusing herself, she rose from the table and cornered him at the far end of the bar, out of her escorts' sight.

"Monsieur, do you have a vacant room in this hotel for a few days?" She glanced around as she spoke trying not to show how nervous she felt. A drunken dispute between several French officers nearby forced her to raise her voice, making it difficult to be unobtrusive. Fortunately, plenty of rooms were vacant now the fleet had departed, and Annette swiftly settled the matter. As she returned to the table her old shoulder bag caught on the chair. The long since broken clasp flew open, allowing the contents of her bag to fall onto the floor and table. The men rose and helped her right the problem. Annette's face flushed as she stuffed conspicuously out of period items such as her Yale keys and address book back into her bag. As she sat down again, she noticed Ken's phone sitting open on the table where it had fallen. Ken had disabled the entry code for her and when it hit the wooden surface the screen slowly scrolled through the late 20th century Mediterranean nautical charts. Grabbing the smart phone, she returned it to her bag and sat down, her face red with fear and embarrassment.

The officers appeared oblivious to the unusual object as they resumed their conversation. Annette forced herself to relax; surely if they had noticed anything strange they would have questioned her about it.

The meal over, Granon was dispatched with the bill, leaving Reynard a moment alone with Annette.

"Mademoiselle, it has been a wonderful evening. Perhaps I could call on you? We have yet to receive our sailing orders."

"That would be most generous of you, Monsieur Reynard."

"Please call me André. But how shall I find you?"

"Monsieur André I am staying here, at this inn. Until I have dealt with my family affairs, you understand?" Reynard nodded his head gravely, and she added: "You may leave a message for me." Granon reappeared, and the officers took their leave.

Her extensive studies of the period could not prepare Annette for the reality of an 18th century inn. The smells were strange and slightly disgusting, and the stairs creaked as she was shown up to her attic room. She ducked, through the low doorway leading to a delightful old chamber. She was not so thrilled with the chamber pot under the bed and still worried about the smart phone incident, but her excitement overshadowed her concern. It was not so often one travelled two hundred years in a single day.

Tuesday 19th June 1798 7:30 pm — Ken and Sarah

Ken and Sarah walked into the June sunshine of the old fort only half an hour behind Annette. As they took in their surroundings, Ken whispered to Sarah.

"Oh Toto, I have a feeling we're not in Victoria anymore."

"We're in some kind of castle. No doubt we want to be on the other side of that wall," laughed Sarah.

She pointed through the big, heavily guarded iron gate. A number of uniformed men, dressed not so differently from Ken and Sarah, moved purposely about their business, but fortunately the courtyard was crowded and they were not noticed. The couple mingled with a group of locals and French officers heading towards the castle gate. Ken walked out of the old fort with a bit of a swagger, and Sarah followed, surprised nobody challenged them. Although they spoke little, not wishing to draw attention to their French, it did occur to Ken that his Acadian French bore many similarities to the language spoken by the soldiers.

Sarah's memory of Valletta was different from the city that greeted her, especially the smells and sounds of life around them. Horses clip clopped on the old cobbles, and the smell of car exhaust was replaced by that of horse dung. The colours seemed dreary compared to what she remembered of her visit in the 21st century, and the smells and sounds of 21st century life were entirely missing.

A French army patrol passed, looking grand but hot in their blue coats and white breeches. Sarah, thinking it best to avoid the busy places in case they were questioned, led Ken off the main avenue. After walking for twenty minutes, they found themselves in a deserted street where they felt safe enough to discuss their next move.

"First we must find out exactly when and where we are," said Sarah.

Ken looked at her, his eyes sparkling in triumph. "How about at the Taverna St. Ursula, Valletta, and this is St. Ursula Street, at least that's what's written on this sign."

Sarah was still a little dazed by their walk through time and space. "So you're sure this is not some kind of illusion?"

"Look around you! This is definitely not Canada! Do you think Valletta looks like this today?"

"Have you been there? It's hardly any different," sighed Sarah.

Ken gave a derisive laugh, and Sarah countered: "Ok the people are different, but the streets look more or less like this now, at least Saint Ursula Street does. I was here last year."

"So where're all the cars? No way this is 21st century Valletta, and it's certainly not Victoria. I was right! That door has led us back in time. Come on! Let's see what we can learn."

Sarah knew that Ken was right. Curious to explore this new, old world, she followed him through the door of the tavern. The inn was crowded, and they walked straight into a group of French army officers. Judging by their degree of intoxication, the officers had been at the inn for some time, and two of them seemed to be having some kind of confrontation over the woman who held each of them by the arm. Sarah eyed the tall red-headed woman's extravagant, low cut dress. In any century it would have been possible to guess her profession.

Ken pushed past the quarrelsome group as if he were in a bar in Canada and leaned on the counter.

"Citoyen!" The army officer beside Ken said with a wink to his comrade. Roughly translated what Ken heard was: "Now the army has taken the town it's time for the navy to provide for us." The man slammed his tankard down on the bar, and he and his companion crowded around the now slightly worried Ken.

Fortunately, the streets of Montreal had trained Ken to cope with this kind of thing. He turned to the bar man, addressing him in Italian.

"Ale for my friends in the army. One for me and my companion and one for yourself, landlord."

He put down the smallest gold piece he could find and pointed to the barrel of ale. The landlord slung the required number of pots on the bar, and the army officers let out a great cheer.

"God be with the brave sailors who embarked today to their destiny."

Ken had won the approval of the army officers, but he was concerned with the commotion his gold coin was causing behind the bar. Ken could understand fragments of the local dialect, which was similar to Arabic.

"How do they expect me to find change for some foreign gold bullion worth half a king's ransom!" The landlord muttered under his breath. Eventually he grudgingly gave Ken some coins in what appeared to be a very inadequate quantity of the local scudos. Ken wisely decided not to question the amount of change, and after some back slapping and general camaraderie from his new drinking companions, he retired to a quiet corner to talk to Sarah.

"Well you do have hidden depths. Bad Italian as well as bad French!"

"Actually my Italian is quite good." For once Ken was being serious. "Did you hear what that guy said?" Ken's face shone with excitement as he continued. "The fleet has sailed. He must mean Napoleon's fleet has already set off for Egypt."

"That makes the date sometime after the 19th of June, and you were right, it's 1798. "

Ken took a sip of his drink and, as he tilted his glass, he noticed that two men in baggy pants were staring them. He whispered in Sarah's ear in French, "Let's not talk too loudly in English. Those two in the corner are paying us too much attention."

Sarah replied in French. "I'm also a little worried about passing as a man. I feel very out of . . ." before she could finish her sentence, one of the army officers fell across their quiet corner table, hotly pursued by his red faced rival. Within a few seconds the whole tavern was joyfully involved in the melee.

A fair number of uniformed French officers converged on the drunken company, and Sarah sensed their disguises would be easily penetrated under even a cursory questioning. Even as this thought flitted through her head, she noticed a large officer heading in their direction.

"Forget the two in the corner," whispered Sarah, her voice cracked with urgency. "Let's sneak out the back door before the huge Capitan comes to question us."

"Okay. You go first, and I'll be right behind you," Ken agreed.

They jostled their way through the crowd towards the back door where Ken followed Sarah. As he stepped outside to join her, a hand grabbed his coat swinging him around. He caught sight of Sarah lying inert on the ground, and then he felt a sharp blow behind his ear. The world spun, but the rush of fear and anger made him hit out wildly at his attacker. He stopped struggling when one of the men he recognized from the bar brandished a large curved knife in front of his face.

Ken's first reaction was surprising, even for him. "Get off! You can hurt somebody with a knife like that!" Although he did not realize it, the fact that he said this in French saved his life. As a Frenchman he was worth keeping alive. The man holding the knife scraped the blade across the side of Ken's neck. The knife dug slightly deeper, and blood ran. It had the required affect on Ken, who went very still, recognizing the man's expertise with his weapon.

His captors were speaking in Arabic and Ken listened, trying to concentrate enough to understand the language of his youth. The two from the bar were officers aboard some kind of craft. As they carried Sarah's limp body, they kept Ken at knife point. One of them muttered about cutting his tongue out if he made a sudden move.

Sarah came to slung over the shoulder of a huge Arab who dumped her on the ground as soon as he sensed she was conscious. Clinging to Ken for support, Sarah scrambled to her feet.

As they stumbled through the dark backstreets, one of the sailors grabbed Sarah's pack and began to go through the contents. Apparently the skin-tight rock-climbing shoes were too flimsy for boots and far too small for him, but the bag containing the climbing chalk was another matter. The heated discussion this unique item instigated was cut short when their officer intervened, curtly demanding that all the captives' belongings be turned over to the captain. Meanwhile the Frenchman could carry the pack. The chalk bag and pack were reluctantly returned. Ken felt the bag of gold bulging in his inside pocket, and wondered when he would be searched. Could he keep it long enough to buy their freedom?

By this time, they were standing on a wooden jetty where an oared vessel was moored. The officer in charge produced an old flintlock pistol, and waved it carelessly in the direction of the captives, pushing them towards the boat. Nobody had ever pointed a gun at Ken and he complied, stumbling on the flagstones as he advanced. This was too slow for the Arabs, who dragged Sarah out of the way, grabbed Ken by the arm and pushed him down into the boat. Ken stifled a cry as he toppled onto a crude wooden bench, where he sat rubbing his bruised arm. He glanced up to see what they would do with Sarah, feeling helpless to intervene.

When one of the sailors lunged at Sarah to haul her on board, she offered no resistance. The man was expecting her to pull back, so he went down, pulling Sarah with him. The boat rocked dangerously as the two landed in a heap on the thwarts. As the cursing men pulled bodies apart and steadied the boat, Ken seized the moment to slip the purse into Sarah's pack.

The oarsmen rowed them away from the dock, and the officer smiled, showing a set of broken and rotting teeth through his black beard.

"Next time you will have to do the rowing!"

Ken understood the words but not the significance of the remark as they pulled out into the dark harbour.

Sarah awoke from a dream of being at sea to find herself lying on a hard wooden deck. Most of her limbs hurt, and her head throbbed with a steady pulsating rhythm, which felt like a ball bouncing on the inside of her skull. She was hot and thirsty and needed to move, so she used a bench beside her to lever herself into a sitting position. Looking down she saw a chain around her ankles and, with a feeling she was in some kind of horror movie, she took in a long, slow breath. She choked on the smell rising from the cesspool at her feet made, and Ken reached down to steady her.

"So you woke up at last."

"Christmas! What's going on?" Sarah replied.

"Christ! You can't even swear when your life is in danger!"

"What? Sorry. Wait. *What?*"

"We're in big trouble, Sarah. This is some kind of slave galley. I thought these things went out with the Romans. Are you sure of your dates?"

Sarah heard the fear in Ken's voice and tried not to panic. "Are we going to be made to row?"

A large African man stepped slowly to the bench and stood looking down at them. Both Ken and Sarah went very quiet. He said nothing, but handed them a stone jug containing water.

"Is it safe to drink?" asked Ken.

Sarah shrugged her shoulders and drank deeply, grateful for the cool liquid. She found she was very thirsty and handed the jug to Ken who followed suit wrinkling his nose at the stale taste.

"Hey Sarah, they left you your pack." Ken reached down and pulled Sarah's pack from beneath the bench. Sarah grabbed it and slung it on her back.

"Thanks, I wouldn't like to lose my climbing shoes."

The startled laughter died in Ken's throat as he noticed two swarthy looking figures in baggy pants and ragged shirts heading in their direction. The Nubian nodded to them and moved away. One of the men unlocked the manacles on the captives' ankles, and marched them up the gangway to the quarterdeck where the officers were assembled behind the imposing figure of their captain. Sarah looked up into the hard, cruel face of the rais who, squaring his shoulders, began to speak in French.

"I am Mohammed Abdul al-Bashir. My grandfather's grandfather's grandfather fought under Turgut Re'is at the siege of Malta in the summer of 1565. He fought alongside his father for the great Mustafa Pasha, commander of the Ottoman land forces." He paused, and Sarah thought he was trying to gauge the effect his words were having on them. Ken's face was pale; he looked as scared as Sarah felt.

"By the grace of God you are now in my service. Freedom may be granted to you in three ways,"

Abdul paused and looked closely at them; a smile of enjoyment played across his face. Sarah glanced down wondering if her disguise would fool anybody.

"First, you can die with honour in battle. Second, your relatives can send me a tribute, your ransom. The third way is without honour, by failing to comply with the rules of our service, or . . ." He paused for dramatic effect and stared into Sarah's eyes, ". . .or if you try to escape, death will follow you."

Sarah stood up on the deck held fast on one side by a burly black haired seaman. She felt the captain's eyes on her and she risked a glance at Ken. He too was held by two guards. Did the captain expect some sort of reply? No words would come. The man stood on the quarterdeck, his officers at his back. Below them, the oarsmen sat at their benches while the hands crowded together by the gangway, carefully watching how their rais dealt with the new captives. Could she escape? Could she break free from the man who held her and jump over the side? She turned her head to look at her captor. He grinned and scratched his hook nose in a knowing way. What was the meaning of such a gesture?

She looked towards the stern and saw the slaves sitting, hot and naked under the burning sun. If they intended to enslave her and Ken, her disguise would be discovered instantly. She looked towards Ken, but no reassurance came from that quarter. He was held fast, and Sarah suspected he would slump to the deck if they let him go.

Abdul barked in her face. "Well! Frenchman! Tell me what you know of the invasion fleet."

She hoped Ken understood they must both play their parts as French officers. She also hoped that Ken would not try anything stupid.

The captain thrust his face towards her. "Speak!"

She cried out in fear and tried to move away to avoid his stinking breath, but the guard stopped her. It was an inescapable response; she looked into the rais' brown eyes and he, in turn, looked more closely at the 'Frenchman'. She saw the recognition slowly dawn on the captain's face. He had penetrated her disguise. He saw she was no man.

She started to breathe in short shallow bursts. Panic was setting in, but she must think if she was to avoid being thrown to the crew as a toy. She must act at once. How could she escape? In that instant of recognition, she forced her brain to process every possibility. The craft was moored in a sheltered bay, a short swim from the limestone cliffs of Malta. They were surrounded on three sides by those steep formidable walls, but her only escape route, perhaps a hundred metres of overhanging rock. She stared at the formations, remembering her visit to Malta two hundred years in the future. Could that be where she had climbed? Yes, that was it! In the centre, a steep "V" shaped groove. The route, slanting from right to left, curved up to an overhanging finish. The steep section at the top had been the crux: the hardest part of the climb. This was the place. She had never seen it from this angle, but there could be no doubt. In two hundred years time, she would rappel down from the top and climb back up the face. The route was more strenuous than technically difficult, except for the last few metres. She had been very fit back then ... no, not *back then*, but rather, in two hundred years. Now she had no harness or safety equipment such as a rope. The bolts that stopped a climber's fall would be missing. It would definitely not be a safe undertaking, but the only other choice was to become a slave or worse, the mistress of this arrogant man staring into her face.

Abdul interrupted her rebellious thoughts. "This is no officer!" he declared with a laugh.

Sarah felt her heart pounding as Abdul moved forward and pulled open her uniform coat. She struggled to stop him, but the hook nosed seaman held both arms tightly. He grasped her shirt and sports bra in his hands and ripped downwards. She screamed and tried to cover herself, but her guard strengthened his grip.

"What do we have here?"

The torn shirt exposed her left breast to the attentive crew. A great cheer went up, followed by laughter. Abdul laughed along with his crew, doing nothing to quiet the obscenities rising from the deck.

The seaman guarding Sarah moved forward to feast his eyes on a white woman but, in doing so, he relaxed his grip. Carpe diem! Sarah kicked upwards between her jailor's legs. He grunted in pain and collapsed to the deck, distracting the others momentarily. Free for a moment, Sarah climbed up on to the taff rail. The reaction from the sailors was typical from males as this act exposed the right breast alongside its sister. Nobody moved for one astonished moment, then Sarah jumped into the sea, to a great roar from the hands. Abdul shouted a few guttural commands, and within a few seconds two men with muskets appeared, just as Sarah dived down. She shed the heavy uniform coat and swam under the stern of the craft. She surfaced by the rudder, well out of sight of the deck. Remembering that swimming was a rare talent amongst sailors of the 18th century, they most likely would be searching for her struggling, drowning body. She must wait before making the dangerous crossing to the shore.

Ten minutes went by, as the crew called out advice to the four musketeers who swept their guns backwards and forwards along the shoreward side of the ship. They made no attempt to launch a boat to search more effectively; instead Abdul summoned two more musketeers. It did not occur to him that she could swim.

With a cry, Omar fished something out of the water. "Allah has received her, she has drowned," Omar proclaimed, brandishing Sarah's discarded coat.

Abdul was a careful man, and so he did not stand the musketeers down. Time passed, the sun beat down and the crew began to return to their routine, while the musketeers kept watch.

Wednesday 20th June 1798 8 AM — Reynard

Reynard entered a large office in the East wing of the old fort belonging to Marcel Langon, a small, thin man who looked even smaller behind his massive desk.

"Ah Lieutenant Reynard. I hope you don't mind my little custom of doing business in the early morning. I find the afternoons a time for repose." He motioned Reynard to sit down. "I have had word the diplomatic mission I spoke of at our last meeting will take place, and I have approval from Paris to appoint you its leader." Langon paused to examine Reynard, who sat passively.

"I trust I am making the right choice? You come highly recommended by Monsieur Taleyrand himself."

Reynard bowed his head in acknowledgement.

"I understand that you earned your promotion ahead of your senior colleagues by exposing a traitor?"

"I did my duty, monsieur."

"Quite so," continued Langon. "You are to take the cutter *Active* to Mersa Matrouh, some 290 km west of Alexandria. You will make contact with one, Atilla bin Samir. This man works for Talleyrand. He will help you get an audience with the Emir Mersa or Mersa Bey as he is known. The Bey is powerful and he also commands a division of Mameluke cavalry. We understand the British have the Bey in their pay. An interesting fellow; he was educated in Paris and London and speaks French and English, so perhaps it will not be too difficult to win him to our side. He has

70

some ships that could cause problems with our Egyptian supply lines. You are to persuade him that Napoleon will conquer all Egypt, and those who support French interests will benefit."

Langon paused and sipped his wine. Reynard sat listening in a rigid posture. It was very early for wine.

"Already I have sent, under guard, a box containing a quantity of gold and silver. This should be aboard the *Active* by the time you return. The details are in the papers I give you now. Here is an agreement we have drawn up. We expect you to return with the Bey's signature and good will. You must provide receipts for any of the gold or silver you deem necessary to leave with the Bey. You will update me with coded reports whenever it is possible to get mail back to Malta. If the Bey will not cooperate I leave it to your discretion to replace him with this Samir. Do you understand?"

There was no point in asking questions. Langon would not have the practical details, and so Reynard replied: "Oui Monsieur, it will be my pleasure to carry out this assignment."

He reached for the document case, but Langon held on to it for a moment. "There is something else." Reynard raised an eyebrow.

"A letter empowering you to act with some . . ." Langon hesitated, lowering his voice before he continued, ". . . certain authorities might question you. Perhaps the navy will try to countermand my orders. The letter explains you are carrying out the work of the Directory. In particular, you are answerable to Monsieur Talleyrand. You will find his name carries some weight." Langon resumed in his usual tone. "After completion you will rejoin the fleet in Alexandria."

Reynard left the building clutching a small leather dispatch case; he could not hide the smile on his face as he went through the castle gate. Life was going well for him. Yesterday he had met a remarkable French woman. She was not only beautiful and fascinating, but he suspected she was hiding something about herself. The very strange instrument she carried had sparked his interest. What was the box? He thought he had seen some kind of picture of a naval chart painted on the front. He couldn't be sure but it had looked as if the picture had changed before his eyes. He needed to get hold of this artefact and investigate it further.

His curiosity about the small box, along with his certainty that such an object might prove useful, was a justification in itself for asking Annette to visit him on the cutter. Once she arrived on board, he would find some excuse to keep her there while he searched her things. After procuring the box, he could investigate it at his leisure. She seemed to keep her valuables in a leather bag, which never left her side. He would have to separate her from that bag. Perhaps he would soon learn something interesting enough to pass to his new master.

Just then he heard a cry behind him,

"Arrêtez-les!"

Reynard saw two fugitives, a man and a woman, running for the gate, and he turned around to stop them.

Wednesday 20th June 1798 8 AM — Duncan

Once again, Duncan dreamed of the girl. She held out her hand to him and pulled him through the bars of his cell. Outside the fortress, they ran together in the rain, but four of the prison guards barred their way with raised muskets. Duncan watched with a resigned fascination as the firearms came level with his chest. At the moment of death, a uniformed figure appeared from inside the shed and thrust his sword at the nearest guard. The blade was bloodied and the soldier went down. "Run you fools," the stranger yelled, but he could not move. His legs felt like they were locked in place.

He rolled across the stone floor and woke up. There was nothing in the cell save for the wooden pallet on which he slept and a small sprinkling of straw providing little comfort. The dream was so real. If he could just clear his head and think about his fantasy escape, perhaps he could achieve his actual freedom. He remembered being captured, but little before that. Two days earlier a French captain had questioned him, wondering how he came to be in Malta at the very time of the French invasion. The captain pointed out that there had been no reports of an English warship nearby, and demanded an explanation for Duncan's presence on the island. Duncan, however, could not remember anything before the butt of a

French musket had fuddled his brains. Even the threat of execution by firing squad had not restored his memory. His naval lieutenant's uniform provided a modicum of protection, but Duncan knew that even his rank could not save him if the French believed that he was a spy.

The lieutenant stared at the stone walls and iron bars around him, but the sound of the girl's footsteps on the stairs distracted him from his gloomy reflections. The food the serving girl brought him was not bad, probably due to the kindness of the girl herself. Unfortunately she was always accompanied by Danton, the fat and disgusting turnkey. Still, Duncan felt the same rush of pleasure he felt every time he saw the girl. She had a kindly, thin face with a small nose, high cheekbones, and long dark hair too luxurious to stay tucked into the pretty head scarf she usually wore. His one attempt to start a conversation with her had ended when her large, brown eyes had sent the message that he must not talk to her. Since it was obvious that she was scared of Danton, he complied with her silent request.

The young woman placed a tray just outside his cell. On it was a bowl of soup, some rough bread, a spoon, and a heavy clay water jug. The turnkey stood behind fiddling with his keys, which were attached to his ample belt. His face wore a complacent smile. Duncan had already seen how the man enjoyed abusing his power. Danton's dark lined face revealed little emotion. The brute's prominent chin seemed to leap out of his face in a most unnatural manner, and reminded Duncan of a fish tail. In his mind, Duncan referred to the man, as Le Poisson.

"Feed the wretch and go about your business." The repugnant bully was as ruthless in his treatment of the girl as he was of the prisoners.

Flustered, the young woman dropped a piece of bread from the tray.

"Hurry up, you little slut," yelled Le Poisson at the girl. She set the tray down on the floor outside the cell and unlocked a small slot in the bars with a tiny key. As she bent down to push the tray inside, Le Poisson grabbed her shapely derri ère with both hands.

"Monsieur, please," she said.

"I always please," said Le Poisson. "Perhaps life here could be much better if you, too, would please."

He spun her round and tried to kiss her. Although the girl fought back as best as she could, she was no match for her attacker. Despite the fat, Le Poisson was strong. He smothered her protests with his mouth. Duncan got to his feet and, in two strides, was gripping the iron bars.

"Mademoiselle, can I help you?" He asked more to distract Le Poisson than as an actual question. By this time, Le Poisson was oblivious to Duncan or anything else. With his free hand, he was busy pushing up the girl's dress, and Duncan realized the fat man had no intention of stopping. His victim twisted her head round to face Duncan, her innocent eyes pleading for his assistance. The professor wondered what he could do, and, casting about for a weapon, his eyes lit upon the heavy jug.

He put his hand through the bars and lifted it up, passing it from bar to bar until it was directly above Le Poisson. The ugly turnkey was too preoccupied to notice as Duncan brought the jug down as hard as he could on the man's head. There was a dull thud. The jug broke, and water poured out over Le Poisson who made a violent screeching sound, fell hard, and passed out on top of his victim.

With a determined grunt, the girl jerked herself from under the enormous body of the turnkey. She kicked his inert form with all the force she could find in her dainty foot before bending over, gasping for breath. When she straightened up, she turned to Duncan.

"Quickly monsieur, before the guards come running."

As she said this, she grabbed the keys from Danton's waistband. At first, he was too concerned about the girl's distress to take in what was happening.

"Are you all right?"

Instead of answering him, she unlocked the cell, then stepped back, fear in her eyes.

"Thank you, mademoiselle. To whom have I the honour of addressing?" Duncan asked in imperfect French.

"My name is Marie-Paule Bonneterre. We must go at once, please Monsieur, the guards . . ."

A flight of stone steps led upwards to the reception area. Beyond that lay a guardhouse and then a courtyard sealed from the outside by heavy wooden gates. Once outside he would be in French occupied Malta. As he passed by, he checked on Le Poisson, and saw the fat man would not wake soon.

"Here help me," he said. They dragged the turnkey's heavy form into the cell and covered him with some straw. At first glance, he looked like any other sleeping prisoner.

"A patrol was sent out this morning. There was some trouble in the town. The few guards are too busy eating to notice you. We have a good chance of getting out. I know a way." Marie-Paule set off down the stone corridor.

"We?" questioned Duncan, "Why do you risk being caught helping me?"

"Perhaps we stand a better chance together."

"Who are you?" Duncan asked.

"A friend who wants to escape the tyranny of the revolution."

"You think you can get us out of here?"

"I have been planning for this moment; will you help me to freedom?" Still Marie-Paule's voice held traces of doubt.

"Mademoiselle, we are on an island, a possession of the revolutionary council. How can I help you?"

"I have a friend outside. Somebody who was known to my parents, and I can trust him. You are a sailor, so perhaps we can find a ship and escape. Shall we go?"

Duncan was not sure it would be so simple, but the first job was to get out of the castle, so he followed her up the stone stairs. At the top, there was a long corridor leading past the guardroom. At the far end, a uniformed soldier stood looking towards the courtyard. They stopped out of sight of the guard reminding Duncan of his dream.

"Marie-Paule, is it raining outside?"

"No, it's the dry season. Wait here!"

She approached the soldier and whispered in his ear. The guard reacted by grabbing his musket and dashing back along the corridor towards Duncan. At first, he thought Marie-Paule had given him up to the authorities, but at the last minute, the guard turned off down a side corridor and disappeared from view.

"What did you say?"

"I told him the commandant had ordered a count of the prisoners."

"He'll find one missing!"

"It will take time. Now we must run." Duncan followed her into the guard house. Three guards sat eating at a long wooden table. They did not question Marie-Paule as she walked past them towards the kitchen while Duncan ducked down out of sight behind a cabinet. Soon shouts of alarm came from the direction of the kitchen and a cry of, "Fire!"

The guards left their meal to go to Marie-Paule's aid. Duncan seized his opportunity and ran across the room and out into the courtyard. It was raining outside, and when Marie-Paule joined him she laughed in wonder.

"How did you know it would be raining?"

"I dreamed it," Duncan answered. Had he been here before?

"Stay here," she instructed him, and she ran towards the gate yelling, "Fire!"

The gatekeeper stumbled out and followed Marie-Paule to the kitchen. Once he was inside, she returned to Duncan.

"Two men guard the gate. I will have to try and get you past them."

"Not so fast, four more guards will come from behind the ammunition shed."

"How can you know that?" So saying she made a dash across the courtyard towards the gatehouse.

"I was right about the rain," called Duncan, catching up with her.

Four guards emerged from behind the magazine and raised their muskets.

"They are from my dream."

Marie-Paule looked at Duncan with such a classic open mouthed expression that, despite the circumstances, Duncan had to smile.

"Trust me," said Duncan. "Help is on its way."

As he said this, the door of the shed opened and a figure emerged. Duncan smiled in triumph and, grasping Marie-Paule's hand, he shouted at the figure, "For God's sake, Masthead, keep them off!" In that instant Duncan's memory fully returned. The figure was indeed himself. He had fallen victim to the fluctuations of the time gate.

The guards started to spread out as the stranger ran towards them waving his sword, and one went down. "Run, you fools," whispered Duncan to Marie-Paule.

"Run you fools!" said the stranger.

As the pair ran to the gate, the alarm was raised behind them. "Arrêtez-les!"

The two gate guards stepped forward. They knew Marie-Paule worked for the prison service and at first they were unsure what was happening. She reached for Duncan's hands and pulled them together, whispering: "Act like they are tied together. Trust me now!"

She turned to the guards saying; "Message from General Vaubois' chief of staff. Please help me conduct this prisoner. His bonds need tightening."

The guards came forward and bent down to peer at Duncan's seemingly bound hands, but he moved as fast as a striking cobra, grabbing each man by the back of their neck. Before they realized what was happening, he banged their heads together in a painful sounding crunch. Down they went.

Duncan and Marie Paule passed through the gate, but a naval officer appeared in front of them. He took in the situation at a glance, and raised a halting hand. Duncan pushed the man off balance and Marie-Paule, still resentful of her treatment by the prison guard, kicked him viciously between the legs. The naval officer cried out clutching himself as he fell. He looked her full in the face as she passed.

All she heard was: "Je me rappellerai vous, Mademoiselle."

They sped out into the cobbled street leaving behind a trail of sprawling prison guards. By the time soldiers assembled outside the prison under the command of an officer, the fugitives had disappeared. The rain stopped as the search spread out in the direction of Valletta.

Chapter 5

Escape

Wednesday 20th June 1798 9 AM — Sarah

It seemed like hours had passed since Sarah's leap into the water. She clung to the rudder, shaded from the June heat, and shivering with cold. Whatever the danger, she must move soon and swim to shore. A large clump of seaweed float by, giving her an idea. Drawing the penknife from her pack, she reached out and cut off a piece of kelp. She lay on her back, letting the waves gently hold her against the stern of the vessel while her hands fashioned the hollow kelp into a snorkel. Ducking her head down, she blew through the tube to clear it so she could take in a tentative breath. The kelp-filtered air was foul but, if she breathed shallowly, her makeshift apparatus worked. Keeping just below the surface, and using the large clump of seaweed as cover, she made her way towards the shore. She crossed to a rock on the shoreline, and let her head come up. All was quiet.

She reasoned that swimming around the headland would bring her into view of the galliot, so her best chance of escape lay in the rock climb she remembered from her recent (actually, Sarah realized with some confusion, future) trip to Malta. Swimming to the foot of the wall, she looked up and located the "V" shaped groove and the start of the route. She pulled herself out of the water onto a small flattish platform to recover her breath and soak up the warm sun. Sarah reached in her pack and pulled out the 20th century tight rock shoes with their special sticky rubber soles. She knew she would never be able to get up a climb like this without them. She laid the shoes out to dry and examined a small bag of chalk, vital to dry the sweat from her fingers. It was, of course, soaked and useless.

Sarah could feel the adrenaline surge as she considered her situation. Could she climb this route solo without a rope? She knew the climb was within her capability under ideal conditions; however, without that safety line, a single slip would see her reduced to a red stain smeared on the rocks. She also realized that, as soon as she started, she would be in full view of the galley, but could a musket ball reach her from such a distance? The more she thought about the climb, the more Sarah began to doubt herself. Before she lost all her resolve, she reached for her now dry climbing shoes, and grimaced as she pulled them onto her feet. They felt very tight after being in the sea, but she bore the pain and stood up, prepared to make the first move. Despite her situation, Sarah felt a jolt of exhilaration at the idea of climbing solo. Just her shoes, her skill, and a half remembered passage to the top; this was the purest and most dangerous form of the sport.

Hand-sized, water-worn holes at the start gave Sarah an extra sense of security and enabled her to climb quickly up the initial groove before the route angled to the right and the face curved inwards, becoming very steep. Now a clear drop into the sea lay beneath her feet, and if she fell, she might well survive to endure life as a slave aboard the *Murad*. The rock was just as she remembered, and she gained the only ledge on the climb. Here a buttress thrust out over the edge, twenty meters above the waves providing her with a tiny, flat resting place.

She sat down, legs dangling, and looked across at the galliot. It occurred to her that the captain might take out his anger on Ken. Perhaps if she found the Professor he would be able to effect a rescue. But how? Trying not to think about such insurmountable problems, she focused on the current task. The steep pitch ahead was harder than the first, but the real challenge was in the final section. She waited another few minutes unwilling to leave the last rest ledge.

Sarah started climbing again with long reaches between deeply in-cut pockets, wide enough to accommodate two of her slender fingers, solid and secure at two knuckles deep. She moved up smooth as a spider, pushing back the fear so it would not cramp her elegant style. She remembered the crux of this route; a mono-doigt move, high up, near the top. When she got there all her weight would be entrusted to a finger-tip sized hole in the rock. She forced herself back to the moment and followed the holds leading rightwards across the steepest part of the wall to a foothold on an outside corner. As she traversed around, the rock swept down and inwards beneath her, like a great concave mirror, stretching into the sea below. In another lifetime she would have enjoyed this tremendous exposure, but now, with no rope and little hope, she could not bear to look down. For one heart-stopping moment, she saw herself as a fragile figure, arms gradually draining of strength, clinging to some tiny protuberances on the mirror's centre. She pushed back these grim thoughts, and stepped up with her right foot onto a small ledge no more than a half inch wide. Keeping her centre of gravity low, left foot dangling over the gulf beneath, Sarah looked up. It was too far to go, and she felt hopelessness overcome her, so much so that she thought of letting go to relieve the awful tension.

A popping noise interrupted her despair, and the second shot dispelled her morbid thoughts. A third bang from the *Murad* prompted her to grasp the side of a tufa, a kind of stalactite stuck to the wall where once water had flowed. She glided up the great dish until a jutting overhang more than three feet wide stopped further progress. Reaching up she found nothing except smooth rock. The horizontal crack five feet above her was just out of reach. More shots made her glance back towards the ship. She could see gun smoke, but no musket balls had come her way. She searched for something she could use as an intermediate hold to reach the crack above, wondering why she had no memory of this overhang from her previous time on the route. Her hand found a fin of rock beneath the overhang, an undercling good for an outwards pull. With her feet braced, she leaned out over the foaming sea nearly two hundred feet below, so that her head pushed past this rocky ceiling. Every instinct told her to stay close to the cliff face, but here she was leaning backwards as far as she could, pushed out by the chunk of rock barring her way. It was the only route forward; her back arched away from the rock, and she stepped back down. This was too much without a rope. She stood for a moment, thinking; there was no choice. With a renewed resolve, she ignored the gaping void below, pulled out over the overhang and, with one hand on the rock, made a slight jump, while reaching with her other hand to the deep crack. Fingers slipped in to the wrist and muscles tightened to keep her tortured hand jammed into the rock. She paused with her arm at full extension, then the adrenaline pumping through her system gave her the needed impetus. With a grunt of determination, she pulled safely onto a small ledge above the overhang.

The crack ran behind the ledge and Sarah could tell that there was not much holding this massive block onto the wall. No wonder she could not remember this part of the climb. It probably would not last 200 years of weathering. Gingerly, Sarah stood up; to her horror sand started to flow from the crack on the left. She instinctively grabbed a hold on the wall in front of her and lifted her feet off the ledge as, with a grinding bang, the whole chunk of rock gave way and slipped downwards. It had not taken 200 years after all! Sarah cried out as the great block fell away, hitting the water with an enormous splash, and turning the sea white with foam. Her frail body dangled from one hold, feet scrabbling, dark against the brilliant white of the rock scar. She could not have drawn more attention to her position if she had tried.

Wednesday 20th June 1798 9:40 AM — Ken

Abdul muttered an order under his breath, and instantly Ken was dragged to a six foot wooden post planted in the centre of the *Murad's* quarterdeck. Dark with age and stained with what looked ominously like blood, it was called the post of compliance. His hands were tied behind him so tightly that he could feel the hard edges of the wood jar his spine. He hung from the post, his face betraying his pain, while he watched the musketeers who were, in turn, watching the water. He knew Sarah was a strong swimmer and, if she could just hold on long enough, perhaps she could get away. Then he looked over to the steep and blank limestone cliffs, and he closed his eyes in despair. A shout from one of the sailors interrupted Ken's dire thoughts, and his eyes flew open in time to see the man fishing Sarah's uniform coat out of the water. Abdul took possession of the proffered garment as he leaned over the stern gazing into the depths. What had the man said about escape? To die without honour? What exactly did that mean? And how would this captain react to the escape of not just a prisoner, but a woman at that? As Ken sweated under the sun, wilting against his bonds and worrying about both Sarah and himself, he could not help thinking that life couldn't get any worse. Then it did, for he smelled coffee, and an incredible longing came over him. The coffee reminded him of the comforts of 21st century life, and he felt tears on his cheeks as he watched Abdul take the tiny cup from his old servant.

"In all my years at sea, I have never lost an escaping slave. I catch them and kill them to set an example to the others." He paused to sniff at his cup appreciatively. "Manu, you always know when my need is greatest!" Abdul walked over to the post.

"Frenchman," he said to Ken. "Your companion has defied the rules and will be caught and given to the crew for sport. It is possible I will spare your life for I am a civilised man. So tell me what you know about the fleet, and perhaps I will be merciful."

"Monsieur, General Napoleon's fleet has put to sea," Ken replied, remembering what he had overheard in the tavern. He hoped his Acadian French accent was in keeping with what Abdul expected to hear.

"Where bound, this mighty fleet?"

"To attack Egypt, Monsieur."

"Egypt! That is not likely."

The rais studied Ken before continuing. "You do not have the bearing of a French naval officer. Tell me truthfully, for your life hangs in the balance."

He drew his jambiya, a vicious looking curved dagger with an ornate handle. Ken considered his answer. Since, strictly speaking, Canada did not yet exist, he decided to stay as close to the truth as possible.

"I am English."

Abdul took a pace across the deck and placed the jambiya at Ken's throat; the boy winced then kept very, very still. "An English spy. Can you procure gold for your release? Or do you prefer life in my ciurma?"

Although Ken could think of little else but the knife, he forced himself to focus on how he might extricate himself from this latest threat. Could he buy his freedom? Then he remembered the purse filled with gold that he had pushed into Sarah's bag. By now it was probably at the bottom of the bay. Still, he managed to look Abdul In the eye as he said, "Capitane, I have funds ashore. If you let me return to the inn, I can collect them."

Without moving the knife, Abdul studied his face, then he seemed to come to some sort of decision. "Your fellow 'officer' was a woman. Are you both English spies dressed as French officers?"

"No, .. that is yes. I er .."

"Well, Englishman? Whose side are you on?"

Ken made a sudden decision. "I am a true Englishman. God save King George!"

"You would die for your King?"

"If you kill me, my king will pursue you to the ends of the Earth."

Abdul laughed into Ken's face. Although Ken couldn't turn for fear of the knife, he winced at the smell, wondering if his last earthly breath was going to be such a bad one.

"I think you are an ignorant boy. You will remain where you are while I decide your fate."

To Ken's relief, Abdul removed the knife from his throat. His body relaxed, and he slumped against the post. The whole crew was motionless. All attention was on Abdul's next move. His eyes gave no sign of any emotion, but looked towards the cliff as he replaced the Jambiya in his waistband. Fingering the handle of a huge scimitar hanging on his left side, he said very quietly, "Now we shall have target practice." At this command the four musket men, who had been watching for some sign of Sarah, came forward.

Ken hung limply, his bonds biting into his flesh as the sun rose higher in the sky. For a moment, he almost laughed out loud at the absurdity of the situation. Here he was, so hot he was convinced he might die of sunstroke, while Sarah was somewhere in the cool water below him. His hysterical consideration of the merits of death by drowning over death by heatstroke was rudely, if refreshingly, interrupted when the huge African who had brought water that morning upended a bucket of sea water over him. As he gasped in shock, the man held a cup to Ken's lips, and he gratefully gulped down some fresh water. Well, Perhaps not so fresh; the taste was horrible, but it revived him.

Four musketeers stood to attention while one of the hands hung a roughly circular wooden target, some half a metre wide, from the yard. Each of the four fell into line, and the captain spoke quietly to them. The first marksman took aim and fired, hitting the target a little right of centre to the general approval of the officers and crew. The next one was not so accurate but still managed to wing the edge of the target. The third fared similarly. The captain turned to the fourth. "Hit the centre, and you may shoot the Frenchman."

The colour drained from Ken's face. Had he understood correctly? The captain could have easily slit his throat but instead had cruelly saved Ken as an incentive for the musketeer? Somehow he must convince the captain he had more value alive than dead. He struggled fruitlessly at the rope, but it had been tied expertly.

A long, jagged scar ran down the marksman's right cheek. He took careful aim and fired. To Ken's horror, a hole appeared in the centre of the target. The man's success was greeted by loud cheers by the crew. The scar-faced man smiled and announced as he carefully reloaded his musket, "I like target practice. Perhaps the boy may be permitted to run?"

Abdul nodded and one of the hands cut Ken's bonds. He fell forward on his knees and rubbed his wrists to bring some circulation back. He was stiff and ached all over. When he looked up, the gunner raised his musket.

"You better run, boy!"

When Ken didn't move, Scarface took careful aim; his fingers drummed along the trigger guard. "Don't you fear death, boy?"

As the man waited for Ken to run, it occurred to Ken that, if he ran, the man would shoot him down. Keeping still seemed to be the best way to stay alive, albeit temporarily. Disappointed, the crew tried to spur Ken on.

"Run! Run for your life!" Ken kept his place.

"Run, or stand to, it is all the same to me," said the musketeer, and he took careful aim at Ken's head.

Ken closed his eyes bowing his head in resignation, when a loud crash made every head turn. The splash came from the landward side. Ken looked towards the cliffs, while Abdul turned to look out to sea, clearly unable to see a cause for the sound. "Where away?"

The lookout replied, "The splash came from the cliff. A falling rock perhaps?"

All eyes turned once again towards the shore searching the rocks for signs of life. Only Ken, knowing about Sarah's rock climbing ability, looked upwards to the cliff face, and only Ken saw the white rock scar, half hidden by a cloud of dust. Then he saw Sarah, frozen to the rocks. For ten seconds he stared at her, unable to pull his eyes away, until he realized he was endangering her life. He turned his head only to stare directly into the eyes of the captain. Ken immediately looked down at the deck, but he was too late. A look of understanding passed over Abdul's face; his eyes scanned the cliff, to settle on Sarah silhouetted in the rock scar.

"Allah be praised! The woman clings to the cliff like a Jinni! Musketeers!"

The musketeers raised their weapons and searched for their target. Ken's face flushed a deep scarlet. His neck felt so hot he thought he could smell his shirt smouldering. One by one the musketeers took their shots, the first three failing to hit their mark. Ken shuddered as the scar faced man raised his weapon. Knowing that he was the best shot Ken, with a mighty effort, launched himself at the musketeer jarring scar face's arm as he pulled the trigger. The marksman cursed as he stumbled forward. As the sailors clubbed Ken senseless, all that he could think of was that he had just killed Sarah.

Wednesday 20th June 1798 9:45 AM — Sarah

Sarah placed her feet carefully, trying to avoid the loose rock that the block had left barely connected to the wall. She looked up to where the pitch ended. This was the last and hardest part of the climb. It was about eighty feet to the top, but her arms throbbed and she knew that the one finger move was between her and safety. She stood balanced on her toes, shaking one arm at a time until she felt them recover slightly. The steep cliff swept down more than the height of a twelve-storey skyscraper into the sea below, where she stood with only one hand connecting her to the rock.

To the untrained observer her position could not be considered relaxing, but to her it was a rest. She looked out into the bay behind her; from that distance, she could not make out any change on board the tranquil *Murad*. Had the rock fall alerted them to her presence? No matter, they had stopped shooting. She deliberately counted one minute in her mind. When nothing happened and, feeling that she had recovered as much as possible, Sarah continued the climb.

The rock yielded up good, but widely spaced, hand holds, forcing her to make long, tiring reaches. A few moves further on she looked up to find nothing but blank rock. She stopped with her feet bridged wide across a shallow groove. With no chalk to dry them, her fingers grew slippery with sweat. Her calf muscles joined her forearms in throbbing complaint. This must be it — the crux of the route. She let her right hand drop behind her back and shook it to get the blood flowing. Soon her left hand could take the weight no more, and she held on with her right giving her left a good shake out. The net result was a slight lessening of the forearm pain, and she found the energy to make one move up on very small handholds. She could stay balanced where she was, her legs taking most of her weight, but now her self-doubt took over. *This is crazy! There is no way I can finish this without falling and breaking every bone in my body!* She could no longer see herself moving through the difficult section above and decided to reverse back to the resting place and wait until she felt sufficiently rested. She tried to back down a move, but felt herself slipping and using too much precious energy searching for tiny footholds. Reversing was out of the question. She would just have to climb the crux. Above, the groove steepened so much that she absolutely had to have a larger hand-hold. The left wall overhung and forced her to lean rightwards, one hand scrabbling for a hold, but all she found was a tiny hole, into which the tip of the index finger of her right hand just fit. The mono doigt! The finger still throbbed with the memory of a recent fall at Horne Lake.

Okay stay calm! I will just make this steep pull on the damn mono. There is no pain in my index finger!

Sarah tried to move her fear frozen fingers and, when she felt the tears coming, she stopped, angry with herself, knowing it was all over the minute she started to cry. Realizing these may be her last words, she quietly spoke: "Oh please God let me finish this climb, and I promise I will never solo anything again!"

Ignoring the voice, which reminded her that she had made such promises in the past and that this time there would be no second chance, she swapped hands and did the shakeout trick again, recovering just enough to feel confident about her next move. Then her left leg started to vibrate as her rebellious muscles demanded relief from this awkward position. "Great! Now I've got the shakes. It can't get worse than this."

She regretted even thinking this while she held her leg in a vain attempt to keep the jitters from shaking her off the wall. Of course it got worse. There was a loud crack and an explosion beside her head. "What the hell?"

The shock almost shook her loose, but she held on with even more determination as she admitted that an 18th century musket could reach the cliff from the ship. Staying put was not an option. She pushed her index finger into the hole as far as it would go and, ignoring the pain, she pulled on it, bridged up another move with her feet. Just as her arms and legs were giving in to exhaustion she found a hold big enough to take her entire left hand. "Yes! Thank you, thank you!" she screamed.

When she pulled up, a second crack scattered stinging rock chips into her face; she closed her eyes in alarm and pain, but she knew she had to keep moving. The angle eased, the crux was over and, as the *Murad* found her range, she reached towards the top. As she grasped for this last hold, she was thwarted when the knob of rock she was holding exploded under her hand.

"Oh hell!" was all her Canadian upbringing would allow her to yell as an expletive. Shards of rock drew blood from her right hand as it grasped nothing but air. One more move to go, and her left hand was still in contact but, without a handhold for the right, she started to swing like an opening barn door. She was going to fall so near the end. Where was the justice in that? There was a brief moment when she felt nothing but anger, like a cartoon character suspended in that instant of realization that her fall and subsequent death were imminent.

Ken came too enough to feel men in baggy pants dragging his aching body to the benches, and chained him by the ankles. He felt sick, hurt, and only barely conscious. His thoughts went out to Sarah. The gun men had seen her because of him, but he hoped she would still somehow make it up the cliff. He slumped across the bench with his head hanging over the side, trying to stay conscious and pay attention. With a great effort, he managed to focus, even as the pounding in his head added distant drums to the drama he was witnessing. She had almost made it over the edge when he heard the sound of the musket fire again, and Sarah seemed to pause. "Oh God, tell me they missed!" Despite his atheist views he silently prayed, asking God to spare Sarah and promising in return that he would think more about his actions that might endanger the lives of his friends. In his heart he didn't trust God or himself to fulfil his prayers or promises. Although Ken was fighting waves of pain and drowsiness, he forced himself to keep watching. The rush of hope kept him awake as she seemed to recover, but then he lost sight of her. Had she fallen? A harsh voice gave an order to launch the boat. They were going after Sarah, and his only hope of freedom. With this thought, his mind let go and consciousness mercifully left his bruised body.

Finding strength in her left hand, Sarah remained in contact with the wall and her swing stopped. She put her fingers onto the large finishing hold, and with the other hand reached into the grass. A firm hand grasped her wrist steadying her so both feet could come back into contact with the rock. She pulled gratefully over the top to escape a fusillade of musket shots. A shepherd boy still held her hand while she lay on the flat grassy cliff top. Choking back tears of relief, she soaked up the life giving smells, the grass and wild thyme.

The boy who had helped her, continued to pull on her arm, gesturing at her frantically. They must get away from the edge and out of range, but she was exhausted, as much mentally as physically. Never had a climb cost her so much in pure effort. She let herself be steered towards a crude shelter and felt the tears flow freely as she lay down out of the sun. The boy put a leather gourd to her lips, and she gratefully drank.

In response to the boy's continued gestures, Sarah looked seaward. A boat had beached in a sandy cove, but where, Sarah wondered, was the crew? The boy put his fingers to his lips and signalled for Sarah to lie still in the shelter and make no sound. To her horror he started waving at a group of armed men coming into view. Were her efforts going to be wasted? Would they capture her again so soon? She could do nothing except stay put. It was far too late to run now, and she was too tired to move.

Chapter 6

The Brig Palerma

The French speaking waiter smiled at Annette as he handed her a note with her second cup of coffee. To her delight it was from Reynard inviting her to tour the cutter, *Active*. All she had to do was find her way to the docks by noon.

She had time to find some clothes more appropriate for her visit so, with the help of her favourite waiter, she found the local dress shop. She loved to wear dresses, and wanted to arrive at the cutter in comfortable but impressive attire. She chose a sky blue affair and, with a pang of guilt, paid for it with the gold she'd grabbed from Duncan's office. At first the high waist made her feel naked, but after a while, she saw the advantage in the June Mediterranean heat.

Getting to the dock was simple on a horse drawn carriage that her favourite waiter had summoned for her. she probably paid ten times the asking price, but she didn't care, loving, at least for the moment, the elevation in status. Two sailors from the *Active* greeted her, and took care she entered the boat without getting her dress dirty. A cry from the shore stayed their embarkation, as a messenger hove into view. As soon as the man handed over a leather dispatch bag, they rowed the short distance over to the cutter. Annette noticed it was a single masted vessel, anchored quite far out in the harbour. Now that the great fleet had departed, *Active* was the only armed

90

vessel in view. Perhaps this was her chance to reach Aboukir Bay before the end of July?

She came aboard to find the cutter's company assembled on deck. She made a brief curtsy to Reynard, who greeted her before accepting the leather dispatch case from the coxswain.

"Pardon, mademoiselle, our orders have arrived. I must take my leave while I read them." As he left he said to Granon: "Monsieur, please show the mademoiselle our humble vessel."

Starting at the great tiller at the stern, Granon took pleasure in explaining the workings of the cutter. "The vessel looks like she is sleeping, but we can put to sea at a moment's notice. There, mademoiselle, our mainsail."

The great boom stuck out beyond the stern rail, and held the huge fore and aft sail, furled and held down by gaskets. At the bow, the jib thrust proudly out over the sea, bearing three furled sails. He showed her the guns, the mast, the sails, rigging, and the hatchway leading below decks. They went down so she could see the cramped space in which the men ate and slept.

"Why lieutenant, a man cannot even stand up below decks!"

"That is true, Mademoiselle, but in the navy we get used to such hardships."

"I expect it is very tiring, Monsieur, being a sailor."

Annette imagined the lieutenant crawling into his hammock soaking wet and cold after spending his watch a hundred feet in the air, out along a spar in the rain and howling wind, trying to put a reef in a sail.

As they came back up on deck, Reynard appeared from his cabin.

"Mademoiselle, forgive us, our orders are to put to sea with no delay. I am sorry but you must remain aboard. Monsieur Granon, we will get under way immediately. Once out of the harbour set a course east by south east."

The colour drained from Annette's face. She was terrified, but knew that this was what she wanted, provided Reynard would take her to Admiral Brueys.

"Monsieur, I . . ."

"Man the windlass!"

In response the hands ran across the deck to start hauling in the anchor cable.

"Off main sail gaskets!"

Men climbed out along the huge boom to release the gaff and main sail.

"Man the topping lift!"

She stood back behind the helmsmen at the tiller, listening to a string of commands that held no meaning to her, feeling lost.

"Sir! I must protest . . . "

"Mademoiselle, my first priority is my duty to the service. You have my word that you will be safe under my protection. Please forgive me, I must get the ship under way."

At his order the anchor was weighed, the hands sheeted down on the main sail, and the brisk north westerly brought the vessel under way. The wind blew harder as they sailed out from the sheltered waters of the Grand Harbour and into the choppy Mediterranean, causing the ship to heel over and she started to pitch. Annette was overwhelmed by the motion and held on to whatever she could find, watching the point of St. Elmo coming up fast to windward. By the time they were round the headland, Annette realized that the nausea she felt was not caused only by fear.

"Please captain, I need to sit down."

Reynard steadied her, quite naturally taking hold of her leather bag.

Reynard took her arm and, as he conducted her into his cabin, Annette was startled to observe her bag on the table and, in Granon's hand, the phone. Reynard must have passed Granon the bag, she concluded. Taking the device from his second in command, Reynard broke the silence.

"Mademoiselle, I believe this is yours? Perhaps you could enlighten us as to its usage?"

Annette sat down looking very green. Reynard waited patiently. She could see in his eyes that she had no choice but to do as he asked, but still she shook her head. He would have to wait until the seasickness passed.

"Lieutenant Granon, please make my cabin available for Mademoiselle. She will feel better once she gets used to the motion."

Any relief that Annette might have felt, crumbled as she heard him say:

"Perhaps the mademoiselle will feel more like telling us about her toy after a day or two at sea."

Friday 22nd June 1798 7 AM — Ken

Ken came to with a parched mouth, and a body that throbbed with pain. Had he been at a party with the engineers? Now he lay on a hard wooden floor with a very bad memory nagging at his brain. As soon as he moved his legs, his ankles hurt, so he stopped, and noticed the chains. He could hold back reality no longer; he was a galley slave.

The *Murad* had lain to in the night and now waited close to shore. Such nights were full of biting insects, and the days spent rowing caused his entire body to ache. Starting with the left ankle, he made an inspection, to find raw and chaffed skin and red patches where the chains had rubbed. The right leg was worse, where he could see blood oozing from a sore spot.

Ken had forgotten about food, but his memory awakened when he smelt something other than the usual ship's stink in the air. Bin Kabina brought him some bread with bean soup. To his surprise he found a large chunk of fish in his bowl and it tasted wonderful to Ken.

"Thank you, I was very hungry," said Ken finishing his bowl.

"The captain allows me to catch fish. Hungry men can't row."

Ken sniffed the air. On the first day, the smell of the ciurma was overpowering, but after two days the odour had apparently faded. He nodded to his oar mate, bin Kabina, the giant African who had been kind to him. The big man instructed him on how to manage the oar without causing undue damage to their bodies, and how to avoid angering the galley master, Ali, who was quick to use his whip at the slightest provocation. Somehow bin Kabina was exempt from Ali's abuse although, for the rest of the crew, the fat galley master did not distinguish between slave and freeman.

93

Ken finished his meal, rejoicing that the silver whistle calling them to work had not yet sounded. He wanted to lie down, but his whole life revolved around that bench and that was the last place he wanted to be. He had got to know every knot and bump in the rough hewn wood; it was his home, his workplace, his kitchen, and his bathroom. So he sat, pondering. What happened to Sarah? How long was he to be enslaved? How was he going to get back to the gate, and more importantly, where were his boots?

When the captain came out on deck, Ken kept quiet. Their bench was close to the quarterdeck, and he worried Abdul would notice him.

"Ali, I have need of you."

Ali came aft, using his whip to wake the sleeping slaves.

"Bring the *French* boy to me."

They both knew he was not French, but Ali went over to Ken's bench. Ken felt the blood pumping in his veins. Had his time come now? He clung to the hope that he might still be of some value. Ali unshackled him and roughly manhandled him up onto the quarterdeck.

Abdul stared at Ken, then spoke to his officers. "Samir, it has been three days since you were sent into the city. Were my instructions as clear as the waters of this bay?"

Samir was not prepared for this interrogation. As far as he was concerned, he had carried out the captain's orders to the letter.

"Rais, I brought you this Frenchmen. The boy had a purse full of gold coins. I saw them in the tavern. His companion must have taken it."

Abdul advanced towards Samir, gripping the hilt of his scimitar, the curved blade of the weapon reflecting the morning sun.

"As Allah is my witness I asked you to bring me men with the following qualities: French, wealthy, and knowledgeable. First, this man is not a Frenchman, second he is not rich, and third his companion is not even a man!" Abdul paused, letting these words sink in to enhance the dramatic effect. "He has no gold, and if he is not a Frenchman he will have no information about the fleet!"

"I have done my duty, captain." Samir stammered, retreating from his rais.

"Allah saw fit to take from us our brother and first lieutenant. I must promote one of you to be first officer," the rais looked at Samir, then turned slowly to Omar. "Omar Hassan al-Munari. Subject to the Bey's approval, you are hereby promoted."

At this announcement Samir growled something inaudible to Ken, and for a brief moment, Ken thought Samir would defy his captain. Instead he turned away his face scarlet with suppressed anger.

"I will deal with this slave another time. Take him away!" ordered Abdul.

To his intense relief, Ken was led back to his bench. He was still alive, and for once he didn't care if he was chained.

"We go now," said bin Kabina in Arabic.

His prediction was correct. The silver whistle blew and the ciurma instantly obeyed. To be slow meant punishment from the galley master's whip, and to refuse meant death. They rowed at a slow pace, and Ken soon got into the rhythm; dip, sweep, pause. Abdul did not want to tire his men; they would be needed if he had to chase a vessel down. A wind sprang up from the northwest, and the captain raised his sail to make the most of the freshening breeze.

What seemed to Ken like a long time later, the ciurma were stood down for a rest. After shipping the oar, he lay dozing on the bench, while bin Kabina sat stoically, his fishing line thrown out over the side. An hour passed in a minute for Ken; then the lookout called something, and the captain altered course. Ken shuddered fully awake to the sound of the silver whistle and took his oar once more, slowly at first: dip, sweep, pause.

Ken sweated and pulled at his oar under the hot sun. He was desperate to rest his hands and hoped the ciurma would stand down soon. A cry from the lookout announced a sail on the starboard quarter, which meant no chance of a rest anytime soon. He heard Omar call for one of the ship's boys,

"Talibah, inform the captain of our change of course and that we have a ship in sight, a goodly sized brig."

Ken dreaded the call to action, and the intense work that would bring to the ciurma. It seemed to him that the only way out was death, and the empty benches were testament to the fact that slaves could die in action. Once again he wished he had not ventured so casually to this dangerous century.

Thirty minutes later they were still rowing, and Abdul stood by Omar's side observing their progress.

"We have gained considerably on the brig. They have not changed course nor added any sail. It would seem they do not feel any danger. They carry 12 guns, no doubt 4 pounders. We can intercept in less than an hour. Remember, the key is to spare your ciurma until the last moment, and then drive them hard. Use them wisely and may Allah be your guide."

Ken listened to the interchange between the two officers, observing how pleased Omar was to be in control of the pursuit.

The hour passed, bringing the other vessel much nearer. Ken kept up with the motion of the oars; dip, sweep, pause. He was beginning to understand how to spare his muscles, and work the oar using his weight. The drum beat grew faster, then stopped. A whistled signal alerted the ciurma to proceed in silence. The brig was getting nearer, but still had not altered sail or tried any evasion tactics. It was possible the galliot, being low in the water, was mistaken for a less war like vessel.

Omar addressed his captain: "Rais, in my opinion it's time to close with the brig."

"The chase is yours. Let's see what our meagre fifteen oars a side can do."

Ken's heart sank when he heard those words. Now he was going to be made to really work. Omar passed the word quietly through the chain of command. The silver whistle called again, and soon the speed increased to six and a half knots. Ken was covered in sweat, and he could feel blisters on his hands.

The oar slipped at every stroke, causing the right hand blister to start bleeding. His shoulders, arms everything was in pain and, with a cry, he dropped his oar and stood up, holding his bleeding right hand. The whip cracked across his shoulders, making him forget all the other pain. Bin Kabina stood up and let the oar trail in the water. With a gleam in his eye, Ali took out his anger on Ken's back, until the big Negro held up his hand to Ali, and glared at him. Ali stopped for a moment to catch his breath, so Ken's companion

96

gently sat him down, wrapped a rag around his right hand, and they took up the oar again.

"Next time I will kill you!" Ali stalked off towards the bow laying right and left with his whip.

The *Murad*, with such a reduced ciurma, was at maximum speed, when the drum beat faster. Ken remembered reading somewhere it took twenty minutes of this kind of exertion to kill an oarsman.

Meanwhile the breeze was freshening, and veering slightly to the North. As the brig changed course, he caught a brief glimpse of their prize. Her crew had, at last, seen the chasing vessel for what she was, so the captain had put on more sail. In a desperate attempt to get more speed out of her, the brig's crew were pumping their fresh water over the side. With a quick glance over his shoulder Ken saw that they also started throwing the brig's big guns overboard. His first thought was relief that he would not come under fire, then he wondered if the lightened brig might have a chance.

"The brig's captain must be scared of a fight. I wonder what she is carrying," Abdul said to Omar. "Now is the time to fire the gun."

Omar called out an order, and there was activity amongst the crew. A few seconds later there was the bang of the bow gun going off and Omar barked out,

"Too short!"

They turned back on a course to intercept, which prompted the brig to cast off a small boat they had been towing. At last the brig started to pull away from them through the water. It was late in the June evening, but the day was long, and there was still plenty of daylight left to stop her from escaping into the night. Every minute Ken watched, the brig seemed to find a new sail to bend on. By this time the galliot had fallen back to a half mile behind. Ken wondered how much longer he had before his heart gave out, then he felt a bump as the galliot bore down on the brig's boat. The side of the small gig was stoved in, but it still floated and Ken saw it drift by.

Omar started to show his frustration and muttered loudly to himself; "Allah, let her lose a spar!"

As if in answer to his prayer, the brig slowed and turned up into the wind. Her captain had tried to put on too much sail to escape the *Murad* in a strengthening wind, and the main topgallant mast could no longer take the pressure. The spar sprung with a loud crack, and the broken spar dangled in a tangle of rigging, bringing a smile to Omar's face, as he saw she was in trouble.

"Prepare boarders to larboard," he ordered.

As the vessels drew ever closer, Abdul was ready with scimitar drawn, the crew quiet and organized, whereas the brig was in total disarray. The weight of the top gallant sail had dragged the damaged mast into the main topsail, but in their efforts to disentangle the mess, the mast had fallen over the side still attached by several lines. Now it was acting as a sea anchor, slowing the brig to a crawl. Just as the sailors cut through the last of the tangled ropes holding the spar, the *Murad* came up with her.

Ken's whole being went into pulling. It was worse than running a marathon. Even a hint that he might be slowing the ciurma, would bring down Ali's whip, so Ken continued to work, even though his hands were raw and bleeding. He counted each stroke, promising himself it would stop if he could just pull ten more. When the ten was done, he made the same promise, so started the count again. At stroke seven, he decided he would die if he had to pull another. Perhaps it would be better to die at the hands of Ali than have his heart blow apart. At stroke nine, the galliot's helmsman put her hard over at exactly the right moment.

As soon as the silver whistle spoke the signal to stop rowing, Ken moved his oar as bin Kabina had taught him, and together they stowed the huge heavy wooden implement. At their peak the oarsmen had reached a count of twenty six strokes per minute. It seemed to Ken they had been forced to keep this pace for an hour, but in fact it had been barely eighteen minutes. He could not express the elation he felt when he stopped. He slumped onto the bench and closed his eyes, listening to Abdul give last minute orders to his officers,

"I will lead the boarding party; Omar will be second. Samir will take over the watch and, if necessary, lead the second wave. Wait for my signal. Perhaps she will drop her colours without too much of a fight."

The galliot supported a large crew of soldiers trained to board enemy shipping. They lined the larboard side of the vessel, armed with cutlasses, scimitars, boarding pikes, and a few pistols. On the quarterdeck, Abdul had stationed his musketeers.

"Fire!"

There was a series of reports followed by acrid white smoke. A great roar went up from the Arab fighters, as they threw their grapnels into the air towards the enemy vessel. Twenty ropes came taut pulling the hulls together, then Abdul led the boarders over the side.

Ken raised his weary head and looked across at the brig. Her crew was putting up considerable resistance. There had been an initial return volley of fire from their small arms, but now he could hear swords clashing, mixed with the shouts and wails of wounded and dying men. He had the feeling that this was not real, but a movie set, and soon the director would call out "cut". Unfortunately these men were not actors and stuntmen with blunted weapons. Any sword wounds inflicted were real, and would likely prove fatal.

He lay back, thankful he was not ordered to fight. He hoped the battle would stay on the brig. As he thought this, he looked up at the quarterdeck where Samir was marshalling a number of men. Ali Peshwar and Ken's other tormentors milled around Samir, who seemed to be giving them some kind of inspirational talk. As Ken listened he realized Samir was stirring up those left aboard; was he hatching a mutiny?

He whispered to bin Kabina; "Can you hear what he said? Do you know what they plan to do?"

"We must stay calm like the sea on a windless day."

"Stay calm?" Ken was far from calm. He watched Abdul's followers swarm aboard the brig, swinging from ropes, climbing over the side, into a volley of pistol shots from the brig's crew. Ken squirmed in his seat, trying to improve his limited view. The smoke was getting thicker, and his instinct to flee kept his blood pounding, and his senses alert. At least the Maltese sailors wore a colourful broad waist sash helping distinguish friend from foe in the fight.

Ken found a suitable eye hole in the wooden side panel close to his bench. He looked upward to the brig's quarterdeck where Abdul confronted one of the brig's pistol wielding officers. The man fired at him just too late; the rais jumped to one side laughing and, before the brig's officer could bring his sword into action, Abdul pierced the man's heart with his scimitar. The officer fell to the deck with a slight sigh as if he was pleased to give up this life. Abdul's men let up a great cheer, as they attacked left and right of him, forcing the brig's crew back.

As Addul dropped from view, Ken saw the newly appointed first officer, Omar, who proved to be very able with his straight sword, sweeping away any opposition as he progressed across the quarterdeck. A man rushed at him screaming, sliding along in a spray of blood. Omar dodged the charge and, with a deft flick of his sword, sent his attacker onwards down an open companionway with a shriek. At the ship's wheel the brig's captain stood firm with a heavy cutlass, held confidently. He stepped back drawing Omar towards him, then side stepped and slashed out under Omar's guard. Omar was caught off balance, but his wild parry luckily turned away the slashing blade. Seizing the opportunity, Omar followed through with a side swipe that made the captain bring his sword across his body in defence. The move was too late to stop Omar from cutting into the man's sword arm, causing him to back off panting. His injured arm hung uselessly by his side. Omar pushed home his advantage, and the captain fell to his knees accepting a quick death.

Ken was surprised it took such a short time for the *Murad's* men to clear the quarterdeck. Without their officers, the Maltese sailors hauled down their colours and put down their swords. The last twenty crew members stood defeated in front of the main mast, where Abdul inspected them.

Ken felt so tired he wanted to sleep on his bench. while he could, but he was fascinated by the taking of the brig, and watched the prisoners being led aboard the *Murad*. Abdul remained in view on the quarterdeck of the brig, watching his crew bring up the first crate from the hold. Abdul crashed his sword down on the first box causing bits of the wooden lid to fly into the air, exposing the contents.

"A fine haul from the Infidel church!" exclaimed Abdul, holding up a great silver crucifix in one hand, and candelabra in the other. "We have been well rewarded for our work today!" A great cheer went up from his crew, and soon the remaining crates were brought up, and the men started to transfer them to the galliot.

Ken sat transfixed by the sight of the silver. He forgot he was a chained slave, forgot Samir was poised ready to take over the ship. All he could see was the treasure. Abdul's gaze fell upon the youngest member of his crew, Talibah, Manu's son. The boy had volunteered to join in the fighting, against his father's advice.

"Omar, take young Talibah, and these other men to help you sail the prize back to Mersa Matruh. A fine gift for the Bey."

Abdul indicated a dozen of his sailors who would return immediately to their home port.

Ken knew something was going to happen and, sure enough, just as Abdul swung across to the *Murad*, Samir's grinning face barred his way.

"Thank you for the infidel treasure."

Abdul dropped onto the deck, staring in disbelief at Samir. The whole crew paused, everybody waiting to see how Abdul would react.

"You will get you share, as will all the crew," Abdul said, pushing past Samir. The galliot started to swing in the wind, the only remaining line attaching her to the brig was belayed right where Samir stood.

"The men have decided I will be their new Rais," declared Samir, who brought his cutlass down on the line slicing it away, thus freeing the brig.

"Treachery!" Abdul cried, turning to face Samir, his scimitar drawn.

Without a pause Abdul swung his curved blade at Samir, who dodged to the left, and brought up his own weapon in response. There was a great clash as the swords locked together, and those still loyal to Abdul rushed to his aid. For a few tense moments, Samir's men tried to keep the boarders on the brig, but too many had already returned with the silver. The brig swung so her stern towered over the galliot's midships, and a line came snaking across the gap between the vessels. Abdul's followers fought hard to keep the connection, and one by one, they came across to join the fight. Soon the galliot was filled with the smack of steel on steel, the smell of gun powder smoke, and the yells of the battling men. To add to their misery, the *Murad* began to roll, as the wind strengthened.

While he watched in full view of the battling factions, bin Kabina guided Ken under their bench. The filth and stink of the fetid water around them was better than being sliced in half by a stray cutlass blow. It was late in the day, and Ken was thankful he would soon be hidden by darkness. Even so he could not help peeking out into the action.

Samir steadied himself, cutlass in one hand and pistol in the other, with his legs astride one of the benches. He brought the gun up to point directly at Abdul's face, but just as he fired, a stray line, weighed down with a heavy block, came swinging through the air. It hit Samir square in the back, so the shot went wide. He picked himself up from the deck, winded but unhurt. Abdul's great scimitar swung at his head, causing Samir to duck down, barely fending off the blow. He jumped back to face the captain on his feet.

Abdul's supporters were not doing as well. Already tired after fighting the men of the brig, several of them were down, and Samir's men were pressing their advantage. As they ran across the benches, a cutlass sliced through the remaining connection between the vessels, preventing any more reinforcements from bridging the gap. Abdul, stronger than any man aboard, pursued Samir relentlessly, hacking down those who dared intervene.

Samir ran towards the stern, hoping that others would slow Abdul down. To his dismay, he turned to find his rais right behind, swinging his blade. The mutineer fell between the benches, his head so close to Ken, that the youth choked at the smell of the man's rancid breath. Samir's whole attention focused on fending off the rain of blows from Abdul. Inevitably, the scimitar smashed through Samir's guard but, the steel slid down his blade with an ear grating scrape, embedding itself into the bench. Ken saw a glint of hope in Samir's eyes, as Abdul struggled to withdraw his scimitar. With a howl of triumph, Samir drew his jambiya, and would have jabbed it into Abdul's face had not Ken, without thinking, reached out and gripped the wrist holding the knife. It happened so fast Abdul withdrew the scimitar and touched it to Samir's throat before the unfortunate man had time to wrench his hand free. Abdul dragged the mutineer out onto the deck where he lay exhausted, waiting to die. The rais cast a glance back to the bench where Ken had put his head up. A brief nod was Abdul's only acknowledgement of his slave's assistance.

Ken was relieved the combatants had moved forward away from him, but then he felt a bump as the waves pushed the brig into the side of the *Murad*. Omar, with two of the hands, emerged onto the brig's quarterdeck. Ken thought they must have been below assessing the ship's stores, and were only now aware there was mutiny afoot. In two strides, Omar led his men across the quarterdeck, jumped up on the rail. "They can't get back, now," muttered Ken. With the lines cut, the ships had drifted apart. The remaining members of the prize crew rallied around Omar on the brig's stern. Within seconds the wind gusted and momentarily pinned the galliot into the larger brig and Ali ran over to help stop Omar from boarding. As he did so there was a cry from Samir, as he went down in Abdul's power. "What the heck?" Ken spluttered. Ali, witnessing Samir's fall, turned on the mutineer next to him, slicing him across the back. The man fell screaming to the deck, and Ali threw a line to Omar allowing him to cross back to the galliot. Ken suppressed his desire to yell "traitor" at Ali. As soon as the prize crew came onboard, fortunes were reversed, and the mutineers were soon subdued.

Once curiosity overcame his fear, Ken left the security of the bench, and looked over the side to see the brig was adrift. In the confusion, nobody had noticed there was no line left to connect the prize to the *Murad*. The last thing Ken noticed as she drifted off into the gathering gloom was the name on the vessel, *Palerma*. A faint memory jogged in his brain, and he remembered Sarah's story. Then he thought about his hand in her death, bringing tears to his eyes. The brig's gig, damaged by the collision with the *Murad*, and still afloat, drifted downwind and came to rest against the galliot's side. Ken looked down at the battered boat, amazed it had not been sunk. A yell of pain and rage from Abdul, drew Ken's attention back to the ongoing drama.

As Samir was dragged forward by Abdul, he managed to draw a hidden blade from his ankle strap, which he thrust into Abdul's left foot. Seizing the opportunity for freedom, and facing overwhelming odds, Samir threw himself over the side. The brig had already disappeared from sight in the dark. Ken wondered if a slow death by drowning was any better than the fate awaiting him. The mutineers were dealt with in brutal fashion, as soon as the fight was over. There were five still alive, and they were lined up on the galliot's starboard side, with their heads held out over the water.

"Who here would follow Samir?"

There was no answer to Abdul's question.

"You are wise to stay silent, your death will be swift,"

He raised his sword and decapitated the first man, quickly followed by three more economical strokes. Their heads splashed into the sea, to be lost in the galliot's wake.

"You believe in Allah, my friend?" He asked the last man.

The sailor managed to lift his head, and summon a few drops of saliva in his parched mouth, to spit pathetically into the sea. Abdul laughed at the rebel's puny defiance and sent him to meet his maker.

A quiet descended on the company. The high sides that protected the slaves ended behind Ken's bench, so he could stand on his seat and be quietly sick over the side. There was no longer any sign of the brig, but Ken distinctly heard the creak of oars from the brig's little boat.

Two days at sea was enough to make Annette feel her life was over. All Reynard would say about their journey was: "We are on patrol." As the rough weather continued to aggravate her nausea, she began to question if this voyage would, indeed, bring her closer to her objective. Despite these woes, she was still determined to carry out her plan. This miraculous opportunity of being thrust back in time was a gift. She must endure the hardships of the French cutter, and make good her promise to her mother. Somehow, she would convince Reynard to take her to join the fleet.

On the third morning, feeling a little better, she stepped out onto the weather deck, just as the lookout warned of an approaching vessel. The ship became alive as Reynard gave out orders in sharp staccato bursts.

"Clear for action! Beat to quarters!"

The cutter closed on the slow moving vessel, and Annette joined Reynard by the steersman.

"Mademoiselle please, you must go below, and stay where it is safer, there may be fighting."

Annette grasped the rail.

"Sir, I need the air for my health."

Reynard was about to insist when the lookout interrupted again.

"The brig's flying the colours of Malta."

"Can you see what vessel?"

"The *Palerma*!"

Annette gasped in surprise. Where had she heard that name? Of course! Sarah's story came back to her. The cutter had been away for four nights so it was now the 23rd of June, Sarah's birthday.

"Monsieur le Capitan, I must tell you something."

"I too would like to talk to you, but we have to first find out if this vessel is friendly; it may be flying false colours. Monsieur Granon, please conduct Mademoiselle below."

Granon held her arm, but she tore herself free. "Monsieur Reynard, you will find that vessel deserted, as if the spirits have mysteriously taken the crew. If this is the true state of affairs aboard this brig, then hear me out."

Reynard looked at her in surprise. He nodded his agreement, then turned back to the task in hand. Granon escorted her below.

Saturday 23rd June 1798 5 PM — Annette

Annette entered the small cabin, keeping her head bowed to avoid the low ceiling. She sat down at the table alongside lieutenant Granon to face Reynard. The officers each had their servants who stood behind their chairs to wait on them. Dinner was substantial by Annette's standards. The chicken was a little tough, the vegetables overcooked, but the exquisite wine soon made her forget the cooking. After a sweet concoction of fruit and Cognac, the officers continued drinking, while Annette contented herself with a pot of freshly made coffee. Conversation was sparse, and Annette waited. At last, the cloth was drawn and Reynard began.

105

"Perhaps Lieutenant Granon would care to share some of his poetry with us?"

Annette was surprised. Granon was a very handsome man, but it had not occurred to her that he had any artistic talents.

Granon stood up. "Mademoiselle Annette, you are acquainted with the English poet and playwright, William Shakespeare?" Annette nodded, and Granon coughed and recited in English.

"Let me not to the marriage of true minds Admit impediments. Love is not love Which alters when it alteration finds, Or bends with the remover to remove —"

At first, his voice was gentle and playful, then full of character and passion. He finished the sonnet and continued with two more. By the end, Annette found herself quite moved. Perhaps it was the situation, at sea, in a tiny cultural bubble where she could lose herself in something as simple as poetry.

Annette clapped her hands as Granon sat down. "Bravo Monsieur Granon, where did you learn to speak English so well?"

The lieutenant was a little embarrassed, as he was not used to such enthusiasm.

"I have relatives in England. As a child I was sent there for holidays sometimes, when there was peace."

Annette warmed to Granon; he had made sure she was well looked after, and she admired his handsome face and kindly eyes. He kept his long black hair in a pony tail nautical style, but when she looked at his mouth she decided she should concentrate on the business at hand and not get side tracked.

Reynard interrupted her thoughts. "Thank you Monsieur. Now let us discuss some weighty matters. I have two questions to put to you, Mademoiselle. First, how did you know the brig would be deserted? Second, what is the purpose of this box?" He set Ken's phone on the table, sat back and sipped his brandy.

Annette had come to a decision. She must take a chance on Reynard, and let him into her secret. As she started to speak, she wondered if they still burned witches in the late 18th century and, swallowing that unfortunate thought, she took a deep breath.

106

"Mesieurs, I have something to say that you will find difficult to believe. I will answer your questions, but my story will stretch your imagination and intelligence to its limit."

Reynard's face betrayed a slight smile. "Perhaps you better explain yourself, mademoiselle, and put our credulity to the test."

"First let me give you a simple answer to your questions, I knew about the *Palerma* being discovered as a ghost ship because I read about it from an original source. In this case it was described in general Vaubois' records. I should say will be described next year, but I read it 200 years from now. I was born in the year 1989, and until a few days ago, I was living in the year 2015. The box you hold in your hand will not be made until over 200 years into the future. It is a kind of machine — one capable of storing information in the form of words or pictures, and has the ability to display this information. Please believe me. I have indeed travelled back in time from 2015 and so has this machine. Let me show you."

She picked up the smart phone, pushing a button so the device sprang to life. With a nod from Reynard, she touched the screen to access the chart app., and displayed the chart of Aboukir Bay.

The reaction was interesting. At first neither Reynard nor Granon could make anything out on the screen. The viewing angle was not right for them. They could see patches of colour, but neither of the officers could organize these shapes into something intelligible. Granon stood up, turned the little computer around and gave it another look. This time he was standing further back and, almost as a second thought in his peripheral vision, Granon again saw the charts he had glimpsed at the inn.

"Now I see it!" He turned to Reynard; "It takes some effort, it is a trick of the light, but there is a naval chart depicted on this box. I cannot tell how this is done. There seems to be light issuing from here."

He pointed to the screen, but he could not find a suitable French word to describe such a thing.

"Monsieur, you know I had knowledge of the brig. Have I convinced you that I come from the future?" Annette asked.

Reynard too stood at the right angle to the screen and saw the naval charts. As Annette watched him, he turned pale.

"On the one hand you have evidence, which could only be explained by fore knowledge of current events. On the other hand, to travel from the future is an impossibility. My father was a teacher, who taught me to be a man of science. I use reason where others listen to their emotions, and I have learned something of philosophy where others have their religion. Mademoiselle Annette, how can you have made this journey? What powers have you invoked?"

Annette laughed, but it was a false, nervous laugh. "Monsieur, I have no mysterious powers. I took advantage of a gateway through time. I cannot control it, I do not understand it; I simply discovered it and made use of it."

Reynard gathered his thoughts. This apparently harmless woman was full of surprises.

"Let us assume you are not mad, and you have indeed somehow managed to move back in time. Why would you want to visit this particular time? What motive do you have?"

Annette drew a deep breath; this was going to be the difficult bit. "Monsieur, I had no control or knowledge of where or when the gateway would take me. Yet I have studied this part of my history. I know something about the past and your future; indeed, the future of Napoleon's expedition."

The two officers were too dumbfounded to speak. At last, Reynard recovered his composure.

"Please go on, Mademoiselle. Everybody wants to know their future."

Granon started to say something, but stopped; then he nodded. His face wore an expression bordering on fear.

"The fleet is going to Alexandria in Egypt. On the first of August, there will be a terrible battle at Aboukir Bay, where the French men of war will be destroyed by an English fleet under the command of Admiral Nelson. Admiral Brueys' flagship, L'Orient will sink when the powder magazine blows up at about 10 PM that same day. I think I can help the Admiral save his ship, and change the outcome of that battle. I believe it is your duty, Monsieur, to take me to Admiral Brueys."

Reynard rose to his feet. "My duty, Mademoiselle? You tell me my duty?"

"Forgive me, Monsieur, I want not to offend. Indeed I wish only for the best outcome for France."

"Mademoiselle, I will consider your request. Monsieur Granon, what is your opinion?"

Granon took a long time to answer. "Monsieur, it is a fantastic story, but she knew the destination of the fleet; a military secret. Her story is of course impossible, and so is her foreknowledge of the brig. These two impossibilities leave me . . ." He paused, shook his head and said: "I would tread with caution."

Annette was quite alarmed at this candid statement, and thought again about her personal safety.

"We are three days sail East of Malta, and if we continue to Alexandria and Aboukir Bay we could be sailing into a trap set by the English." Reynard declared.

"Monsieur Reynard . . . "

Reynard cut her short. "Mademoiselle, you could, unwittingly, be playing a part of an English game." Pausing, he took a long look at Annette's face. "I pride myself, Mademoiselle on judging character. I believe you are sincere in what you say; however it is possible you have been manipulated. Monsieur Granon, is the *Palerma* ready to sail?"

"Oui mon capitan, the prize crew is aboard, and she can return to Malta immediately."

"Good!" said Reynard. "You will take command of the *Palerma*. Report to the fort, and take your orders from general Vaubois."

With a smile on his face, Granon saluted as he exited the cabin, but Reynard brought him back. "Belay that order. At the old fort, I would like you to report to Monsieur Langon. Please tell him what has happened since we met the Mademoiselle. You are not to share this knowledge with Vaubois, but you are to take your orders from Langon, you understand?"

Granon made a short bow to acknowledge his orders, and as he turned to go Reynard stopped him again. "Wait a moment. I want to put a question to the Mademoiselle. I want you to convey the answer to Langon."

"Oui Monsieur."

"Mademoiselle, I believe it is best for France if we proceed to this Aboukir Bay. We shall set a course for Egypt. I have one question to put to you. Who else came with you from 2015?"

"I believe my history professor is a captive of the French general in Malta, you may know him as Lieutenant Duncan."

Reynard looked at Annette in amazement. "Duncan? The English lieutenant? I was visiting the castle the day he escaped, aided by a traitor. I saw them myself, one of them attacked me when I tried to stop them. You say he is a history professor?"

"In the 21st century, but I believe in 1798, he is an English naval lieutenant."

Reynard thought aloud: "What are his intentions, I wonder?"

"I cannot say, but he knows I want to help France win this battle. So he will do everything to stop us."

"In which case, Mademoiselle, we shall have to make it our purpose to prevent him!"

Chapter 7

The Storm

Wednesday 20th June 1798 1:30 PM — Sarah

Sarah stayed in the shelter, keeping as quiet as possible, expecting the sailors to drag her out at any moment. The minutes ticked by, and soon she started to doze, tired from her climb. She woke feeling refreshed. The boy sat beside her in the shelter.

"Pawlu," he said pointing to himself. "Tlaqna!"

Sarah followed him into the sunshine, where she saw that the cliff top was clear of the *Murad's* sailors. Pawlu signed to her that he was taking her to a place where she could rest and eat. Sarah understood him easily; impressed how well he mimed the actions. She exchanged her dry climbing shoes for the damp, but sensible shoes in her pack, and soon they started to walk down a steep, stony track. Sarah had found her first ally in the 18th century.

Sunday 24th June 1798 6 PM — Sarah

Sarah sat outside Pawlu's stone hut, not far from the cliff top. She nibbled at some bread and cheese, enjoying the peaceful surroundings. Under different circumstances, she would have relished this escape from the pressures of university life. There was no traffic noises, no blaring radios, no aircraft overhead. What she could experience here was not to be found in the 21st century. An hour passed while she dozed in the quiet of the June evening, dreaming of a simple, but complete life filled with first ascents of the cliffs, and the subsequent hero worship of appreciative shepherd boys.

She woke up as the boy, Pawlu approached accompanied by a young naval officer with a kindly face. The pair stopped in front of her, and the man made a slight bow.

"You speak French, Mademoiselle?" He asked in French.

"Yes, but my first language is English."

The man shook his head. "My education in Sicily was in French and Italian. My name is Antonio Barbaro. For three days Pawlu has been telling me of a woman who can climb the sea cliffs by magic, and needs my help to find her friend captured by the French. For three days I have told the boy it is impossible to climb the cliffs, and I have no time for his stories. Today he said you were the most beautiful woman on the island, and if I did not come, you would die of sadness. So I followed the boy to find he was right, you are the most beautiful woman on the island, but where are the tears he spoke about?"

Antonio flashed her a most winning smile, and she could not help but laugh.

"Monsieur Antonio, my name is Sarah Malette. Thank you for coming to help. At least part of what the boy said is true. I climbed the cliffs to escape the pirates, who have a friend of mine chained to the benches of their galley."

"And another who is captive of the French?"

Sarah nodded, remembering Duncan and amazed that the boy had understood so much from her attempts at communication.

"I have never met a woman who can climb the unclimbable cliffs."

"One day I will show you."

"Perhaps, in the meantime, I may be able to help with one of your problems, my lady. If you would accompany us."

Without giving Sarah a chance to respond, he walked down the path towards Valletta. Intrigued as to which problem he referred to, Sarah rose and caught up with the dashing young officer. The sea breezes gave way to dry still air as they retreated from the shore into the town. Walking side by side, Sarah felt a flicker of doubt. Could she trust this man from Malta?

"What happens if we meet a patrol?" Asked Sarah, knowing full well Napoleon's invading army had decreed a curfew at dusk, which meant they would be arrested if discovered.

"Mademoiselle, we shall endeavour to avoid them, besides they are not looking for you."

"Meaning it is you they seek? For what reason? Am I accompanying a criminal?"

"I am no friend to these invaders. Do you know something of our government?"

"I know only that Hompesch was head of the order of the ruling knights and . . ."

Antonio interrupted her. "Until the French arrived. A movement against the knights has existed for a long time. The French know we are prepared to fight them to gain control over the country, but we can talk politics later."

They made a curious trio of curfew breakers: the man, the boy, and the young woman. At a nod from the man, young Pawlu darted off into the maze of back streets while Sarah and Antonio proceeded cautiously. About ten minutes later, the boy reappeared, whispered something to Antonio, and dashed off again.

"Take care, Mademoiselle. The boy informs me there is a French patrol ahead. Don't worry they are searching for me, not you."

A short distance later, he held up his hand motioning her to wait while he crossed the street and disappeared. Sarah obeyed; in the distance she heard the tramp of marching boots on the cobbles. They were getting louder and still Antonio did not return. What would happen if the patrol found her? The tramping boots grew louder. When the marching boots were almost upon her, Antonio appeared breathless.

"Mademoiselle, this way, quickly."

They ran down the street until they reached a large fenced property, slipping through a gateway as the patrol rounded the corner. They waited, trying to catch their breath as they crouched behind the wall. The patrol had also stopped. Had they been seen? With a nod from Antonio they raced across the grounds of the big house to a courtyard. As the pair fled into the stable, several blue uniformed soldiers entered the courtyard, and started to make a systematic search.

Sarah saw an old smock hanging over the horse stall, and she slipped it on. "You hide. I can pass for a stable boy," she said realizing that Antonio was endangering himself for her.

Antonio started to protest as they heard the searchers approaching the stable, so she pushed him up a ladder to the hayloft. Two soldiers entered just as she moved back into the shadows beside a chestnut mare. The horse breathed hard, but Sarah was used to these nervous beasts, and gently stroked its mane.

"Lucien, ici j'ecoute quelque chose!"

The second soldier climbed the ladder with his bayoneted musket hanging loosely on its strap. Sarah watched in horror as he started to systematically shove the sharp point into the straw. If they found Antonio, perhaps he would be guillotined. Was her fate linked to his? She emerged stifling a yawn, and adopting her best Montreal accent, she said:

"Messieurs! Why are you disturbing my horses?"

The unshaven soldier stopped probing the hay, and slid down the ladder to join his friend. Both pointed their muskets at Sarah.

"Who are you? What are you doing here?"

"I take care of the horses. I was taking a nap when you barged in making a noise and frightening these animals."

"Are you from here? How come you speak French? Where is your accent from?" The one called Lucien demanded.

"I learned French from my mother."

"Have you seen a young man, tall, dark, and dangerous?"

"That describes most of my friends," said Sarah with a laugh. Then she noticed the tip of the bayonet was red with blood, and her laughter died abruptly.

"We must arrest her for breaking the curfew," said the other soldier.

"She says she works with the horses. She has not gone outside," replied Lucien.

"Do not leave here; it is dangerous," Lucien spoke sharply to Sarah.

Sarah nodded her head, trying not to look at the bayonet. The soldiers were almost out the door when one of them turned back.

"Wait, let me see your papers."

"They are in the house," she said, wondering whose house it was.

The soldier shrugged, then noticed his companion's blooded bayonet. "It looks like you caught something up there after all . . ."

"Sacre bleu! I thought I felt something . . ."

Antonio dropped on the soldier and rolled him onto the floor. The other soldier pushed Sarah out of the way, trying to aim his musket at Antonio, but before he could pull the trigger, Sarah picked up a shovel covered in horse manure, and swung it into his shoulder. The musket discharged with a loud bang into the fighting pair. There was a moment of shock, everybody froze, and then Antonio stood up. The fight had gone out of his opponent, and he gently laid the soldier on the floor, The remaining soldier, beside himself with anger, turned on Sarah, who retreated into the stable.

Antonio picked up the fallen soldier's musket. "Halt! Lay down your weapon!" he commanded.

As the soldier obeyed, Sarah knelt beside his companion. She held the man's wrist and took his pulse, then shook her head. At a word from Antonio she found some chord and bound the remaining soldier's hands. As she finished, she glanced up and gasped. Antonio had removed his shirt to reveal a gash on his left side.

"It is nothing," said Antonio.

"Nothing? You're bleeding. How come you didn't cry out?"

"Our revolution makes us strong."

Sarah tore the shirt into strips, doing what she could to stop the bleeding, before they hurried outside and across the courtyard. The street was alive with shouts from the neighbouring houses, as the patrol continued searching.

"How do they know you're out here?" Asked Sarah.

Without answering her, he knocked on a side door and entered. Sarah followed him into a deserted hallway and up a staircase. A skylight led them onto the rooftops, several stories above street level. They threaded their way through the chimneys, and came to the edge of the building, where a narrow plank formed a walkway to the next rooftop.

"Quickly, we must cross." Antonio held the plank steady for her.

Sarah, who felt fine on a rock face, looked at the plank and stopped. "I would feel safer if you went first, " she said.

Antonio nodded and crossed without a pause. It was a long drop to the street. As she hesitated, a cry came from below.

"Attention! Attention sur le toit. Halt!"

With one foot on the plank, she stared down into the muzzles of twenty muskets pointing up at her. Ignoring the danger from the street, she fixed her eye on the opposite side. She set her other foot on the plank, feeling the board sway beneath her. "At least rock is stable," she thought. "Don't look down!" she told herself as she put one foot in front of the other. Antonio held his hand out to her beckoning, so she put another foot forward, and then heard the order to fire from below. Sarah was not usually given to panic, but she was not used to guns aimed in her direction, either, so she instinctively stepped back to the safety of the rooftop. There was a loud report and several musket balls hit the plank, turning it over. Somehow it still bridged the gap.

"Mademoiselle Sarah, we must go! They have entered the building."

Sarah tentatively put her foot on the plank again, and started to walk across. She had not realized that the evening was so hot until sweat started to pour down her face. With arms spread wide to gain some balance, she did not dare take a hand down to wipe her eyes. A noise behind her made her freeze.

"Mademoiselle, do not look back, you are half way across."

There was the sound of the wood splintering as a musket ball hit the edge of the plank in front of her. Her mind charged ahead, but her body remained still.

"Attention! Halt!" This time the voice came from behind her on the roof.

As Sarah kept moving, something flicked by her shoulder. She ducked, causing the plank to sway alarmingly. Her terrified cry did not drown out the crack of a musket firing. Sarah expected to feel the pain of the ball entering her body, but instead she heard a scream of pain from behind. She could no longer resist the temptation to look back. Two soldiers were down, one writhing in

116

agony on the roof next to a musket that had clearly blown up in his face, and the other one with a knife protruding from his chest. Facing forward again, she concentrated on reaching the next building. She tried to think of the plank as another climb, and managed to take two more steps. She was now one step away from the end when she felt the plank move. The third soldier had grabbed the end and was trying to pull it out from under her feet.

"Jump, now!"

She made a leap as the end of the plank exploded in a hail of musket shots, and found herself safely in Antonio's outstretched arms. He gripped her hand, keeping low as a musket ball whistled past her right shoulder. The rooftop was full of obstacles, skylights, what looked like small sheds, and even a garden. Antonio seemed to know where he was going, and guided her, running faster than she thought possible. He shepherded her around every obstacle, and helped through a trap door in a flat roof. Flinging it open, he beckoned to her to descend a steep stairway, flight after flight, until they reached a cellar, where her thoughtful guide pressed some hidden lever in the wall revealing a narrow opening.

Antonio lit a candle, and Sarah followed him along a silent passageway. Antonio's shadow hid her from the light, so she reached out for the reassurance of his muscular shoulder. He paused at her touch and asked:

"Are you all right, Mademoiselle?"

"Yes, thank you. On the plank I thought I might . . .," Sarah hesitated.

"You are a brave woman, Mademoiselle. We must wait here. The patrol will be doing a house to house search."

Thankful for the break, Sarah found herself dozing when Antonio spoke.

"Come, we are nearly at our destination."

They emerged into the dark streets to walk for a few minutes before stopping in front of a grand looking house.

A uniformed butler greeted them with no sign of surprise at Sarah's unkempt appearance. She entered, staring in wonder at the magnificent vestibule.

"Perhaps madam would care to wash and dress for dinner?" The butler suggested in perfect English, nodding towards a grand staircase. Tired and overwhelmed by events, she did not stop to ask questions, but accepted the welcome invitation to a bathroom. She followed his direction and ascended. At the top, a maid stepped out with a curtsy.

"I think we can find something suitable, Mademoiselle," the woman said as she eyed Sarah's unorthodox garb.

The maid ushered her into a room where there was a porcelain wash basin, a jug of water, lye soap, and towels. As Sarah began her ablutions, the maid returned with a magnificent dress for her.

Sarah emerged twenty minutes later to be greeted by the butler, who actually raised an eyebrow at her transformation. She wore a low cut green dress with an empire waistline. The maid had done a good job with Sarah's short hair, and completed the ensemble with a delicate string of sparkling gems. She walked down the stairs, hardly able to conceal her giggles at the bizarre contrast with her evening adventure. A footman emerged from a room to her right, and she could see past him to what looked to her like a very old fashioned piano. The thought that she might get to play it crossed her mind when the footman opened a much grander door to the dining room, where the butler announced:

"Mademoiselle Sarah."

Some very elegantly dressed and well to do people sat at a long, formal dining table. At the head sat a lively looking, white haired, old man holding a walking cane, while the rest of the men stood up at her entrance, including Antonio. The only other woman in the room smiled warmly from across the table, dispelling the wave of nerves that had engulfed her upon entering. Antonio stepped forward, and escorted her to the head of the table.

"Mademoiselle Sarah, monsieur le Comte," said Antonio.

"So this is the woman who defies gravity? I understand you are a long way from home, Mademoiselle. Welcome to my house; please sit down and enjoy our hospitality," the old man said in accented English.

Sarah felt she should curtsy but could not quite remember how it should be done, so she mumbled a thank you, and gratefully allowed Antonio to guide her to her seat at the far end of the table. A man in a British naval officer's uniform turned round as she approached. Sarah stopped and stared.

Antonio stepped forward. "Mademoiselle Sarah, I think you know Lieutenant Duncan of the British Navy?"

Tuesday 26th June 1798 7 PM — Ken

Ken woke up to the sound of bin Kabina's voice in his ear. "Salaam Mr. Ken. You must wake up now, for soon we shall have to work our oar."

Stirring, Ken looked up at the only kindly face he had found in this accursed century. Bin Kabina called him "Strange friend" and Ken understood his Arabic, which was similar to the Egyptian dialect of his youth.

"Now we shall return to Egypt," bin Kabina said with an encouraging smile.

"Egypt? You came from Egypt?"

Now he was even more curious about bin Kabina. Why was it that Ali, the galley master, never attempted to lay his whip across the muscular back of the Nubian? The backs and shoulders of every other man in the ciurma were covered in wicked red marks, signifying where the whip had gouged away their flesh. bin Kabina, however, remained untouched and, by good fortune, Ken found himself under this dignified man's protection.

"bin Kabina, where are you from?" Asked Ken, hoping that the silver whistle would not come too soon.

"Strange friend Ken, I am Bedu."

"Why is it you are not chained? Why does the galley master never single you out for punishment?

"I came aboard the *Murad* to pay a debt for my family. Their freedom is bought by my labour, but I am no slave and these men know that. When first I sat in these benches, a man tried to put irons on my legs. I picked him up with one hand, and warned him, and all those on this cursed vessel that I, bin Kabina, am a free man. I defied the man who would have chained me, but I left him the use of his legs, and told him it was a warning never to try to make me a slave.

119

Two crew members tried to help the man. I threw his squirming body at them, and they fell to the deck. Since that day they leave me be."

This was by far the longest speech that Ken had ever heard bin Kabina make.

Ali started his rounds accompanied by the whistle blower. One blew, the other whipped. Blood rushed to Ken's face, and his heart pounded. He dreaded their arrival, knowing that even a slight hesitation, a misinterpreted signal, or the sadistic whim of the galley master could result in the whip slashing down.

He arrived at Ken's bench. "You, little Frenchman, move to number five larboard."

Before Ken could move, bin Kabina stood up. He looked down at the galley master, himself a large man. A look of rage passed over Ali's face, but he avoided any eye contact with bin Kabina, and moved on.

"I have decided to let the boy stay."

Ken stayed where he was, astonished at bin Kabina's ability to control the galley master. "I thank you," Ken said. It did not seem appropriate to ask questions, but his face must have betrayed his confusion.

"You were sent to me for a purpose, known only to Allah," said bin Kabina.

The silver whistle blew, ending their conversation. They pulled on their oar for three hours, until they came close to shore. As they drew near, a complicated set of signals indicated a manoeuvre unknown to Ken. Ali was everywhere with his whip. bin Kabina seemed to understand, and showed Ken whether to pull or push on the great oar, as he listened to the signals. Their objective was to back the galliot through the surf to the beach, so that the bow gun protected them against nasty surprises. As they started the turn, there was a disturbance on the starboard side, close to the bow. The inexperienced oarsmen banged clumsily into the oars of their neighbour. The galley master replied with his whip, but it worsened the situation, and a further clash of oars caused the galliot to remain broadside on to the waves, until water cascaded over the side soaking Ali. A ripple of laughter from the larboard oarsmen worsened his mood, and lashed out at all around him. Finally, the oarsmen became coordinated enough to bring the vessel around to beach the galliot. The galley master, however, had lost face, due to the clumsiness of the inexperienced men, and he directed his wrath at the larboard oars. His whip laid the backs of many slaves raw during this incident, but bin Kabina and Ken were untouched.

As usual, Ken slept so soundly it was as if no time had passed at all. That morning the slaves were cleared from the vessel, and chained to wooden stakes driven into the ground. Ken was enjoying the sensation of lying on soft sand, instead of a hard bench, when he was interrupted by a disturbance nearby. One of the captured Brig's crew broke away from the guards and ran across the beach. He did not get far before a shot rang out; one of the marksmen brought the man down. He clutched his arm where blood ran from the wound, but to the surprise of all he got to his feet and resumed his run. A second shot missed, so he managed to gain the harder ground above the beach. Low wooded hills ringed the area, and if he could just reach the trees, he stood a chance. Two of the hands ran after him.

"If he escapes you will die!" The galley master harangued the sailors.

The desperate man ran at a steady pace, barely keeping a few steps ahead of the pursuing crew members, who were also panting with exertion. One of the crew stopped, reached into his belt, and threw his knife at the moving target. The man yelped in pain as the knife drove into his back. He staggered a few steps before falling in front of his pursuers. They dragged him, trailing blood, back to the beach, and dumped him at the feet of the galley master.

Every slave looked at the man, wondering what the fugitive's fate would be. He made horrible sounds as he breathed; Ken suspected that the knife had punctured a lung. Abdul inspected his slave, who looked quite old to Ken. The rais drew his scimitar, and looked over at the slaves.

"Observe! This is the fate of those who try to escape."

He brought his blade cleanly down on the man's neck, and his head rolled onto the beach. This action had the required effect on the ciurma. Not a man moved. The silence was broken by Ken vomiting into the sand.

As the sun set, mosquitoes and vicious bugs began to feed on the ciurma. The man next to Ken was from the Brig's crew. He looked to be about 70 years old, with almost no hair, and a thin rugged face. He swore loudly in Italian at the carnivorous insects.

"It helps to cover your legs in sand," said Ken, also in Italian.

The man nodded his thanks. "How come you to be a captive?"

"I am a traveller, and I was caught in a raid on Malta. My name is Ken."

"I am Francisco originally from Italy, boatswain aboard the *Palerma*."

A man sitting nearby, with the weather beaten look of a sailor, laughed. A large scar ran down his right cheek; he too had seen some action. "P'raps we'll get our chance to 'scape if they go back to Africa now?"

"You're English?" Ken said in surprise.

"Well I can tell you ain't, mate! George Cobbley is me name. Born in London, left for a deserter in Malta, and captured by these pirates these last nine months. Should have known better. Ship left wivout me, due to the drink, and I got taken up, also due to the drink. I must be stupid! What's yer story then, mate?"

"I was visiting Malta when these pirates took me."

Ken thought this might not satisfy George, but as the man started to speak, a clear voice sung to the night sky. It was bin Kabina singing in a language unknown to Ken. The sound was laced with African rhythms, and the men on the beach all kept quiet. George filled the silence after the song.

"Come on me new mate, yer must know this one." He stood up and lifted his head in a tuneful bass;

"Farewell and adieu to you, Spanish Ladies,
Farewell and adieu to you, ladies of Spain."
On the next line Ken joined in. His excellent tenor complimented George's voice. George held the melody while Ken hit perfect harmonies.

"For we've received orders for to sail for ol' England,
But we hope in a short time to see you again."

George smiled at Ken and, without a word passed, they swapped roles. Ken held the melody while George improvised in the bass.

"We will rant and we'll roar like true British sailors,
We'll rant and we'll roar all on the salt sea.
Until we strike soundings in the channel of old England;
From Ushant to Scilly is thirty five leagues. "

A great cheer went up from the whole company. Entertainment was a rare thing in Abdul's service. For Ken it was a happy moment in the midst of fear and hard work. Unfortunately the happy mood was broken, when the galley master appeared with four of the crew.

"This is the one." He pointed at Ken. "Bring him and the other from the brig."

The sailors seized Ken and Francisco, and marched them back aboard the galliot where they were forced to their knees on the deck. Ken could feel the terror rising within him. He'd not had to face any interrogation since the first day.

When Abdul walked up on deck, the galley master said: "Your honour, rais, this is the man I told you of. The Frenchman! He speaks good Arabic, and I saw him talking to the Nubian."

Abdul spoke to Ken in Arabic. "Ali tells me you, who are not a Frenchman, can speak Arabic?" Ken did not know if he expected an answer and kept silent.

Ali gave Ken a vicious kick in the ribs. "Answer the Rais, slave." Ken's mouth was dry but he managed to blurt out, "I was born in Egypt, your honour."

Abdul folded his arms. "Keeping this information from me was not wise. You said you were English."

Ken started to speak only to receive another kick from the galley master. "Say nothing until you're told to do so, slave."

"I find this evening you are a linguist. You were heard to speak Italian with this man from the brig. I wish to know about the French fleet. If the old man is reluctant, Ali will break one of his arms or should we start off by doing that?"

Ali grabbed the unfortunate man, and pulled his arm behind his back. Ken stood up and reached out to interfere. The galley master laughed, dropped Francisco, and took Ken by the throat and shook him as easily as he might strangle a cat. When Abdul signalled for him to stop, Ken fell to the ground, gasping for breath.

"Speak, boy!" Ordered Abdul.

Ken addressed Francisco in Italian. "They want to know about the French fleet. Did you hear any news on the brig?"

Francisco was no less frightened. "The brig was stopped on the 22nd June by Nelson's fleet. Our captain spoke with the English captain. He told him the French left port on the 19th for an unknown destination."

Ken turned to Abdul, thinking the rais would want more than the old man could tell him. "The French are on their way to Egypt, your honour. There is also an English fleet pursuing them. The brig spoke to one of the English ships only hours before she was captured by your honour."

"Take them back to the beach," said Abdul, distracted and deep in thought.

Back with the sand flies, Ken helped Francisco to get comfortable. "My son, Antonio, will raise the ransom money. Perhaps he can find enough for you, too?" Ken smiled. "Unless, of course, we all die first at the hands of Ali," continued Francisco gloomily.

"Ali, the galley master? A big fat coward if ever I saw one. A concerted effort by a few of us and we could have 'im over the side in no time."

"What have you got to live for, old man?" George said with a laugh.

"I have a son, and I want revenge!" Francisco was not joking.

"Revenge is it?" Said George in a light hearted mood. "Are you talking about these pirates or the Maltese knight who did you a favour, and signed you up for the navy? Look at you, a petty officer, a bosun!"

"You don't know what else he did to my family. I heard he left with Napoleon. Tonight this lad told the Arab captain the French are going to Egypt. Perhaps in Egypt I will have the opportunity to kill this knight."

"Perhaps you will die trying," remarked George.

"Not such a bad way to die," muttered Francisco as he drifted off to sleep.

Chapter 8

Passage to Egypt

Wednesday 27th June 1798 8 AM — Sarah

On Wednesday morning Sarah dreamed that she was at sea. The ship was being buffeted by a storm, and the sailors lay on the deck sick or dead. She was the only one capable of altering sail, and all their lives depended on her action. She woke up thinking that she had no idea which sail to use.

Then she remembered that Duncan was alive and free, giving her hope. She was anxious to learn what was going on with her history professor. He had given little away on the previous evening.

She dressed and went through into the adjoining room in time to answer a knock at the door.

"Well, young lady, you're in a lot of trouble," Duncan said, lips pursed in mock anger.

"How so?"

"First, there is breaking and entering, which you must have done to get into my office. Second, there is making use of a certain gateway, which, I am sure, you do not understand. Then you have the audacity to go exploring in the past instead of turning right around, and staying in your own time!" Duncan seemed a little more serious about this point. "Did you do this on your own, or is there anyone else from the 21st century knocking around here in 1798 that I should know about?"

Sarah started to speak, but hesitated, not knowing quite where to begin.

"Sarah, we are alone now. I know I cut you off last night, after you described your cliff escape, but I couldn't risk you shedding light on your origins." said Duncan with a sigh.

"Professor Duncan . . ."

"I am known as *Lieutenant* Duncan in this part of the world." Duncan pulled at his ear; a gesture Sarah had seen before in class when a student had annoyed him. "Have you any idea how dangerous it was to follow me through the gate?"

"Dangerous?"

"Apart from the obvious danger to your life and limb at a time of war, there's the danger of not getting back to your own time, because the gates are not permanent; they disappear!"

"Yes Ken came with me. I escaped from the pirates, but Ken is a prisoner. Have we time to rescue him from those pirates? How long have we got?" Asked Sarah, alarmed.

"The gates are unstable at the time they come into being, and shortly before they disappear. They have even sent me back to see myself already there! Now that's dangerous!"

Sarah looked aghast, not quite understanding. "Are you saying we can't get back?"

"There's a middle period, when they are more or less reliable for two to three months; say about seventy five days," said Duncan with his mouth turned down for once.

"What if we can't get there in time?"

"If you try and go through when they are not stable, there is no telling where or when you will end up! In my experience they disappear after about eighty days. You better be back by the 20th August to be safe."

"Right," agreed Sarah. Uh . . . lieutenant? What other dangers are there?" Asked Sarah.

"There's always the danger of changing events that have already taken place. You know, killing your own grandmother . . . that kind of thing."

"Why would I want to kill my own grandmother?" Sarah asked in a puzzled tone.

"I don't mean that literally. Sometimes you can change time by accident. Fortunately there is something called time momentum; it's the opposite of the butterfly effect. Time tends not to change radically unless you do something extreme. There's a kind of self healing that goes on. It's unlikely you will make accidental changes that will affect your future, although not impossible."

"Is this a kind of parallel world?"

"Perhaps. I have little understanding of how the gates interact with the space time continuum. I do know that I can return through the portal, or wormhole, but I have no control over the wormholes that connect the gates."

Sarah listened fascinated, and then she remembered Annette. "Profes . . . er . . . Lieutenant Duncan, so if somebody really made a major change, it wouldn't matter in our world?"

"Unfortunately that is not the case. It would seem it is possible to have parallel worlds, and to affect your own world at the same time. Or, perhaps, getting to your own parallel world becomes impossible once a change has been made. I don't really know. Either way, the safest thing would be to get back as soon as possible," Duncan answered.

"So some event changed here could be . . ." Sarah searched for the right word,

"A problem? Yes, well that depends on exactly what the traveller did to the time continuum. What do you have in mind?"

"Oh, not me. Annette."

"Annette? You didn't tell me she also came back."

"I'm afraid she came back to change time; she tricked us!" Sarah sighed with relief that she had finally told Duncan what was going on. "It's worse than you think. She has Ken's smart phone containing modern naval charts of Aboukir Bay."

"Don't tell me she actually wants to change the Battle of the Nile!"

Duncan stood up, walked over to the window, and threw back the curtains to reveal a lovely summer day. Then he continued: "If she did reach the French navy in Aboukir Bay, and if Brueys were to know exactly when Nelson was going to arrive it could change the outcome of the battle." He sighed. "Where do you think Ken and Annette are at this moment?"

"That's the problem! I don't know." Sarah admitted. "Annette is somewhere in Valletta. She could be trying to find a way to get to Brueys. As for Ken, I just hope those slavers spared his life after I escaped."

Sarah's voice drifted off. She had hardly allowed herself to consider Ken's fate, but Duncan's presence forced her to wonder if the galley captain had taken out his anger at her escape on Ken. Was he hurt? Or worse? She started to cry, so Duncan came over and put his arm around her.

"Everything is going to be fine. I will make it so."

A knock at the door broke the moment, and Marie-Paule entered. She stopped short, misinterpreting the intimate scene she had interrupted.

"Mademoiselle Marie-Paule may I introduce my student, Sarah," said Duncan rising.

"Monsieur, I'm surprised to find you beat your students so harshly."

Sarah staunched the flow of tears. "Mademoiselle, your concern is not warranted. My tears were of concern for a friend."

Marie-Paule looked from one to the other. "She is your student, so you have both come from Canada?" She said the word "Canada" as if she knew quite well it did not convey the whole truth.

"Marie-Paule has a way of finding out what she wants to know. Yes, I was Sarah's teacher in Canada," confessed Duncan.

"I was just telling the Lieutenant that my . . . " Sarah was about to say 'sister' when she paused, uncertain whether she should reveal her relationship. Recovering, she continued. "Annette, a Canadian friend of mine, is also in Malta."

Marie-Paule looked at Sarah intently. "This woman, Annette, is in some sort of trouble?"

Sarah nodded, and said: "Surely she will be easy to find, a woman from the fut . . ." when she was interrupted by Duncan.

"She may prove very difficult to find in time to avert a disaster. Priority one, we find Annette. Once we have found her we shall direct our energies to rescuing Ken. You present me with many problems, young lady. I will go and make some inquiries." Duncan was deadly serious.

Sarah looked alarmed. "Sir, you will not hurt Annette?"

"Annette will be treated like a lady." With a curt nod, Duncan left the room.

Marie-Paule patted Sarah's hand. "Do not worry, the Comte has spies everywhere, and Valletta is a small place. I expect they'll be able to find out something about your Annette. She must be staying somewhere, an inn perhaps? A woman travelling alone is not usual here."

Sarah nodded. Marie-Paule continued holding Sarah's hand. "So tell me, what do you think of your teacher?"

"Of Duncan?" asked Sarah,

"Yes, what is he like in your lessons? How does he treat his pupils?"

Sarah did not quite know what to say. "He's normal, he treats us well, and everybody likes him. How do you know him?"

Marie-Paule laughed. "The brave Lieutenant saved my life and helped me escape from an enforced service in the prison."

"You were in prison together?" Sarah was confused.

"No, no! I brought the prisoners food. I was no more free than he was! First in the Bastille in Paris, and then here in Malta."

"But why did you stay? Working in the prison?"

"I had no choice."

"Is that why you helped Duncan escape?"

"Au contraire! He helped me to escape! We left together, and then spent the night crammed into a tiny hole hiding from the army patrols. Then we came here."

Before Sarah could ask any more questions, Duncan entered. "The Comte requests the pleasure of taking breakfast with the two young ladies."

Sarah laughed, and the two women left the room arm in arm. Duncan followed, shaking his head.

As breakfast was ending, Antonio returned. "You have some news you wish to impart?" Asked the Comte.

"Monsieur le Comte, I have two important items to report. The first concerns Mademoiselle Annette."

"I am told a woman fitting her description stayed at the Taverna St. Ursula. On the night of Tuesday last, she left some clothes at the inn, and paid in gold for a week. She was last seen going aboard the French cutter *Active*, under the command of a Lieutenant Reynard."

Duncan looked up. "The vessel has left port?"

"The cutter has sailed."

"Perhaps our informants amongst the French have some knowledge of the orders given to that vessel; she did not sail with the fleet," said the Comte.

The breakfast party became quite animated; everybody seemed to want to voice an opinion about Annette, until the Comte motioned for silence. "What is your second piece of news?"

A sad look crossed Antonio's face. "It grieves me to report that yesterday the *Palerma* sailed into Valletta under the command of Lieutenant Granon of the French navy."

Sarah suddenly cried out; "The *Palerma*? The ghost ship!" There was an expectant silence, and she started to feel uncomfortable. "There's a legend about a ship found in Valletta with no crew."

Duncan gave her a warning look, so she finished lamely: "I read about it somewhere."

"Mademoiselle, we heard only last night that the vessel was found without a crew, abandoned." Antonio gave Sarah an intense look. "How could you have read about it?"

"I must've made a mistake. I was thinking of a legend from somewhere else . . . a coincidence," said Sarah, feeling embarrassed by her faux pas.

"Sarah is very perceptive," chimed in Duncan.

The old Comte's eyes twinkled, but he said nothing.

"Monsieur le Comte, do we have sufficient resources to commandeer this ship?" Asked Duncan.

"Commandeer? It is our ship, Lieutenant Duncan," Said the Comte quietly.

"Monsieur, the young woman, Annette, may have valuable information about Nelson's fleet, which she wishes to carry to Admiral Brueys. It is vital that we stop her reaching Alexandria. If not, it is possible that the invaders of your island will rule the Mediterranean for many years to come. If we can cap . . . recapture the brig, we can at least try and find her. Time is of the essence!"

The Comte deliberated. "The ship lacks guns, and many of our most able seamen were in the *Palerma* when she left here a week ago including, I regret to say, Antonio's father."

There was a short awkward silence, then Antonio said: "May he rest in peace."

"Is there no hope for somebody captured by the galley?" Asked Sarah alarmed.

"You are speaking of your friend? My dear, it is possible he is alive, in which case we shall all rejoice; until then, we can but hope." The Comte turned to Duncan. "As to the *Palerma*, we have nobody to command her except perhaps yourself?"

"It would be my honour to command this vessel on behalf of the free Malta Navy."

The Comte nodded his head. "It is also my desire. I will write you a warrant, authorized by my government in waiting. I shall officially second you to our navy. In view of the long standing relationship between your government and my organization, perhaps this paper will help keep you from being arrested by your own navy for desertion." The Comte paused, then continued with a nod to Sarah and Marie-Paule. "I somehow doubt that these women wish to stay behind. They are, of course, welcome to remain as guests of my house." The Comte raised an eyebrow of enquiry.

"Monsieur, Sarah and I have discussed this. We wish to volunteer for the free Malta navy," stated Marie-Paule in a firm voice.

Duncan's eyes lifted in protest, but the Comte silenced his unvoiced comment.

"We are short handed. I see no reason that you cannot both serve our cause. Women at sea will be at risk, so perhaps it would best if you posed as men. Antonio, they will serve us best with the rank of aspirant. You can find uniforms for these brave volunteers?"

"Certainly monsieur," said Antonio.

The Comte leaned forward, speaking quietly to Duncan.

"While we speak of rank, Antonio has passed the necessary exams for the rank of tenente, or lieutenant in your navy. You agree?"

"Of course. I will need a lieutenant."

"Well then, these matters are settled," said the Comte looking first at Antonio and then at the two women.

The men fell into a discussion about how best to capture the brig from the French, and Sarah waited for a quiet moment.

"Lieutenant Duncan, can we reach Aboukir Bay in time?"

"In a fast brig, it is possible," he said with an optimistic smile.

Sarah saw the smile change to a frown, as he turned away from her. If they failed, then the course of history could be changed in an alarming and unpredictable way.

Friday 29th June 1798 9 PM The Grand Harbour, Valletta, — Sarah

Sarah and Marie-Paule made themselves comfortable on a few barrels surrounded by some wooden crates containing their supplies courtesy of the Comte, where they could observe the brig moored nearby. Duncan, in a naval officer's uniform approached.

"Mr. Malette, Mr. Bonneterre, good evening. The Comte persuaded me to take you on this voyage on the grounds that it is better to have you both in a place where I can keep my eye on you. Who knows what trouble you might get up to with me gone. The action will start very soon, and I would like you both to stay out of the way until the brig is taken. Your disguises are to your satisfaction?"

"The midshipman uniforms fit like a glove, Monsieur. Please do not worry, we are not going to get ourselves killed unnecessarily."

Antonio appeared out of the darkness.

"Good evening, Tenente. How many men has the Comte sent me?"

"Monsieur, we have forty eight men deployed around the harbour in small groups, including our two 'midshipman' . Also, I have a report on the condition of the brig from a ship yard worker, loyal to the Comte. With the fleet gone, the invaders made the brig a priority. All spars and rigging have been repaired, and the guns replaced. Her stores and water are completed. She is loaded with Maltese delicacies; perhaps she was destined to supply Napoleon himself."

Sarah saw a gleam in Duncan's eyes. The ship was like a dream, the ultimate prize, fully stocked and ready for sea.

"Do we yet know her strength?" Duncan asked the question with his eyes glued on the brig.

"The full crew has not reported. It is most likely just the anchor watch, and a few French soldiers. We cannot be sure of their number."

Sarah could see two armed guards, and Marie-Paule nudged her as Duncan spoke.

"It would certainly help to know how many are aboard."

"I have an idea, cheri. I will be back . . ." Marie-Paule's voice was lost as she disappeared behind the crates.

A short time later, she returned wearing a dress.

"Mademoiselle, why the change?" Demanded Duncan, a little irritated.

"Look at me," Marie-Paule laughed. "Do you think I dress like this every day?"

Sarah noticed her dress was cut low, and she wore a scarlet scarf.

"I think I can persuade two of the guards to follow me. Antonio and his boys will do the rest." Marie-Paule kept her voice low and alluring.

"Mademoiselle, you cannot risk your life like that. I will not allow it," declared Duncan.

"We are not aboard ship. In Valletta the Comte gives the orders, Monsieur."

Leaving an astonished Duncan, she walked right up to the soldier guarding access to the brig. "Good evening Monsieur. I have come to give you your reward for saving Malta."

The young soldier opened his mouth, but no sound emerged. He gaped at Marie-Paule's ample cleavage before calling to his companion. "Alain, there's a beautiful whore who wants to give us a reward for saving the island."

There was a grunt from Alain somewhere below decks.

"What is your name?" Enquired Marie-Paule.

134

"I am Thierry, Mademoiselle, and this is . . ."

"Alain, I presume," Marie-Paule laughed just as Alain appeared on the deck, looking bleary eyed from sleep.

"Is your offer gratis, Mademoiselle?"

Sarah could not help smiling at Marie-Paule's act. She did not have to try too hard to look sexy. "Of course, my brave boys follow me." She started away from the ship and Alain followed.

"Wait," said Thierry. "What about our guard duty?"

"Are there others on board?"

"Yes, myself and six others," answered the sleepy Alain.

"Good," said Marie-Paule. Let them all come to me after you."

"I will tell them to be ready when we get back." He disappeared below decks, and in almost no time returned with two more soldiers to take over the watch duty. Marie-Paule nodded, and led Alain and Thierry into the darkness. Once out of sight amongst the packing cases Antonio seized Alain while two of his men grabbed Thierry. Soon they were both gagged and bound, and stuffed in a nearby warehouse where they would not be found for at least a couple of hours.

Duncan whispered to Antonio, then turned to Marie-Paule. "You are quite a woman, mademoiselle. I, too, have an idea."

Taking off his uniform coat, he took a few steps towards the ship and called; "I am looking for Monsieur Alain. I work at the Taverna Ursula: he asked me to bring some food for you all, six hungry men, yes?"

The guard looked suspicious. "Where is the food? Are you bringing us something to drink, too? Who is paying for this, Alain?"

"It is paid for, monsieur. I am the head waiter; the other waiters will do the carrying," Duncan gestured to the shadowy figures behind him.

"What have you brought us?" As the curious guard crossed the gang plank to get a better look, Duncan stepped behind him, and, drawing a small bludgeon from under his coat, dealt the sailor a short, sharp, knock behind the ear. While the two women slipped into the shadows to allow Marie-Paule the privacy she required to revert back to her disguise, Duncan and his men pushed past the fallen guard. The next instant two midshipmen boarded the vessel, and stood beside Duncan on the quarterdeck. The remaining French sailors were ushered up from below and were soon bound and gagged on the dock.

The Maltese sailors emerged and started loading their supplies, and launched one of the ship's boats. The sailors knew their trade, and soon the oarsmen put their backs into towing the brig slowly into the windless night.

The old sailor at the tiller broke the silence, his voice ringing out across the water: "Pull harder, you French arse lickers!"

A shout of "Silence!" from Antonio, came too late. As they pulled away from the quay, they could hear the alert spreading. "Tenente, launch the jolly boat to help tow, but send a dozen of your best sharp shooters aloft to defend the ship.

"Ay aye, Sir!"

"Halt!"

Sarah stood in the waist, watching in horror as she heard the sound of a French patrol on the cobbled street. A mounted officer took in the situation at a glance, but was helpless to stop the theft of the ship. There was a round of musket fire from the tops, and one of the French foot soldiers clutched his throat and toppled into the harbour. Another fell with a scream, blood seeping from a leg wound while a third fell silently, his shirt a mass of blood. An order was called out and the patrol ran for cover and started to fire back at the brig, but they soon lost their target as the darkness swallowed the ship. Leaving his men, the French officer cantered off.

Sarah ran up onto the quarterdeck.

"Mr. Malette, unless you know how to shoot a musket, get back below."

Sarah hesitated.

"I want an inventory of everything and everybody on board, get busy!"

Still Sarah would not move, so Duncan called: "If that French officer reaches the old fort in time, the shore batteries will open fire and most of us will die. Get below!"

"Aye, aye, Sir."

Sarah retreated into the shadows, but remained on deck hiding in the waist. As the brig came up level with the fort, she heard faint voices across the water; she thought the whole crew, like her, were holding their breath. By now they had two boats in the water towing, as there was still no wind. Every oarsman glistened with sweat wondering if that French officer had given his warning?

Sarah couldn't resist poking her head up to see what was going on, despite the danger. First she saw a few sparks, then the light of lanterns being lit on the battlements. She gripped the side of the ship, as they slipped past black stone walls. She should get below, but her fascination for the danger outweighed her common sense. Then she saw a flash from the fort, followed by a loud bang that crashed through the silence. A shot hit the water short of the brig, followed by another splash, this time much closer, and two more in quick succession. A great cascade of water splashed on the larboard side, rocking the brig, soaking Sarah. A few minutes later more cannon fire exploded from the fort, and a great crack caused the whole crew to look up to see the main topgallant mast ripped apart. The spar came down in a jumble of rigging followed by screams from aloft and alow. Sarah ran towards the noise in the dark where two sailors had been hit by falling debris. Marie-Paule helped pull a man free from the tangled ropes and broken spars. Miraculously he was alive, but nearby his fellow topman had fallen from the cross trees, and his broken body lay still.

More shots landed in the water close to them. Soon the rest of the guns would be manned, and Sarah could see they were moving as fast as a floating bathtub. There was enough starlight to make them a perfect target. Unless the wind came up in the next few minutes, those guns would blow them to bits.

Monday 2nd July 1798 6 PM — Annette

Granon's departure on the *Palermo* did nothing to change the normal routine onboard the cutter. Annette was surprised that Reynard ignored her presence; he did not even invite her to dine with him. The rest of the crew had been given orders to treat her with respect, as she was allowed to roam the ship unmolested. She paced the deck, eying beautiful Crete, where they had stopped to water and make repairs. She overheard Reynard rant at the shipyard,

137

expressing his frustration at having to make do without the right sails or spars. Annette could not understand his swift, salty words. Clearly he did not have the same power as the wealthier officers and, therefore, whatever was wrong with the ship would not be repaired as quickly as he would like. Annette felt her stomach drop; the delay in Crete, along with the light winds, had slowed the ship's progress, and there was still a long way to go.

This was her once in a lifetime opportunity to change the course of history, and she was determined she would find Admiral Brueys, and convince him she knew something about the future battle. Unable to contain her anxiety any longer, Annette went in search of her captain. On deck she was pleasantly surprised when she felt the strength of the breeze that greeted her.

"Monsieur, a word if you please?"

"Good day to you, Mademoiselle. What is your pleasure?"

"Perhaps you are able to estimate our arrival date in Aboukir Bay, monsieur?"

"Mademoiselle, if the wind remains in our favour, we will be in Alexandria by Wednesday evening. If the admiral is indeed in Aboukir Bay, we can proceed there on Thursday."

This was good news. Annette was about to take her leave, but Reynard stood waiting for her to speak. She tried to make small talk, to avoid the awkward silence.

"Monsieur, your first officer has many talents. I enjoyed his poetry."

"Yes, that is true, but it is unfortunate he has a soft spot for Englishmen."

"What do you mean, Monsieur?"

Reynard had a hard edge to his voice when he replied. "Last year we boarded an English cutter. Monsieur Granon passed an opportunity to put his sword through an English officer. If I had not entered the cabin at that moment, the Englishman would have dispatched the lieutenant."

Annette was shocked. "He owes you his life?"

"Indeed we all rely on each other in war, Mademoiselle." He paused and changed the subject.

"Perhaps you are familiar with reading naval charts?"

"Naval charts? Why no, monsieur."

"I thought not. We should work together. I need some training with this box." He laid the smart phone on the table between them. "It would perhaps be best if I tried to explain to Admiral Brueys how to see the stored charts."

"Teach you to use this device? Yes, I can do that Monsieur, but we must be careful. The power supply is very limited." She would have said more, but Reynard was called away to the quarterdeck.

As the day wore on the northwest wind was interrupted with occasional hot and dusty gusts from the south. Annette started to feel queasy again as the waves grew bigger, so she came back on deck and leaned over the leeward side, noticing the green tint to the sky. The sailors seemed to find this to be a bad omen, but in her limited experience, it was the same with everything they didn't understand. Annette was more concerned with the large waves hitting the ship at an angle causing the vessel to pitch and roll.

She overheard Reynard talking sharply to midshipmen Arsenault, acting lieutenant while Granon was away. The weather had prevented the noon sun sighting, and the captain was worried about their exact position, close to a lee shore. She listened to the conversation, but there was more nautical terminology than she could deal with in any century. She understood they had been blown a little too far to the south, so they would have to weather Cape Ageebah.

The gusty cross wind continued, causing bigger seas as the wind veered to the northwest. It started to rain, cutting visibility.

"Well, Monsieur Arsenault, it is imperative to keep the vessel from being pushed further south. You may suggest a course of action under our current circumstance."

"Sir, perhaps it would be best to heave to, and try to ride out the storm."

"Thank you, for your suggestion, Monsieur; you would see us all dead. Heaved to we would drift inevitably to leeward, and end our lives blown onto the cape. We shall wear ship, Monsieur. We shall fight our way out of this storm!"

The hands knew their business, managing the sails through the manoeuvre, storm or no storm. Annette was terrified. It was one thing to be on board an 18th century sailing ship in perfect conditions, but she could hardly believe it was possible to survive this storm. Reynard stood by the tiller, a smile of confidence on his face, but as the bow swung to leeward there was a shudder. The ship had hit something in the water.

"Damage report," ordered Reynard.

"We have struck some debris. It looked like a ship's mast," reported a crew member. "We are taking on water on the larboard bow."

Reynard ordered the pumps into action, and called for the carpenter. "Ten inches in the well and rising," yelled the bosun. After a few minutes, one of the ship's boys ran to Reynard to report the carpenter had used sail cloth to contain the leak. The hole was large, but with the pumps working, they would not sink. Reynard ordered the hands on the pumps to be changed every fifteen minutes.

"It is likely, Mademoiselle, that we have been forced south, towards the cape. You should return to your cabin. It will be safer."

An hour passed with no change, but she could hear the pumps at work. The wind increased again, and the cutter stayed afloat, steering with a minimum of sail. In the captain's cabin, Annette held her breath as the ship's bow rose high on the next wave, and came crashing down wallowing and rolling into the empty space. At each successive wave, Annette thought the cutter would not recover, but despite the massive forces of the sea on her timbers, the vessel survived.

A larger than usual wave tore Annette from her hand hold, and threw her across the cabin. She would have slammed into the door, had not Reynard chosen that moment to enter, grim faced.

"Monsieur, I am no longer sure that this cabin is my safest option."

"Mademoiselle, you must stay here. It is too dangerous to venture outside."

"Sir, I have no intention of drowning!"

There was a loud crack and a cry from one of the hands. The bowsprit had cracked in two and now, without pressure from both sails, the rudder would not save them from being driven further south. Reynard rushed outside and gave a flurry of orders.

"Breakers off the starboard bow!" Cried the lookout.

On hearing this, Annette went out on deck despite the captain's warning. She could see the white water foaming around the rocks of the cape and crashing over the starboard bow. Was this really happening to her? She felt like she was in some unreal world. A stray line gave her a handhold as the deck rolled to an angle too steep for her to stand. The crew fought to launch the ship's boats.

"Mademoiselle, we must go quickly, the cutter is about to sink."

Annette let go and reached for Reynard, then hesitated.

"Monsieur Reynard, where is the box that gives light? It is the only piece of evidence we possess to convince the Admiral."

Reynard tapped his pocket, then held out his hand. She grabbed hold and they fought their way aft to where the crew already had one boat in the water, trying to keep control of it in the waves. The boat rose a moment before the ship, and Reynard pushed Annette over the side. Arsenault caught her as she fell into the boat, and looked up for his captain, who jumped just as the next wave pushed the boat away from the cutter, leaving him struggling in the water. Annette stretch her hand over the side.

"The box, Monsieur, it will be useless if it gets wet."

Reynard held it up and threw it to her. Annette caught the device and slipped it into her pocket. It was enclosed in a case, which she thought might be waterproof, and she just hoped the momentary immersion had not affected its workings. Before they could retrieve their captain, the top mast tore free and a mass of rigging fell on top of Reynard as he tried to reach an outstretched oar. The crew kept the boat on station, while several leaned out to look for him in the water. Then the cutter rolled towards them with a great crack, nearly swamping the boat.

"There is no time, we must steer clear!" Called out Arsenault.

As the boat pulled away, they saw Reynard clinging to the rigging, blood pouring from a head wound. Another wave hit, and pushed the boat towards the wreck, while the men pulled even harder to get away from the sinking ship.

As soon as the cutter went down, the crew rowed back towards the fallen mast, but there was no sign of Reynard in the darkness.

Friday 29th June 1798 10 PM The Grand Harbour, Valletta. — Duncan

Any minute Duncan expected the air to be filled with angry iron balls intent on sinking his ship, but instead he was overjoyed to feel the blessed wind blown up from nowhere driving the brig out of danger.

With the topmast debris clear *Palerma* surged forward through the black water as the wind filled the main course, the brig swarmed with men intent on squeezing the last knot of her. Duncan was still concerned about Sarah, but she had moved to the starboard side, away from the land batteries, to watch the crew pick up the boats. The hands swayed the boats in over the side in the dark, while the topmen carried out his orders; piling on more sail to power them out of the harbour. The ship was moving well now, but still cannons thundered hoping to blindly hit some vital spar. A lucky shot put a hole in the main course just as they disappeared into the darkness, out of range of the angry guns.

Duncan looked across at Sarah. "Well Mr. Malette, you have my lists?"

He was laughing as he said it, and the steersmen laughed with him, causing Marie-Paule to look quizzically at Duncan. She came up onto the quarter deck and stood beside Sarah.

"A fine pair of midshipmen. I am glad you were able to join the *Palermas*."

"What do you mean, the *Palermas*?" Sarah asked.

"A ship's company is known by the name of their ship. We are all *Palermas* now."

Duncan turned his attention to Marie-Paule. "Mr. Bonneterre, quite the transformation! We owe you our thanks. Where did you get the costume, which made fools out of the French crew?"

Marie-Paule looked a little sheepish. "It was amongst the clothes the Comte gave me. I rather liked that dress."

"Charming, I am sure, Mr. Bonneterre." Sarah saw Duncan exchange a glance with Marie-Paule. "Carry on," said Duncan, and the moment was over.

The ship heeled to starboard in the strengthening wind, which put a smile on Sarah's face. She stood beside the helm fascinated by the workings of the ship. The captain leaned over to the steersman, and said something in Lingua Franca, the language of the Mediterranean. The man was in his sixties, balding and very overweight. "You can talk to me in English, captain, Sir. I been in this 'ere town these last 18 month since the navy pulled out of the Med. and kind of left me 'ere, Sir."

"Lost your ship did you, old timer?"

"Fraid me and me mate were a little four sheets to the wind. We missed our call."

Sarah laughed. "What happened to your mate?"

"Don't rightly know the answer to that one, sir. Old George Cobbley was a topman, but I ain't' seen him these last nine months or more."

She could hear the cockney in the man's voice.

"What's your name, sailor?" Duncan enquired.

"Hidey Smith, sir, quartermaster's mate. Generally they just call me Hidey 'cos there's usually quite a lot of Smiths."

"Sounds like a girl's name to me, Smith." Duncan commented with a smile.

"Well it depends on what yer trying to hide, Sir."

"I see. Well then, Hidey it is! Have you steered a ship of this size before?"

"Bless me Sir, but indeed I 'ave piloted bigger buggers than this 'ere barky."

Duncan smiled and took his rightful place, alone on the windward side of the quarterdeck.

Two hours later they put into a small cove where they were met by two boatloads of Maltese revolutionaries. When they were aboard, their kit stowed, Antonio joined Duncan in his cabin. "How many of those men are sailors?" Duncan asked.

"Capitan, they are all sailors now," replied Antonio.

"Be serious, Tenente. If we have to fight, we need about seventy men, we have about fifty. To sail this ship we need . . ."

"My apologies, capitano. Of our compliment of fifty at least thirty can be considered able. In addition we have twenty landsmen willing to give their lives for a free Malta. One of our topmen is

143

officer material. Pawlu Pullicino is young, and speaks fluent French and Italian; he is a reliable man," Antonio paused. "Also we have one French Lieutenant."

Duncan raised an eyebrow. He did not welcome this complication, and wondered whether he should put the man ashore. "Thank you Tenente, that is what I need to know. We shall hope we don't get stopped by a French frigate."

Monday 2nd July 1798 noon. At Sea. — Duncan

To Duncan, the Khamasin wind was neither good nor bad, but the Maltese sailors whispered loudly enough for him to hear that such a phenomenon was surely a bad omen. The captain had little time for the sailor's superstitions, but he could not dismiss the problem of Granon, the captured French officer. Catching up with Annette was most urgent so the officer would have to remain their prisoner for now.

Antono interrupted his thoughts. "Here is our position, capitan," the newly appointed first officer held out the chart. "We are northwest of Cape Ageebah."

Duncan looked concerned. "We could be in for a rough passage to weather the cape. It is fortunate the ship is in good condition."

Antonio's eyes gleamed with pride. "The shipyard careened her and kindly supplied fresh oakum."

"It is a pity we lost the main t'gallant mast. The replacement is of poor quality, and likely to give us trouble during a bad blow."

"Sir, I will ask Guzepi Gauci, the master carpenter to take a look and report his findings."

Duncan nodded his approval. "You may attend to the carpenter and have the French officer brought to my cabin."

A short time later there was a knock on the door, and Granon was shown in, accompanied by two of the hands. Duncan sat behind his table and addressed the French officer.

"Monsieur Granon, I believe?"

"Oui, Monsieur. Je suis Lieutenant Granon; lately in command of the brig, *Palerma*."

"It is unfortunate you were aboard when we commandeered . . . that is repossessed this vessel for the free Malta navy. Do I have your word not to interfere with the running of the ship?"

Granon hesitated. "It is my duty to escape, Monsieur."

"This is not a British ship, although I am a British officer. I would, in other circumstances, obtain your parole against your exchange. I have no means of detaining you as a prisoner of war. We are bound for Egypt where you may rejoin the French navy. I need your promise in order to give you freedom of the vessel while we are not in port."

"You have my word, Sir," Granon said, and bowed his head in compliance.

"In which case, Monsieur Granon, I would be honoured to have your company at dinner tonight, at two bells in the first dog watch."

"It will be a pleasure, Sir, to attend." Granon saluted and left the cabin.

Duncan followed him out, going up to the quarterdeck, where he stood beside Hidey, who was on watch and taking his turn at the wheel.

"Got your quartermaster's mate ticket then, Hidey?" Enquired Duncan.

"Yes sir, in '95."

"Go on, Hidey, tell me more."

"I was wiv old Jervis, Sir, anchored off Cadiz for the blockade. We fought the Spaniards at Cape St. Vincent, that's when they made him a lord. He used to know quite a few of us top men, and he gave me a chance at the wheel. I knew it see, as I used to be in the merchant service."

"The merchant service, Hidey? What were you doing?" Duncan liked to hear the tales of seamen.

"Gin, Sir, on the Sherbourg run; well, usually it were gin but ovver fings too, brandy and rum."

Duncan laughed. So Hidey was an ex-smuggler: that was how he had earned the nick name.

"What did they rate you on that ship?"

"I was the first mate, Sir. Took a step down when I joined the Royal Navy, on account of them thinking I was not a gentlemen."

"Why would they think that, Hidey?"

"On account of the warrant for my arrest as a smuggler. The navy was kind enough to drop the charge if I volunteered."

Duncan crossed the quarterdeck, laughing quietly to himself, and took his place on the weather side. The waves were coming at them like uneven spiky hills. He loved the feeling of a sturdy ship coping well with the elements. Antonio's polite cough brought him back to his quarterdeck.

"Captain, the carpenter advises the t'gallant mast is sprung, but he has found a suitable spar in the hold. He wishes to inform you, Sir, while he is making it ready, we would be well advised to strike the mule's leg, before the wind gets up."

Duncan sighed. "The 'Mule's Leg? First time I have heard of a bad spar referred to like that."

"The man assures me it will not last a good blow. The barometer is falling and the sailors fear the worst kind of Khamasin," continued Antonio.

"The hands always fear the worst! Make it so Tenente. I will come up on deck shortly and assess the situation." With that, he returned to his cabin.

The dinner went remarkably well. Granon behaved impeccably, and if he penetrated the midshipmen's disguises, he made no allusion to it. Despite the heavy sea, the dishes did not fly across the cabin, and one of the Maltese sailors served them like a professional. The breeze grew stronger as the meal progressed and, as the cloth was drawn, while Duncan was offering his guests port or brandy, their dining room started to rock to the rhythm of the waves. Granon retired to his cabin, and a little later Sarah excused herself, deciding to ride out the storm in the midshipmen's quarters.

Marie-Paule had better sea legs, and sat at the table sipping her brandy in the candle light. The soft shadows played on the cabin wall, accentuating her softer curves. For the first time since their escape from the French prison, Duncan found himself with Marie-Paule without a patrol in pursuit.

"You seem worried," said Marie-Paule, "Do you think we shall sink if there is a storm?"

"My dear, the brig is a weatherly vessel. I have no doubt she will ride out this blow, with some discomfort to ourselves, but I dare say we shall all be alive and well in the morning." Duncan's tone was reassuring.

Marie-Paule laughed, and he smiled at the sound. Even her laughter had a French accent.

"It's not the storm that worries you, is it?" She touched his arm briefly. "You are different."

"Different? Perhaps it is just that I worry about stopping Annette from affecting the outcome of the impending battle. Should she succeed, then the future for both of us is . . ." He paused. "Uncertain."

"Surely that is as it should be? Nobody knows the future. The world is not going to end for either of us because of one battle." She squeezed his hand, and he was struck with the strength in those tiny hands. She started to withdraw her hand, but Duncan held on to it. At first he feared he had offended her, then he felt a tremendous excitement when she gripped his hand tighter and smiled.

Duncan leaned towards her; he could sense her heart beating faster. A knock on the door spoiled the moment.

"About to raise the new t'gallant mast, captain."

"Thank you. Please tell the watch officer I will join him directly."

The door closed, and Duncan spoke again. "My dear, we have become closely acquainted."

"I hope we are . . ."

"You are under no obligation to me," interrupted Duncan.

"Obligation? No, if we are together it is because a bond has grown between us." She spoke quietly, almost a whisper.

"Mademoiselle, I want you to know that I feel that bond deeply."

Marie-Paule leaned her body towards him, with a very soft: "Je t'aime."

Duncan took hold of her hand as gently as he could. "You are strong willed, resourceful, and rouse my passion. If this was peace time I would go to your father and beg permission to pay you court."

147

"But my father is dead . . . " Marie-Paule pulled Duncan close. ". . . and we live in troubled times"

"I cannot offer anything but the life of an adventurer. I will not pretend my quest will pose no danger, but if you want this life . . . if you want me, then I give myself to you in the eyes of God. I am captain on this ship and my word is law. Say yes and we are married."

As he spoke, the ship lurched to starboard as a larger than normal wave hit, and they clung to the table to steady themselves. Marie-Paule let go, and he found her in his arms. As she pressed her lips to his, any misgivings melted away along with the two hundred years separating them. Duncan pulled himself away and held Marie-Paule at arm's length.

"My dear, I must go up on deck."

Marie-Paule nodded. "If you are worried about this ship, then I am terrified."

"Not worried, just doing my duty."

Duncan left the cabin and sought out Antonio. The top gallant mast was in place, but the weather was not improving. When he returned ten minutes later, his cabin was empty and dark.

He sighed as he considered the missed opportunity, then decided to turn in and get what sleep he could. As he sat on the edge of the bed in the dark, he heard a noise. Automatically he reached for his pistol, but stopped when he felt a gentle touch on his hand. The wind howled, and the ship rocked violently.

Duncan laughed. "One of our midshipmen seems to have misplaced her cabin." He reached a gentle exploring hand under the covers. "It seems that she has also misplaced her clothes. Is this your answer to the question I earlier posed?"

"If you will have me, then this is my answer."

"With all my heart."

"Please, Sir, hold me close, and save me from the terrible storm."

Duncan stroked her arm, moving his hand to her shoulder, then up along the side of her neck. When he touched her hair, she reached out with her other arm, and pulled Duncan into the bed.

"I warn you it will be a most uncomfortable night in this tight little bed."

She lay on her side facing him, and curled her leg around, pressing it into the back of his knee. They were wrapped together tightly, so the ship's pitch and roll would not tear them apart. Then she found his lips with her mouth, and they kissed slowly and gently. "Oh Sir, we are still afloat. Have you come to protect me?"

"You did not seem helpless when you brazenly took this brig from the French sailors," chuckled Duncan.

"Perhaps I am a scarlet woman, and those sailors were just to whet my appetite for you."

She clung to him, both of them filled with anticipation, but just as he put his face down to kiss her, the ship gave a violent jolt. He did not know how much time they had before the next crisis would summon him back to the deck. He was cold, but she was still on fire, and she gently stroked him, re-igniting what the ship had taken away. He was not disappointed, and soon they found a much more comfortable fit on the narrow bed. Afterwards Duncan held her knowing the storm was worsening; they had little time.

Later he said: "My dear, I wish to tell you something of my past."

"If you mean that you are here by some kind of magic from the future, then Sarah has kept me well informed."

Duncan looked alarmed. "I will reprimand her for making so free with such knowledge."

"Sir, I urge you to treat her with all dignity. She is somewhat naive and I took the knowledge from her using artful guile." Marie-Paule's eyes sparkled with fun.

"Lady, I bow before your art."

She kissed him softly on the lips and, as if the universe responded, the wind dropped slightly, so the ship lost its violent pitch and roll.

"Tell me about the future, " she ordered. he laughed and they talked into the night, falling asleep before the watch changed.

Up on the quarterdeck, Antonio ordered more sail, but the lull did not last. As the ship was driven eastward, the Khamsin wind blew with renewed strength, and the main topgallant mast proved to be of no better quality than the one it had replaced. There was a great crack as the spar sprung, then one of the hands reported the t'gallant, so newly erected, had come down in the storm.

* * *

Sarah could not stay in her cabin in such wild weather. She came out on deck holding on to whatever she could to stop herself from falling with the roll of the ship.

"Mr. Malette, perhaps you should return to your cabin?" Antonio suggested, without making it an order.

"I feel better on deck. The cabin's so stuffy. I like the wind. It's exhilarating. Something is always flapping. It's as if the wind is playing a tune on the ship."

"We share that thought, Mademoiselle. I love this music."

"Are the sailors still worried about the Khamsin?" Sarah asked.

"The Khamsin has blown itself out, but little makes the sailors happy. The wind has been changing to the North for this glass and a half, so now we are being driven onto the lee shore of Cape Ageebah."

"Should I be worried?"

"Mr. Malette, it is safer below," shouted Antonio over the wind.

The helmsman changed course to take advantage of a gusty cross wind that bought them some more easting. Sarah was not prepared for the softening of the wind's roar, and she yelled embarrassingly loud and clear.

"I need the air."

An awkward silence followed Sarah's outburst, then they laughed together.

"Have you always been a sailor?"

Antonio raised an eyebrow and pouted just a little. Sarah thought she had touched something in him. His reply was lost as he turned back to look out to sea, she said: "Please, tell me about your boyhood."

"My boyhood?" Antonio hesitated, but the wind held steady so he could speak quietly to her. After a while he continued. "We Maltese were always at the mercy of the knights. They could take anything we had. Anything. Le Chevalier Blanc was one such knight. He took a liking to my elder sister, Helena. He entered our home frequently demanding her attentions. One day she hid, so he

150

took my mother instead. Even at eleven years old, I wanted to kill that knight. When next he came to our house I confronted him with my father's sword. This was his answer." Antonio lifted his hat, to show a scar that ran diagonally across his forehead, and barely missed his left eye.

Sarah's eyes widened. She had wondered how he had got that scar, but she said nothing, wanting Antonio to continue.

"My father explained to me I had been lucky, for the man had forgiven the rashness of youth, but a further violent act against this predator would condemn all of us to death. Such was the power of the knights. My parents gave what resources they had to my sister, and she left Malta to live with our cousins in Sicily. Furious at what he considered a slight by our family, the knight recommended my father for the navy, despite his age. Father went to work one day, but did not come back. My mother fell ill and died. I believe it was from a broken heart.

"I had few choices open to me, so I also joined the navy to be near my father, but rarely saw him. I choked back my pride, but always I looked for an opportunity to turn on the knights. Then one day I met the Comte, who invited me to work for him. You would call his organization revolutionary, but all we wanted was to live our own lives without tyranny. We fight for an independent Malta. The French invasion could not have come at a better time for us. At first, we rejoiced as the power of the knights was crushed, but now we realize we have exchanged the rule of the knights for the rule of the French general."

Sarah touched his arm, wondering what had happened to the remains of Antonio's family.

"I will find this knight who has wrought so many wrongs on my family. Through the Comte's network, I found out that he joined Napoleon's army. The man is proud beyond belief. He fights from a white horse, in a white uniform with a red sash, and a white ostrich feather in his hat."

Sarah's face wrinkled in disapproval. "What will you do when you meet this Chevalier?"

"I will kill him."

Sarah let go of his arm and shook her head. "What good will that be to the world when you are hanged for murder?"

"I will die with a quiet soul."

"I would rather you forgive him and live."

"My father was aboard the *Palerma*. This very ship! . . ." He paused, looking at Sarah with a quizzical eye. "How came you to know she was found deserted?"

Sarah laughed, surprised he had remembered her outburst at the Comte's. "I didn't know it. I was confused, I . . . "

Antonio held her hand. "Mademoiselle, you have a secret, which you do not wish to share. I understand; perhaps one day you will tell me everything."

The ship lurched as a wave crashed into her, and the pair were thrown towards the leeward side. He grabbed the rail and held an arm out for Sarah.

"You are not like anybody else I have met. I have told you my secret. Please, trust me with your story."

Sara hesitated, but the wind quieted slightly waiting for her.

"I was born in the city of Montreal. My father works for the government. I have a brother who still lives in Montreal, and my mother is a nurse at the hospital, and I have an adopted sister. I like to climb rocks and play the piano. I wish I could meet Beethoven. There you have everything!"

"Beethoven? I have heard of him; the Comte told me that he is a musician.

"Mademoiselle, that is but the surface. I sense there is much more to your story. Why have you come to the aid of Malta at this dangerous time? You could be at home in Canada, yet you follow Monsieur Duncan without question."

"Yes, I followed Monsieur Duncan. In a way, I am a follower. Climbing was the only thing that made me feel free." Sarah paused, her face wrinkled in confusion. "No, I didn't blindly follow my teacher. I came here for adventure. It was my decision, no one else's."

"How can this be? Antonio was genuinely perplexed. "A woman's lot is to do what she is told."

Sarah looked startled. How could this man possibly understand the progress women had made in 200 years? "Where I come from women are people in their own right. We are strong and control our own destiny." Sarah's tone reflected her strength.

"We all wish to find freedom, Mademoiselle; we from the Knights and now from the French, but . . ."

Whatever Antonio was about to say was interrupted by a huge wave crashing over the side of the ship, soaking them both.

"The barometer is still falling, and if the wind veers further to the North she will start rolling to make your heart break. It would be better if you retired to your cabin."

"Is that my lot, to do as you tell me, Tenente?"

"I pray you, return to your cabin so I can worry about the ship, and not your most valuable life."

Recognizing the wisdom of Antonio's request, Sarah left the quarterdeck.

Fortunately no top men were aloft when the bare main top gallant mast cracked in two. Antonio called all hands to clear the wreckage. The barometer fell, and the wind shifted towards the north, pushing the *Palerma* south. Duncan consulted with Antonio, sending the top men aloft, to take in most of the remaining canvas. Now they were running with a single jib sail, a double reefed top sail on the main, and the spanker.

Duncan was not worried about losing ground to leeward, as they had plenty of sea-room. He adjusted course slightly to take the waves more squarely, then he climbed a short way up the mizzen ratlines to watch the sea. The bow rose to a great height before crashing down into the trough, sending tons of water over the foredeck. A cry from the lookout brought his study to an end. There was some kind of a vessel to the nor-nor-west, but the man aloft was not sure exactly what it was in the gloom.

"Tenente who is aloft?"

"Saluu Bonnici, Sir. He went aloft with the top men. He has the sharpest eyes on the ship."

"Indeed," said Duncan. "Ask him if he can see oars."

A few minutes later the lookout responded: "Galliot ahoy captain."

Through the gloom, the galliot came briefly into view before disappearing in the waves.

"They seem to be closing on us, and they have the weather gage," called Antonio.

Duncan nodded his agreement. "We may have been a little over cautious by taking in so much sail. Order the fore t'gallant to be set, and see if we can gain on them. Clear for action, Tenente."

Fifteen minutes later the brig was rolling like a barrel in the huge waves. The oarsmen had visibly gained. To Duncan it looked like their captain was driving his ciurma into the final frantic twenty minute run.

"If we put the wind on our beam for a short time we might just get off a broadside before broaching," Duncan cried over the wind's roar.

"A great risk, captain," replied Antonio, water streaming off his wet weather gear.

"We must not let them board us. Come, we have one chance, and one chance only. I would speak to the gunner first, Tenente."

As Antonio carried out his orders, Duncan calculated their chances. They had enough men to work the half dozen relatively lightweight six pounders. A well placed broadside of 36 lbs of hot metal could do a lot of damage to a galliot. Just then, the gunner, an older, heavy set Maltese petty officer appeared on deck.

"Aim for their bow gun," Duncan ordered. "Try not to send a ball down the length of their ciurma; we don't want to kill off their slaves unnecessarily. Fire at the top of the roll. We have one chance before I have to turn the ship into the waves. Now hurry, we must fire first!"

The gunner nodded his assent, and left. Every man aboard knew the danger of this manoeuvre. Through his glass, Duncan could see the bow gunner of the galliot make ready. Any minute now they would receive the first ball.

"Helm a lee!" Ordered Duncan. "Fire as she bears."

The waves crashed over the side of the brig as the steersman turned the wheel to larboard, then slowly, slowly she rolled up. Duncan felt his vessel shudder as the guns went off in quick succession; he could feel the curses of the galliot captain. Even as he gave the order to turn the ship back on course, the brig continued her roll and, for one horrible moment, it looked like she would not recover from being heeled over at such an insane angle. Sarah, who had come up on deck when the ship had cleared for action, clung to the rail in the ship's waist as the brig turned. At last the vessel came upright, but when it did she saw smoke pouring from the enemy's bow. The galliot's gun was silent.

"It was a good hit," Duncan observed, coming down to join Sarah at the rail.

She could tell there was something bothering him; he hadn't come to discuss their gunnery.

"How many Mediterranean galliots were there in 1798?"

Sarah shrugged, she could not think about academic questions, only about her heaving stomach.

"Wasn't it a galliot that held you and Ken captive?"

Just then a wave pushed the ship violently to starboard. "For God's sake, reduce sail before we lose a mast!" Ordered Duncan in a voice that penetrated the gloom.

"Capitan, can we weather the cape in this storm?" Antonio asked.

"Tenente, I have inspected the chart. We shall wear ship and head sou-sou-west with the waves. We can put safely into the port at Mersa Matruh."

"It will delay us, capitan."

"Better delayed and still afloat!"

"Aye, Aye, Sir!"

The crew brought the ship about, before continuing into the worsening storm. Duncan turned back and Sarah slowly nodded her head in answer to his question.

Monday 2nd July 1798 — Ken

The repairs to the *Murad* took four days. Abdul sent raiding parties into the nearby hills to find the provisions he needed, as well as a few more slaves for his ciurma. On the fourth day all was complete, and Ken found himself back on the hated bench, thankfully still beside bin Kabina, who informed Ken that the ship had started the long crossing to Egypt. Another day passed: dip, sweep, pause. Ken slumped on his bench unaware of the world. He wished he had never crossed through the gate, and wondered when he would die. The next day was much the same: dip, sweep, pause.

Ali had taken a particular dislike to Ken, and watched carefully for periods when bin Kabina was not there to protect him. Yet another day of backbreaking work, but at last, with the wind filling their sail, the ciurma was stood down. Bin Kabina told Ken to rest and went to prepare dinner. As soon as he was gone, Ali and Ahmad walked the length of the deck inspecting the slaves. Ken thought of them as school bullies, except these roughnecks had no headmaster to moderate the force they used. Ali kicked Ken's bench on the way past and Ahmad paused, tapping his foot on the deck right beside Ken, who glanced down to see his own boots on Ahmad's feet.

"My bloody boots!" Ken yelled.

"The price of my kindness, infidel!!"

Ahmad gave Ken a quick slash across the shoulders with his whip, hardly a touch, but it seemed to Ken as if he had been scraped with nine red hot nails. As Ahmad raised his whip for another gleeful strike, bin Kabina, returning with food, stepped in front of him. For a moment their eyes met, then Ahmad averted his eyes and left without delivering another blow.

Ken took his food gratefully. He never dreamed that basics such as food and sleep could mean so much to him. As they bowed their heads to eat, his oar mate spoke quietly.

"Strange friend, we are returning to the vessel's home base, a place called Mersa Matruh. Your relatives will have the chance to redeem you. Is there somebody who will pay?"

Ken shook his head.

"My instinct told me so," bin Kabina dropped his voice. "You must wait. When we reach Matruh, my time on the galliot is over. Perhaps there will be an opportunity for your escape."

The breeze continued strongly throughout the late afternoon, and they reduced sail to protect the mast. By evening the ciurma was back in action to provide extra power to keep the vessel from broaching, as the waves grew larger.

The wind was dry, dusty, and blowing hard. "A Khamsin wind," said bin Kabina, "straight from the desert."

Throughout the rest of the day, the fickle wind rose and fell, requiring frequent course adjustments. Just as the wind rose again, this time from the northwest, the lookout announced a sail to the east.

An hour passed before Ken caught a glimpse of the vessel.

"A brig? Is it the same one as before? Is that possible?"

"A bad omen," stated bin Kabina, and he said a prayer as they rowed. Ken felt fear in the bottom of his belly. His grim thoughts were interrupted by Omar shouting to the captain to make himself heard over the wind.

"Your honour, it is the same brig we took only ten days ago."

Abdul grabbed his telescope. "It is true. She has been repaired, and flies before the wind at a good rate. The captain is unaware of us. Perhaps he cares more about the worsening storm than the threat from my little ship? Omar, we shall give chase, but be aware we are close to a lee shore. We must be certain that the ciurma can keep us from the rocks. It is a dangerous place to attack. Post a man to watch out for surf."

The order for maximum speed was casually given, but to Ken it was bad news. On the piping signal, he put his back into his oar, and the galliot fairly flew through the water. Eventually the brig became aware of them, but could do little except pile on more sail, as the galliot had the weather gauge. Ken could not see the brig, but simply rowed, trying to pick up the voices from the quarterdeck. The chase was going much as it had before, and he wondered how far this deja vu might go? Would the brig lose another spar? The galliot was now sliding through the water, taking the waves at about 45 degrees. She rolled and pitched forcing the occasional oar to miss a stroke, but as long as the ciurma kept her from broaching, they gained on the brig.

Head down over his oar, Abdul's orders were loud enough to hear over the howling wind.

"If the brig will not lose a spar from the wind, perhaps I can help. Put a shot into her rigging."

Ken felt like his heart would burst at any minute. It was worse than the last time. The drum beat even faster, and Ken's gut cried out to him to stop pulling, but instead the whip cracked, so he pulled even harder. When they were close enough the bow gun barked, only to miss as the brig changed course.

"What a chance that man is taking! The brig will surely broach."

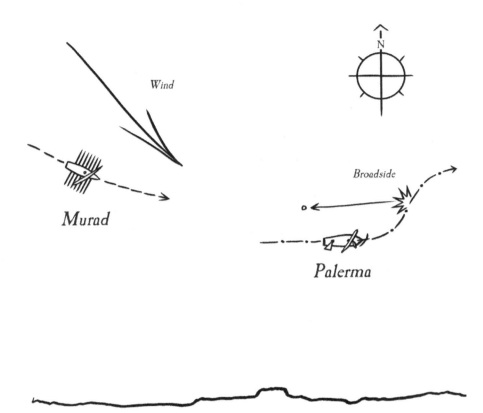

Palerma and Murad meet off Cape Ageebah

The brig's broadside fired, and for an instant Ken wondered where she had got new guns? Even over the storm, he could hear the sound of the four pounders firing. Ken added terror to his exhaustion as he felt the galliot shudder, and heard cries from for'ard where the shot had hit. Would the next broadside leave him screaming on the deck? He was lucky; the single broadside was all the brig could manage before saving herself from the big waves.

That one shot, however, was enough. The entire bow portion of the galliot was a mass of smoke and flame. A lucky ball had smashed into the *Murad's* bow cannon, and red hot splinters of metal had set off one of the powder charges sitting on the deck. Another ball had knocked out the spar holding the sail. Ken reeled back as the galliot bucked due to the sudden loss of power. He couldn't tell how many men had met their end. All he knew was he had an excuse to stop pulling at his oar.

Within a few seconds the silver whistle ordered them back to work. The ciurma resumed rowing in long steady pulls, but the ship was no longer responding. Ken started to look around, wondering why their efforts were in vain. Then it occurred to him they might be sinking. He heard a new order from the quarterdeck.

"Make the boats ready!"

"Surf on the starboard bow."

The vessel was taking on water fast, and he heard the call again to launch the boats. The men were trying, but she was visibly lower in the water, and panic was setting in. All around him, sailors were running up and down the deck, their bare feet making a sharp slapping sound.

Ahmad came running past, heading for the galliot's two boats. Everywhere the slaves stopped rowing, and called out to be freed from their irons. The all-pervading wind howled through broken spars drowning their pathetic voices.

Ken felt the panic rising from his belly. Bin Kabina was his one hope and he yelled to his companion; "For pity's sake, make them release the chains!"

The deck was visibly sloping towards the bow, and the galley master came past, the keys at his waist tantalizingly close. He ignored the pleas of the trapped slaves. Using his whip, he cleared a path, yelling at them over the confusion: "Keep rowing! The ship will only founder if you stop rowing!"

Even to the eyes of a new galley slave, this was obviously a lie. The galliot was on her way down. bin Kabina stood up and grabbed the galley master by the throat, and threw the terrified man onto the rolling deck. Ali scrambled to his feet, fear showing in his

159

eyes, as bin Kabina tore the whip from his grasp and the keys from his waist, passing them to Ken, who unlocked his chains, and followed the big Nubian through the chaos along the deck. An arm grabbed at him from one of the benches,

"Shipmate, help me!"

Ken looked to the larboard side oars, where George Cobbley and his oar mate, Francisco, were appealing to him for the precious key. Stooping down, he unlocked their chains, before passing the key to the slaves on the next bench. The chaos increased as more slaves joined the throng moving away from the rising water. The galliot wallowed, and Ken struggled against the bucking deck, following the uphill slope towards the stern.

Slaves and crewmen were pushing, falling, screaming, jumping. A slave made an anguish appeal, so Ken stopped to relieve him of his chain, which had got tangled out of his reach. The slave jumped up and roughly pushed Ken down onto the bench in his eagerness to get to the stern. As he did so, a big wave swamped the midships, but Ken clung to the bench. When the water washed away, he could see the slave in the water waving his hands and gulping for air. It was obvious to Ken that the man couldn't swim.

Sailors and slaves alike swept Ken along towards the apparent safety of the quarterdeck. He could see the figure of bin Kabina, taller by a head than anybody in the crowd. Without the power of the ciurma, the galliot was just another piece of flotsam. The steersman was still at his station, but it was getting harder to keep her head into the waves, as she took on water at the bow faster and faster.

Ken finally caught up with bin Kabina, who yelled above the howling wind: "Friend, this is my destiny; I cannot swim!"

As he spoke the next wave hit the *Murad* broadside, turning the vessel on her beam ends, and crashing down into the water on her starboard side. Ken went under, but fought his way back to the surface despite the exhaustion from rowing at top speed for twenty two minutes.

Seizing hold of an oar floating on the surface, he rested for a moment. He saw men were everywhere in the water, fighting, grabbing onto anything that would float. He saw Talibah help Manu, his father, both of them struggling to reach one of the larger pieces of drifting wreckage. It looked like they might make it. Ken tried to stay calm. If he was going to survive this catastrophe, his actions in the next few minutes would be critical. Just then, a body popped up a short distance away; it was bin Kabina. The big man looked at Ken, eyes wide with terror, coughing and gasping for air before he started to go back down. Ken barely managed to grab the Nubian by the arm and bring his hand in contact with the oar.

"Kick," yelled Ken.

Bin Kabina's dark fingers closed around the wooden shaft. The *Murad* was gone, leaving only wreckage. Neither was there any sign of the brig, lost from sight in the big waves. Ken focused on staying afloat as the waves pounded over them. Now he had bin Kabina to worry about too. He remembered the last few weeks, and how much he owed his Arab friend. How many times bin Kabina had intervened and stayed the galley master's whip.

The waves drove them south towards the coast, giving Ken a faint hope they would reach the shore before they drowned. Debris floated everywhere and, as they went up on a wave crest, he saw men clinging to oars like himself. He even caught a glimpse of Francisco and George Cobbley on top of some distant wreckage. The oar gave barely enough flotation, so Ken encouraged bin Kabina to keep kicking until Ken saw the galliot's sail, floating just out of reach. It was still attached to a spar providing them a much better chance of survival. It was a chance worth taking. Grabbing bin Kabina by the head, Ken yelled into his ear.

"We have to reach that big spar. When I give the word kick away from the oar, and we will be carried on the following wave."

Bin Kabina nodded that he understood. Ken clung to the oar for a moment feeling tired. The thought occurred to him he could just let go, drift off into an infinite sleep cushioned by the waves. Water splashed over his face, and he let the dismal thought go. It was more than just his own life at stake.

"Now!"

They kicked hard away from the oar, launching themselves towards the sail. The wave crashed over their heads, but they surfaced, gasping. Ken still had hold of the living, breathing body of bin Kabina, perhaps he would reach the sail on the next wave.

Chapter 9

Egypt

Wednesday 4th July 1798 1 PM — Abdul

Abdul left the palace in Mersa Matruh with no conscious notion where his legs were carrying him. He had reported to the Bey only to be humiliated for the first time in his life. Furious about the loss of his ship, the region's ruler had set him an impossible task to capture an infidel brig sheltering in the harbour. Not only this, but he must also enslave the crew, and sell all in Alexandria. This part Abdul could manage, but there was more to the Bey's punishment, and the words still echoed in Abdul's head; "Bring me the gold by travelling overland to the camp of Sheikh bin Kineivisha." He would have to cross the desert like some poor Bedouin.

He stopped and watched such a man at the head of a small camel train leaving a large white house. Abdul's anger mounted when he realised that this was the house of Abu bin Samir, the man he had failed to execute when he had the chance. Now it was too late. He had heard from the local gossip that the mutinous scum had somehow survived jumping overboard fifty miles from shore. Moreover, due to the death of his father and elder brother, Samir had become head of the most powerful family, second only to the Bey.

Several more camels emerged, and on the first, he recognized Samir's servant, Fakhar, and he flushed with anger. A mounted figure on the second camel caught his attention. It was a white woman. The sight of her blew away his anger and replaced it by a hunger he had not felt for a long time. Her hair as black as night and,

162

although her uncovered face marked her as an infidel, she was by far the most beautiful woman Abdul had ever seen in his life. He smiled as he watched her ineptly riding a camel. No longer did he care about losing his ship; he must have this woman!

An old man rode on the last camel of the caravan, and a string of three pack animals tagged on behind. Abdul waved him down. "Where are you bound, old man?"

"Into the desert. What is it to you?"

Abdul rose to his full height and watched the man carefully. "I am Mohammed Abdul al-Bashir, Rais to the Bey. You will tell me what I want to know."

The old man was clearly impressed. "We are bound for the camp of Sheikh bin Kineivisha. The woman calls herself Miss Annette, she is for him."

Abdul nodded his thanks, watched the caravan disappear into the southeast, then struck off to join his crew. It was time to take that brig. He cast a last glance over his shoulder and caught the profile of the woman. He murmured to himself; "Perhaps our paths will cross at Qaret el Matmura beautiful infidel."

Friday 6th July 1798 3 AM On Board The *Palerma* — Sarah

The brig rolled gently in the light breeze, pulling at her anchor and creaking like an old man's knees. In the days she had spent on the ship, Sarah had learned to put these sounds into the background, but something unusual had woken her. It was hot and airless below decks, so knowing she would not sleep, she got out of her hammock and pulled on some clothes. There had been a bump, as if a boat had come in contact with the brig. Marie-Paule appeared out of the gloom and put a finger to her lips,

"Make no noise, there is something bad happening up on deck."

Antonio joined them on the companionway, raising an eyebrow in question.

"We heard something unusual. We were just going to see what was going on, Sir," whispered Sarah.

"I had the same thought. We shall go above . . . " Antonio was going to say "cautiously", when Sarah darted ahead up the companionway. As she came up onto the weather deck, a grimy hand grabbed her shoulder, forcing her to her knees. She started to protest but a flintlock pistol was thrust in her face. Her attacker turned her so she could see the bodies of those who had been on watch. If the warning was not sufficient to stifle further protest, a familiar red beard and hooked nose appeared in the flickering light of the torches. She looked away hoping not to be recognised by Abdul.

Antonio and the others were equipped with cutlasses and boarding axes, but they each faced a man armed with a pistol. At this range, there would be no chance of missing their targets. There was a moment of complete stillness, while Sarah tensed waiting for some act of extreme violence. She jumped at the sound of a shot from the stern section. Then more of Abdul's men gathered around the hatchway, this time pushing Sarah down to join her friends in the darkness below.

A group of Arab sailors went down into the hold, firing until they were sure there was no resistance. The Maltese crouched down, under, or behind anything that could provide protection from the torrent of hot lead. Sarah and Marie-Paule hid behind a huge oak chest, and only came up when the firing had stopped and the surrender was complete. They were immediately grabbed by the boarding party. Sarah and Marie-Paule were herded, along with the Maltese sailors, into a hastily constructed holding pen at the forepeak.

"Where is the captain?" Sarah whispered.

"Not with us. We shall have to hope he managed to get away," replied Antonio.

"If you had just stolen a brig like this, where would you take us?" Sarah asked.

"You mean if I was a Musselman slave trader?"

"Well, yes."

"He will likely take us to the slave market in Alexandria."

"Will they sell us into slavery?" Sarah gasped.

"Or hold us to ransom. It is possible the officers have wealthy families willing to pay a high price."

"But I am not really . . ."

"In your case it would be better to sell you at the market," Antonio's tone was matter of fact.

"Would I rather die than let that happen?" She asked in a naive voice.

"It will take two or three days to reach the city. Who knows what might happen."

A little later Abdul gave the watch over to Omar, and settled comfortably in the captain's cabin. It was perhaps a step down from the luxury he had enjoyed on board the galliot, but to Abdul the captain's bed was soft enough. The woman on the camel nagged at him. He had sent a message out to the Bey's spy network that he was to be kept informed of her movements, but news was yet to reach him. As he drifted off to sleep, he murmured: "long black hair, with a face as white as ivory and dark mysterious eyes."

Sunday 8th July 1798 Dawn — Sarah

Sarah sat in a wooden walled cell in the forepeak. Boards had been nailed up to keep the crew of the *Palerma* hard against the starboard side, giving them an uncomfortable ride as the ship lifted in the wind. There was little light and the heat was close to unbearable, but the prisoners had been fed, so death was not imminent. Beside her sat the French Lieutenant. She smiled at him and was about to say something when a half a dozen Arab sailors came down the companionway accompanied by their captain. Sarah had been dreading a visit by Abdul since the night he had taken the brig. The sight of that hooked nose brought back his words from the galliot: ". . . if you try to escape, death will follow you!"

Sarah stepped behind Granon. "Please, I must not be seen."

Abdul came towards them, larger and even more threatening than she remembered; even his nose seemed to have grown.

165

"Tomorrow we will make landfall in Alexandria. You will be sold at the slave market. If you cooperate, I will make sure that you are sold to good families. You will inform me if you have relatives who are willing to buy your freedom."

The whole crew started to speak. Some asked for a translation, some demanded their freedom, others asked for mercy. Sarah shrank into the crowd, wondering at the futility of avoiding him. Surely he would recognize her tomorrow when she was brought to auction. As if in response to her thoughts, Abdul turned in her direction, and she saw the spark of recognition. He barked an order to two of his men, who dragged Sarah out of their prison.

"I thank Allah that he has seen fit to return you to me. Your famous climb to freedom was worth nothing. Your destiny is set in the slave market of Alexandria, and there is no escape." He turned to his subordinates. "Bring this infidel to my cabin."

As Sarah's captors dragged her to the companionway, the whole ship shook with the impact of a broadside of double shotted eighteen pound round shot. A ball smashed into the wooden sides of the brig, entering the larboard side, just aft of the forepeak. The shot hit the old timbers, which exploded into flying pieces. A jagged, three foot splinter pierced one of Sarah's captors in the chest. He didn't even have time to call out as he fell dead. The screams came from the others, whose injuries would see them die a slower, lingering death.

Spared by the onslaught, Abdul drew his scimitar and rushed up the companionway with a roar, while Sarah was shoved back into the prison. The other Arabs carried their fallen comrades away. The sound of running feet accompanied the call to quarters.

"The enemy ship is very close." Granon whispered. "Looks like an 18 pounder did that, so it is likely a large frigate." He pointed to the jagged hole.

The brig's timbers groaned as the wheel was thrown hard over to starboard. "Whoever is out there tried to put a shot across our bow in the half light, but misjudged slightly," Antonio noted. "Monsieur Granon, I say we forget our differences. If we escape this ship we go as we please."

Granon bowed in agreement. "If it is a French ship, then you are Maltese, and therefore under French protection. Even those from Canada." He looked at Sarah who blushed.

Antonio laughed. "We shall swear that he is Maltese!"

" 'ere I'm English," said Hidey.

"You can be Maltese to save your neck, Hidey," said Antonio with a laugh. The crew showed their approval with a cheer, which was interrupted by a violent explosion above. For the next ten minutes, there was an exchange of gunfire.

"Insanity!" declared Antonio. "We are firing on a frigate. They will sink us easily!"

Two sailors bearing an injured youngster came down the companionway. The boy howled in pain, and the elder of the two Arabs held on to his bleeding left arm, speaking soothingly. The boy's lower arm was shattered, and blood was flooding out. The older man cleared off a table, and laid the young man on top of it. The left hand was gone, and the arm below the elbow hung by a few ligaments and shards of bone. His shirt was soaked in blood. Unless somebody stopped the bleeding soon, the young man would certainly die.

Sarah and Marie-Paule looked on, horrified. "Do something!" Sarah cried. "They are just standing there. They don't know what to do."

The older Arab came over to the prisoners, speaking rapidly in Arabic.

"Can anybody understand him?" Marie-Paule appealed to her fellow prisoners. "That boy is bleeding to death!"

Guzepi, the carpenter, pushed forward and uttered a few words in Arabic. The older man responded, his face a picture of misery. After a moment, Guzepi held up his hand, and turned to the other prisoners.

"This man is the boy's father. His name is Manu, and he says there is no surgeon aboard. He begs us to give any help we can to save his son."

Antonio looked at Sarah. "You are the most resourceful amongst us. You climbed the cliffs of Malta. Can you help the boy?"

Sarah turned white. She had taken a wilderness first aid certificate, but all she knew about serious injuries was to stop the

167

bleeding and seek professional help. Every eye turned to her; she was the help! "Tell him to let us out of here. I will need the strongest amongst you to help me."

The boy's father shook his head; he would only release Sarah. She pointed to the others, but the man shrugged. She looked him right in the eye, sat down, and folded her arms. Another explosion rocked the brig. Above they could hear agonized cries. The regular beat of the brig's broadside had been replaced by intermittent bangs from the occasional gun. The boy moaned, a heart rending sound.

"We have to get out of here." She pointed at the boards that trapped the men. The old man looked at his son, then left abruptly, returning no more than a minute later holding an iron bar. He inserted it into the chain that secured them, and levered a link open. As the prisoners were released, the second Arab fled up the companionway. Sarah went straight to the boy.

"How can I help you?" Antonio asked, as he reached her side.

"I need his knife."

Guzepi said something to Manu, who handed the curved blade to Sarah. She cut away the boy's shirt, and tied it around the injured arm just below the elbow. She pulled hard, but not hard enough, as the blood continued to flow. Antonio took the ends of the strip, and this time the flow visibly slowed.

"Saluu, stay here. You others go up on deck, and find out what is happening. We need weapons," ordered Antonio.

The men rushed up the companionway leaving Antonio, Granon, Guzepi, and Saluu to hold the boy.

Sarah concentrated on the task at hand. "We need a second tourniquet." The men looked expressionlessly at her, so she shouted at Antonio. "Give me your shirt!" He took it off and tore it into strips. She applied a second tourniquet, and the wound stopped bleeding altogether. "I need boiling water and something for him to bite on."

There was a brief conversation between the carpenter and Manu. "The galley fire is out, it will take time."

Sarah thought for a minute. "Sailor's rum!"

"There is plenty of rum on this ship," said Antonio.

Saluu left for a few moments and returned to say that Hidey had been informed, and with a clatter, Hidey appeared with a small cask. Antonio sighed when he saw the rum.

Hidey shrugged. "It's what I do. That's all."

Sarah cleaned the wound with the rum.

"What is that for?" asked Antonio.

"I have to keep everything clean and aseptic as possible," Sarah replied.

"Why? What does that mean?"

Sarah sighed. "Let's just say that the likelihood that the wound will fester and putrefy, will be considerably reduced by keeping everything clean. I know this to be a fact, so unless you would prefer to do this, please don't argue with me."

Antonio shook his head, and Granon stared intently at Sarah. Under his breath he muttered: "Future magic."

Sarah sent Manu to fetch hot water, then took a short pull on the rum in an effort to slow her pulse rate, and steady her nerves. The boy was in shock, unaware of what was happening to him, lying there held down by the three men.

Sarah soaked her hands in rum to get rid of her several days of grime. She remembered reading that in the 18th century many patients survived surgery only to die of infection later. She looked into the cell where the remains of the bread given to the prisoners, had been carefully fostered against a future shortage. An idea occurred to her. "Antonio, please bring me the mouldy bread."

Antonio looked puzzled, as he placed the bread in easy reach, but Sarah had no time to explain. The boy's father reappeared with a bag of surgeon's tools he had found in the captain's cabin. "That's more like it!" Said Sarah who started to rummage through the bag.

She looked up as Guzepi called down from the top of the companionway: "A broadside seems to have killed most of the crew on deck. There is no sign of the captain, or officers. Boiling water, bandages, and chromic gut are on their way, but we should hurry, I think the brig might be sinking."

"What's chromic gut?" Sarah asked.

"Suture material." Antonio answered her. "I believe it is made from the gut of a cat."

169

Sarah shook her head and returned her attention to her patient.

"The French will board any minute," said Guzepi from the top of the ladder.

Sarah looked Manu in the eyes and saw the affection of a father for a son. Nothing else mattered to him anymore. She must deal with the boy and forget their plight. The others seemed to be equally gripped by the boy's fate; everybody stayed put.

"What's his name?" She asked in English, then in French, as she used the rum to clean and prepare the arm.

"Talibah," Manu answered.

"Talibah," Sarah repeated the child's name as she exchanged a quick glance of compassion and understanding with the old man.

She cleaned the wound with rum, then rummaged in the bag to find a suitable saw, pouring rum on it before holding the instrument in a candle flame.

"I am ready," she announced.

The boy stared up at her as he bit down on a smoothed cylinder of wood. Sarah could see the men look everywhere, but at the boy. Granon held him tightly, Antonio stood by her side, also helping to hold the patient still. Saluu turned Talibah's head so he could not see what followed, but moved the boy's arm in doing so.

"Hold still, Saluu!" Antonio glared at Saluu who held on with a firm grip.

Sarah took a deep breath, and placed the saw as accurately as possible. There was resistance, more than she would have thought possible, and still there was blood despite the tourniquet. It was like sawing the bones of a cow, and Sarah thought of herself as a butcher, no better or worse than the average 18th century surgeon. She simply forgot everything around her, and concentrated on getting through the bone, ignoring the blood, the muted screams of her patient, and the turned heads of the so called strong-men holding the boy. She alone saw what was happening, the minute details of the fine toothed edge cutting gratingly, as blood flowed freely. It was the sound, not the cries of the boy through the wooden baton, nor the smell, but the scrape of those tiny metal teeth on the bone that most affected her. At last she was through, and she paused for breath, letting the men deal with the boy. It had taken no more than fifteen seconds.

Antonio wiped the sweat from Sarah's face.

"You must not let the bleeding recommence once the tourniquet is removed," he observed.

There was a moment of panic while Sarah tried to think what to do.

"Will you tie the blood vessels?" Asked Antonio.

Yes of course that was it! Fortunately, Sarah knew her knots from climbing, and instinctively used a square knot with an extra loop to stop it from slipping. She batted away the grubby hand Antonio extended to help hold the blood vessel, indicating instead one of the surgical instruments that she had sterilized.

"Use that please," she said.

Hidey poked his head down the hatchway. "I don't mean to 'urry you, but this brig ain't got long to float. If you catch my meaning?"

"For God's sake, let me finish," shouted Sarah in frustration.

"Orl' right. I'll try and keep us afloat a bit longer. I saw them French ships steering to leeward chasing some flashes that way, and I hears the rumble of guns. One of them frigates was the *Sérieuse*. It's what I calls a serious frigate," he said with a chuckle as the brig lurched, heeling to larboard. "We should get out of 'ere before your work on this boy is rendered useless by the 'oggin!"

Hidey disappeared while Sarah finished her work by packing the wound with the bread mould, which she hoped would help prevent infection. Finally, she sewed the flap of skin she had left to tidy up the stump, without which there would be no healing. Now came the big test. If she had done her job, then it would be safe to remove the tourniquet.

She cut away the first tied shirt and nothing happened. Holding her breath, she removed the second. Still no big rush of blood from the wound. Sarah let out a great sob. For the last hour, she had thought of nothing except helping the boy. Now the reality of the situation started to press on her. She gripped Marie-Paule's hand, shoved some bandages at her and rushed up on deck to the starboard side, where she let the tears flow.

Antonio came up from behind and rested his hands on her shoulders. "You have done well. The boy lives. Even now his colour is returning."

"We have a problem, Sir," Hidey called as he strode towards them.

"Resistance from the Arabs?"

"No Sir, they are all gone over the side or else dead."

"The French?" Growled Antonio.

"They sailed off in pursuit of a larger target, Sir. You should know that we have no boats, Sir. The Arabs took 'em all."

With that, Hidey disappeared to see how fast the water was filling the hold.

Antonio turned his attention back to Sarah. She buried her face in his chest, and tried to hide her tears. He wrapped her in his arms and smoothed her hair. "You are the strongest, bravest woman I have ever had the privilege to meet. It is an honour to stand on the deck beside you. If I continue holding you like this, the men will either suspect your disguise, or suspect me of . . ." he tailed off.

She laughed, and disengaged herself, and turned back to the sea.

Hidey returned, this time accompanied by the carpenter. It was clear that the two men were arguing.

"What is it, Guzepi?"

"This English man, he thinks the ship is sinking, but Tenente, we feathered a sail over the hole, and I have patched it. She will last through the night if we are lucky."

"How much water is there in her?" Asked Antonio.

"Perhaps six feet in the well, but the pumps are working."

As Guzepi spoke, there was a gentle bump on the starboard side. "*Palerma*," yelled a familiar voice.

Hidey looked over the side. "Blimey it's the captain! Good thing he's on the starboard else we'd have to pipe him aboard!"

Antonio met Duncan as he climbed on deck. "Capitan, it is an honour, but what spirit brought you to us at this hour of need?"

"When the Arabs took the Palerma, I jumped ship and commandeered that dhow," Duncan pointed to the vessel moored to the starboard mainchains. "I thought I had lost you in the night, then I saw the two big French frigates, *Le Sérieuse* and *L'Artemise* take the brig by surprise early in the morning. I thought you might be in trouble, so I did my best to keep up, and here I am."

Antonio was astounded. "I hope you are in time, capitan. We may be sinking."

"It looked like she was taking quite a pounding. Is there a hope we can make her serviceable?" At that moment, the ship gave a great lurch to starboard. Duncan remembered the Dhow and rushed to the side, but mercifully she was unharmed. A few of the hands grabbed a line and pulled her round towards the bow as the brig gave another heave.

"That'll be bits falling off the starboard pump. Like I said, she's going down, captain!" Said Hidey,

"Abandon ship! Everybody off this tub, and into the dhow."

The evacuation took place quickly enough, and the sea was calm. The brig seemed to have settled, and was going down steadily.

"Sir, what about food?" Sarah asked, already feeling hungry.

"Thank you, midshipman. See to it, tenente."

Sarah supervised the transfer of the injured boy to the dhow. Somebody tossed in a box of cheese and a barrel of salt beef. They pulled away from the brig just in time to watch the *Palerma* slip gently under the waves. They were crowded onboard the dhow, filling every conceivable space. It was just big enough and, provided that everybody sat down, the craft was stable. Sarah sat in the stern with Duncan, Antonio, and Granon, while Hidey took the tiller. A large triangular sail and a small spritsail adorned the single mast, and the small vessel was soon under way.

"Monsieur Granon you are still my prisoner," said Duncan.

"Au contraire Sir. Le Tenente and I agreed, before this incident, that by giving my help against the Arabs, I would be a free man," Granon spoke with certainty, and Antonio nodded his agreement.

"I see," said Duncan. "Why did you not alert the frigate? We would all be your prisoners."

"Monsieur, it would have been against our agreement; besides, I was too busy helping the brave young midshipman perform surgery on the boy." Duncan looked down into the bottom of the boat where Talibah slept.

"This boy and his father were part of the raiding party that cut out the brig from Mersa Matruh?"

"Yes capitan," replied Antonio. "Guzepi speaks some Arabic. He learned that we were boarded by the crew of a galliot, wrecked Monday night off Cape Ageebah. We fired on them, capitan. Do you understand? It was the same galliot."

Sarah turned pale. The presence of Abdul proved it must be the same vessel in which she and Ken had been enslaved. Had Ken drowned?

The dhow was built for a half dozen sailors and a load of fish, but now fifty people crowded into this floating haven. Duncan navigated through the dark, well aware that they should put to shore as soon as possible. By his reckoning they were somewhere near Al Alamayn.

The captain addressed Hidey. "I want to know if you see whitecaps or hear the surf. In this breeze, it will still be dark when we reach shore, and overloaded like this we may have trouble taking her in."

"Don' you worry yerself, Captain. Saluu Bonnici is on lookout this watch. He can smell land."

There was not sufficient space for Sarah to lie down, but she drifted off to sleep amongst the sweaty sailors, wondering if the dhow would make it to shore.

Sunday 8th July 1798 7:00 PM — Ken

Six days earlier, after being washed up on the shore, Ken had left bin Kabina and wandered along the beach on a foraging expedition. First, he found the drowned body of Ahmad, from which he retrieved his stolen boots. He also found some food and a goatskin of water, all washed up on the shore from the wreck of the galley. When he returned his friend was gone; a set of horse tracks told its own story. The prospect of being alone terrified Ken, so he followed the trail in the sand. Somehow he had made his meagre food supplies last, but on Saturday he drained the last few drops of his water. The next day, from high on a dune, he spotted a dark patch in the distant sand; it had to be water.

174

He reached the dark patch to find the tracks of camels, horses and men, and a water well at the bottom of a crater in the sand. As he filled the goatskin the steep sandy sides of the well collapsed, and he slid screaming into the cold water. He started to make steps in the steep walls of the well, and he was on step three when step two collapsed.

"You sandy bastard!" The curse seemed lame compared to those involving camels. Exhausted, he wondered how much longer he could stay afloat when he heard laughter from above. For no particular reason he called out in French.

"Aidez moi, monsieur, je vous en prie?"

The voice above continued in French. "You want me to release you from the well? How will you pay me?"

"If you leave me in this well, my body will poison the water for many months. It would be easier to help me out."

"There are other wells, some are free of bodies!" From above there was more laughter.

"If you get me out, and give me some food, I will give you my most valuable possession."

"What do you have that is so valuable?"

"Something vital for the defence of your country."

"And what might that be?" The voice sounded genuinely curious.

"Information," said Ken.

"What could you know that would possibly interest me?"

"I have knowledge of your future," said Ken triumphantly.

"Prove it to me!"

"I have information on British and French fleet movements." There was a long pause.

"Tell me your information and I will pull you up."

By now Ken was a little wary. "What assurance do I have that you will not take my information and leave me in the well."

"You have my word as an Egyptian,"

"Is there any other assurance?"

The voice seemed aggrieved. "You insult me Monsieur!" Another silence, then the voice said; "Êtes vous Français?"

"Oui!" Ken did not intend to lie, but it seemed like the only way he was going to get out of the well.

175

A rope came slithering down to him with a loop on the end.

"Tell me something of military value, and I will pull you up."

Ken racked his brain for something. He was not sure of today's date but news travelled slowly in the desert, so he told them what he remembered.

"The English fleet arrived at Alexandria on the 29th June under vice admiral Nelson, but didn't stay. Less than twenty four hours later a large French fleet anchored in Aboukir Bay with an army of 30,000 men under General Napoleon." He heard the murmur of conversation, then the voice recommenced.

"That is not information about the future, but few people know what you know. I am interested how you came by this knowledge. Take the rope, monsieur. I want your information."

From above, Ken heard someone cry: "Yaallah!" He barely had time to grab the loop before he was shot up the side of the well. There was more laughter when he sped several feet across the desert floor before finally letting go of the rope still attached to the saddle of a camel.

Four Bedouin men sat around the well, and a fifth man had hold of the camel's harness. Ken rolled over on his back, soaking up the desert heat. The camel minder reached down and grabbed Ken's right arm, pulling him to his feet in one swift motion. Ken was grateful at first, but then the man whirled him around bending his arm painfully behind his back. Ken found himself face to face with the man in charge. Sly and cold were the eyes that stared into Ken's. The cord that tied his headdress was a little more elaborate, his only mark of rank.

The leader said, in Arabic: "Fakhar there is no need to hurt the boy, let us hear what he has to say. He may be of use to us." Turning to Ken, he shifted to French.

"I am Abu bin Samir. If you provide me with some truth . . ." He paused. "Something useful, you will be my guest at dinner."

"My name is Ken DiPalo."

"How did you come by this knowledge of the fleets? The news only came to me very recently by the fastest dhow from Alexandria."

"I heard it from an impeccable source."

Samir frowned. "But this event is in the past, what do you know about the future?"

Ken searched his knowledge of historical events, wondering if he had made a big mistake with such a promise. "There will be a great sea battle, and many French ships will be destroyed by the British Admiral Nelson. The French general, Napoleon, will reach Cairo with his army and Egypt will be rid of the Mamelukes forever."

"Should I believe you, boy?"

The Arab stared at Ken, who bowed his head, feeling naked under his gaze. Then Samir turned to his companion and spoke in Arabic.

"The boy is correct about the fleet movements, but I know of no other battles. Who is to know if he is wrong about a future fleet engagement? I have heard that a British fleet briefly stopped in Alexandria, but left before the French arrived. Perhaps it is better to feed the boy and make him a member of the raiding force. Later we will interrogate him."

Fakhar relaxed his hold slightly, and his master continued in French.

"Where did you come from, boy?"

"I came from the sea."

"You were wrecked in the French cutter?"

Ken was caught off guard, for he had indeed been wrecked, but he knew nothing about a French cutter. "No I was on board a galley."

At the mention of the galley, the man stared at Ken and the glint of recognition came to him. Ken started at the chill stare, then the man he removed his desert mask revealing the face of Samir, an officer who Ken remembered from the galley.

"I know you boy. We took you from the inn in Valletta." Samir smiled. "Perhaps you remember under the bench, holding my arm and causing me to lose the mutiny."

Ken said nothing, but his mouth dropped open in dismay.

"I should kill you right now but, instead, you will be my slave."

Ken's face turned white through the sunburn.

177

"I am merciful. You can earn your freedom by joining my little army here. The Sammahoulous tribe have been stealing our camels. You can remain in camp as my slave, or fight beside us." Samir turned to Fakhar. "Find suitable robes for this boy, and give him water. We do not want him to fry in the desert heat."

Samir took Ken's arm and guided him towards two groups of men. "My men caught some wild hare, and they have bread."

Ken could hardly believe that Samir had not taken his revenge, but he gratefully hobbled towards the cooking fires, wondering where the hares were being cooked.

Fakhar materialized out of the gloom and handed him a goatskin of water and a Bedouin robe. Noticing Ken's indecision, he said in Arabic: "The galley slaves are to the left."

Ken nodded and followed his direction, gulping water as he walked, smelling the food and feeling very hungry. The men around him were heavily armed; perhaps this was Samir's bodyguard?

"Sit down, Mr. Ken," said a voice in English.

Ken stopped, amazed at hearing his name called. The man threw off his keffiyeh and stood up. "Don't you know me, boy?"

"George — it's you! George Cobbley!" Ken ran to him and shook his hand warmly.

"S'me indeed and 'ere is Francisco. Together we're the survivors of the most brutal storm of the Mediterranean, and now engaged to be mercenaries for Mr. Samir over there, who has been collecting survivors of the *Murad*."

Francisco threw his arms about Ken, who was quite overwhelmed. He felt his face grow hot, and tears came to his eyes. After being alone in the desert, at last, he was amongst friends. He sat down to a plate of food. George with wonderful dexterity, produced a tot of rum from somewhere about his person. "This will warm you up!" He said with a big smile.

Ken soaked up the last few rays from the beautiful, huge orange disk, and ate with the grace of a starving dinosaur. George handed him a blanket, and Ken walked sleepily back to the well to where he had dropped his meagre belongings. He could move no further, so he curled up in his blanket, and closed his eyes. Something nagged at him, but he fell into a deep sleep before he could find an answer.

178

A little before dawn Ken awoke with pains shooting along his right side where he had slept. He forced his eyes open but, on hearing the voices of Abu bin Samir and Fakhar, he closed them again without moving. The pair sat only a few feet away, hunched over the fire. Samir was giving instructions to Fakhar.

"The Bey will camp here tonight. We shall move behind the dunes, over there to the East. It is not so far in a direct line, but if we take the longer route around the dunes, it will convince the French officer that we have gone far enough for the day." He pointed and Fakhar nodded his agreement, Samir chuckled. "We shall rest there and prepare the men. The raid will take place at this time tomorrow, as dawn is breaking. You will lead the men from this camp, including that boy from last night. Make sure they are dressed in the robes of the Jewabis. Let them kill the Bey and his guards, but some must be left alive, you understand?"

Fakhar nodded a silent acknowledgement. "You will break off as soon as the Bey is dead, and retreat back to the dunes. There you must change into the robes of the Sammahoulous. I will bring the second group from the camp of the female slave, to meet you. Together we will rescue the Bey's people from these barbaric raiders."

"Then, Effendi, you will ride to the Sheikh as a hero. But what of the French officer?" Asked Fakhar.

"The French officer and his sailors are our witnesses. They will remain in the dunes camp until we return. We sacrifice a few slaves from the galley in order to gain the love of the Sheikh. We shall be greeted as heroes in his camp at Qaret el Matmura. To comfort him in his sorrow that the Bey is dead, we bring him the gift of the French woman. In his gratitude, I will be acknowledged in the Bey's place. Fakhar, you have your instructions?"

"Efendi, insha'allah it will be done . . ." Fakhar broke off abruptly; Ken could hear the rustle of clothing as someone moved.

"Something is wrong?"

"Forgive me, but I thought . . . perhaps the boy is not asleep." Said Fakhar, his voice betraying his distrust.

"It is of no consequence, the boy cannot understand you; he is English." Ken heard the sound of Samir getting to his feet, and took Fakhar's arm. "Come, we will visit the French officer to make sure all is well."

Ken opened one eye to see the pair move off. On the previous night, Samir had told him to ride with the raiders to attack the camp of the Sammahoulous. What had he said? "The camp of the white slave girl?" Then he had referred to, "the French woman." Could that possibly be Annette? How many French girls were there in this part of the world in 1798?

As the sun rose over the desert, Ken stretched his aching limbs. Francisco approached him, carefully carrying a china cup.

"Say nothing signor, do not ask where I got this, and I will not condemn my soul to eternal damnation by committing the sin of telling you a lie."

Ken laughed and took the cup. It was full of strong, black coffee.

"Is this all for me?" He asked with a huge grin.

"It's yours entirely, my friend."

Ken's joy at waking to a cup of coffee temporarily put his mind at peace. For an instant, he forgot the fate that would overtake them the next day. George arrived with a very hard piece of unleavened bread.

"Yer better dip it in the coffee, else it will be un-biteable. At any rate you could easily lose a tooth or two in that there offering."

George turned to go. "Wait! I have overheard something that I must tell you." George looked concerned, then grim as Ken explained what he had overheard.

"This comes as no surprise, young Mr. Ken," replied George. I have been suspecting for some time that we're being used. Tomorrow we gets up afore everybody else, and I don't think there'll be time for coffee."

Monday 9th July 1798 5:00 am — Sarah

Sarah dreamed that a bearded man with a hooked nose was beating her over the head with a log. When she finally woke up, she found her head smashing into the side of the boat every time a wave

180

hit. She couldn't believe she had slept through it! She looked out to see the sun peaking above the eastern horizon, and the shoreline came in sight to the south.

Within the hour they ran the dhow up onto the beach, and with many hands working, they soon had their supplies unloaded. Sarah looked across the beach to see that it merged into the sand of the Western desert. Antonio took a foraging party off to find fuel and a source of fresh water, while Duncan took Sarah to one side.

"Mr. Midshipman, I had an idea that Manu may be able to throw some light on the fate of your friend, Ken. I am assuming he was part of the galliot's crew that took the *Palerma*."

"You think he is still alive?" Sarah asked with a hopeful smile.

Duncan nodded reassuringly as they approached Guzepi who was sitting beside Manu and his son.

"Your son is feeling better?" asked Duncan.

Guzepi translated. "My thanks to midshipman Malette, and I think he will live. Allah has blessed her hands."

"You mean 'his' hands. You are getting old, my friend. Mr. Malette is one of our young gentlemen," said Guzepi. The pair exchanged a smile; they were not fooled, and Manu had seen evidence of her sex with his own eyes.

Duncan cut in. "Manu, there was a young slave on the galliot. Perhaps you have news of him. He was captured in Valletta wearing a French navy uniform. You remember?" Duncan looked at Guzepi for translation.

"Yes, he remembers. Your friend came aboard with Mr. Malette. He was under the protection of a Bedouin oarsman known as bin Kabina."

"You did not see them after the wreck of the galliot?" Asked Duncan.

"No." The old man paused. "Many of the slaves made it off the vessel. I saw a few of them clinging to some wreckage. The sea was rough, and it was dark. There was chaos and screaming, but it is possible your friend escaped with his life."

"Did you see either of them after you came ashore?" The old man shook his head sadly, but Duncan looked hopeful.

"Mr. Malette, do not lose hope. We shall continue to make enquiries about your friend. It is the whereabouts of Annette that concerns me more. We have only a short time to find her."

Duncan addressed Manu again through Guzepi. "We also seek a young French woman, dark haired and considered to be a beauty. Perhaps Manu has seen this woman?"

After a brief conversation, Guzepi reported. "Manu has not seen such a woman, but two nights ago he went to serve his rais. The captain sat in his cabin looking like a haunted man. He asked him, 'what troubles you my rais?' The captain's eyes burned with desire. 'Manu', he said, 'I have seen the most beautiful infidel girl! She left Mersa Matruh on a camel. Her eyes were as dark as the depths of the ocean, and her long black hair flowed over her shoulders, shining with the light of the waxing moon.' "

"Annette? Where could she be now?" Sarah asked.

"If the galley captain saw her leaving Mersa Matruh, she's somewhere out there in the Western Desert," Duncan replied. "Guzepi, ask Manu if his captain said anything more about the infidel woman on a camel."

"Manu thinks that Abdul knew where she was bound, and he was going to look for her after selling the brig."

"Where were they going to meet?" asked Duncan.

More translation followed. "Manu feels uncomfortable answering your questions. He does not know which side his Bey supports. He is not a prisoner, and feels that he is under no obligation to give away information that may lead you to captain Abdul."

Duncan sighed; this same captain was going to sell his crew into slavery. "Please assure Manu that we mean no harm. I am simply trying to find a friend. She may be the infidel woman that so captivated his captain."

Further interrogation proved to be useless. Manu was clearly afraid and would say nothing more. Duncan drew Sarah aside, but before they could discuss this new turn of events, the foraging party returned.

"Capitan, we found a boat from the Brig. It had *Palerma* written on it. We also found tracks, perhaps a dozen survivors were travelling south," reported Antonio.

Duncan looked determined. "We shall follow them. It is not far to Al Alamayn where we can find some camels."

"Camels!" Antonio looked horrified.

"They are not so bad when you get used to them. I have spent some time in the desert."

Antonio shrugged. "Why do you wish to follow this man Abdul?"

"I have reason to believe he will lead us to Annette. Tenente, you may calm yourself. I still have some gold, and I will hire only nice camels!"

Chapter 10

The Western Desert

The sun had not yet risen as Fakhar led his men down the windward face of the dune. The grey light gave little comfort to the riders. They reached the bottom of the dune, where they were careful not to disturb the Bey's camels grazing near the well. The sand stretched out for another hundred yards to a cluster of tents. Fakhar felt confident as the raiding party advanced in silence not wishing to alert the sleeping Bey, but he could not help wondering why three of the galley slaves had gone missing that morning. One was the boy from the well. Did he know something?

Pushing his dark thought aside, Fakhar signalled to one of the Jewabis to take a few of the men around to the other end of the line of tents. A few minutes later, a brief wolf howl, signalled that the men were in place. Now it was time.

"Yaallah!" Cried Fakhar, as he led his men into the attack.

The raiders charged the tents, replying; "Yee! Yee! Yee!"

They covered half the distance without incident but, as they bore down on the helpless Bey, Fakhar had a premonition that the raid was going to fail. Out of the desert, not thirty yards ahead, twenty men rose up from the sands where they had been buried, and brought their weapons to bear on the charging camels. The first volley took down three out of six men.

His scimitar drawn, Fakhar ran his camel over one of the Sammahoulous warriors. The man went down with a yell under the beast's relentless feet. He could hear the sounds of battle behind him as his men rode into the Bey's defenders. He could see that the men he had sent to the other end of the line of tents were also facing opposition. Two had been cut down by musket fire, and the survivors retreated into the desert. "Cowards!" Fakhar yelled as he charged. "Allah!"

Fakhar knew the enemy would not fire their muskets towards the Bey's tent, his men would rally to him once they had reached their goal. He halted his camel in a cloud of sand, jumped out of the saddle and dashed through the tent's entrance flap with his sword held high. The first person he saw, standing in the entrance way was the boy from the well. Fakhar stopped, remembering what had been troubling him. On the night of his capture he had said something in Arabic, and the boy had understood. It dawned on him that the slave had not deserted that morning, but ridden off to warn the Bey.

"Are you ready to meet Allah, boy?" Fakhar asked in Arabic.

He thrust with his scimitar, but Ken nimbly stepped back, anticipating this move revealing the Bey's personal bodyguards. Fakhar looked behind, expecting to see his men, but none had followed him into the tent. He turned to escape, but was greeted with many smiling Bedouin faces.

Fifteen minutes later as planned, Abu bin Samir rode his camel at the head of his Sammahoulous followers. He had camped with the forward party the previous night, then departed before dawn. A few men were left to escort the woman to the Sheikh. The French naval officer and his sailors were still in their tent when he came to the dune camp. He passed the camp and continued to the rendezvous point atop the big dune. Samir did not want to reveal himself until Fakhar appeared, to reassure him that the Bey was dead.

Time passed. The group waited in vain, until Samir decided it was time for action even at the risk of incriminating Fakhar. He led his party down the dune, and rode into the camp, where the Bey was standing in front of his tent surrounded by his well armed followers. A pile of bodies was the only sign of the raid.

185

Samir dismounted, realising that something had gone terribly wrong. "Greetings, Your Excellency. I see that the Jewabis have been troubling you. Stealing camels no doubt?"

Mersa Bey looked at him, his cold eyes revealing nothing. "There was some minor trouble this morning. It was the will of Allah that no harm befell me. My men dealt with this irritation efficiently." He indicated the bodies.

Samir hoped that there was no evidence to lay the raid at his door. The Bey held Samir's gaze, as one of the guards came forward holding the recently decapitated head of Fakhar high up so that everybody could see it.

"Samir, behold, your servant!"

The warrior threw Fakhar's head onto the sand; it rolled to a stop, eyes open, staring up at Samir in bitter accusation.

Monday 9th July 1798 7 PM — Ken

When the Bey's caravan arrived at the camp of Sheikh bin Kineivisha at Qaret el Matmura, Ken immediately went to search the camp convinced that Annette was nearby. He walked towards the sheikh's tent attracted by the sounds of raised voices, but as he approached the meeting ended and the people came hurrying out. He caught a glimpse of a tall dark haired woman in the centre of a crowd of other women. She flicked the end of her long black hair in a familiar gesture. It was Annette.

"Wait! Annette, it's me, Ken," as he said this he pulled aside his desert face mask.

She spun around in response to his voice. "Ken! I can't believe it! You're here in Egypt!"

"Annette, you're in grave danger," said Ken remembering the term "white slave girl."

Before either could say another word, an Arab of immense proportions came out of the harem tent and pushed Ken to the ground.

"Away with you! It is forbidden to speak to the women of the Sheikh's harem. You are a guest, but if I catch you again, I will cut

186

out your tongue!" All Ken could see of this man were his eyes, staring at him over his desert mask. The huge guardian herded the women away leaving two guards armed with scimitars to deter Ken from further contact.

"She has no idea," muttered Ken.

The next day Ken was shepherded into the council tent, following the Bey. The Sheikh, aged like an old cheese, rose from a huge pile of cushions to greet the Bey.

"Salaam aleikum — Peace be with you, my brother."

As the Bey settled on a secondary peak of Mount Cushion, Sheikh bin Kineivisha continued to address the council.

"The woman you see before us is a gift from the French General Napoleon, who recently landed in Alexandria, and even now is driving the Mameluke armies from Egypt." He indicated Annette who sat in the cushion foothills. "This woman is a symbol of the peace that France seeks between our two nations. Brother, your subject Abu bin Samir was the messenger who has delivered our new wife."

A ripple of appreciation went through the assembly. Horrified, Ken looked across at the oblivious Annette.

"Greetings to the Sammahoulous people from Mersa Matruh," said the Bey, addressing the assembly.

"I have to report that the traitor, bin Samir has fled into the desert."

After quieting the outraged voices, the Sheikh addressed Ken directly. "You risked death to inform the Bey of the onslaught of this traitor?"

"Yes, Effendi," Ken replied.

The sheikh's brother spoke: "This boy saved my life, and risked his own to do so. Our custom dictates that we should reward him."

The Sheikh looked Ken in the eye. "You are an infidel Master Ken, but you have saved the life of my brother, so you may ask of us a boon."

Ken knew what he had to request.

"State what you want boy! A camel? Two camels may be within your grasp."

"My lord," Ken forced himself to speak. "I have a particular friend who stands here today confused, misrepresented and, worst of all, she understands nothing of these proceedings. She is not a gift from the lords of France. That is an invention of Abu bin Samir. I beg freedom for my friend, Mademoiselle Annette."

"The boy is mad," whispered the Bey. "Does he know nothing about our customs? Our father would have his head sliced from his body for such a suggestion. That woman is far above the boy's remotest dreams." The sheikh smiled at his brother, and the whole council held its breath.

"The boy's request is not under consideration. He may step down."

Ken had the sensation that he had completely ruined any chance for Annette. He returned to his station near the entrance and inched as close to her as he dared.

The sheikh continued. "A French officer accompanied Samir in his caravan. I would like him to appear before the council." There was a scurry of activity and, after a few minutes, Reynard was led into the meeting tent. One of the elders stepped forward to translate for the Frenchman.

"Monsieur, please state your name and your mission to the Sammahoulous people."

"I am Lieutenant André Reynard, a representative of the French government."

"We are told that this woman," the sheikh indicated Annette, "is a gift from France to the Sheikh of the Sammahoulous, as a symbol of an alliance between our nations. Is this the truth?"

As this was translated, there was a shriek of protest from the French woman.

"Why is she so upset?" whispered the Bey. "Surely she knew what her destiny was to be? Is this not a great honour? A life of luxury!"

Reynard thought for a moment, and then asked: "Permit me to speak to her a moment, your Excellency."

The sheikh shrugged, and Reynard walked over to Annette. He spoke very quietly, but Ken was standing close enough to hear.

"Give me the magic box, and I will tell them to let you free."

Annette stiffened in protest but, after a moment, she drew the smart phone from the folds of her robe and handed it to Reynard.

"Is the woman a gift for the Sammahoulous?" Asked the sheikh. "If she is not, you must take her back under the protection of the French invasion forces. We will offer you an escort to Alexandria."

"I am a free woman!" Annette cried.

Ignoring Annette's outburst, Reynard continued. "I thank the Sammahoulous people for their generosity. The French government acknowledges its debt to you, and informs the Sheikh that there is some urgency to our journey. We would be obliged if the caravan could be made available at the Sheikh's earliest convenience."

The Sheikh bowed his head in acknowledgement. "We shall grant this request, but the Sammahoulous require an answer to the question of the woman."

Reynard looked at Annette, and a gleam of triumph came into his eye. "The woman is indeed a gift for the Sheikh, as a token of our alliance."

Annette shouted in dismay. She lunged towards Reynard, but was restrained by the guards.

"As you observe the woman is somewhat reluctant to accept this honour. We thought the Sheikh would appreciate a high spirited woman."

The men laughed at this observation, and smiled knowingly at each other. Annette was removed, protesting. When the Sheikh dismissed the French officer, Ken saw his opportunity, and bowed himself out of the tent.

A pair of palm trees leaned at alarming angles due to the pressure of the sand, shading Ken and his two companions from the midday heat. "My friends, I need your help. The Sheikh's new concubine is a woman I know well . . ." Ken trailed off in a meaningful way.

"You have lain with the raven haired beauty from France?" George's eyes were wide with surprise.

189

"No," said Ken carefully, not wishing to lie. "But she is promised to me." This was as close to the truth as Ken thought his friends would understand.

"You are a lucky man, Ken," laughed Francisco.

"First I have to free her, and escape to Alexandria."

George lifted an eyebrow. "You want Francisco and me to risk our lives by helping you to release the girl from the harem, steal some camels, flee unarmed across an unknown desert, pursued by a raging hoard of very angry, well equipped, heavily armed Bedouin warriors in their native territory, every one of them determined to slice us into a million pieces?"

There was a short pause while George's words sunk in.

"Yes, well, I suppose," stammered Ken. "Will you help me?"

George slapped Ken on the back with a great roar of laughter. "Of course. Life is short; we should find adventure while we can!"

"George paints the bad picture, but I see a simple ride across the desert on these four legged ships. As the hero who saved the Bey . . . " Francisco made a grand gesture to Ken as he spoke.

"One of the three heroes," interjected George.

" . . . I have become friends with the camel master. He offered to lend me some animals to visit the nearby ancient ruins. I shall borrow four camels, and load them with food and water. We shall wait until night, then you and George get the girl, and we ride off before she is missed. We shall have four or five hours lead on our pursuers." Francisco folded his arm in a determined manner.

"We shall wait until midnight tonight."

While his friends snoozed, Ken hiked to the top of a dune overlooking the salt flats to watch the sun set. A brilliant orange red ball hung over the desert, and the sky slowly turned to purple as the sun's disk touched the horizon. The desert to the north east was hidden by dunes, some as much as 800 feet high, formidable obstacles that their tiny caravan would have to cross. If they chose the wrong pass, they would have to retrace their steps directly into the path of any pursuer. A single wrong turn could completely eliminate their early start. He closed his eyes trying to memorize at least the part of the route that was in view.

George's loud breathing interrupted Ken's reverie. He sat down next to Ken, holding his chest and gasping from the steep climb.

"Francisco has procured camels, food, water, and a compass. As long as we find grazing, the camels can go thirsty. We have enough for two days maybe three. We shouldn't overburden the camels in case we have to run; besides there are wells, as you well know!" Ken chuckled in response.

"Three men guard the harem. One is larger than a camel and possibly stronger."

"Yes, I think I met him," commented Ken, remembering the huge Arab.

"The other two are not so formidable, and always stay at the entrance. I think I can distract the 'camel-man' while you cut your way into the back of the tent with this." George showed Ken three small, very sharp scimitars.

"What's this? How?" Asked Ken.

George chuckled, he stood up and threw the three swords from hand to hand, and started to juggle. Each sword spun once in the air to land handle first into his waiting grasp. As the pattern stabilized, he started to vary the throws, first a double spin, then over his arm instead of under. He became more ambitious; a sword would disappear behind his back, then under his leg, and still the juggling would continue. He held Ken's attention for about three minutes before a sword fell from his hand.

"Take care!" Ken expected George to grab the wrong end and lose a finger.

George caught the blunt end neatly on his left foot, and kicked it into the air so that it came down handle first into the pattern. He continued juggling without a pause, until he finished by catching all three swords in one hand.

"That's incredible! Where did you learn to do that?"

"At sea, when the work is done, the weather is good, and no enemies are in sight, I practice."

Around midnight Ken waited in the shadows while George went over to the harem tent to start his juggling. Soon he could hear the guards laughing and shouting comments. Ken ran to the back, and threw himself onto the sand. He started to cut the fabric of the tent, but minutes passed, and the layers were endless. The scimitar was not as sharp as he had thought, and often the fabric just stuck to the metal. Then Ken heard the laughter stop, and George's loud goodnight. So he attacked the cloth with increased fury, but froze when he heard a noise to his left. A soft giggling caused him to look up. Annette stood above him, holding a sharp knife. The tent was flapping where she had cut her way out.

"You took your time to rescue me," Annette chuckled softly.

"Sorry, I will organize my rescues on your timetable in future. We better go before Camel-man finds us," he said getting up.

"Who?"

"Never mind." Ken grasped her hand and hurried her into the darkness.

"Where are we going?"

"Trust me. Everything is arranged." Ken led her away from the flaming camp lights, to the rendezvous.

"For once you're organized!" Annette exclaimed.

"Do you mind riding a camel?"

"Yes, but I'll do anything to get away from here."

They reached the first of the big dune barriers two hours later. This one small part of their journey was like a mountain range. The first of several that they had to cross. Brick red by day, these sandy hills became dark, loathsome mountains by night. Each dune seemed worse than the last as they climbed the gentler windward slope, dismounting to lead their camels down the steep side. Shortly before dawn Ken, exhausted, rode out of the ranges he had seen from the camp. It was all he could do to stay on his camel.

"Shall we stop for a rest?" He suggested.

They had reached the shelter of some rocks. George and Francisco discreetly moved behind a low rock band out of sight. Ken and Annette rolled out their sleeping mats, and Ken moved closer to Annette, but the smell of her hair stopped him with a shudder of guilt.

Annette snuggled towards him with a whispered: "Ken, I'm cold."

Ken put his arms around her, and Annette turned her lovely face towards him. As she kissed him gently on the cheek, she whispered:

"Goodnight Ken, thanks for saving me. You're improving."

Tuesday 10th July 1798 8 PM — Abdul

"You bring me news?" Abdul asked the stranger.

"Effendi, she whom you seek will be taken by the sheikh's men tomorrow. They have no choice but to take water at the well at Bi'r Walad, before joining the Sheikh's army at the Nile. Hurry, if you wish to arrive first."

Abdul nodded and passed a coin to the informant who melted into the night. To his companions he said. "Tonight we will ride. Tomorrow we rest, and wait."

Wednesday 11th July 1798 6 AM An obligation fulfilled

Ken awoke to find Annette kneeling over him holding a cup of water. "Here drink this," she said with a twinkle in her eye.

Ken caught the look. "Thanks. Why are you looking at me like that?"

"It's just that I fulfilled my promise," she said with a broad smile.

"What do you mean? What?" Asked Ken.

Annette laughed.

"Did you sleep?"

Ken nodded his head somewhat perplexed.

"So did I."

"I'm glad," said Ken, still not understanding what she was getting at.

"When you gave me the key to Duncan's office, I said I would sleep with you; well I just did!"

193

Ken could not help but laugh. Cuddling up together to keep out the desert cold was not quite what he had in mind.

She interrupted his thoughts. "Ken, what's next?"

"We are going to Alexandria to find a ship to take us back to Malta. When we get there, we have to find a way to the time gate. We go through, and head straight to the 'Bean There' for a coffee and the biggest burger I can find. Sound good to you?"

Annette laughed, and Ken's face fell. He knew that lovely laugh of hers. "Ken, I appreciate you helping me to escape, but I have, well . . . other plans. I wish you luck finding your way back to the time gate."

Ken did not quite know what to say. He could not force Annette to go with him, but he felt instinctively that he should stop her from causing any change to history. Right now, they were together, and he couldn't ask for more.

"S'ok. I get it. If I can't dissuade you, perhaps I can just go along to make sure you're . . . you know, ok?"

Annette touched his cheek. "You are not such a bad guy, Ken. Following me back through the time gate on your own took some guts."

"Well I wasn't quite alone. Sarah came with me."

"What? Where is she? Is she ok?"

A cry made them both glance up at the nearby dune, where they saw tracks going to the top. Almost at once George came tumbling down, spluttering something incoherent through clouds of sand.

"Camels coming!" George yelled, regaining his balance for an instant. Then he rolled and slid down the remainder of the dune in a spectacular ball of sand and limbs.

They went over to pick him up, but he was up on his feet at once, pushing them towards the camels. "We go, now!"

Annette packed her few things away as Francisco frantically loaded their supplies. George ran from camel to camel checking everything.

"How far away are our pursuers?" asked Annette.

"From the top of the dune I could see a cloud of sand from a small caravan. They will pass this place in less than an hour. They must be good trackers to have found us so quickly."

194

"These men live in the desert. They can look at your tracks and know what you had for breakfast, and which of your wives you laid with last night," said Francisco in a resigned tone.

"We should try to hide our tracks," suggested Annette.

"It is not worth the time it would take, and they will find us no matter what," said Francisco in a voice that had given up hope.

"Wait! I have a plan!" Announced Ken. "Annette and I could ride the same camel, and send the other animal off to the left, while we ride to the right."

"Very clever, Sundance, I saw that movie too," said Annette with a sigh.

Francisco merely shook his head.

They quickened their pace until small boulders speckled the sandy desert floor, so they dismounted.

"At least our pursuers will also be slowed by these rocks," Ken commented.

Francisco looked at Ken as if he knew nothing. Half an hour later, they had hardly made any progress. Ahead of them was a range of rocky hills, and behind a dust cloud growing visibly closer.

"Look there's a gap in the cliffs. Once we're out of sight they'll never track us on rocks," Ken didn't sound completely convinced.

They picked their way up a steep rocky hillside towards a dark cleft, and Ken glanced back beyond the boulder choked path. Were the Sheikh's men a little closer? "We must go faster," he called to his companions.

For a full twenty minutes Ken kept his eyes on the pass and hopes of safety. Inevitably, as the ground gave way to steep outcrops of red and yellow baked sandstone, he succumbed to his curiosity, and turned his gaze down the hill. The Sheikh's camels were closer, but still distant. Perhaps the fugitives still had a chance. Ahead was a deep gorge, littered with high rock spires providing plenty of cover.

"We can hide up here."

Full of hope, Ken urged his companions onwards. Annette led her camel without complaint, George and Francisco, a good hundred yards behind them, laboured up the slope. As they entered the gorge, he glanced back again, and saw nothing, no sign of their pursuers, just windswept sand and rocks. Ken could not believe his luck.

"Where did they go?"

She turned frowning. "Let's get into the rocks, and hope they never find us."

They waited for the older men to catch up, and entered the gorge, where they were able to re-mount. The path split into two, then split again. Ken chose the smallest each time, hoping it was the least likely choice. There was space enough for a man to ride a camel between steep, smooth, sandstone cliffs and, in single file, they followed the winding, shadowy trail, cool after the desert heat. Eventually the canyon widened out, and several trails met in a natural courtyard surrounded by high cliffs. A huge rock that reminded Ken of a camel's head blocked their way. As they stopped, Ken felt rather than heard a pebble whistle through the air past his head, and bounce off the rocky walls beside him. He looked up to see a pathway high above cutting across the top of the cliffs.

"There!" Annette pointed upwards to four camel mounted Bedouin warriors staring down at them.

Ken felt a sense of hopelessness but fought against it. "How in hell did they get up there? Come on we have to go on," he said with determination.

They forged ahead choosing the left path around camel head rock. Soon the gap between the cliffs widened.

Annette caught up to Ken.

"We're trapped. We have to hide somewhere."

"I don't think we can. They know these canyons and we are basically lost."

"You're not giving up are you?"

"Of course not! Come on, they haven't caught us yet."

As he said this, a Bedouin warrior appeared from a dark opening ahead, and rode at them yelling: "Yee, yee, yee!."

"Run," Ken called.

They turned their camels in the tight little space, and rode back to camel-head rock. Ken emerged last to find the others stopped in front of four dark skinned Bedouin warriors. At the head was the camel-man, wielding a full size scimitar, a much more formidable weapon than those that George had juggled. The fight went out of

Ken almost instantly. He had failed to help Annette, and the humiliation of being caught by the Sheikh's men was worse than whatever fate awaited him at their hands.

Two of the men dismounted and pulled George, Ken and Francisco from their mounts. There was no point in protesting. One of the others took the reins of Annette's camel; she was going nowhere. A third Arab rushed forward, twisting Ken's arms behind his back, and pushing him to his knees with his face in the sand. Ken still held on to the fact that he had saved the Bey's life. He craned his head around to speak, but nothing but a dry croak came out. He saw Annette sitting on her camel, a look of fear on her face. Of his captor, he could see only baggy pants, and a nasty looking curved blade held dangerously close. He lay immobilized, defeated, waiting for his fate. The camel-man advanced, his sword drawn and mask still in place. The huge black figure stopped directly in front of the forlorn looking youth, and raised his sword to strike.

Wednesday 11 July 1798 4 PM — Sarah

At first, Sarah quite enjoyed riding a camel across the desert, but after three days she had had enough. Each day the riding got harder, until the undulating, gentle sand dunes gave way to rocks and steep inclines. At last they rested under a large outcrop, where she sat dozing next to Duncan. The guide they had hired in Al Alamayn had tracked Abdul and his crew from the brig to the well at Bi'r Walad, but then he had become unsure, and had gone ahead to the South. Sarah wondered if he had left them to die in the desert, but an hour later she saw him returning, and felt slightly guilty for having mistrusted him.

He spoke to the captain then fell back with the rest of the caravan. Sarah urged her camel forward until she was alongside Duncan.

"What news, captain?" Asked Sarah.

"It seems that we are not the only ones following Abdul's trail. According to our scout, a small caravan of eight camels is also following Abdul. They joined the trail last night."

As he said this Antonio came alongside the pair. "What does this mean, Capitan?" Antonio enquired.

"I don't know, exactly. The guide informs me that all travellers are forced into the ancient caravan route. It could be coincidence," but Duncan sounded unsure.

"Everything is possible, Capitan," said Antonio. Noticing that Sarah was having trouble with her camel, he asked: "Can I be of any assistance?"

Sarah was hot, grumpy, and extremely frustrated; she grunted in response.

"Does your camel present a problem?"

"His longer and more agile back legs travel slightly faster and gradually try to pass the front. Since this is impossible, he tends to walk sideways," Sarah grumbled.

"I take your meaning. He drifts to leeward. Take this camel stick, and prod him on the leeward side and he will compensate to windward."

Sarah sighed and took the stick. Despite an initial tentative application, followed by a more enthusiastic dose, the beast continued to drift. Seeing the futility of her efforts, she accepted her camel's peculiarity and rode as best she could. Duncan trotted ahead, and Sarah found herself alone with Antonio. Screwing up her courage, she voiced the question that had been on her mind since hearing his story.

"Antonio, would you really seek revenge if you found this chevalier?"

"It is my duty; I have no more wish to take a life than you have."

Sarah made a sound of exasperation.

He continued: "Perhaps, when we return to Malta, my sister will be back, and you two can meet."

"I would like that."

Antonio reached for her hand. "Please try and understand, I have no choice in this."

She gave his hand a squeeze and he looked at her as if pleading for some understanding. Duncan called him forward, and the moment was gone.

Wednesday 11th July 1798 4 PM — Ken

Ken watched speechless as Camel-man raised his scimitar, and at last, words came to him; "For the love of God, show some mercy. I saved the life of Mersa Bey."

There was something about the big man's eyes that did not carry the malice that Ken expected.

"Who are you?" Asked Camel-man.

It dawned on Ken that this was a formal challenge. His grandmother had taught him well.

"A citizen," he replied.

"Attest the unity of God!"

"There is no deity but God!"

Even as Ken gave the formal response, he wondered why he hadn't been simply slaughtered. Camel-man slowly took off his desert mask and stared at the youth. It was the expression on the man's face that took Ken quite by surprise. His brain slowly assimilated the man's features. He was looking at the face of bin Kabina, who quietly ordered his fellows to let go of their captives. bin Kabina seized Ken giving him an enormous bear hug that might have proved fatal had Ken not shrieked in protest.

"Why didn't you reveal yourself to me yesterday?" Ken asked when bin Kabina finally released him.

"Yesterday I was watched by my enemies. Today I am with my brothers." bin Kabina indicated his three companions whose laughter indicated that the entire incident was the best joke they had ever played.

"Come we will guide you to Alexandria, and help you to find a ship. For it is written that my sailing days are not over!"

"What about the sheikh? Will he not punish you?"

"First he has to catch me. Second, the sheikh's entire army left this morning. I was dispatched to bring you to them," replied bin Kabina.

Annette came down to join the group. "Ken, Who is this man?"

"Annette, this is my fellow galley sailor, bin Kabina."

"Tell her I owe you my life," said bin Kabina.

199

Ken paused but bin Kabina insisted. "I kinda saved him from drowning when the galley went down," muttered Ken.

"I was right, you do have hidden depths," Annette said. Ken couldn't help but smile.

"So Mr. Ken, life is not so bad, and 'ere's our old mate bin Kabina!" George said, nudging Ken gently.

Bin Kabina greeted his old shipmates with a bow.

"What happened? Why weren't you on the beach when I returned for you?" Ken asked.

"I was found by Jewabis horsemen, who traded me with the Sammahoulous. The sheikh gave me employment. Spending time in the desert is like bread."

"Like bread?" Ken did not understand his friend's curious logic.

"Baking in the oven. Allah has guided me to you so that I may I return to the sea. Come, we must be careful not to meet the Sheikh's army. We must journey to the well at Bi'r Walad."

They rode their camels until the sun started to set. Bin Kabina led them silently a short distance up a steep rocky slope overlooked by cliffs. From this vantage point, they could look down on the well.

Ken translated for bin Kabina. "It is safer to camp away from the well, for the road is well used. All travellers are forced to take water here. Tomorrow we cross the valley that was once the ancient bed of the Nile. We will reach the river they call the mother of life tomorrow night or perhaps the day after. Fill the goat skins, for we must carry as much water as we can."

Ken and Annette watched the sun sink, colouring the sky with crimson and gold. Later, as they laid out their bedrolls side by side, he thought that life was close to perfect.

"Now that we are safe, please tell me what happened to Sarah." Annette interrupted Ken's thoughts.

"I don't know where she is. We were captured by slavers — she escaped. They didn't recapture her. It's all I know."

"Slavers? I want the details, man!"

Ken told the story of their capture and Sarah's climb. Afterwards, a silence fell between them.

"So Annette, what are your plans now that you're free?" Ken said breaking the silence.

She looked at him not unkindly, perhaps trying to decide what to tell him. "Ken, I want to make a difference in the world. I have to take advantage of this opportunity." She reached for his hand, and a ray of hope shone in Ken's heart. "Your way of life, your hedonistic attitude is just not for me."

Ken withdrew his hand. "Hedonistic? I went to a lot of trouble to rescue you, didn't I?"

Annette sighed. "Maybe I was a bit harsh. I'm grateful." She hesitated, and then asked abruptly: "Are you in love with me?"

Ken was startled. "I, I don't . . . what a thing to ask!"

"Is it? You were chasing me all term, and now you have rescued me from a fate worse than . . . well anyway a bad fate. Do you have some feelings for me, or is it just my breasts?"

Ken looked at the sand, not daring to show his face. Eventually he said; "I feel that we have a connection. There's some potential for . . ." He paused. " . . . and you have great breasts."

Annette laughed and reached for Ken's hand again. "Would you help me no matter what?"

Ken smiled at her. "Of course, whatever I can do."

"Perhaps I will remind you of that. Look, I have had a wonderful adventure here. I've been terrified, amazed, experienced real danger, but I must try to do what I came for. I think I can make our world a better place." She gave his hand a squeeze.

"By changing the outcome of the Battle of the Nile?"

She didn't answer for a while, staring upwards where the few clouds that dotted the sky had turned purple, streaked with orange; it was a beautiful display. "Perhaps it's too late now. Perhaps that awful French officer will change time for me, although he doesn't know how to operate the smart phone, or know why they'll lose the battle, or how to advise the admiral, or . . ." Annette paused, then smiled. "Thank you, Ken. Perhaps I shall call upon you to help in the future."

Ken thought that he might have done something right, but he knew in his heart that to stay her friend he should leave her be.

She got up to leave. "Ken, I am going to try my best to succeed. I have eighteen days left. Please go back to Malta to find Sarah. See that she is safe. Will you do that much for me?"

"You know I can't just leave you. I care about my future too."

Annette gave his hand a squeeze. "All right. I understand. I'm tired. We can discuss it in the morning. I have to wash myself without the men around me; back in a minute, and you can keep me warm again."

She dropped his hand to search in her leather bag, then disappeared discreetly behind some rocks over by the well, while Ken lay down in the fading light, looking forward to Annette cuddling up to him.

He must have dozed for a few minutes, as an image of Annette leapt unbidden into his mind. She was standing by the well, pouring the cool water over her body, naked in the moonlight. He sat up. Had he heard something? It had sounded like a cry for help carried away on the wind. Could it have been her? He got up from his sandy bed, and ran down towards the well, but there was no sign of Annette. He stopped to listen, hoping for a clue, but all he could hear was the wind howling between the indifferent rocks.

The sun scorched down on the group as they took a brief rest, while one of bin Kabina's companions carefully examined the tracks that had led them through the night to this lonely spot. Despite the intolerable noon heat, Ken urged his companions forward, determined to track down whoever had taken Annette. Perhaps he was doomed to follow her tracks through rocky hills and dunes forever.

"My friend, we have ridden for many hours." bin Kabina's gentle voice broke into Ken's reverie. "The people who took the lady Annette must be close enough to God to keep on riding, but we are mortal. Without rest, we will become slower until we drop. Our camels are getting weaker; their humps are soft and flop over. They must graze or die. See here is camel fodder; it would be a good thing if you decided to stop here."

Ken saw only a few rocks and some scrubby bushes. If the camels would eat these thorny plants then so be it. He nodded his head and bin Kabina called a halt.

The camel savvy Arabs hobbled their animals, and led them to the grazing, while Ken curled up in his robes in the shade of a huge boulder. He had hardly closed his eyes when somebody shook him awake.

"If I ever get out of this desert I pray to God that I never have to smell a camel for the rest of my days!"

"Friend Ken, when first you rode a camel it was like watching a fish climb a palm tree. Now, you are like a gazelle in a pool of olive oil."

Ken had a feeling that bin Kabina might be trying to pay him a compliment, but he couldn't be sure.

"There is a large party of perhaps fifty Bedu heading this way."

"We can hide ourselves in the rocks." Ken pointed off the trail to the left.

"We cannot stand against a large force. If we try to hide and they find us, they will be suspicious. I am known to the Sheikh's men. I shall tell them that I have apprehended you and your companion, but the girl escaped. Later we shall leave them."

Ken agreed, so they waited for the caravan to appear. The sun was setting, casting long shadows over the desert. A narrow trail led between large boulders on one side, and a wall of rock on the other.

"Sarah would like that wall," Ken's breath caught for a moment as he allowed himself to contemplate Sarah's fate. Although he had told Annette that he believed Sarah to be alive, in his heart he doubted it. He put this thought aside as the Bedu caravan paused 200 yards away, and showed their weapons. Bin Kabina went forward with his hands open. He knelt down and, grabbing a handful of sand, he threw it in the air in a symbol of peace. Two robed figures dismounted and advanced towards them. Bin Kabina beckoned to Ken, and they walked out to meet the advancing pair.

One of them threw back his face covering and Ken found himself looking into the smiling face of his history professor, Masthead Duncan.

Chapter 11

Down the Nile

The caravan made its way through a gap in the rocky hills to a perch overlooking the River Nile, where Duncan called a halt.

Sarah and Ken dismounted and joined Duncan and Antonio as Hidey approached bearing a very small cask of rum, which he generously distributed.

"Beggin' yer pardon, Captain, Sir, and Mr. Barbaro, if I may make so bold. Fate wrecked us all in the same storm, and fate directed us to the only caravan route across the desert. So I would like to propose a toast to fate!"

"To fate!" The company replied as they drank their tots of rum.

"Look there!"

Duncan pointed to the head of Napoleon's army, marching south with the Nile just behind them. The column was led by the hussars on their fine horses, their red uniforms an oasis of colour against the brown of the desert.

Sarah sat on the sand beside Antonio, dazzled by the display below her; the green clad fusiliers, the dark blue of the elite carabiniers, and the mass of infantry in light blue appearing out of the baking desert. Even from a distance, she could tell that they were suffering in the heavy serge coats better suited to an alpine campaign. Loaded with heavy packs and rifles, some had already

204

succumbed to the heat, and lay prostrate on the desert. She recalled from one of her many history classes that twenty five thousand troops followed Napoleon. She knew they were thirsty as water was strictly rationed, and the wells along the way were guarded by the French army.

"The knight is out there somewhere my son. I heard that he went with the French general to seek glory." Francisco murmured from behind them.

"No doubt to increase his fortune with looting," growled Antonio. Sarah remained silent.

The van of the army was approaching a small village, and the watchers on the hill could see that the French were about to meet some resistance.

"Friday the 13th of July; the day that Murad Bey, general of the Mameluke army, will attack the French column." Duncan paused and watched as they approached the village. "That must be Shubra Khit."

"Something is happening on the river," Sarah observed.

"The Mamelukes are attacking French gunboats with armed feluccas." Puffs of smoke, and the sound of cannon supported Duncan's explanation. "Magnificent!" continued Duncan, and they watched the Mamelukes streaming along the banks of the Nile. "This is Murad Bey's elite force, they do not know defeat."

The expression on Duncan's face told Sarah that this was why he had come back, to see such sights. She crouched low, as a company of moustachioed Mameluke warriors rode within a hundred yards of their hiding place in the dunes. The sun glistened off their commander's coat of chain mail. He was a colourful sight with his voluminous red pantaloons, leather gauntlets, and red pointed slippers.

Sarah borrowed Duncan's telescope to make out the details below the man's large yellow turban. He was adorned by a brace of pistols, a mace, a sheaf of arrows, and an English carbine. As they watched, the warrior raised his long curved sword, and with a yell started the charge down the slope towards the French column. The men of his company followed behind and, behind them, twenty other companies of Mameluke cavalry. So started the battle of Shubra Khit.

She turned the telescope to the West bank of the Nile, where Napoleon's forces, flowing like a blue stream, left a trail of fallen men, victims of the harsh climate. The sudden advance of the Mameluke cavalry gave the French generals little time to deploy their big guns. Sarah knew from her studies what to expect as General Desaix's forces started to form squares around the mounted officers and equipment. The sides were at least six men deep, with their bayonets pointing outwards like some giant prickly porcupine.

The Mameluke cavalry advanced in all their finery, dealing death to any lagging, blue-clad soldiers, but their triumph was short lived. As they met the first square, the big French field guns cut a swath through their ranks. The horses, trained in battle, turned and rode along the side of the square, only to be cut down by French muskets. Sarah did not want to watch men die, but her eyes were held, fascinated by the sight of the Mamelukes falling on those deadly squares. This was no history text, no movie set, nor was it red paint that stained the desert around each of the fallen Mamelukes; people were really dying.

Then, from the centre of one of these human fortresses, a small troop of French cavalry rode out towards the enemy. At their head, seated on a pure white horse, rode a tall, imposing, white uniformed officer. A broad red sash of office adorned his uniform, and in his cocked hat a white ostrich feather added even more to his height. Antonio reacted to the sight, and leapt onto his camel. He raised his sword in salute to his father; "Le Chevalier Blanc!"

"Antonio, please — come back!" Sarah yelled as he rode off.

A single word wafted back on the breeze: "Duty!"

She sat down on the sand to watch his progress, hoping that he might somehow come to his senses, while Duncan shouted uselessly at his retreating figure: "Return immediately, Tenente. That's an order!"

"He doesn't hear your orders," Sarah said quietly.

"And I have no legal authority over him. He's a volunteer."

Marie-Paule came and stood by Sarah. "Blood and sand! We are near enough to see men fall, without the horror of hearing their screams or seeing their faces."

"Come, we don't have to watch this battle. We can't stop these men trying to kill each other," Duncan said, sensing her horror at the scene.

Then they heard the sound of the French artillery again. What chance did a man on a horse stand against such fire power?

Hidey interrupted: "Begg'n yer pardon, sir, but we'm gone and lost the frog officer."

Duncan looked distracted, and then remembered Lieutenant Granon. "Not your worry, Hidey. He has our permission, and indeed a duty to rejoin the French forces."

When Duncan looked back to the battle, Murad Bey had started to withdraw his defeated cavalry. "I'm sorry, Marie-Paule, you should not have to endure this sight. The Mamelukes are discovering that their medieval ways have no place in the modern world. The bravery of each Mameluke warrior is irrelevant in the face of the coordinated indifference of the French fighting machine."

Marie-Paule looked at Duncan and touched the lines etched into his sand blown face. "Nevertheless, you came to see this, did you not?"

Sarah saw the captain lower his eyes to the sand. Perhaps he felt ashamed of his fascination for battle. She turned to Marie-Paule.

"Can you still see Antonio?"

Marie-Paule handed her the captain's telescope. "I am sorry, cheri, I lost him, but look, down there towards the French stragglers, it's Monsieur Granon!"

The lone figure of Granon rode his camel down out of the hills to head away from the Mameluke action, to the North.

"The Frog's heading back to join his own people," called out Hidey.

He was easy to pick out, riding against the tide of stragglers from Napoleon's army and, through the telescope, Sarah could see him look around, perhaps trying to search out an officer. Suddenly there was a terrible war cry. A mass of Bedouin warriors were heading towards the ragged column with knives and scimitars drawn.

"The forces of the Sheikh! They will kill the stragglers until there's no more resistance, then take the rest for slaves," declared bin Kabina.

As bin Kabina said this, the leader brought his scimitar down across the back of the first of Napoleon's weaker soldiers, who died without a sound. Seeing this, Granon spurred his camel into action to escape the charge. The French lieutenant had little skill on camel back, but held on grimly. Just as it looked like he would outdistance the Sheikh's men, a grinning Bedouin dashed ahead of the others. The man rode alongside Granon, then slashed out with his blade, cutting the saddle from under him. Granon slid backwards off the animal, landing hard on the desert floor.

Sarah held her breath, wondering if this was the end for Granon, when she saw him stagger to his feet, only to stumble to his knees, right in the path of the oncoming Bedouin attack. Shrieking a war cry, they came charging towards the Frenchman, who curled up into a ball to present the smallest target to the flying hooves. To her surprise, the Frenchman's camel, now free of his burden, stood over Granon, patiently protecting him from the flying feet of the oncoming charge; standing unperturbed. The Bedouin raiders passed, leaving a trail of dead and dying French soldiers, but Granon survived.

Much relieved, Sarah turned the telescope towards the Nile bank hoping to catch a glimpse of Antonio, but she found no trace. When she turned back towards Granon, he had jury rigged the saddle and mounted. He rode north through the carnage.

Just then Sarah heard the Bedouin war cries. "Yee, yee, yee, yee!" They were coming back. Once again, Granon fled before the onslaught, a prime target now as little else was moving, but he rode off into the hills, and nobody followed. She lost sight of him amongst the dunes.

"What will happen to him?"

Duncan shook his head. "It's wartime. Some will live, and some will die. My job is to catch up with Annette, then make sure you all return to Malta; not chase French officers." Taking Sarah's arm, he led her a short distance off from the main group. "Perhaps you have some insight into Antonio's strange behaviour?"

"He has a personal feud with the officer who led the French troop away from the square."

"I don't think we can count on him returning from such an unequal fight. That officer has an entire army behind him. I'm sorry . . ."

Sarah nodded and bit her lip. She turned away, trying to blink back the tears. Duncan let go of her arm, and returned to the group, leaving Sarah to cry alone in the desert.

A little while later Sarah recovered herself and determined to forget about the hot headed Antonio. She looked up to see Marie-Paule close by with Duncan. Not meaning to eavesdrop, she could not help but hear their conversation. It made her smile despite her grief over what might have been.

"Can I ask something of my captain?"

"I am at your disposal, my lady."

"I have spoken to Sarah."

"So you informed me."

Marie-Paule looked troubled. "I want to know if you are my lord and master or my equal partner under God?"

Duncan laughed. "The North American woman has done her work, I see. My darling, we are partners. A leader amongst us will emerge depending on the situation. Back in Malta at the docks, you took the initiative. You were the leader. Here, I am your captain."

Sarah quietly withdrew. Settling down beside Ken, she took his arm.

"Hey what's up?" he enquired.

Sarah merely shook her head and remained silent. Confused, Ken respected her silence until Duncan strode up to them.

"Tell me again when you last saw Annette?" Duncan asked, looking directly at Ken.

"Two nights ago, when we camped up in the hills beside the well at Bi'r Walad. Annette went to wash herself and never came back. We rode all night trying to follow whoever took her."

"Sarah mentioned that Annette had your smart phone. Does she still have it?"

"A French naval officer, a Lieutenant Reynard, took it from Annette. The Sheikh gave him some kind of safe conduct back to the French lines. He left a few hours before we did."

Duncan was thoughtful. "If that French officer knows something of Nelson's future movements, and manages to convince Admiral Brueys to take appropriate action, then it could tip the balance at the Nile, just eighteen days from now. Perhaps this

Lieutenant Reynard, armed with a 21st century smart phone, is a bigger threat than Annette. If we are unable to track Rais Abdul and find news of my star student, then we must rethink our plan of action. I suggest that we find transport down the Nile towards Aboukir Bay. Perhaps we could commandeer a ship, and warn Admiral Nelson. It will be a dangerous mission. It would be best if I found a safe haven for you ."

"Monsieur, I have lived with danger since my parents were taken at the time of the Reign of Terror. We will not hide like children when there is work to be done."

"You're not going to leave us behind, either" as Ken spoke, Sarah nodded vigorously.

"That's settled then," Duncan sighed.

Ken lay in the shade waiting with the others until dusk before making their way down towards the Nile, heading well to the North of the battlefield. When they came to Ramaniyeh, a village of low mud brick buildings, they found the headman.

"We wish to trade our camels for these two large boats." Ken translated Duncan's instructions to the headman.

A tirade of rapid Arabic followed from one of the men who sat with the headman. Ken raised his hand requesting a break to translate.

"They are willing to sell the boats; they are called djermes. This man is the owner of the djermes, and captain of the larger vessel, He already has a passenger, a wealthy merchant, and they are obliged to transport him to the village of Rosetta, some distance downstream." Ken paused and in confidence to Duncan said: "He said he will wait on shore for his passenger. You may take over the *Caliph* now, and use the cabin on the *Nile Sheikh* tonight. I don't think he will be open to persuasion on this one, but he assures me the vessel will be ours once his mission is completed."

"Agreed. Let's get on with it," said Duncan, but as stepped away the captain of the *Caliph*, and the headman were clearly bent on observing their custom and drinking quantities of rakh, the local moonshine. It was another fifteen minutes before they could escape the hospitality. A great deal of laughter followed.

"What is the source of their mirth?" Asked Duncan, with an eyebrow raised.

"Apparently the vessels are old, and would be retired soon. We paid more than twice what they are worth," said Ken. Duncan shrugged his shoulders and smiled.

"Mr. Smith you are the most experienced man I have, since our first officer took his leave of us. You know your navigation?"

"Aye, Sir. Ten years in the merchant service as first mate."

"Good. I doubt you will get lost on the river!"

Ken laughed along with Hidey, who shook his head without being disrespectful to his captain.

"You will take command of the smaller vessel. I am making you up to Master's mate."

"Thank 'ee kindly Sir. I won't let you down," Hidey responded with a smile on his face.

Saturday 14th July 1798 1 AM — Annette

Annette sat in her tent, hoping that her guard would fall asleep. They had made camp in a sheltered spot surrounded on three sides by large boulders. It was a fine site by a rocky ridge running north towards the Nile delta. She waited until all was quiet, knowing that her tent would be guarded, as it had been every other night. She had deliberately shown no signs of rebellion before this night, but now that they were in sight of the Nile, she thought there was a good chance of finding some French soldiers. The man calling himself Abdul had been civil enough, but she could see lust for her in his eyes, and she was not sure what was holding him back. Perhaps it was the fact that she technically belonged to the Sheikh, a prohibition that would not hold him off for long. More importantly, she still had two weeks to reach Admiral Brueys.

She could see the guard through a crack in the heavy tent material, and she could hear the man's breathing as he sat dozing beside the fire. His head nodded once, but he jerked himself awake. He stood up and made a pile of small stones on a boulder, holding them in place with some kindling. He carefully tied a length of twine to the tent support about six inches off the ground. The other end he attached to the twig that was stopping the stones from falling. Annette smiled as she watched him work. The guard settled down to sleep, believing that if she left the tent she would trip on the twine and wake him up.

Annette waited until she heard the guard's even breathing. Moving quietly, she stepped carefully over the twine. The sleeping guard stirred slightly; instinctively, Annette stepped back, remembering too late about the trap. She tripped the snare causing a small avalanche of stones. Annette darted forward, avoiding the grasp of the awakened guard. The man stumbled after her in the darkness, but was brought to a halt by a sharp crack, as a rock bounced off the canyon wall. He turned towards the sound as Annette slid into the shadow of a huge boulder.

Gripped with fear she paused, trying to outthink the guard, when suddenly a hand covered her mouth, and she was pulled into a cleft in the rock. As she struggled, a voice whispered in her ear in French:

"It is I, Granon. Stay quiet and perhaps we can escape. Do you understand? Nod your head and I will remove my hand." Annette nodded.

"How did you find me?" She said as quietly as she could.

Granon pulled her further into the shadows, where they could hear Abdul, bellowing like a bull, organize his followers to search in all directions for Annette.

"I was looking for a hiding place from the Bedu, and these rocks gave me shelter. It is the first sizeable outcrop I came across, no doubt a favoured campsite. We should wait here until they are all gone."

Annette nodded warily. She was grateful that the terrain had led Granon to her, but wasn't he Reynard's man?

She watched Abdul mount his camel, while his followers searched on foot. As soon as the sounds of the search quieted, Granon emerged from their hiding place. Annette hung back, watching him go straight to the camels. He didn't see the guard who had been squatting behind one of the animals. The burly man grabbed Granon's right arm, put his own arm around his throat. As he tightened his grip the Frenchman started to gasp for breath.

212

Annette slipped behind the struggling men, and grabbing a rock she brought it down on the guard's head. Leaving him senseless, she moved towards the camels.

"Come on, it's our only chance," Annette said removing the hobbles from as many camels as she could.

Granon nodded his thanks and they mounted. Annette still held the reins of several animals, so the whole herd followed them down towards the river. Annette let go of the riderless beasts, and they cantered away into the night.

At last she was free, riding hard across the desert with the cool night air rushing past her at an exhilarating speed. The moon was just one day past full, bright enough to make the going easy, and they were soon down on the plains. Even the fact that her mount was yet again a hated camel could not ruin her joy. The sound of crashing hoofs behind caused her to glance back.

Abdul, brandishing his scimitar, and yelling a terrifying war cry followed them in the moonlight. They urged their camels on, but they could hear their pursuer gaining on them as they came to the banks of the Nile.

"Mademoiselle, I saw gunboats flying the French flag. Can you swim?"

As Granon spoke, he took off his shirt and boots while Annette, too tired and frightened to protest, kicked off her shoes. They plunged into the Nile as Abdul arrived at the riverbank and, in one practiced motion, levelled his musket at Granon and fired. The shot went wide, but the sound spurred the swimmers to make more effort while, behind them, Abdul cursed as he loaded his gun again.

"Mademoiselle, we must reach the nearest boat, perhaps ten minutes more," Granon slowed his strokes to remain right beside her.

She was exhausted from the ride and her clothing was soaked, weighing her down. She swam on resolutely, until a musket ball splashed into the water beside her. It had taken Abdul less than thirty seconds to reload.

She stopped to tread water in order to catch her breath. Granon swam onwards, and she tried to call to him, but swallowed water instead. An ugly, terrified squeak stopped Granon, and he came back to her.

"Mademoiselle, I am sorry, but it is vital we keep moving, however slowly."

She felt incredibly limp. It was as if she was watching the drama that was unfolding in the water. She wanted to relax into the silky smooth yellow waters of the Nile, and just drift with the river. She took a gulp of water, then started to cough. Then another. She barely had the strength to keep her face out of it, when suddenly she felt Granon's strong arms around her. She made no resistance as he turned her onto her back, and continued his swim pulling her along after him.

Another shot rang out, and Annette clung hard to Granon., who gasped and let go of her. Annette started to struggle. She spun around in the water and saw blood leaking from Granon's shoulder. He'd been hit. She could see a French gunboat approaching, and she waved frantically. It was too far away, and Granon was hardly able to stay afloat.

A local fishing craft appeared from the landward side. With the wind on its beam, it fairly flew through the water, reaching them before the gunboat. It came right up alongside Annette, and she felt hands from above grab her arm. "Granon!" she yelled, terrified that he had gone under. This man had risked his life for her, and she felt guilty that she had judged him as one with Reynard. She broke free from the sailors, and turned round, looking desperately for any sign of her rescuer, but he was gone.

Hands pulled Annette from the water and she fell exhausted amongst the fish. A wizened fishermen smiled at her through a thin grey beard and steered off into the night.

Monday 16th July 1798 7 AM The Nile — Ken

The two djermes stayed in convoy, throughout the day on Sunday, and early on Monday morning they followed the *Caliph* into Rosetta where the former owner and his passenger disembarked. Ken listened to their conversation, and caught the words; 'A dark haired white woman of exceptional beauty.' Leaping to his feet he grabbed Duncan's arm.

214

"Sir, they are negotiating over a white woman discovered by some sailors two days ago," said Ken. His urgent tone spurred Duncan into action.

"Mr. DiPalo are you suggesting that the woman could be our missing student?"

Ken's eyes widened, and was about to speak, when Duncan took his arm, and jumped ashore, calling out to Hidey to follow him with half a dozen of the crew.

"Come armed if you please," ordered Duncan.

They pushed their way through a crowd of fishermen, to approach the merchant.

"Where is this white woman?" Said Duncan, looking at Ken to interpret.

The old man with the thin grey beard turned away from the merchant.

"She is safe, effendi."

"Tell him we wish to meet her and we will pay well for her safe return," instructed Duncan.

At first the fisherman preferred to negotiate with the merchant, until Duncan produced some gold coins. The presence of the armed crew members caused the merchant to retire leaving Duncan to make the bargain.

Ken sat with Annette all day, even though she simply shook her head when he asked her about her adventures. Despite her refusal to speak, Ken remained by her side after the two djermes met midstream, and it was this tense silence that Duncan interrupted.

"I am relieved to find you safe. Have you been injured in any way?"

"No I am quite well, thank you, professor. How did you find me?"

"My dear, the presence of a lone white woman is a rarity in these parts."

"Am I free to leave this vessel when I choose?"

"Mademoiselle, your love of history has caused some serious problems. I think it is time we started the journey home."

Annette did not respond, but hugged her knees to her chest as she stared out at the muddy green waters of the Nile.

"Come on, Annette, can't you see it is for the best?" Sarah asked with a smile.

"I am relieved to find you safe, Sarah," replied Annette. "But you and Ken should never have come here in the first place."

"Who knows what terrible consequences might have followed your attempt to change history." Ken said slowly.

Annette continued to gaze towards the horizon

Chapter 12

Aboukir Bay

Tuesday 17th July 1798 5:30 AM Aboukir Bay — Sarah

When Sarah opened her eyes, she looked out to see a red line marking their passage from the muddy waters of the Nile into the clear water of the Mediterranean.

"Aboukir Bay!" exclaimed Hidey loud enough to startle her.

It was late afternoon before they could see the crowded masts that marked the fleet at anchor on the west side of the bay. She watched the elegant seventy-fours became distinguishable in the maze of spars that confronted them. There it was, the French line of battle drawn up just as he had read, with the massive 120 gun *L'Orient* in the centre. If everything remained unchanged that ship would explode during the battle, killing hundreds of sailors. They sailed slowly along, not two hundred yards away from the great ships — the *Timoleon, Guillaume Tell, Mercure* — in all thirteen great ships of the line. Many small craft bustled about the war ships.

"I read that vice admiral Brueys is having difficulty keeping his navy fed, or even adequately watered. Those small craft are supplying the French navy for a high price," Informed Ken, his internet-fact crowded brain working overtime.

The two djermes anchored in the shoal waters offshore where it was too shallow for the fleet. Sarah stayed with the silent Annette while Ken went across to the *Nile Sheikh* to negotiate for victuals with one of the small craft, but returned to the *Caliph* to settle down for their first night in Aboukir Bay.

The sun had barely risen when Sarah stood up stiffly from her night spent in the bottom of the boat with Annette. They talked about their experiences since coming through the time gate, but Annette simply diverted the conversation if Sarah mentioned her future plans. In the morning Duncan sent a message for Sarah to report to him in the larger vessel. Sarah motioned Ken to her side and, after extracting a promise from him to watch over Annette carefully until her return, she hastened to the other vessel.

Duncan was standing in the stern talking to one of the hands, but broke off to greet her. "There you are Mr. Malette. Your companion will be needed shortly to interpret; he has not yet reported aboard."

"Ken will be here shortly, Sir. He is instructing a crew member who is standing guard over our colleague."

"And how is the charming Annette?"

"She refuses to move from her sleeping quarters aboard the *Caliph*, Sir."

Duncan's eyes softened. "Mr Malette, I would like you to stay with her. You are to make sure that she does not make contact with the French fleet."

Sarah was about to say something when Marie-Paule emerged from the rear cabin.

"Good morning Mr. Midshipman, did you sleep well enquired Duncan.

"Not as well as last night, Monsieur."

Sarah listened to the exchange and looked closely at Marie-Paule. Her expression said everything that Sarah wanted to know, so she discreetly withdrew. As she backed away, Ken blundered past her, and went straight to Duncan despite Sarah's subtle protestations.

"Now that I have found all of my adventurous students we could leave this dangerous place, were it not for your damnable phone!" Duncan spoke softly. "I don't suppose the battery has run down by now?"

"It was fully charged when I left, and as long as it hasn't been left switched on it is probably fine. Perhaps the French lieutenant who stole the phone has not yet arrived at the flagship?" Ken said hopefully.

"Much as I would like to sail to Alexandria to find a ship to take us to Malta, I cannot leave here with the possibility of that instrument falling into the hands of the French. We have to find out if the damn thing is onboard the flagship."

"And if it is?"

Duncan took a deep breath. "What does this French lieutenant know?"

"Annette said he has no knowledge of the device. He would have a hard time finding the relevant navigational charts."

"He may not have to show much," murmured Duncan. "All he has to do is to produce some images to convince the admirals the device is from the future to validate his knowledge, in which case Brueys might modify his current plan."

A fresh morning breeze ruffled the waters of the bay, rocking the djerme gently. Duncan looked across at the French ships strung out along the border with the shallow water. He reached a decision and beckoned to Hidey who, after a whispered conversation, went off giving orders to the men.

Ken and Sarah waited patiently. "We shall have to find out how much Annette told Reynard about the battle, won't we?"

A little later in the day Duncan addressed the senior members of the crew who were crowded into the stern of the anchored djerme.

"Does anybody here speak French with a convincing Arab accent?"

Ken laughed and gave his best impression: "Capitan, J'habite au Caire."

The crew applauded; they thought Ken sounded convincing, despite the fact that many of them spoke no French.

"What should I say, captain?"

After a hasty conference, Duncan directed the djerme to take their turn in approaching the huge three decker, *L'Orient*. They pulled up in line to pass aft of the flagship. Ken looked up fascinated by the stern gallery, a series of designer windows set into a curved

219

wooden wall. He couldn't help but wonder what was happening in the spacious quarters of the admiral with his multiple rooms. Ken remembered that the ordinary seaman had no more privacy than that afforded by the length of a hammock, hanging alongside his messmates with a mere fourteen inches to call his own. At last they drew level with the entry port, just like any another small craft selling everything from fresh food and water to hashish. Soon they were hailed.

'State your business,"

"We have fresh fish and clear water." Ken's translation and accent was poor enough that he sounded convincing to the French sailors.

"Stay there. I will come aboard and examine your cargo."

A burly sailor whose uniform distinguished him as a petty officer, possibly even the purser's mate, came aboard with two of the hands. Ken showed them the fish in boxes piled up in the bow and a few barrels of water amidships.

"Is that all? Not enough even to feed the wardroom!"

"This is our best quality fish, suitable for the table of the capitan or even your admiral," Ken protested.

"What do you know of our admiral?" The purser's mate looked doubtful.

"This is the biggest of your ships; I assume that he lives on the best?" Ken had just the right amount of hurt pride in his voice.

"You are right, my friend, but we need meat for the crew; can you bring us some mutton?"

"Of course next time, but see here we are two boats, and there is plenty more fish in the other."

"Fish that is ripe enough to give us all some terrible sickness," laughed the French petty officer.

"Send the admiral's cook to us; he will know good fish when he sees it! Perhaps you have visitors, officers from the other ships? We can bring you even better than this at a special price!" Ken smiled as he thought up this subtle probe.

The petty officer looked at him suspiciously. "You must always bring your best to the flagship."

Duncan whispered something to Ken who turned to the Frenchman and said: "Only last week we talked to Lieutenant Reynard. He knows good fish."

The petty officer looked puzzled.

"Not on this ship, my friend; he is not one of our officers. Come. I will take your fish, but it does not smell so good; half price for this fish. You are lucky that I am a generous man."

After unloading their cargo, they sailed to the Eastern banks of the bay, away from the eye of the French ships.

"It looks like Reynard has not been to see the admiral," said Ken.

"Or else that man knew nothing about Reynard's visit," Duncan added gloomily. "We need to put a man on the flagship to discover what is known, and to report to us if Reynard comes aboard. It is a pity that not one man here can pass for a Frenchman."

Marie-Paule stood before Duncan, and said in a very quiet voice intended only for him: "There may not be a man, but there is a woman."

Duncan dismissed the crew, and waited until he was alone with Marie-Paule.

"I am sorry, my dear. I do not want to endanger your life for our struggle."

Marie-Paule looked him straight in the eye.

"I am the only one who could get aboard that ship safely. I am a French citoyenne! Perhaps I was kidnapped from the prison on Malta by Lieutenant Duncan during his escape attempt. He sailed to Egypt in the *Palerma*, which was subsequently destroyed by one of our brave frigates. I managed to escape his clutches and these kind Arabs have brought me to report to the senior French officer."

Duncan was stunned into silence. Twice he tried to speak but could not. At last he said: "Did you just dream up this story, or have you been thinking about it for the past week?"

Marie-Paule laughed, but Duncan continued in as stern a voice as he could muster. "Are you seriously thinking that you can go aboard *L'Orient* with this thin cover story of yours and spy for us?"

Marie-Paule tossed her long brown hair back and folded her arms defiantly. Duncan glanced forward where the crew were straining to hear what was going on.

"What is your plan?"

"It is simple; you 'Arabs' put me aboard *L'Orient*. I tell them the story. I find out if Reynard has been aboard. You keep watch, and if he arrives I will hang my petticoat from a gunport." At this Marie-Paule produced her best French lace from under her Bedouin robes.

Duncan looked at her, his left eyebrow raising itself automatically, as it did so often when he was trying to resolve internal conflicts.

"This is not going to work. You could be thrown off the ship or, worse yet, incarcerated. I cannot ask you to betray your country."

"I am not betraying my country. I am betraying the regime that killed my parents, and would have killed me were it not for a turnkey who took a liking to a little girl."

"You must swear to me that you will leave before the night of August 1st," said Duncan.

"So, mon brave, you have to make sure that I am off the ship before the English come?"

"Nelson's ships will arrive late in the afternoon of the first. We shall wait on the flagship's larboard side, for your signal."

She laughed. "I may not be able to find a larboard side cabin from which to hang my petticoats. But don't worry, if nothing has happened by noon of the first I shall find my way on deck and jump over the side into your arms!"

Duncan laughed and placed his arm on her shoulders. "You are a very brave woman, Marie-Paule; the people of Malta will be indebted to you, and perhaps the entire future of the planet relies on your bravery."

Marie-Paule laughed. "Like all men, you love to exaggerate."

In a very firm voice Duncan said: "You must be off that ship by noon at the latest on the 1st August. Nelson's fleet will round Aboukir Island lead by Captain Foley in the *Goliath*."

"Seventy-four!" Ken interjected.

Duncan looked up to see Ken standing close by.

"Very good Mr. DiPalo, yes indeed a seventy-four gun ship. At five o'clock the battle will commence, and at 9 PM *L'Orient* will catch fire and, at 10 o'clock, explode. You understand the importance of being far away from that ship on the evening of the 1st August?"

Marie-Paule nodded and felt her whole body tense as she acknowledged the dangers she faced.

Duncan beckoned to Ken and Sarah.

"We shall have to find you and Mr. Malette some midshipmen uniforms, and I can't present myself looking like this."

"To whom are you going to be presenting yourself, professor?" Asked Ken.

"Why, Admiral Nelson, of course. Do you think we are going to sit here for the next two weeks?"

"You don't propose sailing to Malta in these djermes do you?"

"While our man . . . that is our person on *L'Orient* keeps a watch for our enemies, we shall go and steal a more suitable ship to get us back to Malta."

"Which ship are you going to take, captain?"

Duncan looked to the South, inshore of the line of the battle ships, where four French frigates were moored.

"We shall take our pick of those smaller vessels, and slip away at the dark of the moon. That gives us ten days to plan our action. Perhaps we will also catch this Reynard by then."

A troubled look crossed Hidey's face.

"Capitan, you mean to take a French brig?"

"Perhaps a frigate."

"One of those big frigates? Capitan, she will require perhaps 250 men to sail and fight her. If Ken and his friends are willing to fight we have but 60 men. Enough to handle ten guns if we are at anchor. Our power to sail her . . ."

The captain interrupted.

"Mr. Hidey, I know where to find a large number of British sailors. All we have to do is to find Nelson before the battle."

The overcrowded conditions on the two djermes had been relieved when they left a large number of the hands at a caravansary close to the outlet of Lake Etko. Ken returned with Hidey and George, and spent a hard working hour on the beach getting a lesson on the "use of the cutlass," as Hidey put it. In the coming days of waiting he welcomed the lessons from Hidey and ignored Sarah's comments on blood sports.

On Tuesday morning, with a new load of fish, and Ken and the crew decked out in their Bedouin robes, the djerme moored alongside *L'Orient*, it was Ken's turn to play his role again. He found himself speaking to the same petty officer as on the previous day.

"Effendi I have something special for you today." Ken spoke again in his delightful French with the almost stage Arab accent that seemed to pass unnoticed by the French sailors.

"We need fresh fruit and vegetables. What do you have to offer?" Asked the petty officer.

"Monsieur we have a French woman here. She was kidnapped by an Englishman, and has escaped. What reward will you give to me, her rescuer?"

"A French woman? A rare kind of vegetable indeed!" The petty officer said for the benefit of the idling sailors sitting around the forecastle.

"Perhaps she is a flower of France," laughed one of the sailors.

The petty officer ignored him on the principal that only officers were allowed to make jokes.

"Where is this French woman? Show her to me, and I want none of your tricks,"

"Effendi, she is here in the boat, but first give me my reward for finding her."

"Monsieur, I can call upon the help of several hundred armed men. You see this gun . . ." He pointed to the 24 pounder carronade by his feet. "My men here could put a hole in the bottom of your boat before you could get two lengths from the ship. Now show me your French woman, and then perhaps we can talk of rewards."

Ken shrugged his shoulders and called down to the stern of the boat. Marie-Paule was led along the djerme, and as she approached mid-ships she struggled free of the men holding her, calling out to the petty officer:

"Monsieur, help me please. I have been a captive for more than a month."

The sound of Marie-Paule's Paris accent took the officer by surprise.

"Mademoiselle, where have you come from?"

Marie-Paule hesitated; her story seemed so thin now. Ken saw her difficulty. Cutting in directly, and holding Marie-Paule's arm, he said: "Effendi, you cannot take her without some reward for my crew."

"Unhand her, Monsieur, before I command my men to blow you out of the water!"

Ken bowed, and backed off, while the crew of the djerme helped Marie-Paule up the side of the French flagship, and the petty officer threw Ken a coin. Ken bit the coin, waved his thanks, and the djerme pulled clear.

Tuesday 24th July 1798 4 PM — Marie-Paule

Once on board, the purser's mate, Jean-Marc, made Marie-Paule comfortable on the flagship until an officer could deal with her case. The purser's mate communicated with the purser who, in turn, informed the 6th lieutenant of Marie-Paule's existence. She was by no means the only woman aboard; in fact, many women lived on the ship, some illicitly, and some as wives of crew members.

Marie-Paule's experiences as a prisoner had taught her that survival depended on knowledge. She knew she could adapt herself to new situations and the 3-decker was no different, just another kind of prison. In a matter of days, she fitted herself into the ship's routine and could talk to any of the women on board. She would soon know if any new officer arrived. She was put to work in the

225

sick bay where there was no shortage of patients even though the ship had not fought an action for a long time. One afternoon, as she sorted bandages, liniments, and ointments, she was interrupted by one of the ship's boys.

"Mademoiselle Marie-Paule?"

"I have heard you called Giocante, is that your name?" asked Marie-Paule with a smile.

"That is correct, Mademoiselle. Commodore Casabianca sends his compliments and requests your presence in his day cabin as soon as you are able."

Marie-Paule's heart began to beat faster. Her presence had been communicated up the chain of command. Perhaps now she would be able to find out whether it was too late to stop Reynard. As she turned to follow the ten year old, she realized the connection.

"Wait, your name is also Casabianca?"

"Oui Mademoiselle, he is my father."

The boy conducted Marie-Paule to the captain's cabin. The room was set up as an office, and smaller rooms for sleeping and dining adjoined on the stern side of the great cabin. Two officers sat eating, but rose to their feet as she came in.

"Mademoiselle Marie-Paule Bonneterre, I hope you do not mind if I finish my lunch? Perhaps we could offer you something?"

"No, thank you, Monsieur. I wish to express my gratitude to you and your men for sustaining me during this difficult time."

The senior man, Casabianca, looked at her with a vaguely bored expression.

"Mademoiselle the circumstances of your kidnap and subsequent escape must have been a terrible experience. Unfortunately, we are not an hotel. This is a ship of war. It is possible that we could find ourselves engaged with an English fleet at any moment. I gather that you have already made yourself useful, but are you prepared to stay on a fighting ship in the time of war?"

"Sir, I am prepared to work and help the brave boys that are fighting for all of us, for the revolution."

Casabianca laughed. "Were you not a child of the aristocrats? I look at you: at the proud way you hold yourself and your refined Parisienne accent. Why would you help the revolution?"

"I have worked hard for the revolution both in Paris . . ."

" . . . and in Malta, Mademoiselle?" The junior officer interrupted her.

The mention of Malta put Marie-Paule on alert. The younger man, sensing her discomfiture said slowly: "Mademoiselle, we have met before."

Marie-Paule looked more closely; there was something familiar about him. Without showing any outwards sign of distress she started to feel cold and trembled inside. She remembered a rainy day in Malta when she had escaped with Duncan. On the way out she had kicked an officer who had stepped in their path. That same man was facing her across the table.

He smiled a cold, humourless smile and looked directly into her eyes. "Bonjour Mademoiselle Bonneterre, I am Lieutenant André Reynard of the French navy. So nice to see you again."

Wednesday 25th July 1798 8 AM — Annette

On Wednesday morning a French longboat, with *Franklin* written on the stern, pulled alongside, and asked if they had any fresh meat. Duncan had made sure they were well supplied in case they needed to find an excuse to visit *L'Orient*, so two of the sailors came on board to inspect the cargo. A price was negotiated and, as had happened several times during the preceding week, the Arab sailors helped put the barrels aboard the French boat.

As was their custom, one of Annette's guards had tied her hands and feet while everybody was busy moving stores. Sarah came over to her and sat down.

"Good morning, Annette. Can I get you some breakfast?"

"Just how do you suggest I eat it?" Annette asked sarcastically.

"I was only trying to help . . ."

"Help whom? Certainly not me. If you wanted to help, you would untie me."

Sarah got up, eyes wet with tears.

"I'm sorry. You know I can't do that."

She stalked off to help with the cargo, and Ken walked up, ignorant of their tiff. He addressed Annette with his most winning of smiles.

"Anything I can get you?"

Annette's face lit up, as an idea occurred to her.

"Ken, how are you holding up to life in the 18th century? I expect you miss your burgers?" She asked warmly.

"Well, I had a bad time as a galley slave and in the desert, but now I am beginning to enjoy myself," he replied.

Annette slid closer along the bench.

"I underestimated you, Ken. You have more depth to you than I thought. I feel very safe knowing that you are here, and that you keep looking out for me. I appreciate that."

"That's nice of you to notice. I do my best," replied Ken reddening slightly.

Annette placed her bound hands on his.

"Would you mind getting me something to drink? I heard that one of the sailors has a supply of coffee."

"No problem, Annette. I will ask Francisco."

As he turned to go, she held up her hands to him.

"Do you really think this is necessary?"

Ken paused uncertainly, and Annette pressed her hands into his.

"Do you remember in the desert? You said you loved me and would do anything for me?"

"I said no such thing," protested Ken.

"You definitely said you would help me, and I just want to drink the coffee you offered. Some sailor tied these knots way too tight."

"Ken. The ropes are hurting me." Annette continued.

"Look, even if I could escape, where can I go? There are Duncan's sailors everywhere."

"All right. I will loosen the ropes so they don't hurt you, and I'll be right back with your coffee."

"Thanks so much, Ken," Annette said, her head on one side drawing his attention to her eyes.

Ken was captivated by that face, and hardly noticed what he had done to the knots. "Thanks, that is so much more comfortable,"

Annette said clenching her wrists as tightly as possible against the ropes.

She blew him a kiss as Ken disappeared into the crowd. Annette relaxed her wrists and slipped her hands easily through the loops of rope. She pulled her Bedouin robes around her to conceal her hair and face, shouldering a small barrel, she made her way to the French boat. She handed the barrel over, grabbed the sailor's hand, and showed her face to him.

"Please help me, I'm a captive of these Arabs," she said quietly.

The sailor nodded his head, and let her pass onto the small craft. Once in the French boat, she went to the stern where an officer sat. She took off her hood, revealing her flowing dark hair. The aspirant in charge was astonished to see a woman.

"Mademoiselle!"

"I am a free French woman, made captive by these Arabs. Please take me to your superior officer."

"Oui Mademoiselle. Sit down please, and we will try and get away before they realize you are missing."

To Annette's relief the boat pulled away without a hue and cry being raised. As soon as they were on board the 80 gun *Franklin*, the aspirant took Annette down to the midshipman's cabin. Hammocks were rigged on the first gundeck, and a multitude of different smells told her she was aboard a ship where hundreds of men lived in close proximity.

She was not left with the Aspirants for long. Twenty minutes after coming aboard she was taken to see the officer of the watch, the second lieutenant, to whom she gave a brief version of her story. He seemed somewhat indifferent but, when the watch changed, brought her before Captain Saulnier.

"Mademoiselle, I would be obliged if you would tell your story to my superior, Rear Admiral Blanquet. Today he meets with our commander in chief, Admiral Brueys on *L'Orient*. I myself have to go there. But first, Mademoiselle, I think you should be more suitably attired."

"Captain, is it possible to find a woman's dress on board a French man-of-war?"

Saulnier smiled and, fifteen minutes later, Annette was presented with a choice of several dresses, which he told her were found among some theatrical costumes. Relieved to swap her robes for a dress that would cover the sailor's duck trousers and blue striped cotton shirt that served as her underwear, Annette swiftly changed and eventually they set off, with due ceremony, in the captain's barge. Finally she was going aboard *L'Orient*. Unfortunately, when she arrived admiral Blanquet sent word that he was too busy to meet with her, but would attend to her in due course. Meanwhile one of the lieutenants would be happy to give up his small cabin for a few days.

The days passed, and still Annette waited. Blanquet left the ship so she applied to see Admiral Brueys himself, but received firm but polite refusals from his secretary.

"Perhaps next week, Mademoiselle. I am sure the admiral will have time for you next week."

"I have vital information that could change the course of the war with England."

"Yes, I am sure that you have Mademoiselle. Next week!"

Despite being put off, Annette continued to spend her days in the wardroom, hoping to gain an audience with the Admiral. As she sat wondering if she would still be in there after the battle started, Lieutenant Reynard strolled in, and stood looking down at her.

"Ah! Mademoiselle Annette. May I sit down?"

Annette regarded Reynard as if he was some kind of small worm that had crawled out of her lunch.

"Monsieur, you may go to hell where you belong. I have no use for your pretended chivalry."

"Ah I detect that you are a little upset by our last encounter in the desert. You were not comfortable in the Sheikh's harem?"

Annette folded her arms and glared at him.

"It is a good thing that I found you, Mademoiselle. Come, we are practical people and we have the same goal. We both wish to see France win the coming battle."

Annette continued to sit without speaking.

"I will take your silence as agreement. I presented Admiral Brueys with the device that you so kindly gave to me . . ."

"That you stole from me!" Annette interrupted.

"As you wish, Mademoiselle. Nevertheless, I could not make the device show the charts, or convince Brueys that he needed to take action to guard against the danger of the advancing English fleet. I do not have the details that you have learned, Mademoiselle. It is details that win wars. When I learned of your presence, I accepted that we must act as a team."

Annette merely looked at him without acknowledging this statement.

"You will find that Admiral Brueys is a very busy man. The chances of you getting an appointment with him are very small."

Annette said nothing.

"Very well, we can continue as enemies, and let the battle take its course, or we can declare peace, and go together to convince the admiral. What say you?"

Annette sat very still. This man, who had abandoned her to life as a slave in a harem, was now offering to conduct her to see the Admiral. Perhaps the smart phone was the key that allowed a mere lieutenant to get access to the fleet commander, but without her knowledge it was useless. He needed her and she needed him. She just had to make sure that she could put as much distance between them as possible after the meeting.

Very slowly Annette nodded her head in assent.

Chapter 13

Prelude to Battle

Wind NW. Lat. 34 deg 56 min Long. 23 deg 4 min. Fresh breezes & clear weather. At 7 Cape Mantipan E & S 7 leagues. At 5 AM S Wt point of Candia S & E Dist. 5 or 6 leagues. Killed two bullocks at 3 PM the Culloden *cut a French brig out of harbour attended at Divine Service Fleet in company.*
Lieutenant's log, HMS *Vanguard* 29/July/1798

Sunday 29th July 1798 2 PM — Annette

It was not until Sunday that the fleet commander acknowledged Lieutenant's Reynard's request. He had a meeting with the senior men of the fleet but, if there was time afterwards, he would grant the officer a brief interview. He understood that the lieutenant's female companion was in possession of information that may be of interest. The pair was conducted to a small anteroom outside the Admiral's quarters below the flag captain's cabin.

"You better let me do the talking, Mademoiselle, unless I ask you to fill in some detail. Is that understood?" Reynard said firmly.

"Very well," said Annette. These two words carried the loathing she felt for this man.

Two officers, accompanied by a young aspirant of about ten years old, entered the room. The senior man whispered into the boy's ear, and he scuttled off to some other part of the ship. Annette assumed that the officer who brought his son to war must be the flag captain, Casabianca. She looked at him and remembered what she had read about the battle. Annette experienced a wave of sadness as she recalled that the boy would perish with his father on the burning deck of this very ship.

The captain's deep voice reminded her that she might be able to change that bleak future. "Lieutenant, Mademoiselle, I understand from Captain Saulnier that you wish to speak to the fleet commander. Normally this would be impossible, but some recent events have brought your case to his attention. You will be permitted a short interview. You will speak only when directed to do so, and you must answer questions posed to you with the truth. Only under these conditions will you be permitted to approach Admiral Brueys. Is it agreed?" These remarks were mainly directed at Annette.

She smiled. "Yes, oh yes!"

"Lieutenant, you will follow me. Mademoiselle, we shall call you."

Annette stayed seated, anxious that she may not get her chance, but ten minutes later she was summoned into the admiral's cabin. The spacious room was built for a man at the pinnacle of his career. Two 18 pounder guns dwarfed the furnishings. Even this cabin would be cleared and used when the fighting started. She was directed to a chair in front of four admirals, who sat behind a desk that was barely large enough. She was grateful for Casabianca's presence beside her, offering a small measure of support.

"I am Comte Honoré Joseph Antoine Ganteaume, rear admiral and chief of staff to Admiral Brueys. We have heard from Captain Saulnier something of your incredible story, mademoiselle, a story supported by this officer." The admiral indicated Reynard. "It seems that others are convinced by it and of course there is this . . . ." He paused, obviously searching for the right word, and finally settling for: "bauble," as he pointed to the table where the smart phone lay.

Annette could not tell if it had been switched off, or if Reynard had run the battery down.

"This object was given to Commodore Casabianca by Lieutenant Reynard." He looked at Reynard scathingly and continued, "It is unfortunate that this officer could give no satisfactory demonstration of its function, otherwise we would not have to trouble you, Mademoiselle. The Commodore here does not believe in your story. It is difficult for men of action such as ourselves." He paused and looked at the other officers before continuing.

"Mademoiselle, you have come here of your own free will?"

"Yes," Annette said simply.

Admiral Ganteaume was used to addressing a court martial, and he continued in a ponderous style: "Lieutenant Reynard has told us that you have come with knowledge of the English fleet. The manner by which you gained this knowledge seemed rather strange to the officers, but . . ." He turned to address the admirals. "We have agreed that we shall hear evidence from this woman?" There were general noises of assent around the cabin. "Mademoiselle if you please."

Annette got to her feet and rather nervously turned and addressed herself to the assembly before her. This was what she had been waiting for. She had one chance to make a difference. This was her opportunity to avert what she saw as an historical tragedy that should never have happened. She picked up the smart phone from the desk and switched it on. She held it up and, when the device powered up, sent a silent thank you that the battery was not dead. She pushed a few buttons to bring up the chart of Aboukir Bay. As she did so a small man with somewhat pointed features walked into the room. He removed his naval hat to reveal long, prematurely white hair.

"Admiral Brueys, this is the woman of our discussion last evening. Mademoiselle Annette, Annette . . ." said Ganteaume.

He broke off to shuffle through some papers on his desk when Brueys spoke. "Please gentlemen won't you sit down. I must apologies for my lateness. The dysentery takes all my strength. Mademoiselle pray continue with your story. We are most intrigued."

Annette breathed deeply, relieved that in this cabin the ship's human smells had been replaced by a fresh sea breeze blowing through an open stern window. She cleared her throat. Admiral

Brueys looked pale and sick. She was shocked at his appearance, but stayed focused on the task at hand.

"Thank you Admirals and Commodore for letting me speak. This device contains charts of every navigable waterway on this planet. She pressed some more buttons and held it up again.

"This is the chart for Aboukir Bay." There was a stirring and Ganteaume started to say something but Brueys held up his hand for silence, so Annette continued. "This chart is dated, and if you gentlemen care to look at the date you will see that the survey was made in 1997, 200 years from now."

The voices broke out again, and again Brueys raised his hand. He gently took the device from Annette, looked at it, and passed it round, nodding at her to carry on.

"You will observe, gentlemen, that it would be impossible to build this object today, yet it is merely a machine. A machine that can store information, words, pictures, and even sounds. This is all made possible by," she paused and ended rather lamely with: "electricity."

Somebody muttered something about Benjamin Franklin then, after a long silence, Admiral Brueys finally spoke. "Mademoiselle, how old are you?"

"I am 26 years old, I was born in 1989 and I travelled here through a doorway from 2015. I have no understanding of it. I found it, and I took advantage of it."

This time the outburst lasted several seconds before Brueys again called for silence.

"We find it difficult to believe such a story, Mademoiselle, yet it does provide an explanation for the presence of this device. Lieutenant Reynard was convinced that you have information about English fleet movements. We are all most interested to know if they will attack us?"

"Gentlemen, in a few days from now, on the 1st of August, at about 2 PM lookouts will sight a fleet of English ships of the line, under the command of Rear Admiral Horatio Nelson, approaching from the direction of Aboukir Island. At approximately 5 PM these seventy-four gunships will sail into the van of the French line in ideal sailing conditions with the wind on their beam out of the northwest. The first ship will lead an attack on the shoreward or larboard side of the line. The English ships will double the French line, and destroy the first few ships followed by those at the centre. A few hours later only four French ships will be in seaworthy condition and able to leave Aboukir Bay. The rest of the fleet will surrender or be destroyed."

Admiral Brueys smiled at Annette as he spoke: "My dear, you know little of naval tactics; the English will most likely attack the rear of our line, and they will certainly not launch an attack so late in the day. Fleet actions cannot take place at night, as there would be nothing to stop a ship from firing on his own fleet! Besides the line is protected by the fort, and the shoals will prevent an attack from that direction. When I fought under Admiral De Grasse against the English in '82 I learned how to form an impregnable line at St. Kits. The British admiral Hood showed how it should be done, and in doing so his fleet withstood our advance for days. An 'L' shape with the heel of the 'L' into the direction of the wind is an impregnable position and that is what we have!"

"Admiral, I am not telling you what might be. I am telling you what I learned in my history books. The shore batteries are in poor condition and cannot protect your line. Furthermore Nelson is not a conventional tactician, and his ships will attack in an unconventional manner; he will ignore the onset of night. Three lanterns at the stern of each English ship will distinguish them and let them be known to each other to avoid accident."

Admiral Ganteaume coughed and leaned towards Brueys speaking in a low conspiratorial tone that Annette could barely hear. "Francois, I have a report from Brigadier Potevin; the woman is correct about the shore batteries."

Brueys looked concerned. "Why are you telling us these things you say are in your history books? Are they immutable forces of nature that we have no power to change?"

Now Annette was not sure of her ground, and the admirals heard it in her voice. "I believe, Admiral, that you can change these events." She pointed at the smart phone. "This device is not mentioned in the history books. I have caused history to be changed by simply bringing it here. I believe you can change the fate of the fleet and, indeed, the fate of the world."

This last statement provoked considerably more comment from the admirals, but Brueys exerted his authority with his quiet voice. "Mademoiselle, we are interested in what you have told us. Pray tell me everything about the battle you remember from your history books."

Annette took up the tale. "From my studies, I have indeed learned some things that may be changed. I have a number of points, Monsieur that you will not like because they are contrary to decisions already made, however these . . ." she paused and searched for the right words, ". . . items have been identified after 200 years of scrutiny by others, better qualified than myself to judge naval tactics."

Admiral Brueys laughed. "I am not a proud man, Mademoiselle; already my colleague Admiral Blanquet believes that our fleet should be mobile rather than fight at anchor. I am bound by General Napoleon's orders, but I am interested to hear what history will say about us, so pray continue."

"Admiral, there are many reasons that the English fleet, according to my history books, triumphed over the French. First the frigates are the eyes of the fleet, yet you have not sent them to find Nelson, whom you know to have been in Alexandria the day before your own fleet arrived."

"Mademoiselle you have already told us when the English will arrive!" Ganteaume looked around for support. Annette was encouraged when his colleagues did not respond, choosing instead to focus their attention on her.

"Monsieur, I understand that many of your men are ashore at this moment?"

"It is true that the fleet is undermanned, because Napoleon has taken so many of our sailors for his army." Brueys was almost apologetic.

Annette said matter of factly: "I believe you are reduced from 11,000 to 8,000 men. Many of your shore parties will not return in time for the battle unless you make it so."

Brueys nodded. "Very wise Mademoiselle, a surprise attack at this moment would be very bad. What else have you noted?"

"The ships are moored too far apart, and although you ordered it, not all of the ships have set cables to their neighbours. So it is possible for an English ship to break the line. Moreover, some have not properly affixed cables with springs to their anchors, or indeed anchors at each end of the ship. These vessels can swing at anchor instead of providing a stable platform from which to pound the enemy. The English can easily sail between the ships and around the van of the line. There is space enough for an English seventy-four to slip between the *Guerrier* and the shore, and . . ." she paused for dramatic affect: ". . . they will!"

Brueys looked up briefly: "I sent *Guerrier* and *Conquerant* to fill the gap in the line between *Spartiate* and the shoals." Almost to himself he added: "Perhaps this was not enough."

There was a brief pause, but before any of the admirals could speak Annette continued. "*Le Conquerant*, is 50 years old and her timbers are so weak that she can only mount 18 pounders on the lower gun deck and yet she sits as number two in the line as Nelson will attack from the er . . . wrong end."

Annette paused for breath and Reynard interrupted. "Messieurs, my young friend presumes to tell you your business. Perhaps I should take her back to her quarters now?"

Brueys stared at him. "You will do no such thing, lieutenant. We are fascinated, are we not messieurs?" There were sounds of agreement. "Please do not interrupt further, or I shall have you removed. Pray continue, Mademoiselle."

Annette saw the anger in Reynard's eyes, but she did not need him now. "Nobody expects an attack from the shoreward side. Indeed many of the ships will not clear for action on the larboard. The debris left on deck will make it slow for each ship to bring its guns against the British. Tins of paint on *L'Orient* will cause a fire. *Le Peuple Souverain* will come out of line and allow the English to break the defensive position." She rushed on, letting everything she knew pour out. "Many of the ships are equipped with 36 pounder guns. The shot is so heavy that it takes twice as long to load and the rate of fire falls below an acceptable level."

"Wait, Mademoiselle," it was Villeneuve who interrupted. "You said that the *Conquerant* mounts only 18 pounders not 36; now you say that this is a good thing?"

Brueys came to Annette's rescue. "I believe Monsieur Villeneuve, that this woman is only reporting on what she has read about the forthcoming battle. She does not claim to be an expert on naval battles; am I correct, Mademoiselle?"

Annette looked gratefully at the Admiral, and nodded.

"Pray continue," said Brueys.

Annette took a moment to better recall what she had read on the subject. "The history books record that the guns are triggered using slow-match rather than the faster gun-locks. The delay causes the shot to be sent high as the ship rolls up. This is good for destroying the English rigging, but with the English ships at anchor it is important to aim low to hit their guns. Nelson will take advantage of the wind direction blowing from the van to the rear of the French line. He will attack the van, knowing that his ships can easily sail down the line but the French ships at the rear cannot sail against the wind to meet him. An alternative disposition may be to anchor the first ships as close as possible to the shoal in the north, with the line running south-west from there, turning through 90 degrees, to run south-east. Any attack from the east or the south would be facing a contrary wind. Nelson will round Aboukir Island from the north-west, so an attack from the north-east is unlikely as Nelson would have to tack."

The torrent of words ceased leaving Annette slightly breathless. It was as if she had run out of words. She sat upright and still, feeling her heart beating faster than she had ever known.

Brueys pondered Annette's words. The eyes of the admirals upon him, and at last he spoke.

"Do you happen to remember, mademoiselle, the composition of the English fleet?"

"From what I read, Nelson will arrive in command of thirteen English seventy-fours and the Leander, an older 50 gun ship; he has no frigates."

Admiral Blanquet cleared his throat. "Francois, if there is truth in what she says, then perhaps it may account for the behaviour of two English frigates sighted by our fleet on the 21st. What was it they were doing? Why did they flee from us? We thought perhaps it was a want of victuals. If they had been in contact with the larger portion of the English fleet they would have investigated further. Perhaps they were working alone, seeking the English ships?"

Admiral Brueys looked grim. He nodded his agreement to Blanquet, then turned to Annette whose face was quite pale. She looked exhausted.

"Thank you Mademoiselle for your frank and candid assessment of the battle, and for the opinions, that you voice. I have never before heard such opinions, or indeed such knowledge, over matters of battle from a woman before. You may leave us. Please take your rest." He rose and so did all of the officers. "Vive la France."

Tuesday 31st July 1798 6 PM seventy-four — Ken

Ken sat in the stern of the *Caliph*, while the crew, sensing that punishment was imminent, cleared to the bow.

"Perhaps Mr. DiPalo you would care to explain how Annette was able to leave this ship despite being bound at hands and feet?"

"I am very sorry, Sir. I believed that she was sincere when she promised to stay where she was; she pleaded with me to loosen the ropes."

"In this century, under the articles of war, the punishment for aiding and abetting an enemy, is death."

Ken went white with shock. He hadn't thought of the consequences, or that Annette would be seen as an enemy.

"Your future depended on preventing Annette reaching the admirals. When and if you get back, you will be facing the unknown."

Ken looked at Sarah, who seemed to him to show little sympathy. He said nothing and Duncan continued.

"You are fortunate this is not technically a vessel of the British navy, and I am not bound by the articles. The crew expects me to punish you, so I will. You will scrub the ship from stem to stern, including the heads."

With that remark Duncan went forward leaving a crestfallen Ken to go about his duty.

"I would probably have believed her too," said Sarah trying to help.

Ken brushed away her proffered hand. "No you wouldn't!" He stalked off amidships half way between Duncan and Sarah.

Sarah followed him, worry lines creasing her brow. Ken was sitting staring over the side at the French ships of the line. He ignored her, but she sat beside him anyway. "Ken, I understand how you feel about Annette. Nobody blames you for being taken in by her," said Sarah in a soothing tone.

"It isn't just that. I feel we have become a burden to Duncan and when we came here, I wanted to . . ."

"Wanted to what?"

"You know, I wanted to make a difference, be somebody in this century, leave my mark!"

"Have your name in the history books so you can read about it when you return?"

"Something like that," he admitted sheepishly.

"Ken you are a vital part of the organization, you are the one responsible for negotiating with the fishermen. Without you we would not have any connection with the Orient."

Ken smiled at her. For once he realised that she was not only sincere, but also trying to be a friend to him.

Tuesday 31st July 1798 7 PM — Sarah

As the sun set Sarah sat in the stern of the *Caliph*, her eyes drooped, and her lips turned down. She put her head in her hands and sighed. The last days of waiting had been almost unendurable. She worried about Annette and her friend, Marie-Paule. She could not help thinking that if the French discovered that Marie-Paule had helped Duncan escape the prison on Malta, she would suffer the harsh retribution of the navy. Above all was her fear that Antonio was lying dead somewhere — another unknown soldier. Now she had Ken to worry about too. She knew that Annette had reached the admirals because, a few days after Annette disappeared, the whole fleet started to move. First, the frigates and brigs weighed anchor and left the bay, then the great ships of the line repositioned further West. The new line changed direction and composition so that the ships were moored closer to each other and much closer to the shoals. She watched the great battleships manoeuvre into line just to the East of Aboukir Island. *L'Orient* was again in the centre, with half of the ships in line to the north, and the rest angled to the south east.

"Another few hours and they should all be in place," Duncan noted. "You can see that the leading ships are much closer to each other than previously, and all their springs and anchor cables are set. Tomorrow Nelson arrives, but the rest of the French ships will be at anchor, waiting. We shall see if this has an effect on the outcome.

"You think the Admiral would listen to a young woman?"

"I do not claim to know how she achieved her goal, but it is clear that Brueys has been warned of Nelson's approach. By the looks of the fleet disposition, he's corrected his former errors. He's even sent out his frigates."

"Except for the smaller one," remarked Sarah.

"That's the 36 gun frigate *Sérieuse*," muttered Duncan with his telescope pressed to his right eye.

"There's been a lot of activity this afternoon. Boats leaving and returning," she added.

Duncan seemed interested. "Has there indeed? I have been too busy watching the ships of the line. That is very smart of you to notice, Sarah." He paused, looking around to make sure they were alone, but most of the hands were on shore to avoid the overcrowding aboard the djermes.

"What did you observe?"

"I think the frigate's crew is being ferried over to the larger ships of the line."

"Quite right! Now, if I just had my first Lieutenant here I could make a plan to take her!"

Without thinking Sarah said: "Yes, I miss him too."

While they talked the *Nile Sheikh* arrived and dropped anchor beside them. After a few minutes Hidey arrived on board.

"Report," said Duncan curtly.

"Nothing more than you can see, Sir. We have been keeping a good look out for the flagship since the ships started repositioning." Duncan looked at him expectantly. "Sorry to say, Sir, but there is no news from Marie-Paule."

The captain nodded his understanding. "We need a ship. It is most vital that we find Nelson, and warn him of what is waiting for him in this accursed bay. We dare not put to sea in the *Caliph* or the *Nile Sheikh*!"

"Them smaller craft, including the frigates, left the night afore last. Only the thirty-six gun frigate, *Sérieuse* has returned, and if I may make so bold, Sir, it is my observation that in the last few hours more than 150 men transferred from her in the direction of *L'Orient*."

"Well done, Hidey," said Duncan. "Our midshipman here has been watching the transfer also. If the frigate had been at full compliment then there could be a hundred sailors left in her, perhaps too many for our band of sixty men to overpower. It would still be easy for them to cry for help to the neighbouring ships; nevertheless this is our best chance yet."

Duncan leaned over confidentially, while Sarah edged closer. "Mr. Smith, your job is a good deal harder than mine. I have only to cut out a highly undermanned frigate. You have to deal with the largest warship in the world with a full complement of fighting men. Our work is done here, I am sorry to say we have failed in our task. We shall cut out *Le Sérieuse*, find Nelson, and return with him. When we return I want you to take the smaller djerme and half a dozen volunteers. Perhaps you can find a way to take Marie-Paule off *L'Orient*."

Hidey laughed. "Have no fear capitan, she will be safe, and what would be the point if there was no challenge?"

The moon was waxing, a thin crescent in the sky; he had missed the dark of the moon but it was still dark enough for his purposes.

"Am I to come on the cutting out expedition?" asked Sarah.

"If I had my way I would put you ashore out of harm's way," declared Duncan. "But I suppose you'd better come along."

Tuesday 31st July 1798 1 PM — Marie-Paule

Marie-Paule had been transferred to a small cabin. She stayed behind the locked door worrying what Reynard might do to her. On day three there was the clunk of the key in the lock, and she backed away from the door, more afraid than she had ever been in her life. The lieutenant, accompanied by a man in Arab dress, walked into her cell.

"We meet again, Mademoiselle."

She couldn't help but step back away from the lieutenant, but the Arab moved behind her.

"That man behind you is Monsieur Samir. He is quite ruthless and will stop at nothing to get to the truth. I am telling you this because I want you to help me find your friends. I am sure you will cooperate. Now, tell me, are you acquainted with a Mademoiselle Annette?"

Marie-Paule was confused. What did Reynard want of her?

"I do not know her," she lied.

"Perhaps you have not met her," continued Reynard, "but your friend whom you helped escape, Lieutenant Duncan I believe he is called, knows her well."

"Monsieur, I have nothing to hide from you. I was attacked by the turnkey Danton. That pig would have killed me were it not for the Englishman who came to my aid. I saw no option but to flee the prison to get away from the turnkey." Her instinct was to stay as close to the truth as possible; even giving away the fact of Duncan's presence may be fatal to him.

"Indeed Mademoiselle, you have told us you were a prisoner of Duncan. He forced you to leave Malta on the brig, *Palerma*. Now you are back with us."

Here Reynard paused and sat down on some small spars beside Marie-Paule, taking her hand. She immediately pulled away, repulsed by this man with the large nose and unkind eyes, but he was stronger than he appeared and held her hand hard, crushing her fingers. "Mademoiselle, you are not telling me the whole truth. I can sense these things. This woman Annette told me something very strange." He paused and looked at Samir, who nodded his agreement.

"It is a curious, almost an unbelievable thing, but she said she came from a future time. She believes this wholeheartedly. Annette

244

told me that there will be a battle right here in Aboukir Bay. It will be a victory for the English. ”

She leaned forward slightly, trying to move further from Samir whose presence at her back frightened her more than did Reynard.

“Moreover, Monsieur Samir here met a boy called Ken, who told him about some fleet manoeuvres, confirming him to be one of Annette's companions from the future. Now my child . . .” Reynard leaned his body closer to Marie-Paule. She could feel the warmth of his breath in her face, and smell the garlic and wine he had consumed for his lunch. Reynard looked into her eyes, as if searching for the truth. She squirmed, but could not break away. “You will divulge what you know about Lieutenant Duncan. I think you are reluctant to tell us, but I want you to know that this is for France, and if I have to cause you some discomfort to persuade you to talk to me, I will.”

At this moment he squeezed her hand very hard, causing her to wince in pain. She tried not to cry out, but a soft gurgling noise came unwittingly from her lips. She turned her body to escape from his crushing grip, but she could not, so she raised her other hand to push Reynard away. Samir grabbed her arm, twisting it behind her back and forcing her to her knees. Reynard sat astride her back, causing her to feel pain in three places at once. Marie-Paule sucked air into her burning lungs, feeling that her back was about to break.

“I know nothing of this man. He helped me to get away from Danton, and I helped him to get out of the fortress.”

Reynard smiled at Samir. “La redoutable poire d'angoisse?” He enquired.

Marie-Paule had heard of the 'poire' and knew that its use would lead to a painful death. She felt as if she would give her life to protect Duncan, but withstanding pain was a different matter. She twisted her head around to see Samir take up a red velvet bag. He held the bag almost lovingly, reaching in to withdraw a large metal device with four prongs that were currently closed together. Samir worked a small handle, making the prongs slowly move away from each other. Such a device could be inserted in some body opening and made larger inside. Marie-Paule did not want to know where they intended to put the poire, so she screamed as loud as she could.

The men seemed to be too interested in their new toy to be bothered by Marie-Paule's screams, and Reynard held the violently struggling woman down while Samir inserted the device into her mouth. She shook her head from side to side in an effort to dislodge the horrible metal prongs that hurt her tongue and dug into her gums, but most of all she did not want to give Samir any opportunity to turn the handle that was geared to push the metal arms away from each other, enlarging the whole gruesome gadget in its place.

Reynard held both her arms very tightly while Samir caught the poire, and held it fast. Any movement Marie-Paule made now would only cause her more pain.

"Mphmmm mmm !!" She exclaimed trying to look pleadingly into Samir's cold, grey eyes.

"Perhaps the woman has something to tell us? Perhaps she does not? We shall test her courage a little further to make sure that she knows we are men of purpose." With that Samir turned the handle a few degrees, and the sound of excruciating pain that escaped from Marie-Paule could be heard some distance away in other compartments on the orlop deck.

"She is in extreme pain, there is no doubt," Samir said with a smile.

"Perhaps we should relax a little and see what she can tell us now," replied Reynard. Marie-Paule hoped that she could detect concern in his voice.

"I think not my friend," Samir. "I have known women withstand several more degrees of angle before I hear their jaw break. I will turn it a little more to make absolutely sure there is no doubt in her mind that she must tell us everything she knows."

As he began to twist the device further the door burst open, and an officer accompanied by several crew members, walked into the cell.

The first lieutenant held his sword to Samir's throat. "You will stop and desist or else suffer death." As Samir removed the poire, the lieutenant continued. "Arrest that man!" Two crew members moved forward and held Samir's arms.

"On what authority do you disturb our investigation?" Reynard protested. "I represent the Directoire, I represent France, I am France!" As his voice rose out of control, Commodore

Casabianca entered the crowded cell accompanied by his son. Marie-Paule started to weep, and the boy rushed forward to give her some water.

"That is as may be, Sir; however, on this ship I am the law. In the French navy we do not entertain torture or torturers," said Casabianca.

"I am in charge here," Reynard argued. He reached into his pocket for the letter from Langon, and placed it in the Commodore's hands. "This letter confirms that my orders come from the highest levels!" He turned quickly to the men holding Samir. "Release that man; he is an emissary from a powerful sheikh. This woman is a traitor to France, she is being held on the orders of Admiral Brueys."

The sailors held their ground and did nothing. Reynard moved forward and yelled at the sailors. "Release that man I said!" Still they stood silently.

"Monsieur Reynard, if you try to countermand my orders I will consider it incitement to mutiny, and have you arrested. These men will obey me, as will every other man on this ship. I suggest you lodge your complaints to the Directoire when you return to France," Casabianca spoke quietly and as he turned to go, he added: "Monsieur, you have lost your ship, and must face a tribunal. In the mean time you are assigned to the frigate *Sérieuse* under Captain Martin. You will report to him immediately. Am I understood?"

The cold realization came to Reynard that he was still a mere lieutenant facing a senior officer. He bit back his anger and saluted. Casabianca took in both of them as he spoke.

"You may take this *emissary* with you," and to his first lieutenant he said: "Please restore the mademoiselle to her former cabin," He turned and followed his first officer, who was gently guiding Marie-Paule out of the cabin.

The sailors started to lock the cell behind them, and Reynard had to move fast to escape being locked in. Soon after, the torturers and their dunnage, were ferried over to the *Sérieuse*.

Tuesday 31st July 1798 11 PM — Ken

A few hours later the djerme slid silently through the darkness and came to rest under the bow of *Le Sérieuse*. The frigate was still transferring some of its stores, so the boarding netting had been temporarily cleared. The French crew had rigged a number of lanterns to enable them to work in the darkness. Ken could see now that Duncan's timing was perfect. The sailors on board the frigate were unlikely to observe them hidden under the bow, and Duncan had manoeuvred his vessel so that their mainmast yard touched the big ship's starboard anchor.

Duncan led the boarders over the yard onto the anchor. He gained the cathead and disappeared onto the deck of *Sérieuse*, while Ken and the others followed him as silently as possible. The group was silent, but Ken became aware of the sounds of fighting from the stern of the vessel.

"What the hell is going on? Is the vessel already under attack?" Ken whispered.

"Perhaps there are others interested in cutting out this ship. We shall work our way sternward and find out. Remember, use firearms only as a last resort; we do not want to alert the rest of the fleet." Duncan was gambling on the other ships being fully engaged with repositioning.

Hidey caught Ken's arm and held him back. "Never mind lad, just remember to hold yer cutlass like I told yer. It's a heavy weapon, so use the weight. Don't forget yer footwork; try to create an opening. Tempt the bugger in and if it ain't working, and all else fails, chuck the bloody thing point first and hope it sticks the enemy!"

Ken was shaking with anticipation. It was not just the enemy that scared him. He was horrified by his desire to join the fight and this newfound lust for blood. With a shout, some French hands came swarming up a companionway directly behind them. Ken turned and parried a vicious blow as a French sailor swung at him with a cutlass. He could not believe how hard the man had struck; the blow spun him around causing him to drop onto one knee, temporarily confused. The sailor lunged and, as the blade sliced towards him, Ken felt adrenaline flood his body. He reacted quickly with a parry as hard as a blow, following through by pushing on his own blade giving him the impetus to roll out of the way.

248

Ken had never faced people intent on ending his life. He felt an insane anger build within him. He must kill his attacker at all costs, so with a war cry from his belly, he ran back into the fray. He never found his original opponent for a new blade swung from his left. He cut downwards, pushing the enemy cutlass out of his way and ran into the waist of the frigate. The enemy was a hardened topman, who had boarded ships on many occasions and he came after Ken.

From the corner of his eye, he saw both bin Kabina and Hidey coming to his rescue.

"Christ! They think I'm an easy target," thought Ken, the bloodlust growing stronger at every attack. His brain told him to run, but instead he watched the man carefully, and feinted to the left, so his attacker drove into the gap on the right. Anticipating, Ken turned the blade with his own and let the momentum carry the blade forward towards the topman's unprotected side.

Caught by surprise, the topman brought his cutlass up, stepping to the left to avoid the blow, His inexperience catching up to him, Ken raised his weapon to deal a lethal blow, but this time it was the topman who changed direction at the last minute, catching Ken with his cutlass still high in the air, leaving his body unprotected. Fortunately the young man had learned his lessons well from Hidey and, arching his body to avoid the blow, he spun around to catch the Frenchman unawares on the right arm. The topman went down howling with pain. Sweat poured into Ken's eyes. He could barely see, and his heart pounding so much, it felt to Ken as if his life was over unless he killed his attacker. He dashed towards his opponent, who was up on one knee, so Ken drove his blade into the man's torso, screaming as he did so. Death was instantaneous, but Ken could no longer control his body. He hacked at the dead man, again and again, long after he was dead.

Hidey grabbed Ken's arm. "Enough! Vent your rage on the live ones."

The youth got control of himself, breathing so hard he felt like he was running a marathon. He advanced on the nearest group of resistance with Hidey beside him and Francisco not far away. The flat side of a wildly swinging boarding axe caught him in the shoulder, pushing him towards the larboard rail. The bay was calm, but there was enough of a roll that he missed the rail, falling against the side of the ship.

A French sailor saw him slip, and seized the opportunity to hit a man who was down. This time both bin Kabina and Hidey were engaged. As Ken started to rise he caught sight of the whirling blade coming towards him. He threw himself out of the way, sliding across the deck, and rolling into a crouched position. The sailor changed direction continuing his charge, but Ken's blade came up swiftly. The man was going too fast to stop, and he skewered himself on Ken's cutlass, falling on Ken with the blade imbedded in his chest. Blood soaked into Ken's shirt, and he struggled out from under the dead man in horror. He stood on the deck unarmed, and slightly dazed as another Frenchman ran towards him. Before the man struck, Francisco jumped in front of Ken pushing another cutlass into his hand while he fended off the attack.

Ken stood without an opponent for mere seconds before a man twice his size, who handled his cutlass like it weighed nothing, addressed him with a guttural challenge. The young man fended off a blow from the giant, although he knew that he could not last long against such an opponent. Deciding that discretion really was the better part of valour, he ran across the deck, but the huge man followed. Ken was desperate; he couldn't survive another blow from that man's blade. Hidey's words came back to him and, as the French sailor rushed forward, Ken threw his cutlass at him. The man kept coming, bowling Ken over, crushing the breath out of him. Ken struggled, thinking this was his end when, with a mighty heave, he escaped from under the weight, and realized that his throw had actually worked. His cutlass was embedded in the man's neck. As he shook his head in amazement, bin Kabina advanced to help saying: "You fight like a camel in heat."

Ken smiled and, still not knowing if he was being insulted, he grabbed his cutlass, and ran towards the sounds of clashing blades. By now they had reached the semi-lit quarterdeck, where the sailors were already engaged with another attack. He joined Duncan by the ship's wheel as Hidey and George came up beside them.

"Wot's goin' on 'ere captain? That there is Abdul, from the slave galley, and they got him pinned to the wheel!" George exclaimed.

Ken looked across the deck to a most confusing scene. A group of men were engaged with the French crew but these were real Arabs, not Maltese sailors dressed up. Abdul was fighting for his life against two opponents; it was only a matter of time before he succumbed.

Fear gripped Ken as he saw Abdul's face, remembering every awful minute on the galliot, and the bloodlust drained out of him. He felt so tired he just wanted to sit down. It was a strange sight, Abdul fighting two men; a uniformed French lieutenant, and an Arab.

For a brief moment, Ken was back on the slave galley. His old enemy, Samir stood fighting once again with Abdul. Feeling almost too tired to understand the scene, he fell in behind his companions, who circled behind the combatants. His attention diverted, Abdul slashed out towards Duncan, who, aided by Hidey, quickly disarmed the Arab captain.

Abdul stepped back, but Samir was close enough to draw blood with his sword point. Abdul turned to face him, so Samir pushed Abdul back towards Duncan, while the French lieutenant seemed content to watch. Duncan called out to Ken: "to me!" So saying, he pushed Samir aside into the hands of the Maltese sailors, while George and Hidey held the French officer at sword point. Samir threw down his sword.

"Captain Duncan, the galliot that held us captive continues to haunt us. That's the galley captain and that there other Arab was 'is second in command until there was a mutiny," said George pointing with his cutlass.

The combination of the two attacking forces had driven the French crew below decks. With the hatches guarded, there were now two roughly equal forces facing each other across the quarterdeck. The bulk of Abdul's sailor's, having subdued the French crew, rallied behind their Rais. They faced Duncan and the Maltese sailors.

"Put this man in irons," he ordered, pointing at Samir, who was led away, with no complaint from Abdul.

At that moment the French lieutenant who had been fighting Abdul was brought up under guard, along with his superior officer. The captain bowed briefly to Duncan, presenting him with a rather bloody sword.

251

"I am Captain Martin, and this is Lieutenant Reynard. The other lieutenants are dead."

Reynard straightened to attention, a half smile on his face. "Monsieur Duncan, we meet again."

Ignoring Reynard, Duncan accepted the sword. "Sir, you may remain at liberty if I have your parole that you will not fight for the enemies of his Britannic majesty."

Martin laughed. "Sir, the tide of battle may turn at any time. You are in the midst of the French fleet. We will remain with the crew below until the outcome is certain." Duncan looked at Reynard who started to say something, but a glare from his superior officer shut him up. Duncan nodded, and the pair was led below.

Sarah, who had been amongst the reserve force, came aft to bind Abdul's wounds. The Rais brushed her aside, addressing Duncan, to whom he undoubtedly owed his life.

"I am Mohammed Abdul al-Bashir, my grandfather's, grandfather's, grandfather fought under Turgut Re'is. Who by Allah are you?" Ken stood in his robes and thought that in the dim light with the Bedouin robes, Duncan had been mistaken for another Arab. No doubt the Arab dress had been the only reason that a three way fight had not developed. When Duncan did not understand, Abdul reached forward and uncovered Duncan's head. He let out a great roar of laughter when he saw that he was facing an Englishman. He raised his cutlass to salute Duncan. Mistaking this action Manu came forward, and threw himself between the two men with a yell.

"Rais, I owe this man my life, and that of my son Talibah. I beg you by the love of Allah to preserve him. Take mine if you must have a life."

Abdul lowered his cutlass and stared incredulously at Manu. "By Allah, I thought you were drowned on that accursed brig! How came you to this French ship?"

"The same as you, Rais, we are here to take the ship. These men are the crew from the Maltese Brig that was sunk by this very frigate!"

Abdul threw his great bearded head back and laughed again. "Still I am plagued by the ghost of that accursed brig!" To Duncan he said; "You are indeed the captain of the brig?"

Ken, looking battle weary, translated and a conversation developed between Abdul and Duncan.

"By what right are you taking this French ship?" Duncan demanded.

"I have more right than a Christian has to betray other Christians! You may leave this ship and go in peace, or fight to the death with my crew."

It was clear that the two sides were fairly evenly matched in numbers. Duncan said: "Alone neither you nor I have enough men to work this ship. Together we can at least fight with the guns on one side."

This thought had also occurred to Abdul, and he said quite reasonably. "Captain, we are surrounded by enemies; perhaps if we cooperate we can at least leave Aboukir Bay."

"Since we are the only fluent French speakers, I will take *Le Sérieuse* out of the bay, and then we can negotiate. Agreed?"

"Agreed!"

With the French crew secured below decks, Hidey took the helm and Duncan very quietly gave orders to get under way. Meanwhile the sailors did what they always did, they weighed anchor and let fall the sails. Neither language nor culture prevented them from accomplishing their tasks. The large djerme at the bow, and Abdul's two djermes at the stern, were taken under tow. The sailors knew they might be useful and were easy to cut loose if necessary. Captain Martin informed Duncan that he had very little chance of sailing out of the bay without being stopped by one of the French seventy-fours. In answer to this Duncan posted a number of hands to guard the French sailors.

"If any man tries to raise the alarm, shoot him."

"Aye, aye, Sir."

Le Sérieuse got under way with whispered orders. The fore lacked a top mast, so she quietly slipped her anchorage with reefed topgallant on the main.

The big warships were on the move, and the frigate had to sail before the wind, parallel to the line of seventy-fours. If any of the enemy ships noticed anything unusual about their night manoeuvre they might be stopped and questioned. They came about to put the wind on their larboard quarter ready to round to the rear of the line of ships to escape the bay. The stern lights of *LeConquerant* hove into view, her boats out with a kedge anchor to haul her against the wind, following the admiral's orders to reposition.

The leadsman of the *Sérieuse* whispered their depth to the next man, and so it was passed to the quarterdeck. They followed a narrow channel with the dangerous shoals to leeward and the French ship to windward. When they were thirty yards sternwards of the seventy-four, a voice rang out in the darkness,

"Qui est la?"

There was a pause and the captain said very quietly,

"Who has the best French accent?"

"That would be Mr. Malette, Sir." Hidey emphasized the Mr. and looked knowingly at Duncan who smiled in agreement.

"Please tell them who we are, Mr. Malette."

"Aye Sir," Sarah whispered quietly before she called into the night, *Sérieuse*."

There was movement on the French quarterdeck, and a voice said in French: "Admiral Ganteaume would speak with Capitaine Martin."

"He is indisposed, Monsieur," Sarah responded after a moment's hesitation.

"Indisposed? We spoke with him only yesterday. Heave to. We shall send a boat."

"Monsieur, we have special instructions from the commander in chief. We must make all speed." Duncan looked at Sarah in admiration.

"What is your mission? I have not received these instructions."

"It is Admiral Ganteaume, he is the chief of staff, and would have been informed. Tell him, ... Tell him something," whispered Duncan.

Admiral Ganteaume was alert and suspicious, and replied before Sarah had time to think. "Heave to, Monsieur or we will fire upon you!"

"Put your helm down, Mr. Smith and run before the wind," ordered Duncan.

"Sir, we shall come under their stern chasers, in less than one minute," Hidey warned.

"If the wind holds we will be out of sight in under five minutes, time for two rounds."

There was no doubt that the French ship had not been fooled. They heard men running across the deck, and commands rang out to prime and load the nine pounders that were mounted in the stern gallery. Two minutes passed and no shot was fired. *Le Sérieuse* was almost lost in the darkness when the wind died and she stalled. She was still a dim white shape to the gun crew of the seventy-four.

"Get down!" shouted Duncan as both nine pounders fired simultaneously and they heard the shot whistle overhead, flying through the rigging. "That was a warning, most likely the next shot will be grape or canister."

Ken stood beside Sarah, willing the wind to return to take them out of danger. Meanwhile the night was so still and silent they could hear the sounds of the nine pounders being reloaded. Duncan silently pointed aloft where the tattle tales on the main topgallant sail flapped slightly as the breeze came back. Very slowly, the ship started to pick up speed. For a brief moment Sarah gripped Ken's hand in the dark, as they heard the rumble of the French guns being run out again.

From the vantage of the French ship, the stern of *Le Sérieuse* must have been disappearing into the darkness. The French did not know whether they would turn left or right. Duncan said very quietly: "Helm alee Mr. Smith. Gentlemen, lie flat on the deck."

If the French captain had outguessed them, they would be sliced to bits by grapeshot at any second. The report came, the guns fired and Sarah heard the shot spin away into the night and splash harmlessly into the sea on the starboard side.

"'Ee guessed wrong 'ee did!" laughed Hidey.

Le Sérieuse headed out of the bay under cover of darkness, and came about on the opposite tack beating against a contrary wind on an interception course for Nelson's fleet.

"Will they pursue us, Sir?" Asked Ken.

"Not with a ship of the line. We are lucky the other frigates are not in the bay," replied Duncan.

As they sailed to safety, Abdul appeared out of the gloom, unmistakable with his great bushy beard, and they all knew it was time to talk.

The officers retired to the great cabin to negotiate the basis of their cooperation. Ken understood that there was a choice, Duncan must either fight Abdul or settle with him. Ken summed up a long speech from Abdul. "Sir, the Rais wants the vessel as a privateer, but he is happy to have the English captain's expertise as a sailor, and will make you second in command. He will not release control of the vessel to you."

Duncan shook his head. "I will not release the vessel to this pirate!" They ate and drank in the cabin late into the night while unknown to Abdul they sailed towards the rendezvous with the English fleet. Finally, they reached a tentative agreement.

Duncan, tired and exasperated stood up and the room fell silent. "Rais Abdul, I require this ship, under my command, for two more days, and afterwards my officers and I need passage directly to Malta. In two days you are most welcome to take command, and to employ any of the Maltese sailors who wish to ship with you."

Ken translated and heads nodded around the table; this could work. Abdul, ignorant of the coming battle, said: "It is agreed then. In two days the ship will be mine, and provided I take you to Malta, you will make no more claims to it?"

Duncan looked him right in the eye: "I swear to you as a British officer I will relinquish command to you and you alone. Until that time I need complete control."

Abdul bowed slightly, clasping his hands together as he did so. "There is one more condition. The man who was attacking me when you so fortuitously arrived is a criminal by the name of Samir. You must understand that he is my prisoner."

Duncan agreed and soon after, Abdul made his berth in the gun room with the other officers, while Duncan took possession of the amply appointed captain's cabin. Just before the meeting broke up, Ali, the galley master from the galliot, quietly moved, unnoticed by anyone, from his listening post outside the door of the great cabin.

Wednesday 1st August 1798 10 AM — Sarah

Moderate breezes and fine weather. Saw Alexandria bearing south. Set driver and main sail and haul'd to the wind.
Lieutenant's log, HMS *Vanguard* 1/Aug/1798

A cross wind caused the ship to roll more than usual waking Sarah. Her red rimmed eyes gave evidence to a very long day followed by a short night. One of the Maltese hands relayed some gruff orders, which Ken translated.

"A duty roster has been prepared, and Mr. Malette is wanted on the quarterdeck."

She reported for duty, but Duncan barely acknowledged her, as he paced the windward side relentlessly. Hidey stood beside the helmsman, keeping a close eye on the sails.

"The captain is a-exercising 'is brain, and if I were you I would not disturb him."

"Thank you, Mr. Smith, Sir." replied Sarah with a smile.

"Mr. Malette, being as how we don't actually have a purser aboard, the captain has ordered me to take stock of the ship's stores. I would be obliged t'ye if you would do some clerking and write up what we has and what we has not."

For the next few hours she did her duty for Hidey, writing down everything they found. When they came back on deck the former owners of the frigate crowded the companionway past a phalanx of muskets and over the side into the waiting djermes. Duncan watched them go and pointed to the south.

"I trust you are not worrying about our French foes, Mr. Malette? We are within sight of the Pharaoh's tower, and the djermes will carry them there safely. They will not be able to return to Aboukir before tomorrow."

"Sir, We have done an assessment of the ship," said Sarah.

"Rais Abdul wanted to dump the French sailors over the side," said Duncan, his mind still upon the French crew until Sarah handed over her notes. "Thank you, Mr. Malette. Our worst problem is lack of men. Not much we can do about that until we meet the fleet. I see we are missing some spars. Is there nothing we can use to replace the fore topgallant mast?"

Hidey looked apologetic. "The ship's stores have been stripped. Without doubt it was to supply the needs of the larger ships."

"Very well; It would seem it is my fate to be in command of a ship lacking some vital spar. We shall see how well she sails without."

"On deck there!"

Sarah stood on the quarterdeck watching the green seas battering against the ship as they made their laborious zigzag course northwest into the prevailing wind. The ship rolled and pitched in the brisk Mediterranean chop. They were still in sight of Alexandria, near enough to see the French tri-colour flying from the town. They tacked frequently, and Sarah kept out of the way staring up at the rigging on the mainmast, wondering if she would get the chance for some climbing exercise when one of the Maltese topmen indicated she should follow him.

She reached the main top, exhilarated and the topman pointed up to the main cross trees, where they were very short handed. He had no idea that this midshipman lacked any training, but Sarah had no difficulty keeping up with him. A hail from the lookout attracted her attention, and she saw the masts of a large ship a long way off to windward. Pawlu Pullicino saw Sarah and whispered in her ear in French.

"Please tell the captain, and only the captain, that it could be a man-of-war."

Sarah returned to the quarterdeck and informed Duncan, who responded to the news by spending some time studying the approaching vessel.

"What do you say to that Mr. Malette?" Duncan asked as he handed his telescope to Sarah.

Sarah saw the sails of a three masted ship to the northwest. "Is it Nelson?" she enquired, quietly.

"That is an English seventy-four gun ship of the line bearing a lot of canvas including her royals. I have just informed Abdul that

258

we are intercepting a merchantman; please don't say anything to disillusion him on this point. We are downwind of the fleet, so that seventy-four has the advantage, the weather gage as it is known."

By the time it was clear to all on board it was a British man-of-war approaching, there was no escape. A scuffle broke out by the fo'c's'le and Sarah thought the Arab sailors might try and seize control of the ship, when a splash in the water a few feet off their starboard bow put a stop to any thoughts of insurrection.

"That would be *HMS Goliath* under Captain Foley sending a shot across our bow. Mr. Smith, I must have left the French flag flying and in the face of such a superior force, you would oblige me by lowering our colours, and check the flag locker for something British."

"Aye, aye Sir."

Abdul clambered onto the quarterdeck and Sarah, sensing trouble, nimbly got out of his way. Before he could speak, Duncan said: "I am a British navy lieutenant. I will tell them that this ship is our prize, Rais Abdul, and the Royal Navy will honour that. You will be compensated."

Abdul shrugged, apparently accepting the situation; there was nothing he could do with the seventy-four so close. A boat was lowered from the *Goliath* and as it approached, Sarah heard a cry from the boat's crew. A midshipman in the stern pointed up at the mast. Duncan smiled at her and looked up to where English colours now flew above the French, indicating that *Le Sérieuse* was an English prize.

"Must be a little disappointing to *Goliath's* prize crew."

A lieutenant from the *Goliath* came aboard and addressed the quarterdeck. "William Laurence, first of *Goliath*."

"Welcome aboard Mr. Laurence, I am Lieutenant Duncan in command of *Le Sérieuse*, thirty-six gun frigate, late of the French navy. Your admiral will be pleased to learn that vice admiral Brueys and thirteen ships of the line are moored in Aboukir Bay."

"Am I to understand that this French ship is your prize?"

"Indeed it is, Sir."

"Why then, pray, did you fly the French colours?"

"Perhaps it were better if I explain in person to Captain Foley."

Duncan turned to his officers. "I am going aboard the *Goliath*. Mr. Smith, you will assume the position of acting lieutenant; the ship is yours until I return. Mr. DiPalo you will accompany me."

"Lucky bugger," Sarah whispered as Ken went over the side. "I'll never forgive you if you meet Nelson."

Wednesday 1st August 1798 2 PM — Ken

By the time they ferried over to the *Goliath*, several of the English ships of the line had caught up. After a brief conversation Captain Foley took Duncan and Ken over to the flagship, *Vanguard*.

Ken could not believe his fortune. Here they were on the day of the Battle of the Nile in Nelson's cabin. He took in the comfortable quarters, saw the sea sparkling through the Admiral's ample stern windows. Everything seemed so unreal. Within a few moments, Nelson appeared from his inner sanctum and greeted them. He was a short man with a very large hat. When he spoke, however, Ken sensed the quiet power behind the voice.

"Mr. Foley, the French flag was sighted in Alexandria, and now we learn that the entire French fleet has turned up in Aboukir Bay. Who brought you such a secret?"

Foley bowed slightly. "My lord, may I present Lieutenant Duncan, responsible for cutting out a French frigate, and bringing us the good news."

A smile played across Nelson's fair face. "With what force, Mr. Duncan? Tell me more, but first are you a relative of Lord Duncan of Camperdown perhaps?"

"Only a distant cousin, my lord," replied Duncan.

"What an action your relative fought last year eh what? How d'ya come by the frigate? By God we could have used some frigates last month!"

Foley interjected, "He was in Aboukir Bay last night, my lord. Cut her out from under the Frenchies' noses!"

"Where did you get a crew for her? Or is this midshipman your only officer?" Nelson chuckled at his own humour.

"Mr. DiPalo is one of two midshipmen who helped with cutting out *Sérieuse*."

Ken saluted by raising his hat, in the fashion taught him by Duncan, and wisely said nothing while his captain continued.

"The hands are Maltese and Arab sailors, my lord."

Nelson frowned. "Really? Pressed men are they, Mr. Duncan?"

Duncan cleared his throat. "I was on a mission to Malta when the French invaded back in June. I managed to escape their prison and followed their fleet in a brig supplied by the Maltese revolutionary navy. We were attacked by this very same frigate, and she sunk the brig. We survived, trekked across the desert, and took our revenge by cutting out *Le Sérieuse* in Aboukir Bay."

Nelson laughed and shook Duncan's hand. "Well done, and welcome to our band of brothers. Mr. Duncan, I am going to put you back aboard your frigate with an epaulette." Turning to his clerk he said, "Make a note of that mister. Remind me to put it into the next admiralty dispatch. How many hands do you have aboard, eh Duncan? Can't let you have too many more, barely got enough to man the guns in the seventy-fours. What d'ya say, Foley?"

Captain Foley nodded his agreement, and the admiral looked expectantly at Duncan. "I have near 20 and a hundred my lord, including one Maltese and two British petty officers," he paused and added almost as an afterthought, " . . . and two midshipmen."

"Half a crew is better than no crew. Your guns will be of little use against their seventy-fours. I will send you a signal lieutenant. I want you to keep station on the *Vanguard*, and relay signals to the fleet while the light holds. It is late, but I intend to attack tonight. Now Lieutenant, pray tell us what you know about the French disposition? Aboukir Bay, you said?"

They moved towards a chart of the region laid out on a large table. Ken stepped towards the table when Nelson said: "Ever been aboard a seventy-four, young man?"

"No Sir, I have not."

Nelson turned to one of his attendants. "Perhaps the duty lieutenant would find somebody to show the young gentlemen around the ship while the senior officers confer. Oh, and signal the fleet to prepare for battle!"

261

A few minutes later a smartly dressed midshipman appeared. Ken thought the boy to be no more than fifteen or sixteen years old, yet he was an officer, with power over the men. His uniform coat was immaculate, and he held himself smartly.

"Richard Walker, midshipman. On our way into battle, I am to show you the ship, Mr. DiPalo."

Ken reddened at the sarcastic tone, but nevertheless enjoyed the conducted tour around the *Vanguard*. The ship was a giant compared to *Le Sérieuse*, and Ken was interested in every aspect.

"You do well for space aboard a ship of the line," said Ken.

"You have not been at sea for long Mr. DiPalo." It was not a question.

They returned by way of the quarterdeck where the duty lieutenant was writing in a large log book. The officer was expecting him. "Well Mr. DiPalo, the word is that you and your shipmates cut out a French frigate."

"Aye, Sir, we did!"

"I will attend to my duty, Sir," Walker glared briefly at Ken before he left them.

An idea occurred to Ken. "What happens to the log book, Sir?"

"It is just our daily record of events on board."

"But what happens to it, Sir, once the book is finished?"

"It's admiralty property. They have a huge archive of them in the cellars under the Ripley building."

At that moment Nelson and the other officers appeared on the quarterdeck. The duty lieutenant saluted the admiral. "Lieutenant we should record this historic event. Allow these two officers to enter their names in the log. Duncan stepped forward and signed his name as bidden and Ken followed suit.

Nelson looked to sea before observing: "We'll be at Aboukir in under three hours, and we shall attack before the light fades. Better call the men to eat, we'll clear for action — then up and at 'em, eh?"

Chapter 14

The Battle of the Nile

At 55 minutes past 8 the Orient of 120 guns took fire. The ships ahead still keeping up a heavy fire on the enemy. At 10 the L'Orient blew up with a violent explosion — The enemy ceased firing. 10 past 10 perceived another ship on fire which in two minutes was extinguished and a fresh cannonading begun. 20 past ten a total cessation of firing for 10 minutes when it was renewed again.
Lieutenant's log, HMS *Vanguard* 1/Aug/1798

Wednesday 1st August 1798 5 PM — Sarah

Sarah stood in the main crosstrees high above the deck watching the magnificent seventy-fours under full sail heading into battle. The fleet formed a line fully ten miles long, with *Goliath* and *Zealous* out ahead of the trailing ships. They were quiet and gentle, like elegant antelope out for exercise, their deadly purpose still hidden. The excitement mounted with the sound of the drummer beating to quarters, the flags flying, and the white caps dancing on the water under the brisk northwesterly.

Vanguard kept her place in the centre, sixth in line, her signal flags in view from *Le Sérieuse* as ordered. Sarah remembered what she had read about the fate of the last ship, HMS *Culloden*. She was slow because she towed a prize, a merchant vessel containing some much sought after wine. Soon Nelson would order *Culloden* to

263

abandon the wine and catch up with the fleet, so she would be the last ship to round Aboukir island. Not having the others in sight, Captain Troughbridge would run aground due to his reliance on an outdated chart. Sarah thought she could help prevent this calamity, so she came down from her perch via a backstay as Hidey had shown her, and presented herself to Duncan on the quarterdeck. They were sailing close in to the shoals, and the leadsman kept calling the depth. The rest of the hands were busy wearing ship to round the island.

"Sir," said Sarah eager to share her idea.

"Mr. Malette, you have something to say?"

"Might we drop a marker buoy to keep Culloden off the shoals, Sir?"

"My compliments, Mr. Malette, the order has already been given. We think alike!"

At the five fathoms call, there was a shout of: "Marker buoys away."

Duncan called out: "Mr. Kydd, if you please, hoist a signal to warn the following ships to keep to windward of the buoys."

Ken had spent the last few hours learning as much as he could of the signal book. He had been ordered to assist lieutenant Kydd, the signal officer sent by Nelson. At Kydd's command, he picked out the signal flags and ran them up the mizzen halyards. The signal was relayed by *Swiftsure*, and then taken up by *Alexander* and *Leander*. Sarah just hoped that it would reach *Culloden*.

They stayed more than a mile to the North of the island, more to avoid the dangerous shoals than to stay out of range of the ineffective shore batteries. A few mortars landed harmlessly short of the ship as they came about on the starboard tack to enter the bay.

"Signal from the flagship, Sir," said Kydd to Duncan, then to Ken he said, "What do you see, Mr. DiPalo?"

"Number forty five at the main and forty six at the mizzen."

"What does that signify, Mr. DiPalo?"

Sarah ever trying to be helpful, murmured quietly: "Attack the enemy's van and centre."

"Shut up, I know," hissed Ken. He repeated the order to Mr. Kydd, who relayed it to Duncan.

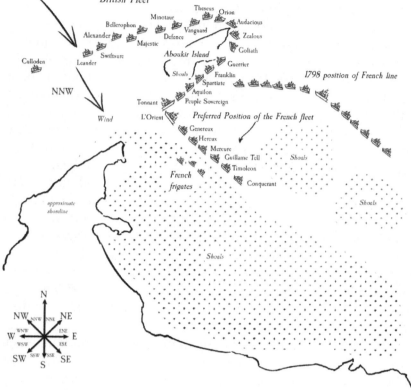

The frigate was positioned in the van, ahead and larboard of *Goliath*. Sarah sucked in a lungful of air, aware suddenly that she had been holding her breath as they approached the French line. The crew was silent; their ship would be first to come into range of the enemy guns. It would not take much for a nervous gun captain to fire a 36 lb shot at the frigate.

265

Hidey whispered in Sarah's ear: "Don' yer worry, Sir. Them Frenchies have got bigger fish to catch. They won't waste time with this little 'un."

As Hidey spoke, Duncan ordered the ship to steer out into the bay, to the west of the fleet where they could get a good view of the battle, and relay signals from the *Vanguard*.

The French ships formed an inside corner, two lines of warships set at right angles. The *Guerrier*, first in the French line, pointed her bow to the northeast. Her broadside packed a punch of over 1000 lbs of high speed hot metal. Sarah thought about the poor sailors of both navies waiting for the onslaught, each man praying he would not be obliterated by shot from an enemy ship. Captain Foley in the *Goliath* piled on more sail, urging his ship to be first to reach the deadly line. She was sailing directly at the *Guerrier's* bow, so neither ship could bring their massive broadside guns to bear on the other. *Goliath* slowed as the wind dropped suddenly and there was quiet. Sarah rubbed her sweaty palms on her jacket sensing a fast approaching disaster. The *Sérieuse* was close enough to *Goliath* that she could hear orders being given as Foley's ship manoeuvred towards the enemy. She heard the flap of a mismanaged sail on the seventy-four's foremast, and a sharp rebuke from the quarterdeck. Sarah remembered from her studies that it was Foley's brilliant move to go behind the enemy line of battle that had helped win the day, but what would such a move bring now?

The great ships drifted silently, almost in slow motion, when the *Goliath* slewed around to starboard, crossing the *Guerrier's* bow. In reply the French ship erupted with the sound of frantic calls and running feet as the crew heaved on the cable that would turn her to starboard. It was too late, and *Goliath* shattered the peace with a broadside that raked the *Guerrier*. More than thirty iron balls tore along the length of her gun decks, shearing off man-sized splinters of wood as they came through the wooden walls. The round shot turned over guns and cut away sheets and lines on her weather deck, while the splinters speared unfortunate sailors. At last the *Guerrier* came round on her cable, and the two decker fired all the guns that could be brought to bear on the English vessel. There was a tremendous roar as the French ship let go her broadside into *Goliath*.

With a great shuddering crash Foley's ship jarred to a halt. She had sailed too far inshore of the *Guerrier*, and despite frantic signalling from the frigate, the *Goliath* had rammed into the shoals. Now Sarah knew for certain that events had changed. What had originally been the move that made naval history had ended in disaster. She watched in horror as Goliath's foremast visibly shuddered on impact and the top mast rocked forward tearing rigging and stays alike. Lack of mobility did not deter Foley's gun crews, who were soon ready with the next broadside aimed low at the French gun decks.

Even as the British continued to pound the *Guerrier's* larboard side, the *Zealous*, second in the British line, sailed up on the French ship's unengaged side, dealing lethal blow after lethal blow. The *Guerrier* fought bravely as best she could on both sides, helped by the next French ship, the larger 80 gun *Franklin*, who had hauled on her cable to bring her forward guns to bear. The *Franklin* let fly at *Zealous* relentlessly. From her relatively safe position, Sarah's imagination pictured the terrible carnage on the ships of both sides.

Sarah thought about Marie Paule still aboard the flagship, stationed where the line turned to the southeast; at that moment the *Orient's* gun decks woke up to poke their muzzles out bristling like a porcupine. Positioned at the base of the French 'L' with her guns pointing straight at the bows of the British ships, she could rake each one as they made their way down this avenue of death. The raking fire was only slowed when the English flagship, *Vanguard*, dropped anchor across the corner, simultaneously taking heavy fire from the larger 80 gun *Tonnant* and *L'Orient*. The strategy worked, however, as *Vanguard* fully distracted *L'Orient*, preventing her guns from raking the remaining oncoming ships in Nelson's navy.

Le Sérieuse took her station by the *Vanguard*, feeling her way through the great foggy whorls of smoke, to get near enough to read any signals Nelson's ships might fly. Even to Sarah's untrained eye, things did not look well for the British fleet that night.

Wednesday 1st August 1798 5:00 PM — Annette

A few minutes after the order to clear for action, two burly sailors struck down the thin walls of Annette's cabin, and she was sent to help the surgeon in the cockpit on the orlop deck. She sat in a dark corner with her head down when the great guns started. Everybody in the cockpit, including Annette, was waiting anxiously, dreading the moment when the first sailors would be brought down. She was not looking forward to witnessing the kind of injuries that occurred in battles of this period.

As she brooded on the possible outcome of her interview with the admirals, she heard a heavy rumbling sound, like distant thunder, as the great guns were run out. She put out a hand to steady herself, braced against the storm to come. Then they started firing. It was loud enough that she prayed for it to stop, glad she wasn't on the gun deck. It took another fifteen minutes before one of the British ships was in position to fire a broadside at *L'Orient*. When the enemy shot hit, she and the ship shuddered with the impact. If history was unchanged, this ship would catch fire and blow up within a few hours, so she had better get off while she could.

The pounding of the guns echoed through the ship as Annette climbed a companionway to the lower gun deck. The gun crews were sweating, shouting, working at an unbelievable rate. She watched two men heft a 36 lb iron ball into the nearest of the great guns. Men swarmed around adding a wad, pushing down the wooden ramrod, and stepping swiftly aside so the rest of the team could heave on the ropes to pull the gun up to the gun port. The gun captain touched a burning piece of nitrate-soaked rope, the slow match, to ignite the charge, and the gun roared and came rolling back as it recoiled. Men swarmed around once more to prepare for the next round. The smoke from the gun powder hung in the air, and Annette wrinkled her nose at the smell. She could hardly see the next gun, so dense was the smoke. As she watched, a return broadside from their unseen enemy smashed through the side of the ship and hit the gun that had just fired. The wooden gun-carriage was split in two, and the huge gun came crashing onto the deck rolling towards her. She ran aside but the gun had already stopped, crushing a sailor's leg in the process. The man screamed and, horrified, Annette fled up the companionway to escape the nightmare scene.

She emerged on the weather deck and ran forward. At the bow two big guns, the bow chasers, lay idle, as they could not be brought to bear on the British fleet. Earlier in the week a sailor had told her the larboard gun was affectionately known as "Le Chien" and the starboard was "Le Chat." When the ship was cleared for action these two were not considered so important. Some items had been pushed beside the guns for storage, including a coil of line and a few blocks along with two buckets of paint tucked in beside Le Chien. Annette remembered that they could be a fire hazard. She was wondering if she could warn somebody, but the crew seemed fully occupied. As she processed these thoughts a marine roughly shook her by the shoulder saying; "Non! Ce n'est pas sûr. Vous devez retourner ci-dessous."

"This paint . . . it must be cleared!" Annette pointed wildly at the offending buckets.

"Yes, yes, we will take care of it, but now, Mademoiselle, you must return below decks," the sailor replied, waving his arms agitatedly.

Annette reluctantly returned to the orlop, and for the next few hours worked steadily, shutting out the sights and her fears as best she could.

Anxious about the time, Annette asked the surgeon, who told her it was almost 9 PM. These people had one hour left to live. As she thought about how she might issue a warning, Jean-Marc, the quartermaster's mate, called to her to help carry one of his gun crew to the surgeon. A giant splinter had embedded itself in the man's lower leg, and she tied a bandage below the knee in an attempt to stem the blood pouring from the wound.

Jean-Marc grabbed her and pushed her towards the surgeon with a pleading gesture, but the prévôt d'équipage, a large man with an apron, covered in blood stains, grabbed Annette by the arm, and ordered: "Wait your turn!"

". . . but my friend is bleeding to death," cried Jean-Marc in despair.

The surgeon looked up. "Quickly, apply a proper tourniquet to that man!"

The prévôt pushed Annette aside, and she watched him apply a tourniquet that actually stemmed the blood flow from the injured sailor. Annette's instinct told her he was unlikely to survive despite this effort. She was jolted with the reminder that everyone in the orlop would die at 10 o'clock and, if she didn't get off this ship, her life was over, too. As she tried to slip away, a man ran into the cockpit, barring her escape.

"Monsieur, the admiral has been hit. He will not leave the quarterdeck, please come quickly."

The impact of the news hit her. The admiral had been hit, and events were following their historical course. Annette felt the panic rising within her as the too well-remembered passage echoed in her mind: "At 9 PM *L'Orient* will catch fire and within the hour will explode."

The surgeon finished his latest amputation, wiped his hands on his bloodstained apron and beckoned to the prévôt to follow him. The pair hurried away past the clamouring cries of injured sailors on the companionway.

Annette tried to follow when she felt a hand grasp her skirts, pulling her back.

"Mademoiselle, please help me!"

She tore herself away only to find her path blocked by a burly sailor carrying his messmate into the orlop.

"Where shall we put this man? Please, take his legs."

Annette staggered back, nauseous at the sight of the sailor's wound. An iron ball had virtually cut him in two, so that his guts were visible in the bloody mess around his mid-rift. Nothing could be done for this man, so she stopped long enough to help lay the injured sailor at the bottom of the stairs as there was no room anywhere else. She then bolted for the companionway, wanting only to get out of this hell hole.

As Annette made her way above deck, some chain shot brought *L'Orient*'s fore topmast crashing down around Le Chien. Sparks flew as hot iron scraped along the barrel of the cannon. The paint bucket was overturned, and the sparks ignited the spilled paint. Flames licked across the deck and caught the sailcloth before it could be cleared from a fallen yard. Three sailors rushed to the scene and poured water over the embryo fire. They had almost succeeded in putting it out when one of them gasped and crumpled to the deck, felled by a British sniper on the *Vanguard*. His companion barely had time to see where the shot came from before he, too, was hit. He gave a gasp as his life ran out. A third sailor came to their aid only to be taken down by another British sharpshooter from what was left of *Minotaur*. Temporarily left unattended, the flames escalated. Seeing the danger, the sailors rallied to put out the fire, but were thwarted, slammed to a halt by wave after wave of deadly grape shot. They were all dead if they could not stop the flames, and one sailor after another broke from cover and dashed in with buckets of water only to be shredded by tiny iron balls. Soon the fire spread, licking the bodies of the fallen men, and sticking to the highly flammable tar covering the foremast. A freshening breeze hastened the blaze in a feeding frenzy that spiralled upwards to consume the whole structure.

Annette watched it all, knowing that her efforts were useless. She had not changed a thing, history was history — the ship would explode.

Wednesday 1st August 1798 9:10 PM — Sarah

Sarah guessed that it must already be after nine o'clock when she saw the fire starting on *L'Orient*. Duncan had left in one of the boats to answer a summons from the flagship, and she breathed deeply knowing that the next hour would be the longest since the battle started. She was still on the quarterdeck watching the deadly fighting and listening to the sounds of broadsides rumbling in the night air. She watched Hidey shouting orders for a boat to be made ready. The boats had been busy all night, and Sarah concluded that he was at last fulfilling his promise to the captain and attempting to rescue Marie-Paule. She went below and filled a bag with bandages, ointments, anything that might be of use in the case of burns, and ran back up on deck just in time to see Hidey climb down to the waiting long boat. She stood at the rail trying to attract his attention.

"Permission to join the party, Sir?"

"You have no place here, midshipman, return to your station."

"My watch has finished and my medical knowledge may be of use in the case of burns."

Hidey pondered. Duncan had not given him any direct order concerning the midshipman, and her medical knowledge had been proven. "Come aboard," he said curtly.

She stepped down into the boat as he yelled: "Shove Off! Ship Oars! Give way!"

Nobody spoke as they pulled towards the sound of the big ships, pounding each other relentlessly like giant fire breathing monsters in the dark.

They pulled around the stern of the *Vanguard*, fire erupting from the guns in her belly sending hot metal into *L'Orient*. The British flagship paid no attention to the longboat, but now they had to cross the enemy cable hanging between the bow of the *Orient* and the stern of the *Tonnant*. The oarsmen on the longboat kept their silence. If either of the French ships recognized them as an enemy they were lost. The shoal water was a short way ahead and, once they were on the unengaged side of the three decker, there was little likelihood of anybody noticing them. The boat raced across the gap, aiming for the centre of the sagging cable where it touched the water. There was no challenge, but still Sarah kept quiet while the boat crossed the dangerous gap. Just as she thought they were safe, a stray ball from the *Vanguard* ricocheted off the wooden side of the French ship and smashed into their tiny, frail craft. The bow exploded into splinters, and within seconds Sarah found herself under water. She kicked off her shoes and struggled to break free of the inexorable pull of the sinking boat. She felt her lungs burning and, just as she was convinced she would drown, she broke surface with a pop. She could hear sailors struggling all around her, but could see nobody in the dark. She called out several times but to no avail. Reluctantly, she struck out for the nearest vessel, *L'Orient*. As she reached the towering side of the French ship, somebody threw her a line. She struggled up the side and swung over to a gunport level with the foremast. The thought occurred to her that it was a lot of work to climb aboard a doomed ship.

Wednesday 1st August 1798 9:30 PM — Ken

By 7 PM it was too dark for *Le Sérieuse* to read any of *Vanguard's* signals, so they sailed within hailing distance and anchored, ready to use the ship's boats to convey orders to other ships. Duncan launched both the cutters and the jolly boat in readiness. The boats were tethered on the leeward side so that the ship protected them from stray French shots. This strategy did not stop Ken from feeling vulnerable, sitting so exposed in an open boat. The guns roared and the night sky brightened with their flashes. Smoke drifted down the French line, here a thin mist, there so thick that it was hard to tell which ships were French and which were English. Occasional glimpses of the stern lanterns ordered by Nelson as the English signature reassured Ken that there were still English ships afloat in Aboukir Bay that night. The flagship signalled through the mist using two mizzen lanterns, and Ken took the boat over to *Vanguard* where he was given a message for *Orion*. Nelson wanted her to go to the aid of *Bellerophon*. Ken urged the boat crew to row with all speed, but when he got there, it was too late. The larger and more numerous armaments on *Le Genereux* had left her enemy mast-less, and all but silenced *Bellerophon's* guns, but he passed the message as ordered.

When Ken, sickened by all the death he had witnessed, returned to *Le Sérieuse*, he was almost dropping with exhaustion. He gratefully obeyed Lieutenant Kydd's order to grab some rest and made his way below to find some peace away from the endless sound of gunnery.

The hands were mostly engaged around the forecastle watching the battle, so the lower decks seemed strangely deserted as Ken descended to the midshipmen's berth. He was now accustomed to the low headroom on the gun deck, and kept his head down as he walked sternward in the dim light. He was passing number six gun, when somebody grabbed him from behind, covered his mouth, and jerked his arm behind his back in an expert fashion. He looked up into the eyes of a second man who rammed a pistol into Ken's face. Ken stiffened as he realized his captor was Samir.

"The boy who can read the future! Indeed you foretold of this battle."

Ken kept very still as his old enemy held the pistol close to his head.

"You look surprised. Possibly you did not know I was a captive on this ship? Perhaps you remember Brother Ali?" Ali Peshawar relaxed his grip. "You may release the boy. If he moves, I will shoot him."

For a moment the sight of his old tormentors sent him back to the galley and the bite of Ali's whip. Ken felt sick, and his eyes started to water. He forced himself to breathe.

"Here also is the man who turned you into a slave." Samir pushed Ken behind the great gun, where Abdul lay on the floor, his mouth gagged, with some thin ship's line binding hands and feet.

Ken's face turned pale remembering his stay aboard the galliot. He had kept himself apart from the Arab sailors since they boarded the frigate, but now he was forced to face Abdul who, even helpless, frightened Ken. Samir took a knife and loosened the rope on Abdul's feet until he was merely hobbled like a camel. He motioned Ali to the open port and, at gun point, Abdul crept out and down into a waiting jolly boat. Samir seized Ken by the arm and, waving his gun threateningly, pushed him out into the night. As he climbed down the tumblehome, the sound of the big 32 pounders from *Vanguard* and the other nearby seventy-fours was so loud that he found it difficult to concentrate. He looked past the *Vanguard* to the *Orient* where the fire was blazing with an unstoppable fury, lighting the whole bay with a red glow. Ali cried in alarm, even though there was a line of ships between them and *L'Orient*. Samir seized Ali's arm.

"You cry like a woman. The battle continues; it is usual for such things. Come I have accounts to settle."

Wednesday 1st August 1798 9:45 PM On board *L'Orient*.

The unstoppable fire swept through the upper gun deck. It was only a matter of time before it reached the magazines. By this

274

time, many of the sailors had already taken to the waters of the bay. The guns on the lower gun deck pounded away into the night as the ship died piece by piece. Despite this, Captain Casabianca would not lower his colours.

Annette was unsure of the exact time, knowing only that she must find her way off the ship. The smoke both obscured and choked the living, and two more steep companionways were between her and the weather deck. The first was so far unaffected by the flames, but as she climbed the second a boy, sitting on the stairs with his head in his hands, blocked her path. There were flames everywhere, preventing their escape upwards. Her first thought was to push her way past the boy but, as he looked up at her, she saw that he was the captain's son. Annette tore her eyes from his sorrowful face, and continued for two more upwards steps, but she could not just leave him there to die.

As she turned back to the child, she spied a bundle of unburnt sailcloth crumpled to the ground. Reaching into her bag, she took out a knife and cut two strips from the cloth. She soaked the makeshift masks in water from a nearby scuttlebutt, and threw them over the boy's, and then her own, head.

"Run!" She commanded as she grabbed his hand and pulled him to his feet.

The smoke seemed to be drawn to the companionway, but this was their only escape route. They raced through the flames up the stairs. When the boy paused, seemingly unable to move, Annette placed his hand on the strap of her leather bag, and instructed him to not let go. She led them on until, as they approached the exit, she saw that a flaming timber blocked their path.

Annette wrapped her hands in the water soaked sailcloth, and heaved at the burning spar until she had made a large enough space to crawl through. She popped her head up to find the weather deck was impassable. Even over the sounds of the ship's guns, she could hear the crackle of flames, and the screams of the fire fighters. Below, the smoke stung her eyes. It was getting worse; she knew she would asphyxiate long before the ship blew up.

She dropped back down the companionway coughing and spluttering, pulling on the strap of the bag, but the boy was gone. She called out into the smoke, but there was no sign of him. The fallen beam burned fiercely in front of her, preventing her from going back up, so she slid further down the steep steps, away from the flames. Stifling panic she ran deeper into the belly of the ship. The lower gun deck was still in operation, and the guns were firing regularly. Unbelievably, the men were hard at work barring her way. The smoke was different here, burnt gun powder rather than burning timbers. She retreated up to the middle deck where the guns had stopped, but she was faced with nothing but flames and smoke. The heat and lack of air combined with the dark broke her resolve and tears poured down her face. Still holding the wet sailcloth over her mouth she fell to the deck, sobbing.

Sarah was frantic, trying to find Annette, when there by a companionway her adopted sister lay coughing, cheeks streaked with tears. "Annette, I've been looking everywhere for you. Thank goodness you're okay. I have found a way out. The sailors have cleared the hatchway up there."

Annette coughed and spluttered, as Sarah pulled her to her feet. "Look you have to help me. One of our companions, a captive on this ship is trapped under a beam. I can't move it on my own."

Sarah led Annette deeper into the darkness, through the smoke. She saw a woman with her leg caught under some debris. Sarah found a wooden rammer, which she jammed under the heavy beam. In a daze, too shocked to ask questions, Annette helped push with all her strength, but the rammer broke in two, and the two women fell to the deck. Near the floor, the smoke was not so dense, and Annette's breathing was a little easier. She caught only a glimpse of the woman's soot covered face. Perhaps it was the smoke addling her brain, but she knew that face. She tried to say something, but her voice was dry, clogged with smoke. Just then, a sheet of flame exploded beside them sending Annette sprawling.

"We must find a bigger lever," said Sarah already disappearing into the smoke. She returned with a long piece of timber that looked as if it had been torn from the ship's side. This time, when the two of them leaned their weight, the beam shifted slightly. The woman trapped below screamed as they relaxed for a few seconds, then Sarah rallied and they tried again. It was enough,

276

and the beam moved releasing its victim. Out of breath, Sarah crouched down low to the deck.

"Marie-Paule! Are you all right? We have to get out of here. Annette, help us," Sarah's voice was as loud as she could be between the gun shots. Annette had been breathing too much smoke for too long, she was exhausted and dazed. She didn't move, but stared at Marie-Paule in confusion, so Sarah took charge and propelled the two women towards the stairway.

"If we don't get off this ship in five minutes, we'll all die. Annette, I have Marie-Paule. Go!"

Annette pulled herself together and ran up the stairs but, as she did so, the leather strap on her bag caught around the jagged timbers. The precious bag flew from her shoulder and fell to the deck. Annette turned to go back for it, but Sarah urged her forward.

"Keep going, I will get it."

Marie-Paule automatically picked up the bag and put it over her shoulder, while Sarah took care of the spilled contents. She threw some things in the bag, realized she was wasting precious seconds, then noticed one last item, Ken's little anachronistic smart phone. She put it in her pocket and returned to the stairs, but as she did so an air current from somewhere sucked the flames into the opening, and she and Marie-Paule were driven back. When they looked up, the way was hopelessly blocked, and Annette was gone.

Two French sailors pushed roughly past them and headed towards the bow section with faces that revealed their panic. Sarah grabbed Marie-Paule by the hand and searched for another way out from the dark, smoke filled, ruined gun deck. It must be nearly ten o'clock she realized. They had only minutes left.

The air seemed slightly fresher towards the stern, so they ran aft on the engaged starboard side, where they could see better. She could still feel the ship shudder to the irregular rhythm of the lower deck guns, along with the explosions as round shot from the English ships found their targets. Everywhere there was the chaos of overturned guns, smashed gun ports, smoke, and flames. Sarah's face was red with the heat and patched black with soot. A tear left a clean pathway down her left cheek as hope faded.

"Damn this dark century!" she cried making one last effort.

Marie-Paule, limp and dazed, followed mechanically behind her. The semi-dark hot, nearly unbreathable atmosphere only added to Sarah's confusion. She stopped as a huge flaming beam crashed down in their path; turning, she saw that the way they had come was also blocked by flames. The women shrank back from the heat and climbed over a ruined gun. The three nearest gun ports had been battered into one, but she would need an axe to make an opening big enough for a person to escape. She felt the clock ticking the final few seconds towards ten, and she pounded the side of the ship in frustration.

"Permit me, Mademoiselle. I think this axe will have more effect than your bare hands."

Sarah blinked in disbelief as a tall, uniformed figure swung hard and accurately at the weakest spot.

"Antonio!" She exclaimed, as recognition dawned. "Is it you?"

"We have more pressing issues to concern us," Antonio grunted without a pause.

It took only three accurate blows from the axe, and one by one the huge splinters fell away. Antonio pushed the two women through the opening, out of the burning hot nightmare. They dropped through the swirling smoke and into the cool water of the bay.

How Sarah had managed to clear the companionway, Annette did not know, but the opening had closed again behind her, and Sarah and the woman had been lost in the flames. She fought her way through the smoke to reach the weather deck. The ship was going to blow up, and Annette would have to swim for it. For a brief instant, she waited again for the other women, hoping they would appear, but they were sealed below decks. She knew that she must go over the side or die. Avoiding burning rigging, and fallen sails, she mounted more stairs and saw that there were still areas of the quarterdeck that were yet to be consumed. She ran towards the rail that guarded the side of the ship but tripped on the body of a badly burned seaman. Gagging at the sight, she picked herself up trying not to look at other bodies strewn across the deck. The fire had swept through the midships section, but when it reached the quarterdeck, the sailors had managed to put it out, despite the gunfire from snipers. This small haven was temporary, and she could see the flames creeping back. Below decks, it was moving inevitably towards the magazine.

She climbed up onto the bulwark and looking down saw that it was a long way to the water below. She hesitated, feeling that she had failed. Failed to save this ship, failed to save France, she had even failed to save her own sister. She looked back one last time at the fiercely raging fire and saw a boy standing alone amidst the smoke and flames. Was this the same boy she had tried to save earlier? Words from some half remembered poem sprang to mind.

The boy stood on the burning deck, whence all but he had fled.

She could not tell what made her run towards the boy, but she just couldn't leave him looking so helpless. Annette reached out and grabbed him.

"Quickly, we must get into the water."

The flame that lit the battle's wreck shone round him o'er the dead.

It was the same boy she had met before. He seemed bewildered.

"My father?" was all he said and made no move to leave.

The flames rolled on-he would not go without his Father's word. That father, faint in death below, his voice no longer heard.

"You must come now!" She grabbed his hand and, without a second thought to the awful drop, she pulled the boy to the rail. "Jump!" she yelled, and they took to the air. The impact with the water made her lose the small hand that had given her his trust. She kicked strongly, but the surface was far away. Her lungs were bursting when she finally breathed air. She looked around her.

"Where are you, boy?" She called.

There were men struggling in the water, and some boats had put out to try and take off survivors. She could see one of them close to her. Perhaps she had a chance, but where was the boy?

An English voice called to her: "Over here mate, grab my hand." Annette shook her head; the English had poured death into these ships for hours, then they send boats to take off the survivors? What a strange world. Ignoring the sailor's hand, she looked back into the water. "What happened to the boy?" Without thinking, she dived down, below the surface. Although she could see nothing in the churning, dark water, her arms thrashed wildly until, by great good fortune, she felt something rising towards her. She grabbed a handful of hair and kicked strongly for the surface. The entire episode took less than a minute and her rescuer was still close by as she reappeared above the water line. She pushed the half-drowned boy into the English sailor's hands, who passed the boy to his comrades and turned back for Annette.

"In you go sailor," then his eyes widened in shock."Er, begging your pardon, I mean, M'am!"

Wednesday 1st August 1798 10 PM — Ken

The jolly boat pulled steadily towards the shore, and Samir, still with a smile on his lips, sat in the stern holding a pistol in each hand pointed at the rowers. Ali sat beside him working the tiller. They pulled past the stern of the burning *L'Orient*, as Abdul and Ken heaved at their oars.

"You are the boy from the well?" Samir asked.

"Yes," said Ken.

"You speak Arabic," Samir stated more to himself than to Ken. "How did you know this battle was coming?"

Ken was not sure what to say. He knew that this man would kill him given any provocation, now as before, when he was stuck in the well. Perhaps he should keep Samir guessing so he would not pull the trigger. Samir laughed at his hesitation. "You are another one from the future?" Ken was so surprised by this remark that he missed a stroke and fell over his oar. Abdul seized the opportunity and jumped towards the stern, only to find Samir's gun in his face. "Not yet Rais! You will die when I think the time is right."

Samir threw his head back and laughed, slightly lowering the gun aimed at Abdul. The other remained pointed at Ken's head. "Perhaps this is the time to kill you both." He looked at Abdul, but his words were directed at Ken.

"The boy means nothing to me. I have no interest in keeping him alive, but you, Rais. Oh yes I want my fun with you!" He squeezed the trigger, but Ken dropped down in the boat. He cried out as the ball made a furrow in his dense black hair, but he was unharmed and lay still listening for an opportunity to slip over the side.

Abdul sat still, as Samir waved the second gun at him, thinking that Ken was dead. "I have changed my mind. You should thank me, death will be swift. He held the gun at arm's length, and was about to pull the trigger when there was an enormous explosion from L'Orient. They were frozen in that moment, Ken on his back, Abdul, and Samir half standing, the sky as bright as day, and the noise so loud that everybody in Aboukir Bay cowered in fear. Abdul and Samir fell simultaneously into the boat. There was a moment of stillness. Not a single gun fired in the bay, and every ship was silent as if time's own clock had stopped. Then the debris started to fall. It was like being in an avalanche. Ken covered his head, hoping that nothing big would fall on him.

Men in boats all over the bay looked up as the sky above them was filled with pieces of L'Orient. The crew of an English long boat that had ventured too close to the French flagship saw the colossal main topgallant spar come tearing through the air, part of a scorched sail still attached keeping the yard upright like a giant spear. It came from so high up that the men had time to watch its path, with the awful certainty that death from the missile was their destiny. The spar went clean through the bottom of the boat dragging lines and sheets, and tangled sailors to the bottom of the bay. Those who were left were tossed like pieces of a puzzle coming apart in the hands of an angry child, spilling them screaming into the water. A boat full of French sailors with *Genereux* written across the stern, watched silently, grateful for their luck as part of the bowsprit landed in the water to larboard. The tremendous splash rocked the boat and showered them with water. A man laughed at his good fortune as the entire spinning capstan splashed down beside him without harming a hair on his head. Then a comparatively tiny truck from one of the ship's great guns hit him a glancing blow on the shoulder, pushing him over the side of the boat, where he struggled for a moment before disappearing below.

The forward magazine on L'Orient was right below Le Chien, and at the moment of the explosion the big gun shot upwards

281

separating from its gun carriage with a force so strong it must have cleared twice the height of the main mast. The wind rushed past the mouth of the spinning cannon, making a sinister whistling noise. It described a parabola through the air, and fell back towards the bay. That same whistling sound was the last thing Samir heard as Le Chien slammed into him, cutting the jolly boat in two, landing Abdul and Ken in the water.

When Ken rose to the surface, he saw that Abdul was struggling.

"Help me!" Unbelievable to Ken, the man could not swim.

Abdul grabbed at Ken, and they both went under. As soon as he got water in his mouth, Abdul let go his grip. Ken came to the surface, looking about warily for Abdul. There was no sign of the man, and Ken grabbed at a floating oar, then turned at the gurgling rush of water right beside him and was suddenly in Abdul's iron like grip. For a moment he lost hold of the oar, and they both started to go down again, with Abdul kicking in all directions like a mad goat. As Ken felt the inexorable pull downwards his fingers touched the oar again, and this time he managed to hold on as Abdul's grip faded.

"Over 'ere! Two more, come on lads let's be having you."

Ken kicked out for the English long boat, and willing hands pulled him aboard. He gasped for air and looked down into the water, but there was no sign of his old foes from the galley.

Chapter 15

Escape from Egypt

Thursday 2nd August 1798 11 AM Aboukir Bay — Sarah

When Sarah awoke she was so stiff she couldn't move. Her journey from the water to the ship had gone by in a daze, but she did remember being picked up by a long boat. Finally she found the strength to climb the companionway and report to the quarterdeck where Duncan greeted her.

"Mr. Malette, I am very glad to see you recovered. What news of our people aboard the unfortunate French flagship?"

"Sir, I saw Annette very briefly. It is possible that she escaped the burning ship. Marie-Paule was in the water with me when *L'Orient* exploded, but I don't know where she is now. Mr Barbaro . . ."

"You saw Mr Barbaro and Marie-Paule in the water? What happened? Was she picked up?" Duncan grasped Sarah by the shoulders, his face a picture of desperation.

"Sir, there was so much flying debris . . . I lost track of them. I'm sorry."

"Well you survived, Mr Malette. Let's hope that your companions were also picked up," Duncan said, his face betraying no emotion as he let her go.

"She survived the explosion, I am sure, Sir."

Duncan nodded his head and turned to go.

"Sir, I have to report that Mr. DiPalo is not to be found on board," Sarah said.

"I am aware of this. We have lost more than our signal midshipman. The jolly boat is gone along with Abdul and an Arab prisoner who, incidentally, was last seen chained in the orlop."

"Are these events connected, Sir?"

"That is something we will have to investigate. I have sent . . . ."

At that moment a British officer from the *Vanguard* appeared on the quarterdeck. "Captain Saumarez sends his compliments, Sir, and requests your immediate presence aboard the flagship."

"Very well, Lieutenant. Mr. Malette if you're quite well enough, we shall take the barge."

"Yes, Sir. Thank you, Sir," replied Sarah eagerly.

As they neared the *Vanguard*, Sarah saw the appalling damage that she had received. Both her fore and main top gallant masts were gone, and her mizzen had been shot down to a stump. The weather deck was swarming with sailors clearing away damaged spars, tangles of rigging, and sails. The boat came around the ship to the starboard, the side that had been engaged all night. Many of the gun ports were battered into gaping holes, and Sarah caught occasional glimpses of chaos on the gun decks. Later she heard that less than half of the great guns had been functional when a cease fire was finally called.

Hidey, acting as the captain's coxswain, called: "*Sérieuse*" indicating that the captain was aboard. The hail was acknowledged, and soon they were tied up alongside. Sarah felt thrilled she might actually get to meet Britain's greatest hero. They were piped aboard and, to her joy, they were shown immediately to the admiral's quarters.

They entered a spacious day cabin, restored to order after the battle. The door to the sleeping chamber was open, where a number of officers were conferring around the bed. She leaned forward and peered through a gap in the crowd. At the sight that greeted her, she let out a small, but audible: "Oh!" There was Nelson, lying unconscious. An older looking, stern faced officer addressed a surgeon tending the admiral.

"Well, Sir, what are your findings? What is to be done? Is there yet hope for the admiral?"

The medical man looked up from his work, his face deeply troubled. Sarah wondered if the man was worried that his own fate was intertwined with that of his patient.

"Captain Saumarez, Sir, you wish my report on my patient, Sir Horatio Nelson Rear Admiral of the Blue?" The surgeon did not await an answer, but continued in the same official tone. "He has suffered a wound on the forehead, over the right eye. When he was brought to me, the cranium was bare for more than an inch; the wound three inches long. I brought the edges of the wound together and applied strips of . . ."

"Yes, yes, man, but give me your prognosis!" The medical officer started a long diatribe on purgans and anodyne, disculient embrocation, much to Sarah's amusement, when Captain Saumarez interrupted again.

"You will tell me what I ask, or I will eject you from this ship, Sir!"

The medical officer finally stuttered: "The blow to the head is likely to have been the cause of a concussion from which he may recover. His responses are conformant to a condition of coma. It is the body's way of slowing down sufficiently for the internal wound to heal. If the admiral receives complete rest, and is cared for in a hospital, his chance of recovery will be improved."

Saumarez addressed the other officers. "Do we have a vessel capable of conveying the admiral to a position of safety where he can receive such care?"

"Sir, I asked commander Duncan, who has command of the French frigate to join us," said captain Foley.

Saumarez turned to see Duncan and Sarah waiting just outside Nelson's sleeping quarters.

"Well, Duncan, it is necessary to convey the admiral to a position of safety. Is your vessel in good order?" Asked Saumarez, walking over to them.

There was a pause. It continued for long enough that Sarah was worried that Duncan was unwell, then she understood. Changes had occurred that clearly shocked Duncan. Sarah remembered that Nelson had indeed sustained a head wound. It was recorded in her history books, but it was minor, not something to put him into a coma. 'It is not written, time can be changed,' she told herself.

"Sir, the ship is in good order, save for the fore topgallant mast. Our company is but a 120 men, but I am glad to say that many of the men can hand, reef, and steer." Duncan reported.

"You have officers also, Mr. Duncan?" Saumarez asked.

"The crew is recruited from Maltese patriots and some Arabs, Sir. It is somewhat unconventional, but they made a fine job of cutting out the French frigate. We lack a sailing master, but I have an excellent first lieutenant, currently missing in the line of duty. We are hopeful for his prompt return. I have a second lieutenant loaned from the *Goliath*, and a few junior officers. We are well for petty officers, Sir."

Saumarez thought for a few seconds. "Very well, Mr. Duncan; you are confident this 'Unconventional' crew is capable of sailing the frigate to Naples?"

"I have confidence in the Maltese crew, sir. Captain Foley spared us a few hands."

"I can't promise you too many men, Mr. Duncan; we have repairs to make to get what remains of the fleet back to sea. We shall see what can be done. Transport for his lordship to your vessel will be arranged at the doctor's discretion. Foley here will find you a sailing master, and a few experienced hands. Perhaps Mr. Foley can give you a platoon of marines to make sure his Lordship is well guarded."

"My pleasure, Sir, but I will trouble you for the return of my signals lieutenant," interjected Foley. Duncan nodded his agreement.

Saumarez held up his hand and continued. "You will proceed with all dispatch to a safe haven for his lordship. The nearest would be Naples. Lord Hamilton, the British ambassador, is acquainted with the Admiral, and will no doubt provide his support. Last night the rear of the French line under Admiral Villeneuve escaped from the bay with six ships of the line. You will avoid contact with the enemy if possible. If you are unable to reach Naples, then continue to Gibraltar. You will await further orders once you have reached a safe port. You are watered?"

"*Sérieuse* is ready to put to sea, Sir."

"You will make all the necessary arrangements for the embarkation of your ship. Yes, what is it?" This last was directed to the medical officer.

"Perhaps by the morrow it will be safe to move him."

Saumarez nodded his assent. "Duncan, you will wait until you receive word that it is safe to transfer his lordship, at which time I shall give you your written orders, understood?"

"Aye, aye, Sir."

Saumarez softened a little. "It is possible Lieutenant, on successful completion of this mission your step will be confirmed; Godspeed to you."

Duncan could not prevent a broad smile from lighting up his face. He had his own ship, and the possibility of permanent promotion.

"One more thing, Mr. Duncan. Should your first Lieutenant have been lost to the battle . . . keep me informed."

They left the cabin and returned to *Sérieuse*. Duncan said nothing to Sarah, but she could sense there was something wrong, and wondered if it was merely worry about the journey or the fact that the past had been changed.

Once back on board, Duncan asked Sarah to come to his cabin.

"Annette has caused a significant change to the history of the world. Captain Villeneuve should only have two ships of the line, not six, and our fleet has been reduced to mast-less hulks. I cannot guarantee that things will be the same when you return to your own time."

Sarah stood there silently, what could she say?

"I have realized a personal dream. I am in command of an 18th century frigate, but I now have two problems. My first duty is to Lord Nelson. Getting you and your friends back to the gate will have to take second place. You understand?"

"Aye, aye, Sir," Sarah replied as she considered the implications of Duncan's words.

"For you and your companions to journey to a fortress held by enemies, on a hostile island where I have no business to go . . ." Duncan paused, significantly. "Is . . . is not going to be easy."

Sarah felt her heart sink. How was she to get home?

Thursday 2nd August 1798 2 PM — Sarah

When their meeting was over, Sarah left the cabin to find Ken waiting for her.

"Ken! What happened, I was worried about you?"

Ken gave a short bow, and took her arm. As they made their way to the weather deck, he said in his usual ironical style : "No need to worry on my account, dear lady. I was but taking the night air with a pistol or two shoved in my face by a desperate man."

"What? Who?"

"It was just one of our prisoners who broke free. I took care of the problem."

"How did you manage that?"

Ken took her arm, guided her to the larboard rail, and pointed to the gap where once the mighty *L'Orient* had floated. "I dropped a rather large gun on his head courtesy of the French flagship!"

Sarah decided that Ken was teasing her, but as she opened her mouth to remonstrate, a boatload of men came on board. Ignoring their grumbles, she pushed the men aside to see who it was, her heart beating so hard she could almost hear it. Antonio stood on the far side of the crowd, but before she could reach him, he caught Sarah's eye, and she knew something was amiss. He shook his head, and went off in the direction of the great cabin.

Later, when Duncan came onto the quarterdeck, Sarah could see that the smile had gone out of his eyes.

"Captain Saumarez will make our number when we are to sail. Please have me informed," with that he left the quarterdeck abruptly.

On Friday morning Sarah noticed the ship was becoming part of the Royal Navy. A marine stood guard outside Duncan's cabin, so she had to negotiate an audience.

"This came into my possession on board *L'Orient*, Sir. I don't know how she came by it." She handed Duncan the missing phone. They both knew to whom Sarah referred.

"Thank you, Mr. Malette," said Duncan. "One more loose end left."

Sarah was surprised that he asked no questions; perhaps he had already spoken to Antonio. Before she could speculate, the captain was called on deck, and she followed.

The patient was swung aboard the frigate with infinite care. The carpenter was ordered to remodel Duncan's cabin to accommodate the invalid, while the surgeon who accompanied him, moved into the gun room.

At three bells in the forenoon watch Sarah was up in the cross trees helping the fore topmen get the ship prepared to sail, when she heard a call from below: "Midshipman Malette needed in the captain's cabin!"

On her way she was stopped by an older, balding officer who spoke with a gruff voice.

"Mr. Midshipman, the name's Whillans — sailing master. I would be much obliged if you would conduct me to the captain's cabin and take care of my dunnage." He pointed to a large wooden box.

"Aye, aye, Sir."

She ordered one of the sailors to take Whillans' box to the gun room, and they made their way to the great cabin, where the captain and first officer were pouring over a chart. Introductions were made, and Duncan began.

"Gentlemen, I must stress the need for secrecy. On no account should the patient's true identity be revealed. If we are unfortunate enough to be captured, the invalid officer is to be called Captain Jones. You are the only ones in possession of this secret, and I want it to remain this way."

There were general nods of agreement, and Sarah was dismissed. She just hoped that Nelson would survive to fight Copenhagen and Trafalgar.

Just before sunset, Sarah met Duncan emerging from his cabin. She was about to ask him when they would sail when Manu ran to the door.

289

"Beggin' pardon, Sir, *Vanguard* she fly number, Sir."

"You speak some English now, Manu?"

"Mr. Malette, she teach me." Sarah had primed Manu carefully, and stood right behind to hear her prodigy practice.

Antonio's eyes met Sarah's briefly. "I have given the order to weigh, Sir. The topmen are already aloft," he said in a hushed voice.

"Thank you, Mr. Barbaro. We shall take her out together. I believe you are also on watch, Mr. Malette." Duncan grabbed his hat, and they followed him up to the quarterdeck.

While the sailors heaved on the anchor chain, Sarah stood by the wheel, hoping to find a moment to speak to Antonio. A launch arrived with a small company of red coated marines, led by two very young midshipmen.

"Your names, gentlemen?" Asked Duncan.

"Walker, Sir." The older one, who was no more than sixteen, responded.

"S-Smith, Sir." Stuttered the younger sailor, who looked around ten years of age.

"Admiral's orders, Sir," piped up Walker. "We are to place ourselves under your command, along with the hands, the sergeant, and these marines. In addition we have a prisoner to be taken to Gibraltar for interrogation, Sir."

Duncan turned to the marine sergeant. "Very well, bring him aboard."

The sergeant looked uncertain. "He's not actually a he, Sir."

"I am not following you, sergeant?"

"She's a she. Possibly a spy, Sir."

He signalled to the marines, and they brought their captive to the quarterdeck. Sarah felt a great weight of fear leave her as she recognized Annette. She smiled and tried to signal with her eyes, but Duncan stood between them.

"She will be treated like a lady, so long as her behaviour warrants it. There are some available cabins off the gun room."

Finally the ship got under way, and Duncan read the crew their orders, promising them shore leave in Naples as reward for a job well done. They slipped out of Aboukir Bay under the last rays of the setting sun. *Le Sérieuse* beat up into the northwest wind tack after tack. She looked a little forlorn, still lacking a fore topgallant mast, but there was not a spare spar to be had from the fleet. The evening wore on without incident, and at last Sarah's watch was finished. She left the quarterdeck with Duncan, closely followed by Manu, who seemed to have assumed the role of captain's servant.

"Make sure that I am called by six bells in the first watch," Duncan ordered.

Saturday 4th August 1798 11 AM — Ken

Moderate breezes clear weather. Employed getting up sheers to get up a jury fore mast. Came off from the shore several French boats for their wounded men. Sailmakers repairing sails.
Lieutenant's log, HMS *Vanguard* 4/Aug/1798

Before the day was very old, *Le Sérieuse* started to pitch and roll from the brisk Mediterranean chop. She was sailing as close to the wind as possible for a square rigged ship, and Ken felt seasick in the moderate breeze. He was off watch, leaning over the side of the ship with Sarah in support, when Walker appeared with a smirk on his face,

"The captain would like to see you landlubbers in his cabin."

His superior tone reminded Ken of a cheeky young school boy, but he felt too sea sick to care. He couldn't understand why the boy had taken a dislike to him.

"Keeping him waiting will not prevent you from being bent over an 18 pounder to feel the weight of the bosun's strap." With that, Walker disappeared about his duties, while Ken and Sarah answered their summons. The guard let them into the captain's cabin.

Duncan left them standing while he spoke. "We are sailing for Naples. I have the needs of the service to consider. Malta, as you know, is in the hands of our enemies. We cannot go there in any safety until the island is recaptured by the British."

"But that is not for two more years!" interjected Ken.

"Mr. DiPalo, you are in the navy now, you will pay me the respect due to the legal captain of this vessel."

"Sir, I am sure you are as keen on getting back to our time as we are . . ."

"Our time?" remarked Duncan.

Sarah and Ken exchanged glances. They had both caught the stress Duncan placed on the word "our."

"I will endeavour to get you back when and if it is safe to do so. I suggest that, in the meantime, you spend some time learning your new profession. I intend to give some lessons on navigation at noon today. If you brought your calculator along with you, Mr. DiPalo, I would advise you to keep it well out of sight and also to watch your words. Private conversation is just about impossible on a frigate like this. Just remember that they still burn witches in this century."

"Yes, Sir."

"I have asked Mr. Whillans to arrange the watches. You understand our system?"

"A bell is rung every half hour, and at eight bells the watch is changed," said Sarah.

"The exception, Mr DiPalo?"

Ken was mystified. "Sorry, Sir, I have no idea."

Sarah muttered quietly in an imitation of a dog barking.

A faint smile came to Duncan's eyes. "I think what Mr. Malette is trying to tell you is that two short watches follow the afternoon watch. At only two hours apiece, they 're known as the dog watches."

"Yes, Sir," said Ken. "I remember now from our lectures."

"Very good, gentlemen. The watch assignments will be given shortly. You may go."

Sarah and Ken made their way to the weather side of the bow, where they could count on the strong breeze to blow away their words.

"So you were right." Sarah spoke into the wind.

"Yup! The same Masthead Duncan from 1720. He certainly belongs in the here and now, unlike us!"

"You seem a little depressed. Are you homesick for the 20th century?" asked Sarah.

292

"Dunno — I'm not really suited to sailoring."

Sarah chuckled. "Well, we only have to live like this for a month. On September 2nd there will be an insurrection in Malta, and the French will take refuge in Valletta."

"Sure, the French will retreat behind the walls of their stronghold, which, by the way, is exactly where the gate is located, remember?" Ken was definitely not happy.

Saturday 4th August 1798 6 PM — Duncan

The sailing Master, Mr. Whillans, commanded the larboard watch, and at the end of the first Dog Watch he knocked on Duncan's cabin. Duncan and Antonio were pouring over their charts.

"Sir, we have re-arranged the officer's watches as you requested. We will all do our duty including the midshipmen. Mr. Malette and Mr. Walker have relieved the starboard watch."

"Thank you, Mr. Whillans."

Whillans stood awkwardly in silence by the cabin door.

"Was there something else, Mr. Whillans?" asked Duncan.

"May I speak freely, Sir?"

Duncan smiled to put Whillans at his ease. "Of course, Mr. Whillans; we all want what is best for the ship."

"The young gentlemen are keen, Sir, but they are inexperienced. Well, I trust young Walker with the sail handling, and the breeze is holding steady, but . . ." Whillans hesitated.

"Pray continue, Mr. Whillans."

"Well Sir, there's a French fleet in the area and I thought . . ." again Whillans paused.

Duncan saved him further embarrassment. "You assigned an experienced bosun's mate to stand watch with the midshipmen?"

Whillans nodded, and Duncan continued reassuringly. "At the slightest hint of trouble, Malette will beat to quarters, and the senior officers will be notified. Now, take a look at this chart. The French frigates, *Diane* and *Justice*, will not be far from the ships of the line that also escaped from Aboukir Bay, hoping perhaps to encounter a lone English frigate like ourselves."

293

Duncan paused and exchanged a glance with Antonio, who had just the glint of a smile in his eyes. "Any sensible man would set a course well to the South of Malta, where there is plenty of sea room. That is exactly where a French admiral would station any force under his command, such as six ships of the line, and any number of frigates out of Malta. We will surprise them, gentlemen, by running between Malta and Sicily through the Malta Channel. They won't be expecting that. We must keep clear of the Sicilian batteries and possible enemy ships in Valletta."

Whillans looked incredulously where Duncan's finger lay on the chart. "Sir! That is exactly where she lies!"

"You are not making yourself clear, Mr. Whillans."

"On the chart off Cape Passaro," he paused for dramatic effect. "The Passaro Reef! Sir."

Duncan smiled and tried not to sound condescending. "Before you raise an objection Mr. Whillans, while the wind is from the northwest, we have nothing to worry about as far as the reef is concerned. Sixty miles of open water at a depth of 50 fathoms separates Malta and the reef. We will be out of sight of the shore batteries at Cape Passaro and we shall sail safely to the south of the rocks."

Whillans muttered something about not wanting to endanger an undermanned ship.

"I agree, Sir, the only risk we take is of the wind shifting to the South, and putting us close to the Sicilian shore," warned Antonio.

"Or backing to the West and driving us onto the reef," Whillans muttered darkly.

Duncan put away his chart. He noted the date on it, 1775.

"Gentlemen, I would like to talk to our prisoner before we eat. I trust you will be joining me for dinner?" They nodded their assent. "Good, I'm more than ready for it." He knew he had better alert Manu to the extra mouths. He opened the cabin door, and to his surprise his servant was standing waiting.

"Ah Manu," he said, frowning. Manu had appeared so quickly that there was no pretence that he hadn't heard every word of their conference, although it was still unclear exactly how much

English he understood. "We will be entertaining these gentlemen for dinner at two bells in this dog watch."

"Ay, aye Captain, I make food."

Duncan interrupted before Manu could continue with further details of dinner. "The former captain of this ship had an exceptionally good collection of clarets. Tonight he will share a few of them with us."

The officers dispersed, while Duncan continued to the cabin where Annette was being held. The red uniformed marine guard came smartly to attention, and ushered his captain into the cabin.

"All quiet in there, Sir."

Annette lay on her cot but she jumped up smartly when Duncan entered.

"You are full of surprises, Miss Salvigny. I am told that you are a French spy. Perhaps you would like to enlighten me as to how you got to be arrested by Nelson's navy?"

"I suppose they didn't like my Quebec accent, Professor."

Duncan looked at her incredulously. "My dear girl, just because this is 1798 does not mean you are up against imbeciles. You were arrested and brought before men serving under Nelson, one of the greatest military minds that ever lived. Don't believe that you fooled any of them for one minute. Why were they so interested in you?"

Annette thought for a while. "I really don't know. One of the French prisoners identified me as having been aboard the *Orient*. That seemed to be enough. "

Duncan shook his head.

"What will happen to me?" Asked Annette.

"I will deal with your case in due course."

"I should like to go back."

"To see what havoc you have wreaked? You want me to help you now?" Snapped Duncan.

"Captain, I have known for some time that you came forward to this time, and that you started perhaps as far back as 1700?"

Duncan hesitated. "You will not compromise my existence here, young lady. I have the power of life and death as far as you are concerned."

"But you're a gentleman."

"Yes, well sometimes we gentlemen have to take extreme measures in times of war."

Two bells struck, and Duncan left Annette to consider her situation.

Monday 6th August 1798 Forenoon watch — Sarah

Sarah stood on the quarterdeck, on duty with Mr. Whillans, the watch officer. She watched the luff in the sails as the helmsman kept the ship as close to the wind as possible. Despite the food, a hammock to sleep in, and having the devil of a time getting the tar out of her uniform from the standing rigging, Sarah was beginning to enjoy herself. Her disguise as a man was thin, but she reasoned that no man disputed what the captain held as the truth. Most of all, her old enemies from the *Murad* seemed not to recognize her, which was just fine. If only she knew that Marie-Paule was safe, Sarah would have been content.

Just after four bells, the wind backed slightly towards the West, and Whillans ordered the sail trimmers on deck, just as Duncan came up to take the air. She watched the sheer pleasure in his face, as he delighted in the movement of the ship and the salt spray.

A call of "On deck there," interrupted her thoughts.

"Sail four points off the starboard bow."

She knew that Walker was on lookout duty, and she watched as the signal flags flew and a gun was fired to larboard. The private signal to ensure that any ship they encountered was under British command.

"Sir, she's the *Preston*, a British sloop under Captain Brackley." Walker reported to Duncan as he strode towards them.

Like everybody on board, Sarah waited for the ships to close the gap, interested in any news that they might convey. Finally, *Preston* heaved to within hailing distance, and Duncan spoke to Brackley.

"We came directly from the English fleet in Aboukir Bay under Captain Saumarez. We are bound for Naples."

"What of the French fleet?" Brackley asked.

"Seven French ships of the line sunk or captured, and six escaped Aboukir Bay, along with some frigates," replied Duncan.

"Two French men of war were seen by local fishermen off Crete two days ago," Brackley warned.

"What force do we have to watch for?"

"We understood they were *Diane* and *Justice*, 40 gun frigates. Thank you for putting us on course. I carry urgent mail for Nelson's fleet, so we shall take our leave."

It didn't take long for the sloop to get underway and head towards Aboukir.

As the sun began to set, Sarah came off watch tired and damp. The relentless northwest wind saw to it that she did not have a dry change of clothing. Her hammock was not inviting, so she started up the companionway to the ship's waist, where she met Antonio on his way down.

The so-called moderate wind howled through the rigging, and ripped across the sails with enough noise that they might have a private conversation, so she took a chance. "Mr. Barbaro, I . . ." She could not tell if the turbulence in her belly was due to the rough seas or the presence of the first officer. She plucked up courage.

"Would you prefer to continue without speaking or . . ."

"Your pardon, midshipman, I have had no time to speak with you since our brief meeting aboard *L'Orient*."

"You survived I see."

"As did you."

It seemed to Sarah that his voice had changed, matured, deepened. His uniform was immaculate; she couldn't understand how he looked so good. The fire in her belly grew fiercer. "Did you take your revenge? What happened at the battle of Shubra Khit?"

"I confronted the knight. He had been sent to warn the gunboats not to let the Mameluke reinforcements across the Nile. I met him on the river bank."

"You called him out?"

"That was my intention, but when I saw him, and his ragged band of followers, something happened. He was so much older, greyer, a tired old man. He was weary from the desert, and he did not know me. His men were going to kill me there and then, but he stopped them, and sent me under guard to the fleet. The rest of the time I spent in confinement, ironically aboard *L'Orient*."

"If the soldiers hadn't stopped you, would you have killed him?"

"He was a confused old man, who remembered nothing of my family. No, I could not kill him in cold blood. I failed my father."

Sarah did not know what to say, so she held her hand out to him in the darkness, and they held each other until torn apart by approaching footsteps.

Saturday 11th August 1798 6 AM — Ken

Six bells sounded in the Middle Watch, and Ken clenched his fists, wondering if he would get into trouble for punching young Richard on the nose.

"All right, I give up! How do you raise the elevation of the muzzle?" Ken's voice cracked in frustration. He wished that Richard Walker would just tell him what to do, instead of making everything a personal comment on Ken's ignorance.

They stood beside a nine pounder mounted on the quarterdeck. Walker laughed at Ken's naive question. "That is what we call a hand spike, these are quoins . . ." Walker tailed off as Duncan approached them.

"Sir!" The midshipman chorused.

"Mr. DiPalo, a word if you please."

Ken followed Duncan over to the weather side, hoping he had not unknowingly committed some crime.

Duncan leaned against the bulwark and nodded towards the northwest. "We'll be sailing quite close to Crete. It's a treacherous place for a ship, and if the wind backs further to the South we could be in serious trouble."

"I am aware of that, Sir. I have been learning a great deal in these last few days. Our progress is very slow."

Duncan made sure that there were no hands close by, and that their voices were carried away by the wind. "There is something I want you to take a look at. You are good with computers aren't you?"

"Computers, Sir?" Ken was puzzled by the mention of something that was not from the 18th century. "I have taken a few computer science courses, Sir."

"Good. Take a look at this, but don't let anybody from this time see it."

"Yes Sir."

Duncan passed him the smart phone, and Ken picked it up with a smile on his face.

"This is my phone, Sir. It was er, on loan to Annette."

"As you are probably aware by now, we were fortunate enough to be reunited with Ms. Salvigny. See what information it contains. I want to know why somebody would have brought it back to 1798."

By the look on Duncan's face, Ken knew better than to pursue questions concerning Annette. "I can tell you that, Sir. It contains charts of the Mediterranean coasts. These are surveys dated in the 1980s and 1990s."

Duncan shook his head."In 200 years the sands shift, and the charts will not reflect the reality of 1798, at least not in Aboukir Bay. The device itself may have been enough to convince Admiral Brueys that he should listen to Annette." He paused to think.

"Sir, since we are alone may I ask a question concerning the gates?" Ken asked.

"They are not a phenomena I know much about. I can only assume they are wormholes. I built the doorway with the voice operated password in Victoria, but otherwise they are a natural phenomenon with a grey, shimmering appearance."

"So they could occur anywhere?" Ken's eyes lit with wonder.

"Indeed, Mr. DiPalo, but they have a limited lifespan and are extremely hard to find. You may carry on, and please inform the duty officer that we shall have gunnery practice at his earliest convenience."

Tuesday 14th August 1798 10 AM Off the coast of Libya, — Ken

On the morning of the fourteenth day, Ken came running up on deck, where Walker and a seaman blocked his way.

"Aloft with you, and look lively!" Commanded Walker. "The man's drunk!" He said to Ken, as he and the sailor went up the companionway to the mainmast.

Whillans, the watch officer, and Hidey were breaking in a new helmsman when Ken came running up onto the quarterdeck, eager to talk to Duncan. He stood impatiently watching the captain take his exercise, not daring to disturb him. Whillans smiled gently, making Ken even more agitated.

"Christ ! I am waiting as fast as I can," muttered Ken under his breath.

Eventually, Duncan strolled over to talk to Whillans. "Good day to you Mr. Whillans." He noticed Ken hopping on one leg. Is there something troubling you, Mr. DiPalo?"

"Sir, I think I have discovered something of importance concerning the . . . er . . . bauble you gave me."

"Very well, Mr. DiPalo, see me in my cabin, in . . . "

A cry of man overboard interrupted him. Duncan called out: "Heave to! You may use my gig, Mr. Whillans; it will be quicker."

"Make ready the gig!" Whillans called out. "It looks like one of the topmen fell from the main." Whillans muttered in a soft voice.

Ken watched the men swing the gig out over the water, when there was a cry from the direction of the forecastle.

"Young Mr. Malette overboard! There'n two of 'em in the briny!"

As the ship heaved to, they drifted past the bodies in the water. Ken ran to the stern rail and there was Sarah, swimming over to where the topman was struggling to stay afloat. She reached him and managed to keep his head up long enough for the pair to be rescued.

There was no doubt in the minds of all who saw Sarah's wet body that she was female. Ken knew how the stories of Sarah's bravery had spread through the lower decks; no one could deny her courage, and Ken knew that nobody would question her gender. It also meant that he would have to wait for a better moment to reveal his discovery.

"All hands on deck!"

It was the middle of the night, and Sarah wearily climbed to her assigned station on the foremast. She was tired, and frustrated at the ship's lack of progress, continually beating up against a contrary wind. Now that they entered the Malta channel, they were forced to tack every two hours while keeping a little north of Malta, and well south of the Passaro reef.

The change of tack was followed by the thunder of feet as the crew returned to their quarters. Sarah and Ken found themselves alone.

"Rough night?" Sarah asked, sympathetically.

"Hell yes, but it doesn't matter because we are going to get blown out of the water by those French frigates. So why bother? "

"Somebody got out of the wrong side of the bed, I think!"

"Thank you, Miss 'I'm always right'. Some of us need our sleep."

"That would be 'Mr. I'm always right'. Fine, see you in the morning."

They got into their hammocks before Ken broke the silence.

"Look, I'm sorry, okay? You're much better at this sailing business than I am."

He couldn't hide the emotion in his voice, and Sarah reached out and found his hand in the dark.

"Are you worried about Annette?"

"No. Well, yes."

Sarah chuckled. "You know she's aboard."

"I know she is. Duncan told me, and anyway I saw her."

"You got past the sentry?"

"It was only for a moment. I think they were taking her for exercise."

"So you're still in love with her?"

Ken withdrew his hand hastily. "I never said I was!"

Wounded, Sarah stared into the dark. When she called his name, he remained silent.

Chapter 16

The Battle of Passaro Reef

Monday 20th August 1798 7:59 AM The Malta Channel.

Eight bells rang like an angry alarm clock, and the running feet sounded like a heavy metal drummer. Because Ken could not bring himself to drink the foul tasting liquid that passed for fresh water on the ship, he had consumed his entire allowance of navy-issued grog the previous night. He groaned as he realized he was late for his watch.

Throwing on his clothing, he ran all the way to the quarterdeck, where Whillans was waiting with a dark scowl on his face. "You are tardy Mr. DiPalo. I fancy it is time for a little exercise on the main mast, to remind you of good timekeeping aboard one of his Majesty's ships. Will you count the vessels you see from the masthead, then report your findings to me? Look lively now."

"Aye, aye, Sir."

Ken dreaded the long climb, but he tried to look a lot livelier than he felt as he set off up the larboard shrouds. Clinging grimly to the ratlines, he neared the formidable overhang that formed the big platform of the main top. Since the shrouds leaned backwards, a sensible person would have stayed close to the mast and squirmed up through what was known as the *lubber's hole*. Seasoned sailors, however, went up and over, and Ken knew that taking any other route would expose him to ridicule and loss of status. Ken took hold of the first rung. Keeping one knee hooked into the shrouds, he let his bodyweight hang on both arms. One foot at a time, he climbed outwards towards the edge of the platform. Against all his mother's safety instructions, and despite the cruel drop to the deck, he launched himself out into space. His left arm, weaker than his right, started to hurt so much that he let go involuntarily; his weight tore his right hand free, leaving him hanging by his legs.

"Yon lubber's goin' to mess up me clean deck."

Ken couldn't tell where the taunt came from, but he urged his weary muscles to hoist his body against gravity and through space to reach the edge of the platform. The men on the main top could hardly contain their laughter at his antics, but one of the hands grabbed Ken by the arm and heaved him up with a smile. At least he had done it the man's way. Ken nodded his gratitude and looked out to find that the ship was becalmed, shrouded in early morning mist. He would have to climb still farther to see above the cloud to satisfy Whillans. To a background of cheers from the topmen he gained the cross trees. It was peaceful up there on a tiny foothold a hundred feet above the weather deck. The ship drifted through the mist shielding him from the drop and he made a few more steps upwards. He was thankful that there was almost no wind to make the climb more difficult. Even as this thought came to him, he felt a gentle breeze on his face and the ship started to roll, slowly at first, but gathering momentum, as the breeze gave way to a strong gust of wind. Ken clung on, frozen with terror, not daring to move.

"On deck there!"

He looked up, to where the highest sails, the royals, hung limply. Standing right up on that lofty, swaying spar, one hand for the ship, and one for his telescope, was Walker, the lookout. Ken watched the young midshipman's body strain to get a glimpse of something moving in the mist beyond the bow.

"Sail to windward. Nay, two sail."

"Where away?" It was Duncan, calling from the quarterdeck.

"One point off the starboard bow."

"Can you see their colours?"

"Could be those French frigates," called Walker.

Distracted by the lookout's grim news, Ken was unprepared when the ship rolled to starboard, and he swung like an opening barn door from his left hand. Hauling himself back to the topgallant shrouds, he clung on in sheer panic.

"Don't like it up here, do ye?" Walker grinned, casually hanging from the main royal yard. As if to emphasize his disdain, he danced along the footrope that enabled the sailors to go right out to the extremity of the yard. "Why don't you come up here and ride the horse, city boy?"

Ken was momentarily incensed by the challenge, and his ego might well have overcome his fear had not the mist swirled about them. Afraid of what Walker might do to him, hidden as they were from the sight of the weather deck, Ken scrambled down the mast as fast as he could.

La *Sérieuse* had almost finished making her easting before turning north to follow the Sicilian coast towards Naples when the news spread through the ship that the French frigates had been seen.

Sarah ran up onto the quarterdeck, stopping to ask permission of Mr. Whillans, officer of the watch, she strode over to Duncan.

"What are our chances, Sir?"

Duncan looked at her with a grim smile. "This is a big frigate, but those Frenchies are even larger. They have more guns and more men to work them, and they have the weather gage."

Sarah puzzled over this for a moment. "You mean the wind is in their favour?"

"Exactly so," replied Duncan. "They are northwest of us. We cannot sail upwind of them before they cross our path, so we shall try to outrun them. Mr. Whillans, please call all hands, prepare to tack ship."

Antonio approached Duncan. "I heard the lookout, Capitan."

"Two sail, Mr. Barbaro, possibly those French frigates."

Duncan glanced aloft noting the activity in the tops necessary for tacking. "Well, Tenente, is the company fit to fight them? The Maltese seem to be working well alongside the Arabs."

Antonio laughed. "It was not such an easy task, Sir. Careful matching of skills, but now the watches are well balanced."

"And the gun crews?"

"They have been improving at target practice."

"Those ships are still hull down, and the wind is growing in strength. We shall have to see who is the better sailor. Mr. Whillans, as soon as we are on our new course, shake out the reef in the main top sail, and set the studding sails if you please."

Whillans nodded his agreement, but Sarah could see the look in his eye. With the breeze strengthening, it would not be long before they would be shortening sail again.

"Aye, aye, Sir."

The "helms a lee" command was given, and the frigate came about on the opposite tack.

"Mr. Whillans, the Passaro Reef is north and east of us. A dangerous place for the night passage." Duncan observed.

"Aye, Sir, we should avoid that place."

"On the other hand, perhaps the French will not follow us into such waters." Duncan paused, then made his decision. "Set a course to the north east, Mr. Whillans."

"Aye, aye, Sir."

Ken had returned to the safety of the quarterdeck and found his way to Sarah's side. "I think I've had my fill of sea battles," he muttered discreetly.

With the wind almost on their beam, they could feel the ship move faster through the water.

At the next heave of the log, Whillans called out: "She's doing near on nine knots, Sir."

Duncan looked pleased. "Mr. Whillans, come with me aloft. Take the deck, Mr. DiPalo."

With one foot on the companionway, he turned back to Sarah. "Mr. Malette, fetch my best glass from Manu and follow us to the maintop." To one of the able seamen he whispered quietly: "The new midshipmen are yet to find their sea legs, and Mr. Malette is to be escorted through the lubber's hole."

"Aye, aye, Sir."

Duncan waited for the somewhat elderly, but still nimble, Mr. Whillans on the maintop. The captain squeezed past the two one pounders mounted on swivels, and glanced forward to see the bow wave as the ship started to pick up speed.

"So now we are the fox," muttered Duncan.

The ship carried as much sail as she dared, and *Sérieuse* was fairly flying through the water. Duncan was astonished to see Sarah, with a huge grin on her face, coming down from the cross trees, with his telescope tucked into her uniform coat. "How did you . . .?"

"Rock climbing, Sir. I have spent a good deal of time up here since we left Aboukir Bay."

"If you please, Sir?" Able seaman Walter Wiley had come up alongside Sarah.

"You may speak, Wiley."

"The top men tried to watch out for the officer, Sir, like you said, Sir. He was too . . ." Wiley did not finish his sentence before Duncan's raucous laughter was heard by every man working on the main.

"Too quick for you, Wiley?"

"Aye, Sir."

"We'll make a sailor of you, yet, Mr. Malette. Mr. Whillans, we'll take our sightings from the cross trees. Carry on Mr. Malette."

Sarah, looking completely at home, climbed out along the topgallant spar and observed the sails in the distance. The French vessels were now hull up, and Wiley said to her: "Look at yonder sails, Sir. Them's men of war, French frigates for sure."

The lead frigate was indeed carrying a great deal of sail. Duncan took in the details trying to get a measure of what he was up against. He sniffed the air. Was the wind still strengthening? The leading frigate was sailing with the wind on her quarter on the starboard tack. As he watched, she started to wear ship.

"She's coming about to give chase," said Duncan. "There she goes! The lead frigate has put the wind on her beam. That's a tight ship. Those French hands know their business."

Whillans nodded his agreement. They watched the second frigate come round in a parallel course. A few minutes later, despite the strengthening wind, the topgallant studding sails billowed out, driving the pursuing frigates towards them at even greater speed.

"The lead frigate is *Le Diane*. We came up against her only last year, Sir. That time she ran from our seventy-four. The way she's moving it looks like she's been careened since we met with her."

"You are right there, Mr. Whillans, and I think she's gaining on us."

Duncan took out his stop watch and made some calculations. Sarah listened to every word, wondering what would happen if the frigates caught them.

"Curse those damn Frenchies for taking away our fore topgallant mast! They are making twelve or even thirteen knots! If we do nothing they will catch us in a little over five hours." Duncan noted after a few minutes of observation.

"Aye, Sir, we shall most likely be dead by three bells in the afternoon watch." Whillans had been doing his own calculations, with a somewhat less sophisticated time piece.

The officers descended to the deck as the glass turned and the bell was rung.

"How do we go any faster, Sir?" Sarah asked innocently.

Duncan laughed. "A good question Mr. Malette." He turned to address the sailing master who stood beside the helmsman, "Mr. Whillans, we will do better with the wind a little more on our beam. Take us to two points to windward, if you would."

Whillans called out the order to the helmsman, and they altered sail accordingly.

"Can we rig something to replace the missing fore topgallant stay and flagstaff stay? We might get another knot out of her if we can make more sail on the jib boom."

"I'll see what can be done, Sir." Whillans went forward to inspect the foremast.

Duncan saw Whillans returning to the quarterdeck, and noted that whatever magic their sailing master had worked, enabled the ship to carry more sail, and she was picking up speed slightly. Duncan was impressed.

"Well Mr. Whillans, you have been busy."

"It's like this, Sir. I rigged an extra stay from the top of the fore topmast to the jib boom to replace the missing fore topgallant stay. To take up any extra strain, I strengthened the main topgallant stay . . ." He paused and, addressing Sarah, explained: "That's the stay that ties the fore mast to the main." He returned to Duncan. "We have set both the sprit topsail and the flying jib, Sir. Just the small one, so's not to interfere with the jib."

Sarah understood they had more sail up, but little more.

Duncan noticed that Ken was still hovering. "Mr. DiPalo, I would like to see you in my cabin, if you please. You have the quarterdeck, Mr. Whillans."

Ken entered the great cabin, where two nine pounder stern chasers occupied much of the space. Duncan was staring at a chart spread across the dining table. "You have something important to tell me?"

"Yes, Sir, concerning the modern charts," said Ken, handing over his phone. "Here Sir, the exact position of the reef. I don't think there would have been any changes in 200 years."

Duncan looked back at his own charts. "The Captain of *Le Diane*, no doubt has this old chart," and he held it up for Ken to see. "These naval charts were prizes in war time, and a prime target for spies on both sides."

"Sir, if you would compare the longitude of the Passaro Reef on the smart phone to that on the old chart."

Duncan examined the two. "The old French chart puts Passaro two miles east of the position shown on the smart phone. The survey captain must have had an error in his chronometer. Young man, this may well work in our favour!" He carefully marked the corrected position on his own chart, and a smile broke out on his face. "Thank you, Mr. DiPalo. We are currently west of the reef, and in fact a little closer than I thought."

They returned to the quarterdeck. "What is the situation, Mr. Whillans?"

"Still losing ground, Sir. We have increased our speed to eleven knots, but if we keep the present course nor nor east, they be like to catch us before nightfall, if we don't run aground afore then on the reef."

"Very good, Mr. Whillans, carry on." Duncan turned away, ignoring Whillans' obvious confusion.

At five bells Whillans approached Duncan. "Those frigates, Sir, will be on us about the same time as we reach the Passaro Reef. On this course it will be directly to our lee, and this wind will lay us right on the rocks."

"Thank you Mr. Whillans. Inform me when the lookout sees white water."

"That is just it, Sir. I know these waters, and the reef is hidden in all but a bad sea, Sir. We will not see the reef until we are stuck upon it."

"Well, then neither will the French frigates!" Duncan laughed. "Keep your course, Mr. Whillans."

"Aye Sir."

Ken had no idea what Duncan intended and wondered if they would sink on the rocks or be blown out of the water by French frigates. Neither choice was appealing.

At six bells the enemy frigates were clearly visible from the quarterdeck. Ken likened the ships to bloodhounds on the scent of *Sérieuse*, gaining at every clock tick. The everyday sounds of shipboard life did not jibe with the tension he felt as the French gained on them. With the creaking of her timbers as the wind whistled through her rigging, Ken couldn't help viewing the ship as a living being who, like him, was fleeing for her life.

Whillans appeared to make one of his gloomy periodic updates on the progress of the chase. "I give 'em seven mile, yet. We'se got another couple of hours to live, young gentlemen. We'm may be lucky and get blown out of the water before the reef rips out the bottom of this barky."

"Mr. Whillans," Duncan ordered. "We shall keep this course until the watch changes. You can start to clear for action, but wait until my say so before you beat to quarters. We have some time at our disposal, so leave the galley fires until the men have eaten. Inform the surgeon that he must move our patient, and send the carpenter down to make sure there is a secure and comfortable berth for him in the orlop."

Instantly the ship was turned into a kind of ordered bedlam. Every hand aboard had his assigned work to do as they turned the frigate into a floating fortress. Everywhere clutter was removed, the officer's bulkheads were struck down, and the furniture carried below. On deck, splinter netting was rigged overhead, and the decks were wetted and sanded. The scuttlebutts were placed so that the men could easily find water when there was time during the fighting.

In fifteen minutes, the running feet stopped. The ship was ready to fight.

Monday 20th August 1798 12 noon The Malta Channel. Afternoon watch — Duncan

Eight bells marked the change of watch, and Antonio took over.

"Good afternoon, Mr. Barbaro," Duncan greeted him. "I estimate we'll see some action before four bells are sounded in this watch. In the meantime, let's tempt those Frenchies in a little closer. When I give the word, drag a sail in the water, on the lee side; I don't want them to see it. I wish them to follow us very closely near the reef."

Whillans was still on deck, and he exploded with indignation. "Sir, there is a great risk due to the rocks."

He tailed off when he saw the expression on Duncan's face. "I beg your pardon, Sir."

"Mr. Whillans, you will just have to put your trust in me. I know something that you do not."

Duncan stared across the choppy water, imagining the captain of *Le Diane* on his quarterdeck. What could he learn that would give them some advantage? The French captain had the weather gage, and a stronger, faster ship. No doubt he was convinced that he would have the *Sérieuse* in less than two hours. Still Duncan kept his course.

By this time Antonio had the log running continuously, and there was a lookout posted to swing the lead and declare the depth. They maintained their speed and, thanks to the smart phone, the captain knew exactly where the reef was located. A beep sounded on his twentieth century time piece at the same moment the ship's bell was rung. It was time.

"Mr Barbaro, you may drag the sail if you please."

At the captain's word, the sail was discretely dipped into the water, and the ship slowed down slightly. Duncan heard Whillans

310

quietly muttering his misgivings, and even Antonio looked worried. Ken looked as baffled as the rest of the crew.

Duncan addressed his midshipmen: "Where are your positions at quarters?"

"Gun deck, Sir," said Ken.

"With the top men, Sir," said Sarah.

"You may remain here until I tell you otherwise. We will not be firing the great guns just yet."

A half hour passed, and the frigates were less than two sea miles behind and slightly west of them. They heard the pop of a gun from *Le Diane*, and saw a splash well to sternward. Ken was relieved they were not yet in range. Despite the dragged sail, the ship sped through the water. Duncan looked at his watch and spoke to Hidey, who was at the helm. "On my mark we will turn to starboard until we are heading due east."

Whillans could not keep silent. "Sir!"

"Yes, Mr. Whillans?" Ken thought he detected some humour in Duncan's tone.

"The Passaro reef is two miles south east of us."

"Thank you, Mr. Whillans."

This near the rocks everybody on the quarterdeck listened out for the leadsman, " . . . by the deep 20," a pause then, "11 fathoms, Sir, shells and soft shale on the bottom."

"Take her round now, Hidey."

"Aye, aye, Sir."

The ship came round easily and the French ships changed course slightly to produce an interception to the south. Duncan again listened to the leadsman and waited.

"Gentlemen, I need your attention. Tenente, on my command we will turn to starboard until your compass points South East."

Whillans looked completely mystified. "Beggin' your pardon, Sir, but by my calculations, the new course will take us directly to the reef in under fifteen minutes."

Duncan laughed. "It is time for me to enlighten you as to our plan of action."

He addressed the quarterdeck, and all those officers and hands near enough listened very carefully. "Gentlemen, we have done everything we can, but there is no way we can avoid the French

311

frigates." There were nods of agreement all round. "My orders are to avoid contact if possible, and that is exactly what I plan to do. This is the way we are going to do it." Duncan continued speaking for several more minutes and finally he said: "Any questions?"

"No, Sir!"

The officers and men hurried off about their assigned duties. Duncan mopped his brow with a large linen handkerchief. There was only one thing left for him to do. He went below, and entered Annette's cabin.

"We will soon be engaged in action, so you cannot stay here. We will move you to the forepeak, where you will be safe."

Annette looked at him with fear in her eyes. "Captain, I will give you my word that I will not interfere with your action, but please, don't shut me in some horrible small space. If those ships sink the *Sérieuse*, I would rather die swimming than die fighting to get out of my prison. Put me below. I will help the surgeon with the lolly boys."

"The loblolly boys," corrected Duncan. "An 18th century surgery at sea may not be a very pretty sight."

"I have seen blood before," she said simply.

"Very well. Make it so." He said to the marine sergeant.

"Wait!" Annette was firm.

"Quickly now, I have a battle to command."

"There is something else, something important I have to tell you. It was when I tried to escape from *L'Orient*, that terrible fire. There was a boy . . ."

"Yes, you rescued Casabianca's son. I heard about it from the *Vanguard*. I congratulate you on your bravery, Mademoiselle. You have come a long way from that classroom in Victoria."

Annette took on a worried frown. "There was something else, before the boy, in the smoke, there was a woman . . ."

At that moment there was a crash and the whole side of the ship shuddered. Without waiting for Annette to finish, Duncan rushed back to the quarterdeck where there was much commotion. A ball from *Le Diane*'s bow chaser had gouged a hole in the side of the ship, above the waterline. Duncan realized they had been going a tad too slow. "Get that sail out of the water!" This was not going to be easy.

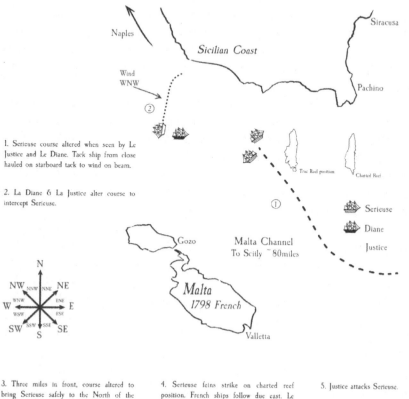

Battle of Passaro Reef - Wednesday 15th August 1798

1. Serieuse course altered when seen by Le Justice and Le Diane. Tack ship from close hauled on starboard tack to wind on beam.

2. La Diane & La Justice alter course to intercept Serieuse.

3. Three miles in front, course altered to bring Serieuse safely to the North of the reef. Justice and La Diane follow.

4. Serieuse feins strike on charted reef position. French ships follow due east. Le Diane strikes true reef, Justice follows safe path of Serieuse.

5. Justice attacks Serieuse.

Captain Villeneuve of *Le Justice* stayed precisely on station as directed by his superior, Captain Solen in *Le Diane*, and looked intently through his glass at the English frigate. He did not understand the manoeuvres that the English captain had made. Surely, they would cause the *Sérieuse* to lose ground.

"C'est la vie!" He shrugged.

313

After all, he would share the prize with the senior captain. Perhaps they would promote him for the recapture of a valuable frigate? What a fine prize to take back to Valletta. He adjusted course with *Le Diane*. They would intercept in the late afternoon. There would be a brief battle; perhaps the English captain would drop his colours before there was too much bloodshed. Afterwards, they could dine together on board *Le Diane* that evening; she had a fine chef. Villeneuve licked his lips in anticipation.

As he watched, *Le Sérieuse* turned to the south east. What was this mad Englishman doing? Villeneuve could tell from his charts that the *Sérieuse* was heading directly to the Passaro reef. As *Le Justice* flew through the water at thirteen knots, he saw Solen fire his bow chaser and do some damage. The *Sérieuse* slowed, then recovered, and perhaps even gained a few lengths. Then something went seriously wrong.

"Mon dieu, *Le Sérieuse* has hit the Passaro reef!"

The stricken ship heeled over to leeward, aground on the reef. She must have been trying to avoid it when the *Diane's* bow chaser took out a spar, and caused the *Sérieuse* to lose control. A smile spread across his face. The ship was theirs, and he had not fired a single shot! All they had to do was float the prize clear of the rocks. Now they knew exactly where the rocky reef was located, so they could sail directly to it, and heave to in good time.

The French ships turned in unison. Silently the minutes ticked by as they sailed towards the enemy ship. *Le Diane* was some 200 yards ahead when there was a terrible sound, like the bottom of the ship had been ripped out of her. The force generated by 300 tons of large French frigate coming to a sudden and undeniable halt caused the fore topmast to break in a harsh cracking sound as jagged timbers came crashing down.

As *Le Diane* hit the submerged rocks, Villeneuve thought he could hear the cries of the top men, clinging to the cross trees, on their last journey to the sea below. The fore topsail covered the deck, creating chaos amongst the crew. He imagined the scene as the survivors tried to move the gear off the screaming victims. As if this was not sufficient to put the ship out of action, the crashing foremast dragged the main topgallant forestay along with the flagstaff stay, and tore the main topgallant mast away. It fell over a hundred feet into the tangle of sails, rigging, and men below. Sails were ripped, yards came down, and many hands were crushed beneath the mess that had once been the best frigate in the French navy.

Villeneuve shouted: "A gauche, au Nord!" The ship slowly turned. At any second he expected to feel the reef ripping holes in his ship, and he clung to the rail waiting for the jolt. Now he understood why the English captain had sailed so far north before he turned. Were there two reefs?

Le Justice, close hauled against the unchanging wind, fought her way northwards to come within a few feet of the hidden rocks. Now Villeneuve had to make a decision; should he stop and attempt to help his superior in *Le Diane* or try to take the prize? He decided on a middle ground, launching the ship's barge with strict instructions to the boat crew to take off only the captain, officers and chef of *Le Diane* if she should sink.

He followed the course taken by *Le Sérieuse* and, believing now that there must be two reefs, he ordered the sails to be clewed up leaving only the fore topsail to allow him control of the ship. With the leadsman calling out the depth, they cautiously followed the path of the enemy ship.

On the angled deck, Duncan heard the crew cheer as they saw *Le Diane* strike the reef. The escape of *Le Justice* was not so welcome. She made her turn after sailing north around the reef, and came directly towards them, unafraid of a ship that was stuck on the rocks. The *Sérieuses* were restless, wanting to get the ship back upright, but Duncan knew he had to wait until the last minute. Their only chance was to send a raking shot down the length of the approaching ship at close range. The guns were already loaded with grape, well wadded to keep the shot from spilling. The enemy ship approached, 300 yards to the north-west, cleared for action with her gun ports open, and her gun crews at the ready.

"Wait for it lads," Duncan ordered, thinking of the carnage they would cause on the enemy ship by their broadside. "It's us or them!" Everybody on board clung on to something trying to stop themselves sliding down the deck. Ken held fast on the gun deck, concentrating on the part he must play to ensure the guns were properly run out and fired. At last the enemy crossed the two hundred yard line; it was time. "Now!" he called. Axes came down on the anchor cables and, as if resurrected from the dead, *Le Sérieuse*, captured by the English, aground on a reef, sprang upright, her starboard broadside pointed along the length of the French ship.

"Open ports!" commanded Ken, proud to be in charge of the forward division. He stood by number nine gun, an 18 pounder. One of the Maltese sailors pushed the wooden gun port door open and secured the flap; no easy task as the ship was still swinging. There was a frantic thunder of running feet as the men ran from cutting the cables to the gun deck. Less than a minute later, the guns were run out. *Le Justice* was still approaching with her bow pointing directly towards *Le Sérieuse* amidships, unable to react quickly to the resurrection of their enemy.

"Fire starboard guns!" The order came just as the French ship started to turn to show her larboard broadside.

"Forward division, fire as they bear," ordered Ken. The great guns fired and, before *Le Justice* could bring her guns to action, she was raked from bow to stern.

Ken held on and tried not to listen to the screams of the injured and dying French men. The devastation from the raking shot did not stop the French ship. She had enough way on her that in less time than it took the *Sérieuses* to reload the starboard broadside, *Le Justice* was ready with her own.

Despite a headscarf and ear pads, Ken's head was throbbing from the explosions of the first broadside. The wind blew the smoke straight back into the gun ports, and now they worked in a thick fog. He could neither hear nor see, but remained bent over, covered in sweat with his head pressed against the low ceiling.

"Sponge!" Shouted Aziz Pasha, the gun captain.

A one armed Arab boy brought the next cartridge, waiting while one of the gun crew plunged a wet sponge on the end of a wooden pole into the gun barrel.

"Powder!"

Taking the cartridge from the boy, one of the Arab sailors stepped up and placed the dangerous looking grey cylinder into the muzzle. He treated the cartridge respectfully, carefully placing it bottom end first, seam down. Stepping aside in a well rehearsed manoeuvre, a wizened old Maltese sailor took his place. The old man rammed the charge home until Aziz, with his finger over the touch hole, nodded that it had seated properly.

"Wad!"

The wad was rammed home, then, like a dance step, the old Maltese sailor moved away so that a younger man could load the heavy iron ball, followed by a second wad to keep it in place.

"Run out!"

As one, the team pulled on the tackle, and the huge gun trundled forward. Before the barrel filled the port, Ken got a view through the swirling smoke. Not a hundred yards away across the green blue Mediterranean chop, the enemy ship had come about, and now they faced twenty open gun ports. To Ken they were gaping black windows revealing the death stocked muzzles of a long row of twenty-four pound guns. Shaken, he turned away from the gunport to find Richard Walker glaring at him.

"Were you thinking of swimming over to your friends?" Richard hissed.

"What? Piss off!"

Walker shoved Ken to the floor. It was probably this uncharitable act by the younger man that saved Ken's life as the sound of the enemy broadside burst like thunder, followed closely by the crack of breaking timbers as the balls, aimed low, smashed their way through the wooden side of *Sérieuse*.

Ken was oblivious to the noise and the stinging smoke. He howled as he felt a searing pain in his left shoulder as he was flung along the deck. As he struggled to get up, something large landed on his back.

A French twenty-four pound iron ball, fired from about a hundred yards away, had penetrated the oaken side of the ship. The wood had exploded under the impact and split into huge jagged splinters. One seven feet long spear of death drove through the men of number nine gun. It neatly cut the master gunner in two, and it was his bleeding, twitching torso that had fallen onto Ken. The last impression Ken had before passing into darkness was the figure of

Walker, miraculously spared any injury, slinking past Ken's prostrate form.

Sarah had read up on this enemy ship; a frigate forte, equipped with thirty twenty-four pounder guns as well as fourteen eighteen pounders. Her broadside weight of metal was nearly 500 lbs, and the shock to *Sérieuse* was similar to being at the epicentre of an earthquake. Sarah, not yet in the tops, grabbed whatever she could to steady herself. An order from the quarterdeck sent her to render assistance on the gun deck, and she ran to obey. The sooner they could get the great guns back in action the better their chance of survival. She slid down the companionway to arrive in hell.

Seeing nothing but smoke, she could hear the shrieks and groans of dying men. She yelled as she slipped on the wet deck and brought her hand up covered in blood. A steady stream of blood coursed along the deck beside her. A man fell to her right, blood pouring from a leg wound where a splinter had gouged its way through the flesh. Recovering, she ordered two sailors to get him below to the Orlop. Then she started to help clear the guns. When she reached number nine, she tried to ignore the rising bile within her, working with the surviving crew to pull away the debris and bodies that were blocking the gun. With a great heave the crew moved the torso of the dead Aziz; to Sarah's horror, Ken lay beneath the mutilated body.

"For Christ's sake he's still breathing. Give me a hand there!" She felt a steady hand on her arm, and looked up into the kindly eyes of bin Kabina, who picked Ken up as gently as he could and took his bloody body below.

When the injured started to come down to the Orlop, Annette took one look, and rushed up the gangway gasping for air. She arrived on the chaotic gun deck, weeping in fear and disgust as she stepped in the blood pouring through the scuppers. She saw Sarah working hard to get the injured out of the way, and drawing some courage from this, she went over to help get Ken down to the orlop. Below, he was dumped in a line of moaning, injured men. The surgeon moved along the line of bodies, deciding whether it was worth spending time on each victim. When he saw Ken covered in blood, he was about to move on when Annette stopped him.

"Please, Sir, it's not his blood."

The surgeon paused to take another look.

"Dislocated shoulder, non-serious head wound, and possible concussion. I will restore his shoulder, you may attend to the wound."

Up on the quarterdeck Duncan could see that there was little chance of his students and the comatose Nelson surviving a bloody battle with the French, broadside to broadside. The enemy had more guns, and a lot more men to fire them. Eventually they would board his ship. Both ships had lost spars, but the superior weight of numbers would end in defeat for *Le Sérieuse*. The ships had taken devastating broadsides and, as he watched, *Le Justice* narrowed the gap between them, turning so that her bow sprit crashed into the waist of his ship. There was such a tangle of rigging that it looked like the ships would be permanently locked in combat. As the French crew came storming over the side, Duncan decided it was time to bring a halt to the battle, and he lowered his colours amidst a hail of musket fire. Abruptly the firing stopped, and the fight was over.

Tuesday 21st August 1798 2 PM The Malta Channel — Ken.

Ken was feeling a lot better by Tuesday afternoon, despite a very sore shoulder. The doctor had immobilized his left arm with a sling, with strict orders to rest. They were well on their way to Malta under a French prize crew. Duncan had given his word they would not try and seize control of the ship, so a dinner was held for all three sets of officers. Even the larger gun room on *Le Justice* was barely big enough. Some junior members were excluded, but Ken and Sarah were on the guest list along with Omar, Antonio, Duncan, and Whillans. As they entered the gun room, Ken was amazed that

319

Duncan received a round of applause from the French officers. The camaraderie seemed no different from on board the *Sérieuse*, when the British had been the owners of the ship.

Ken looked around for Annette, but there was no sign of her. Why was she not present at dinner? Before he got a chance to ask any of the French officers, Captain Solen of *Le Diane* called for silence and addressed the table.

"Captain Duncan, a glass of wine with you, Sir?"

Duncan stood and they toasted each other with the excellent Haut Medoc that Villeneuve had produced. Solen called upon the servants to clear the last few dishes before he continued. "Monsieur, I congratulate you on your bravery and cunning. You deceived us with a ruse de guerre, but I am confused. I believe that our chart is the most accurate, and yet you knew that the reef was not in the marked position. Pray tell me how you discovered this?"

"Captain Solen, I am honoured by the excellent treatment that we have received on board this ship, and we thank you." There were sounds of "hear hear" from his officers. "I was indeed using the chart that I found in Le *Sérieuse*; no doubt the same chart that is in your possession, Sir. But I have something else, I have this boy . . ." To Ken's surprise he pointed straight at him. For a second Ken wondered if he was going to disclose the secret of the smart phone? Duncan continued: ". . . who spent his youth in Sicily and knows every inch of this coast!" This was in fact true, and Ken was much relieved by Duncan's truthful, if somewhat devious, response .

"Well then Monsieur, how did you execute your ruse de guerre?"

"We were fortunate to know the real position of the reef, from the chart made by our midshipman. A chart, I might add, that I committed to the deep before surrendering."

This was greeted with a few chuckles, and then Captain Solen placed the salt cellar in the centre. "It is of no consequence. I discovered the reef's true position!" He continued after much laughter: "Here is the marked position of the reef. Captain, pray continue."

"I knew there was an error in the French chart," declared Duncan, "because we had a copy that was stolen from the French navy!" He planted an empty wine bottle on the table a short distance from the salt cellar. There was a chorus of laughter from the officers on both sides of the table.

"The bottle marks the real position of the reef, nearly two miles to the north west of the charted position. Having successfully sailed around the actual reef, we reached the false position as given by the chart." Duncan moved a knife around the bottle, to stop by the salt cellar.

A young French lieutenant from *Le Diane* stood up, and pointed to the knife. "Monsieur, was there no reef where your ship was heeled over?"

"Indeed not. We heaved to and prepared both larboard bow and stern anchors. Using both capstans to heel the ship over, it appeared from the starboard side exactly as if we had struck the reef. We just needed to persuade *Le Diane* that we were caught hard, so she would sail towards our ship, directly into the rocks. We drifted to leeward until the cables were taut, then Mr. Whillans here used his sails to heel her over. To heel her more, we added a third anchor, set abeam with a line tied to the top of the main mast, and we winched her to leeward. Monsieur Solen, you were well to the west, when you saw us apparently strike the reef. You sailed into battle, not realizing that the Passaro reef lay directly in your path. The outcome you know."

"We kept the pumps going most of the night on the reef, but she finally succumbed when a change in the wind brought some larger waves. She rolled off the reef to sink in twenty fathoms. My thanks to captain Villeneuve for taking us all off safely."

"Here. The pepper pot is *Le Diane*," called the same lieutenant, as he pushed it across the table where it banged into the wine bottle with a loud clang, to turn over and spill its contents.

A great cheer went up from Duncan's crew and the French officers stood to toast his ingenuity.

Eventually the members of that happy company were led to bed by their servants, and the ships bore off for Malta.

Chapter 17

Return To Malta

Upon arrival in Valletta, the English prisoners were handed over to General Vaubois' staff. The officers were transported to a very impressive old house close to the Grand Harbour, where they had three rooms assigned to them. Sarah tried to speak to Duncan, but he cautioned them to silence until they had privacy.

"What happened to our patient, Sir?" Sarah asked.

"Captain Jones and our medical officer travelled in a separate carriage. The surgeon was most insistent on a direct passage to the hospital," said Duncan.

Sarah wondered if Nelson would survive to fight his future famous battles, such as Copenhagen and Trafalgar. She looked around the room, a large reception room of a once very fine house. The walls, were bare and the high ceilings held an ornate plaster centre piece; clearly a family of wealth had owned this house. Sarah's imagination was interrupted when a handsome captain entered in full dress uniform accompanied by a civilian.

"Sorry, Cinders, he is going to the ball without us." Sarah greeted Ken's remark with a withering look.

"I am Captain Crespin of General Vaubois staff. The general conveys his apologies, but he is not able to meet you. He is especially sad to miss the brave and resourceful English captain, but he has to attend to affairs of state," Crespin stated with a bow.

"He is already at the ball!" Ken whispered to Sarah, who dug her elbow into his side to keep him quiet.

"The general has sent a message to the British allies in Naples, and it is likely that an exchange will be arranged at the earliest convenience. Until that time the general has generously agreed to give you the freedom of the city provided that you give him your parole."

The captain continued to speak, ignoring the sudden commotion of marching soldiers just outside their window.

"Monsieur Duncan, please convey these papers to your officers, and have them sign and date them. I will bear witness to these signatures. They are your parole that you will not serve any of the enemies of France until there has been a formal exchange. I take it these terms are acceptable to you?"

Duncan nodded. "Indeed, Sir. Most civil!"

The papers were handed round amongst the officers. The noise outside seemed to subside as papers were signed and duly verified, dated, and witnessed. As the formalities were completed, even the imperturbable captain could no longer ignore the ruckus from below. He collected the documents and handed them to his clerk just as the door burst open.

A naval lieutenant with several marines marched into the room. The officer immediately addressed himself to the captain and his clerk, handing him a letter. "I am Lieutenant Reynard of the French Navy. This letter is written by the foreign minister, Monsieur Charles Maurice de Talleyrand. I am on a special assignment for the minister, and you are advised to grant me every assistance or Monsieur Talleyrand will want to know the reason." He waved a second piece of paper in front of the captain. "This is an order signed by Monsieur Langon, the local representative of the Directory, for the arrest of these enemies of France." He slammed the paper down on the table.

The captain picked it up and studied it before passing it to his clerk. "Monsieur Reynard, I have my orders directly from General Vaubois, the governor of Malta. You will recall that Bonaparte himself appointed the General. The same Bonaparte who took the island on behalf of the Directory. You will find the army is the power here, and if you wish control of these prisoners, you must first seek the permission of General Vaubois. These men have given me their parole, so they have the freedom of the city."

Addressing Duncan he said: "Messieurs, you are free to leave this building, provided you remain within the city limits. You will report to my office at the barracks for information as to your exchange. Good day, Messieurs."

He turned to go, but the infuriated Reynard blocked his path. "Captain, I have a squad of soldiers with me; they will escort these men to the old fort where they will be held for questioning. They are enemies of France and possibly spies!"

The captain remained calm. Sarah looked from one to the other, wondering who would win this power struggle, but inevitably right was on the side of might, and Reynard had a force of marines at his back.

"Very well, Monsieur. I will inform the general of your request. If you insist on taking these prisoners, you will agree that my clerk here goes with you to keep me informed as to their whereabouts." Crespin gave a short bow and left the building.

Wednesday 22nd August 1798 8 AM — Sarah

Sarah opened her eyes to see cold stone walls. Ken was curled up in the straw, with a ragged blanket covering him, while Duncan sat upright, asleep with his back against the wall.

"Ken, what is the date?"

Ken sat up. "Date? It's about 3 weeks since the battle." After a brief pause he said: " I think it is the 22nd August."

"According to Duncan, the gate is now unstable, and may not be there at all!"

At mention of his name, Duncan stirred. "I can't say with any certainty, I have never known a gate to be stable much after 75 days."

"How the heck are we going to get to it?" Ken slumped back on the straw.

Duncan stared silently through the bars.

"We have to find Annette. " Sarah said half to herself.

324

"Ok, don't worry about it. I have a plan for getting us out of here." Ken sounded serious.

"Another of your great plans," Sarah sighed.

"No, really, this is a good idea."

At that moment four armed guards marched into the cell and ordered them out into the corridor, where Reynard waited. "So Monsieur, our roles are reversed."

Duncan looked more closely at this French officer. "We have met before, monsieur?"

"Indeed! On the deck of the frigate *Sérieuse*, where I was your prisoner."

Duncan's eyes grew wide and his mouth opened slightly, and they continued walking. They finally came to a halt in front of another barred cell. At first glance the cell appeared unoccupied, then Reynard held up the lantern revealing a woman curled up asleep on the straw. As the light fell on her face, she stirred slightly but did not wake up. It was Marie-Paule.

Duncan cried out when he saw her, and Sarah laid a gentle hand on his arm, which Reynard pushed aside, and hissed: "I wanted you to see this; it may help you to be forthcoming with information that I require."

The Englishman held himself at full height, looking down into Reynard's cold eyes. "Sir, you need to torture innocent women to fight your war?"

Reynard raised an eyebrow. "You remember a rainy day here in Valletta, when you and this woman escaped from this very castle? I was the unfortunate officer who tried to stop you. Marie-Paule showed her contempt for the French authority at that time. After the battle I was sure she had perished in *L'Orient*; however, she did not appear on the list of dead. A few enquiries led me to the ship to which she had been brought after escaping the explosion. I was still under orders from Malta, so I returned with my prisoner at the first opportunity."

Reynard nodded to the marines, and they marched their prisoners up a flight of stairs into a small interview room.

"I will ask your friends to wait outside, so our conversation remains private."

Sarah watched the door close and wondered what he wanted.

"I know who that man is. There is only one thing that he could possibly want," whispered Ken.

"What do you mean? You know him?"

"Annette told me that she sailed to Egypt on a cutter under the command of Lieutenant Reynard."

"So? What does he want?"

Ken smiled and tapped his nose, and the guard told them to be silent. A few minutes later the door opened, and Reynard beckoned the pair of them into the interview room.

"Captain Duncan has requested that you be present for this interview and I have acquiesced to his wish." Sarah and Ken said nothing, waiting for Reynard to continue. "Monsieur Duncan, you escaped from this prison on the 20th June. You were here on a charge of spying against France."

Duncan protested. "No such charges were brought against me. I was a simple prisoner of war."

Reynard sat down and put his hands on the table. "You are far from simple, Monsieur. May I speak freely before these aspirants?"

"I have already said as much."

"Very well, I would like you tell me how you can travel from the future? More importantly, I would like to know how I may also travel."

Ken nudged Sarah and smiled.

Reynard waited until the silence was uncomfortable, then he said, "Monsieur, I need not remind you that Mademoiselle Bonneterre lies in a cell below us. I don't think you would like to see her suffer."

Sarah saw the pain in Duncan's face at the mention of her name. He would give Reynard whatever he wanted to gain Marie-Paule's freedom.

"I have already interrogated Bonneterre." Reynard continued. "From what she says, I gather that she is in love with you. It is clear to me that you have been foolish enough to let yourself fall in love with her. Come, come Monsieur, I know everything: your daring escape from the fort, your romance on the *Palerma*, the storm, the battle off the African coast, and the long trek across the desert; I can personally attest to her bravery. Aboard *L'Orient*, she faced myself, her torturer and finally she escaped from the flagship only to be plucked from the water by a boat from a French ship."

Sarah saw the fire in Duncan's eyes as he looked directly into Reynard's. "Very well, I will show you what you want, but I have some conditions."

Reynard could hardly keep the smile from his face. "What, pray, are these conditions?"

Duncan stood up and leaned over the table. "First I would like you to release myself and my companions. It is perfectly legal, as they have given their parole."

Reynard laughed. "I doubt that I would be able to keep you much longer against the wishes of Vaubois."

"You will allow Mademoiselle Marie-Paule Bonneterre to come with us." Reynard silently nodded his agreement. "There is another woman, Mademoiselle Annette Salvigny, who was on board *Le Sérieuse*. No doubt her whereabouts are known to you. I would like to see her before we take our journey. Can you arrange this?"

"Certainly. I was expecting as much. Will there be anything else?"

"Yes, we are transporting an injured officer. I would like to ensure that he is given good medical care. I will personally guarantee the expense. He may be exchanged in the ordinary way. I will take these two midshipmen, Mademoiselle Salvigny, and Marie-Paule if she wishes. Lastly, I need your word that you will come alone, and will tell no one of this journey."

"You wish for me to keep private all that I discover? I must use this knowledge only for my own advantage, and give nothing to anybody else? Well, I accept your conditions, Monsieur. You may rest assured that the General will command the best doctors to attend to your patient. He is already being well looked after in the military hospital. A prisoner exchange will be arranged as soon as practicable. Is that assurance sufficient?"

Sarah wondered if Nelson would be better off in a twentieth century hospital, but Duncan nodded his head in assent.

Reynard rose. "First, I will fetch Mademoiselle Salvigny. You will have to wait just a little longer before we disturb Bonneterre."

He closed the door, and they heard the marines come to attention outside. "She's still alive, Sir. Marie-Paule, I mean!" Sarah beamed as she spoke.

Duncan smiled warmly and grasped his student's hands. "Thank God she was pulled from the bay." He started to laugh. "A woman's love has made me soft. I have spent most of my life hiding the existence of the time gates, and I will sacrifice the secret for the life of Marie-Paule."

Reynard soon returned with Annette. She looked pale and frightened, but she faced Reynard with some courage. She took a document from her dress and held it out for him to see.

"This is my parole taken by an English naval officer, Captain Ball. His boat saved me from the burning wreck of *L'Orient*. The parole states that I will not help the enemies of England until I have been duly exchanged. That exchange has not yet taken place, and I am bound by my oath until that time."

"My dear you have already done your work for France. I have brought you here so that Monsieur Duncan can take you home. You would like to go home?"

"Monsieur, my mother raised me, and she is gone. I will go back, but I don't consider that I am going home."

Annette put her face on the table and burst into tears. Sarah put her arm around her sister.

"Sarah, at least you have all you need to return." Duncan stated.

She shook her head. "I need to see Antonio before I go anywhere."

Reynard conducted Annette out of the room, and the others were led back to their cell.

Thursday 23rd August 1798 6 AM The Old fort — Reynard

Reynard chose the busiest time in the morning to release his prisoners.

"I have special orders from the Directory. These prisoners are to accompany me." Reynard spoke harshly to the turnkey as he carelessly displayed Langon's letter.

The fat turnkey took a pull of wine from his glass and wiped his mouth with the back of his hand. "Monsieur, I have received orders only today. I am sorry, but I cannot release the prisoners into your hands without written instructions from the governor.

"You do not need that; Langon is senior to the governor of the fort."

A worried look came over the turnkey's face. A confrontation with an officer would lead to trouble. "Monsieur, I cannot do anything without the governor's orders. He is in attendance today. I have seen his personal assistant; it will not take long, Sir."

"It is not important," said Reynard. "Give me the key, and I will continue my interrogation of the prisoner from yesterday."

The turnkey turned pale. "Sorry, Sir, but I can't do that. I was not on duty yesterday, and this notice came only today from the governor himself, Sir."

Reynard ignored the whining of the turnkey. "In that case, I would like an escort to conduct some prisoners to the interrogation room."

"Sir, during this hour there is only myself on duty."

Reynard struggled to keep calm. "You shall help me then. Come along." He seized the turnkey by his arm and marched him down to the cell where Duncan and the others had spent another night on their beds of straw on the hard floor. The turnkey came panting along the corridor after him wheezing and complaining.

"My duty is to obey the governor, Sir. I cannot permit you to move prisoners without the required paper, Sir."

The lieutenant took the key from the protesting turnkey's belt, and inserted it into the lock. Danton looked aghast. He could not lay hands on an officer, but even an officer should not touch his keys. He stumbled into the cell after Reynard, his high pitched voice continuing with a litany of complaints. He stopped when he realized he was looking at Marie-Paule and Duncan.

"You two!" he said. Marie-Paule got unsteadily to her feet, her face grey. As she staggered Duncan supported her.

The turnkey stared incredulously at the pair of them. "This was the woman who helped the English officer escape not three months ago," he said, rubbing the back of his head where he had been struck and rendered unconscious.

"The governor is not aware that you two have been recaptured. Take a care, Monsieur. These criminals are dangerous. I shall be back with some help." Danton waddled away as fast as his stunted legs would take him.

Reynard held up the keys. "We must move quickly before he returns."

Marie-Paule lent her weight against Duncan. "My dear what is wrong?"

"It is nothing, captain. I was feeling a little sick this morning, but it will pass."

"Sir, what about Annette? We should try and find her," said Ken.

"She will be here shortly. Must we leave the castle grounds?" Inquired Reynard.

"No, all we have to do is to cross the courtyard on the North side. Get us there and you will learn our secret." Duncan said in a quiet voice.

They stopped in the courtyard, and Duncan looked across to the old munitions shed. Nothing had changed. "We will not go without Annette."

"You have my word. She will join us in a few moments." They waited, and just as Reynard was growing impatient, a party of officers joined them. "Captain Duncan, in fulfilment of my part of the bargain, here are the rest of the British officers."

Duncan addressed them. "Doctor, Tenente, we have to say goodbye." They made no move to leave, so Duncan added conspiratorially: "Naval secrets, gentlemen. Perhaps you will find out when the war is over."

The doctor smiled at Duncan and gripped him by the hand. "I understand, Sir. I received good news from the hospital this morning. Our patient has regained his senses, and was talking coherently to the staff."

"Good news, indeed, Doctor. " Duncan shook hands with the officers. "Mr. Whillans, Mr. Barabaro, I take my leave of you."

The sailing master looked quite surprised, while Antonio simply bowed his head, then turned to Sarah.

"Will I ever see you again, Mr. Midshipman?"

Sarah could not believe their journey was nearly over. She had been living on the edge for so long, she was afraid that a return to her normal life would be mundane. Once, her most pressing worry had been what grade she was going to get in her next history course. How could such a life compare to the adventure she had found 200 years in the past? She no longer felt like the hard working B+ student she had been just three short months ago. She had escaped solo up the cliffs, saved the life of a boy on the *Palerma*, helped rescue Marie-Paule from a burning ship, and learned something about sailing. She looked at Antonio, her eyes blurring with tears. Despite her misgivings she knew she had also found love. She accepted the kerchief he held out to her, then threw her arms around him. "I will be back, Tenente. I don't know how but I promise you I will be back."

Duncan coughed politely. Two of his officers hugging in public would never do. "Ken, Sarah, go now. Do not look back. I will wait for Annette." Feeling like students again, they crossed the courtyard to the munitions shed, and disappeared inside.

"Don't say a word, Captain. I am going with you," said Marie-Paule in a soft voice.

"I am sorry, my dear, but it is impossible. The future is not for you to see, and I don't think you will be happy there."

Marie-Paule grabbed Duncan by both arms, giving him a no nonsense look. "Listen to me, Captain. I am going with you, and I will hear no argument. It's true — I love you, but it is not for me that I have to go."

Duncan looked puzzled. "What are you speaking of? I don't understand?"

"You stupid Englishman, can't you tell? I carry your child!"

Before Duncan could say anything Annette came running towards them saying something in an urgent tone. Duncan looked up to see soldiers were assembling behind her. She caught up with them and said breathlessly: "Quickly we must go. Danton has alerted the guard. There will be a hue and cry any moment."

"Tenente, leave the castle while you still can. Just walk away from us and do not look back; it is me they want." Duncan commanded.

"Of course, Captain. Until the next time." Antonio gave a brief bow, and, taking Whillans by the arm, marched away.

Duncan turned to go only to find Annette stalled, staring at Marie-Paule. "Come we must go I will make the introductions later."

"Professor, you do not understand this is the woman I saw on *L'Orient*, she is. . ."

"Arrêtez-les!"

"Do not look back!" Ordered Duncan, hurrying the group forward.

Danton emerged from the arched cloistered wall of the castle and pointed at them. Four soldiers stopped, kneeling on the ground, and unshipped their muskets. Three more drew their swords and ran after the fugitive, keeping well to one side to avoid the line of fire.

"Halt — or we fire!"

Reynard waited as Duncan urged the women forward, then drew his sword and ran as if pursuing them.

The command "Fire!" rang out, and the muskets cracked. The early morning staff had just entered the castle grounds and several stopped behind the kneeling marksmen to see what the noise was about. Not one but two bystanders fell forward, tipping two marksmen off balance as the men pulled their triggers. With great apologies, Antonio and Whillans picked their victims out of the dust. The remaining two musket shots were targeted on Duncan, one hit his left side at waist level and the other winged his right leg. He gasped in pain, but somehow kept moving until he was only a few feet from the door. At the far end of the courtyard, more soldiers arrived, and more musket balls thudded harmlessly into the woodwork.

* * *

By this time Sarah, Ken, Marie-Paule, and Annette had the door open and pulled Duncan inside. "The captain is hurt. Help me get him to the gate," said Sarah.

Ken grabbed Duncan's right arm as he struggled to his feet, with Sarah supporting his other side. Marie-Paule slammed the door closed, and kicked a piece of wood underneath, hoping it would act as a wedge.

"Go with them! Quickly, find the gate. I will try and delay them," she called to Annette, who seemed dazed.

"Don't you know me?" Annette was almost crying.

Ken pulled at her sleeve. "Annette, help us with Duncan. He can't walk."

She pulled herself away from Marie-Paule and grabbed Duncan by the legs. At that moment a fusillade of musket fire hit the shed door, dislodging the wedge. There was a scream from outside.

Still holding Duncan, Sarah watched Reynard stagger through the door. "What happened?" She screeched at him, but his bloody face said everything. A musket ball must have hit the stonework beside him as he came through the door, a sharp splinter of rock had embedded itself in his left eye, while more rock chips spoiled his good looks forever. A second ball had struck Reynard in the throat, perhaps from a ricochet, narrowly missing the carotid artery. He was bleeding profusely, his whole face a mass of blood. With what strength he possessed, he stumbled inside, slammed the door closed, and fell against it. Reynard slid to the floor blocking the door.

"I will help him, please take Duncan to the gate," Marie-Paule said in a firm voice.

The students stumbled through the darkness with Duncan propped between them. The noise and commotion by the door receded, giving way to the sound of wind. Ken moved ahead to the source of the noise.

"I've found the opening. Let's go through," Ken called out with relief.

"You go. I must go back for my mother," said Annette.

"What? What do you mean? When did you have time to find your . . . wait, that's it. Marie-Paule is your mother, isn't she? Ken exclaimed.

"Yes. And I assume that Duncan is my father!"

"Help him, please," Sarah cried as Duncan slumped heavily against her.

With an effort, Duncan raised his head. "That sound . . . like the wind, . . . the gate is changing. Where is Marie-Paule?" He started to struggle, barely able to stand on his own and he staggered away from the gate calling, "Marie Paule!!"

After a few steps he fell against the students who dragged him back.

"Help him. I'll go back for her," Sarah took off into the darkness.

"Oh God! Soon nobody will be going back. Marie-Paule!" Duncan wailed in pain.

Ken said "Open sesame" in the general direction of the gate and, to his intense relief, the door slid open.

"The gate hasn't changed yet. Go through, quickly!" Duncan recovered slightly, urging his students forward, but an older man with a scarred face pushed his way out from inside the office and stood, barring the way to any who wanted to enter.

"Who the hell are you? For God's sake, man, let the young people through, can't you see the gate is changing," gasped Duncan, sagging visibly.

"Remember me, Monsieur?" The man seized Duncan by the collar. Duncan, however, had finally succumbed to the pain, his weight fully on the students.

"Get out of our way!" called Ken, but the man pushed past into Annette, who froze at the sight of the man, "Uncle André!" She whispered, almost dropping her professor. The old man stared at her for a moment, then sidestepped and shouldered his way into the darkness of the shed.

As they were about to go through, the sound of the rushing wind reached a climax and there was a loud popping noise as a shimmering greyness, barely visible in the darkness appeared next to the original gate.

"What is that?" Asked Ken.

"I have seen this before. The timeline has bifurcated. It is a second gate," said Duncan. "One way leads to the world we know, the other to some parallel universe. A world has changed by what has happened here. Soon both gates will disappear forever." With these words his head fell forward, and he passed out.

Ken grabbed Duncan's arm and jerked him towards the doorway. "Come on, Annette, help me." The two students swept Duncan through the doorway into the professor's outer office.

At the entrance to the shed, Marie-Paule was still trying to hold the door closed while the soldiers crashed against it from the other side. She pushed with all her strength, but it was useless until Sarah joined her and flung her weight onto the door, gaining them a precious inch.

"Go!" Sarah cried. "You should be with the one you love."

"You must also follow your heart. You came back for Antonio. Go to him." Marie-Paule kissed Sarah and ran into the darkness.

At that moment, Reynard sat up. The door pounded into him once more and, recovering somewhat, Reynard set off after Marie-Paule. The door finally succumbed and several soldiers burst through; one took hold of Sarah while the others swept past into the darkness.

Less than a minute ahead, with some faint light guiding her, Marie-Paule almost stepped on an old man. He grabbed her arm and pulled himself upright. "Your captain is gone forever, Mademoiselle, but you know me?"

Before she could answer Reynard, with one eye covered in blood, seized her by the arm.

"Monsieur, can you see them? I have sent for some light," called one of the soldiers.

Reynard held his hand to his face, blood oozing out and dripping down his shirt. He squinted out of his good eye and saw an old ruined man holding Marie-Paule, standing between them and the open gate. With a burst of strength he seized the older man's coat.

"Ogt od oer wig obd moon!" His damaged voice sounded like an angry crow.

As Marie-Paule cried in anguish: "Capitan! Capitan! Open the door!" A second opening confronted them; it was nothing more than a faint grey shimmering.

"You fool, Reynard! Don't you know me? I am you!" The old man gasped, still lying on the ground where Reynard had pushed him.

"I know you not, o!" Reynard said harshly.

"Don't go through! It isn't what you think!" croaked the old man.

The old man blocked the way through the left-hand gate, so Marie-Paule stepped through the right into the unknown.

The old man clung to Reynard's leg, but the lieutenant shook him off and with one hand still clutching his injured face staggered through a second before both gates disappeared.

A group of soldiers holding both Sarah and the old man returned to the daylight, where Antonio and Whillans stood in their path.

"Leave that officer alone. He has given his parole, and has the freedom to leave this place. Show them your parole document, Mr. Midshipman," said Antonio pointing at Sarah.

Sarah produced the letter and passed it to the corporal. The man didn't pretend to be able to read it, but stared at it blankly.

Antonio continued. "Go back inside. A French officer is hurt."

"These two were all we found," said the corporal.

"Take the old man for questioning. I will deal with the aspirant," said Antonio.

The corporal shrugged and took the old man into the barracks, leaving Sarah with Antonio.

"I have seen him before." Said Sarah pointing after the old man.

Antonio smiled. "He is of no importance. What I care about is that you came back."

"Yes, I did."

"You are certain you have made the right decision?" He asked, unable to wipe the smile from his face.

She nodded.

"Come, we best leave. Show the guard your parole document."

They joined the throng at the castle gate, and slowly made their way into the town. Sarah followed Antonio down a familiar street, and hand in hand they made their way towards the house of the Comte.

Thursday 23rd August 1798 9:30 AM Victoria — Annette

Annette and Ken helped Duncan into his office chair, and Ken tried to help him get out of his uniform, but the professor waved him away. They all turned to the inner office, and waited for a few seconds, but nobody else came through the gate.

"Who was that old man? Where is Sarah? We have to go back for her." Ken's voice betrayed his panic.

Annette looked to be in shock, she mumbled: "She went back for Marie- . . . for my mother."

"Well we better go and get them both."

Duncan put his arm on the young man's shoulder, trying to speak through the pain. His words came out in short bursts. "It's too late. The gate has changed. We were fortunate to get back. It's happened to me before, a long time ago. I heard the sound of wind, where there was no wind. The gate no longer led to where I thought it would."

"So Sarah is . . .gone?"

"Yes. I think she stayed on purpose. She followed her . . ."

Duncan searched for the right word, but Annette completed the thought: ". . . her heart."

A university security guard burst into the room interrupting their silent contemplation of Sarah's decision.

"Je suis desole, Professor. C'est vous bonne nuit."

As the man turned to leave, Ken asked: "What's the date?" but the guard did not understand, so Ken repeated his question in

337

French. The man shrugged his shoulders and handed the newspaper he was carrying to Ken, and then walked off down the corridor.

"Strange, he spoke English before . . . I swear." He glanced at the newspaper. "August 23rd, 2015. This newspaper is in French."

Annette looked at Duncan's wounds, then picked up the phone.

"Send an ambulance to . . . desolé, une ambulance, merci . . ."

Duncan reached over and stopped the call.

"Professor you need medical help."

"I will be fine, if you just give me a little help, please."

Annette looked puzzled as she put the phone down. "Something's going on. The receptionist only spoke French!"

"I don't need an ambulance. There is a first aid box under my desk; perhaps you would get it for me."

Annette busied herself patching up Duncan's wounds. "The leg wound is superficial, but a ball took a chunk of flesh away at your waist. You need stitches and a doctor to take a look at this wound." She paused in her work and said: "Professor Duncan, what happened to that woman?"

"You mean Marie-Paule?"

"Yes. I demand to know."

Duncan's caterpillar eyebrow rose characteristically. "You demand, Ms Salvigny?"

"You should know, Professor, my mother's name was Bonneterre. We used Salvigny to avoid being found by Uncle André."

"You mean . . ."

"Yes, Marie-Paule is my mother. Are you my father?"

His mouth stayed open for a few seconds, then he nodded his head. "It is most likely true. I am trying to work out exactly how."

"It's easy, you had sex with her!" Annette said with a shrug.

Duncan said nothing.

Ken wrinkled his face as he tried to take this all in. "That is too much of a coincidence. How could the Professor have been at Victoria all these years with you, his daughter?"

"I think you Mr. DiPalo are partly responsible," Duncan said with a spark of humour.

"What'd I do?"

"About ten years ago I was at the naval museum in Greenwich, doing some Library research, when I came across an entry in the log of the HMS *Vanguard* for the 1st August 1798. It read: 'Came aboard Lieutenant Masthead Duncan.' Underneath was a second entry; 'Accompanied by Midshipman Ken DiPalo. University of Victoria, Clearihue Building, room 354, 2015.'

At first, I thought the entry must be a joke. I had never heard of Ken DiPalo, but nobody else has the name Masthead, so that surely was myself. I thought it was a fraud, but I had the ink checked. It was the same ink and the same pen as the rest of the entry for that day. Moreover the handwriting on the former entry was definitely my own.

"But I wrote that a few days ago!" Ken exclaimed.

"No, you wrote it in the year 1798. Time is a strange thing. What you did then has an effect on today. Some things, like that entry, are never noticed. It was serendipity that I came to read it."

Annette asked: "Is that why you came to Victoria? To find the time gate?" Duncan slowly nodded his head.

"But I exist! If you had not come to Victoria, not travelled back, I would not exist?"

"Let's not try and understand the intricacies of the space time continuum before breakfast, young lady."

"Professor, were you born in the twentieth century?" Ken interjected.

Nobody said a word, waiting to hear Duncan's answer. He cleared his throat a couple of times. "I did not say that I was. I just said that I read the entry in the *Vanguard* log in 2005."

"What year were you born, professor?"

"It is rude to ask a person's age. I think that the relevant date is when I came across my first time gate." There was complete silence. "It was the year 1787, and I was seventeen years of age."

The two students started to speak at once, but eventually Annette's voice cut in above Ken's.

"Where is my mother?"

"Believe me, I wish I knew. I received this letter. It was delivered in May of this year by a Quebec firm of solicitors. I have read it, but could not make any sense from it . . . " He tailed off and

Annette picked up the letter. It was in French, dated and addressed to Annette care of Duncan.

She translated it aloud.

1st April 2000, Montreal
My Dearest Annette,

When you read this letter, you will know something of our history that I have never been able to tell you. You may even be reunited with your father, and I hope he is able to look after you. As I write this you are ten years old, and after years of searching I have found a gateway through time, but I know not where or when it leads. I knew I must make provision for you my darling. I would not take a child back to the 18th century but go I must. So I agreed with a good Quebec family that they would take you in if anything happens to me. I have to leave you for a while, but if my dreams are realized, I will come back for you very soon. I am sorry for any wrong you think I may have done you, and I only hope that evil man you know as your Uncle André will never find you. I am confident that Monsieur Malette will be a good parent.

Your loving mother.

Marie-Paule Bonneterre

They stood spellbound by the letter until Annette, sobbing, turned to Duncan,

"Monsieur, is there any chance that my mother is still alive?"

Duncan bowed his head, taking a very long time to answer. "Annette, I cannot say."

"How do I find her?" Annette asked in a harsh voice.

"I have used the time gateways when the opportunity provides. Finding them is not easy."

"Then I must find a way." Annette sounded determined.

"Who was that old man?" asked Ken.

"I think that was Uncle André," said Annette. "He managed to find me, but all along he was looking for the gate. I am almost sure he is what became of Reynard. I think my mother and Reynard,

340

the 1798 Reynard, went through the gate, and it shifted in time and space."

Again nobody spoke for a long time, then Ken broke the silence. He glanced at the headlines. "I didn't know there was a French newspaper in Victoria, but the headlines are strange. Has anybody heard of an organization called the 'Western Alliance Liberation Front'?"

Duncan took the newspaper out of Ken's hand, and read a few paragraphs. "Well young lady," he said to Annette. "it would seem that changing the course of history is possible after all. Perhaps it's also possible to find your mother."

"What do you mean she's changed history?" Ken asked indignantly. Nobody answered him.

"In that case I'm going to join this Western Alliance, and change it back!"

Epilogue

Marie-Paule walked out into an October night in Montreal. It was cold like she had never known before. The world had gone mad. She had never seen anything like this. The noise, the smells, everything was so very different from what she knew. She waited for the others to appear, but they did not. A few minutes earlier, it had been summer in Malta, but now she was in some kind of frozen nightmare. Reynard emerged, blood covering his ruined face, unable to speak due to the damage the musket ball had done to his larynx. Marie-Paule screamed as he collapsed on the sidewalk beside her. People gathered around the prostrate Reynard, and Marie-Paule was pushed out of the way, as he extended a hand to her.

"What's your name Monsieur?" asked a man who bent down to help.

"Bonneterre," he croaked in a raspy imitation of his own voice, before passing out.

Marie-Paule found her way out of the crowd into the street. She hated Reynard, and did not care what happened to him. She wanted to get warm, and find out how to escape this nightmare. She stumbled into a café, where the owner took pity on her, seeing her distress. He gave her a cup of coffee. She sat down and sipped, glad for the warmth it gave her. She wondered if she would ever see Duncan again and thought about his baby that she carried. She was still holding the leather bag that she had picked up a lifetime ago on *L'Orient*. She looked at it more closely. When she saw the name 'Annette', burned into the leather, she started to cry.

Marie-Paule was lost in her thoughts. "What happened back there? Where am I now? Where is he? Have I just been abandoned by Duncan? He did not want me with him so he sends me here, alone to this nightmare."

A man with a droopy moustache sat down beside her, and addressed her in French. "My name is Jacques Parizeau. Do you believe in freedom from the English oppressors?"

She looked at the stranger, and laughed in an ironic sort of way. "Oh yes, I believe in freedom."

The man looked surprised. "Where are you from, Mademoiselle, not Quebec?"

"I am from Paris,"

"Ah Paris! Perhaps you have heard of the Parti Québécoise?"

"I know nothing of this parti, I don't even know what year it is," said Marie-Paule shaking her head, tears flowing.

The man put a gentle, soothing hand on hers. "It is a beautiful October night in 1988."

Historical Notes

The historical context of the Second Gate is accurate. The Maltese did cover their church silver in black paint, thus saving it from being looted by French soldiers. There really was a massacre of Greek sailors by the Maltese although the provocation of a French officer is my invention. Thanks to my Maltese correspondent, Alexandra Bonnici for pointing me in the right direction for these details, and supplying some Maltese names. For my climbing readers, Sarah was already leading mid 5.12 (Fr. 7b), and the climb she does on the cliffs of Malta I saw as around an 11b level with an 11c crux, not impossible for one of Sarah's ability, but certainly the climb of a lifetime for somebody not used to soloing. The Ragusan brig did speak to Captain Hardy as per the starting quote, I elaborated on the fate of that brig (snow).

The reconfiguration of the French fleet at the battle of the Nile is as suggested in Brian Lavery's excellent book; *Nelson and the Nile: The Naval War Against Bonaparte 1798*. Annette's outpouring to the French admirals follows Mr. Lavery's interpretation on the reasons the French lost this key battle. The frigate, *Sérieuse* was sunk at the Nile and not commandeered as in my story. The events of the subsequent replay of that battle are fiction, except that the fire on the *L'Orient* and subsequent explosion happened more or less as I describe it, and inspired the famous poem, "Casabianca", by the English poet Felicia Dorothea Hemans. "The Boy Stood on the Burning Deck" is well known to every British school boy of a certain age.

Brian Wyvill
Victoria, British Columbia

344

23584069R00192

Made in the USA
Columbia, SC
13 August 2018